seven deadly sins

VOL 1.

ALSO BY ROBIN WASSERMAN

Hacking Harvard

The Cold Awakening trilogy:

Frozen

Shattered

Torn

Seven Deadly Sins 1
Lust & Envy

Seven Deadly Sins 2
Pride & Wrath

Seven Deadly Sins 3
Sloth, Gluttony, & Greed

seven deadly sins

VOL 1.
LUST & ENVY

ROBIN WASSERMAN

Simon Pulse
New York London Toronto Sydney New Delhi

This book is a work of fiction. Any references to historical events,
real people, or real locales are used fictitiously. Other names, characters,
places, and incidents are the product of the author's imagination,
and any resemblance to actual events or locales or persons,
living or dead, is entirely coincidental.

SIMON PULSE
An imprint of Simon & Schuster Children's Publishing Division
1230 Avenue of the Americas, New York, NY 10020
First Simon Pulse paperback edition May 2013
Lust copyright © 2005 by Robin Wasserman
Envy copyright © 2006 by Robin Wasserman
All rights reserved, including the right of reproduction
in whole or in part in any form.
SIMON PULSE and colophon are registered trademarks
of Simon & Schuster, Inc.
For information about special discounts for bulk purchases,
please contact Simon & Schuster Special Sales at 1-866-506-1949
or business@simonandschuster.com.
The Simon & Schuster Speakers Bureau can bring authors
to your live event. For more information or to book an event contact
the Simon & Schuster Speakers Bureau at 1-866-248-3049
or visit our website at www.simonspeakers.com.
Designed by Mike Rosamilia
The text of this book was set in Janson Text LT.
Manufactured in the United States of America
2 4 6 8 10 9 7 5 3 1
Library of Congress Control Number 2013931937
ISBN 978-1-4424-7504-5

seven deadly sins

LUST

For Susie

This momentary joy breeds months of pain;
This hot desire converts to cold disdain.
—William Shakespeare, "The Rape of Lucrece"

Don't put me off, 'cause I'm on fire,
And I can't quench my desire.
Don't you know that I'm burning up for your love,
You're not convinced that that is enough.
—Madonna, "Burning Up"

chapter one

"AND IT WAS THE BEST SEX I'D EVER HAD." HARPER finished off the story with her favorite line and a lascivious grin.

The other girls tanning themselves on the makeshift beach (though chaise lounges plus backyard plus desert sun and margaritas did not an island paradise make) sighed appreciatively. All but Miranda, who rolled her eyes and—just barely—stifled a snort. Harper had already given her best friend the full download on this guy, so she knew very well that the previous evening's encounter had been nothing if not nasty, brutish, and (perhaps mercifully) short.

But Harper knew Miranda would keep her mouth shut.

After all, when had she ever dared ruin a Harper Grace story? Never—which is exactly why their friendship had lasted so long.

"So what now?" Beth asked, tucking her long blond hair behind her ears. Miranda and Harper exchanged a smirk: The hallmark of any good Beth Manning imitation was to get the hair tuck just right, at a frequency of about one per every three sentences. "Are you going to see him again?"

Harper shook her head, a crest of wavy auburn hair whipping across her face. "I told him to call me when hell freezes over. So why don't you keep an eye on the weather report and let me know."

The girls all burst into laughter and, clinking their plastic margarita glasses, toasted—to good stories, and better decisions. In the rock-paper-scissors of life in Grace, California, sex sometimes trumped boredom—but often (given the quality of guys available in Grace) it was the other way around.

But this—sun, fun, and booze, no Y chromosomes allowed—this was the life. They'd been meeting once a week all summer, setting up shop in Harper's back-yard—and given that the rest of the week was gener-ally filled with sweat, lethargy, and dead-end part-time jobs off the highway, serving fast food or gas or porn to skeezy travelers, "beach day" was always a highlight. Even if instead of sexy bronzed lifeguards, they were watched over by a couple of spiny, brownish cacti. Even if the only view consisted of the low-slung hills that loomed on the fringes of town, lumps of dirt and dust irregularly spotted with scrub brush as if they'd been struck by a fatal dose of desert leprosy. Even if the only water in sight sat warming in the pitcher Harper periodically tipped into the mouth of the tequila bottle, replacing what she'd taken in hopes her parents would remain none the wiser. So what? The sun still bore down on them from a cloudless sky, mixing with their carefully applied sunscreen to create the picture-perfect tan. The day was hot, the drinks were cool, and it was still summer. At least for a little longer.

"But the really unbelievable thing—," Harper began again, then stopped abruptly. "Aren't you a little old for the Peeping Tom act?" she called out in a louder voice, flicking a hand toward the sliding glass door of the house next door, where a strikingly handsome face had just shown itself. Harper's neighbor, and another highlight of the week: the handsome, hunky, and utterly unavailable Adam Morgan. It wouldn't be a day at the beach without some scoping time. And there was no one better to scope—too bad he always showed up fully clothed.

Adam crept into the backyard with one hand splayed loosely over his eyes.

"Is it safe for me to look, or have you ladies started up the nude tanning portion of your afternoon?" he asked, as the girls frantically threw themselves into poses that maximized their good parts—not that, in their skimpy bikinis, there was much of anywhere to hide the bad.

"This is reality, Adam, not your favorite porn movie," Harper said. "What are you doing here, anyway? Shouldn't you be off somewhere celebrating your last day of freedom? There's still nineteen hours left before that first bell rings."

"Yeah, good-bye summer, hello torture. Don't worry, I'm headed out to the courts now—just thought I'd stop by to say hello." He ruffled Harper's hair and then squeezed onto the plastic chaise lounge next to Beth, slinging a tan, well-muscled arm around his girlfriend.

"Nice to see you, too," Beth giggled. "Now get out of here so that Harper can finish telling us about her date."

"Another date?" He flashed Harper a knowing grin and took a swig from Beth's drink. "I just hope you're not teaching my girl here any of your tricks." He winked at Harper, then leaned over to give Beth a quick peck on the lips.

That was Adam—equal opportunity friend, one-woman man.

Beth nuzzled against her boyfriend. "Don't worry, Adam—I think Harper's got all the guys in town staked out as her own personal property. I guess I'm stuck with you."

But Harper suppressed the nasty comeback that threatened to leap off her tongue. No reason to let the blah blonde spoil her perfectly pleasant afternoon.

"I mean, come on, Harper," Beth continued, oblivious to the dangerous ground. "After all these years and all these dates, is there even anyone left? Or have you been through every eligible guy in town?"

Harper aimed her most sugary grin at the happy couple, her gaze lingering on Adam's handsomely chiseled face and brawny shoulders.

"Not yet, Beth," she said, slowly shaking her head. "Trust me—not yet."

With a sneer, Kaia wearily waved away the stewardess—or flight attendant, if you wanted to bother being PC about it. Which she didn't. As if she wanted a rancid plate of underdone potatoes and gravy-swaddled mystery meat sitting in front of her for the rest of the flight. She didn't need airplane food to make her nauseous—these days, life was doing a good enough job of that on its own.

She squirmed in her seat, trying her best not to touch the greasy arm of the woman next to her, who'd only barely managed to squeeze her rolls of fat into the narrow seat. Talk about airplane clichés—now all she needed was the screaming baby.

THUD.

Oh, that's right—the universe's central casting office had instead saddled her with a bratty five-year-old who had a bad case of ADD and, apparently, a spastic kicking problem.

"Now, now, Taylor," a weary voice behind her said. "We don't kick the seat in front of us—it's not nice."

Kaia wanted to turn around and explain to little Taylor and his wimpy mother exactly what would happen to "us" if the kicking continued throughout the rest of this interminable flight—but she thought better of it.

Simple math: The in-flight movie (some tedious Ben Stiller bomb) would only last two hours, the flight would last at least six—she needed to save *some* entertainment options for later.

THUD.

Kaia sighed, pulled out her iPod, and tried to relax. As a series of indie pop poseurs warbled in her ear, she practiced the breathing exercises that Rashi—her mother's yoga instructor, life coach, and all-around personal guru— had taught her last year. Breathe in, breathe out. Clear your mind. Go to your safe place.

Of course it was all bullshit—ancient wisdom dished out at $300 an hour, maybe—but bullshit nonetheless.

She just needed to stop dwelling. *Stress causes wrinkles*, Kaia reminded herself, and just because her mother was the reigning Botox queen of Manhattan didn't mean that she was eager to claim the throne anytime soon. She needed to calm down . . . but exactly how was she supposed to do that with her hideous new life rushing toward her at six hundred miles an hour?

It was bad enough she was being shipped across the country like a piece of furniture. Literally. (Last summer her mother had decided that her grandmother's mahogany armoire clashed with the new Danish modern decor and shipped it out to her father. This summer's "out of sight, out of mind" shipment was Kaia.) Bad enough she was going to miss this year's Central Park fall gala, the winter benefit season, *all* the La Perla sample sales—basically, every social event of the year. And she was sure that her so-called friends would waste no time in making her so-called boyfriend (okay, *all* her boyfriends) feel a little less lonely.

Bad enough that she was going to be stuck in the middle of nowhere—literally exiled to the desert, and for a lot longer than forty days and forty nights. That tomorrow she'd be facing her first day at some hick school sure to be filled with a bunch of losers destined for community college or *ranching* school, and who probably thought that Gucci was a neato name for a pet cow.

THUD.

She winced. (One more time and that kid was going to learn about the emergency exits the hard way.)

Bad enough, to sum up, that the plane was hurtling toward a father she barely knew, a town whose name she couldn't remember, a year in hicksville hell—

THUD.

All that was bad enough—but honestly, did they really have to make her fly *coach*?

Kane Geary released the ball from his fingertips and then turned away, as if to demonstrate his lack of interest in following its perfect arc across the court. But he grinned as, a moment later, he heard the swish.

"Check it out," he said. "Nothing but net."

Adam grabbed the ball and tossed it back to his friend in disgust. He should have known his early lead was just a false hope. The last time Kane lost a game of pickup ball, they'd both been about three feet tall. Kane may have been too lazy to show up for practices (so lazy, in fact, that he'd been thrown off the Haven High team in ninth grade, never to return), but when it came to actual games, he hated to lose. And thus, never did.

In other words, trailing by seven points and about five minutes away from utter exhaustion, Adam had no chance whatsoever.

"Okay, LeBron, how about we wrap it up for today?" he suggested. The tiny basketball court behind the high school offered no shade, their bottles of water were long since empty, and after an hour of running back and forth in the searing desert heat, Adam looked like he'd just stepped out of the shower. His shirt, now balled up at the foot of the basket, had long since given itself up to the cause, and his sweaty chest glistened in the sun.

Kane, on the other hand, looked as if he'd just stepped out of his air-conditioned Camaro; only a small trickle of sweat tracing a path down his cheekbone betrayed the afternoon's exertion in 103-degree heat.

Kane tossed up a casual layup, which rolled once around the rim and then tipped away on the wrong side of the net. *At least the guy misses sometimes*, Adam told himself. Small comfort.

"In awe of my superior skills?" Kane smirked, jogging down the court to grab the rebound. "Terrified of going head-to-head against the reigning champ? Worried that by the time the season starts, you'll be so demoralized that you'll have to drop off your little team?"

Adam laughed, imagining the look on his coach's face after hearing that his star forward was too *sad* to play that season.

Adam darted across the court and snatched the ball away from Kane, shooting a jump shot from mid-court and watching with satisfaction as the ball soared toward the net.

Three points. Sweet.

"More like I need to get home and make myself pretty for my girlfriend," he corrected Kane. "I hope all those dreams of basketball glory keep you warm tonight while you're sitting home *alone* eating leftovers and watching *The Simpsons*. Beth and I will be thinking of you—oh, wait, no we won't."

"Very funny. You should take that act on the road." Kane shook his head in disbelief. "I still don't understand what the hottest girl in school sees in a loser like you—you're just lucky I'm too busy to give you much competition." Kane palmed the ball and tossed Adam his shirt, and they took off for the parking lot. In the waning hours of summer vacation it was still empty, Kane's lovingly restored Camaro and Adam's rusted Chevy the only evidence of human life in the concrete wasteland. As they walked, both guys tried their best to avoid looking directly at the low-slung red building that would soon imprison them for the next nine months. Ignoring the inevitable may have been a feeble defense, but it was all they had.

"And by 'busy,' I assume you mean hopping in and out of bed with half the cheerleading squad and three-fifths of the girls' field hockey team?" Adam retorted. With his close-cropped black hair, piercing brown eyes, and impeccable physique, Kane could have any girl he wanted. By now, he'd pretty much had them all.

"Dude, you know what they say—idle hands are the

devil's plaything." Kane gave Adam his best Sunday school smile. "You gotta keep them busy doing *something*."

"You're disgusting, you know that?" Adam slapped his friend good-naturedly on the back. "You give us all a bad name."

Kane shoved him in return, then began idly dribbling the ball as they walked.

"Seriously, Adam, I know she's hot, but aren't you bored yet? There's bound to be some freshman cuties this year. . . ."

Adam bristled and walked a step faster, wondering—not for the first time—how disgusted Beth would be if she knew the kind of guy his best friend really was. Sure, she'd seen plenty of Kane and was already distinctly unimpressed—but that was Kane in good-behavior mode. Kane: Uncensored was not a pretty sight.

"I mean, she's gorgeous and all," Kane continued, "but she seems a little uptight, if you know what I mean."

Adam whirled on him.

"Enough! She's not one of your skanks. She's—" Adam cut himself off. He wasn't about to explain to Kane how Beth was different from all the girls he'd dated before (especially since he still didn't really understand it himself). Wasn't going to tell him about how beautiful she looked in the desert moonlight or how he could tell her things, secrets, about himself and his life and his dreams that he'd never told anyone before. He certainly wasn't telling Kane that he thought he might be in love with her.

They were guys. Friendship—even best friendship—had its limits.

"Whatever," he finally said. "Just give it a rest, okay? She's not going anywhere. Get used to it."

Kane winked and gave Adam an intentionally hokey leer.

"No problem. I guess if I had a girl like that willing to climb into bed with me, I wouldn't want to let her out anytime soon either."

Adam flushed and said a silent prayer to whoever watched over sex-obsessed teenagers that Kane wouldn't notice his sudden silence and obvious discomfort. Beth was willing to climb into the bed, all right. She would lie there next to him, her perfect body nestled against his. She would kiss him, and caress him, and drive him crazy with desire, and—

And that was about it.

Harper heard the old Chevy roar into the driveway and rushed to the window. There he was. Lean. Tan. Shirtless. His golden hair bronzed by the sun, his hundred-watt smile piercing through his obvious exhaustion.

Adam. Her next-door neighbor. Her childhood friend—her partner for swimming lessons, playground dates, imaginary tea parties, and the occasional game of doctor.

And now, years later: homecoming king. Star of the swim team. The basketball team. The lacrosse team. Basically, an all-American high school stud. None of which meant much to her, considering how lame their school was, and the fact that she saw sports as a crutch for the mentally weak. Besides, that's not what she saw when she looked at him. Or, at least, not all she saw, not anymore.

She opened the window, about to call out to him, to wave—then thought better of it and just watched. What she saw when she looked at him was her oldest friend, the boy who knew all of her secrets and liked her anyway—the boy she'd recently discovered was a man she wanted to be with. Might even be in love with.

What a hassle.

The poor little overlooked best friend, languishing in the shadows, the man of her dreams blinded by the bright glare of puppy love. Tossing his true soul mate aside in favor of a human Barbie doll. It was such a pathetic cliché—and Harper didn't do clichés. Nor was she a huge fan of seeing her life turn into a second-rate knockoff of a third-rate teen chick flick. Especially one that starred her as the weepy protagonist too wimpy to open her mouth and take what she wanted.

But on the other hand—just look at him.

Postgame, Adam was hot, sweaty, and shirtless. His

taut body gleamed in the sun. Harper couldn't take her eyes off him—that tan six-pack, those firm pecs, the broad biceps that, if she used her imagination, she could feel ever so gently tightening around her. . . .

There was just one problem with the picture-perfect romance—the picture-perfect girlfriend. Beautiful Beth. Blond Beth. Bland and boring Beth.

Lately, the Blond One was all Adam could talk about, and it was driving Harper slowly but surely insane. He was probably even now heading inside to call her, to whisper sweet nothings in his lilting Southern accent (an adorable holdover from an early childhood in South Carolina). He was probably already planning some sickeningly sweet, romantic candlelit dinner for their last night of summer. He was that kind of guy. It was disgusting. And it should have been her.

Harper slammed the window shut and crossed the room to her bed, which was covered in clothes—a haphazard pile of unsuitable first-day-of-school possibilities. She burrowed through them in frustration, wondering how it was possible that with all these clothes, she never had anything to wear.

The beaded yellow tank top with pleated ruffles and an off-center sash that had looked so promising in the store? Hideous.

The stonewashed denim jacket that hugged her

curves and made her feel like a supermodel? *So* last season.

The tan blouse and matching scarf her mother had brought home as a surprise last month? Yeah, maybe—if she were *forty*. And a desperate housewife.

No. She needed something special, something that would make her look good. *Really* good, Harper mused, fingering a lime-green miniskirt that she knew would show off her tan—and potentially, depending on how far she bent over, a lot more.

It was simple. Harper wanted Adam—and Harper always got what she wanted.

It was just a matter of figuring out how.

chapter two

SENIOR YEAR, DAY ONE.

Harper sighed. An hour into the year, and it already felt like an eternity. At least she'd already managed to snag a coveted Get-Out-of-Class-Free pass, this time in the guise of eagerness to welcome some newcomer to their hallowed halls. Because, of course, she wanted to give the girl a warm and cheery Haven High welcome.

As if.

"Ms. Grace, you're late!" called the school secretary, catching Harper wandering slowly down the hall and hauling her back into the office. "Come in, come in! Meet Haven High's newest student."

Squirming out of Mrs. Schlegel's greasy grip, Harper put on her best good-girl smile. It never hurt to curry some favor with the school's high and mighty (or their secretaries), and besides, a new student was something to see. She just hoped this one wouldn't turn out to be as big a loser as the last new girl had been. Heidi Kluger. With a name like that, a name like hocked-up phlegm, it was probably destiny. But today—

"Harper Grace, meet Kaia. Kaia Sellers, Haven High's newest senior." Mrs. Schlegel beamed at the two girls, as if expecting their lifelong friendship to begin immediately. "Kaia, Harper will be showing you around today. I'm sure she'll be happy to give you all the 411 you need."

Harper barely noticed the secretary's pathetic attempt to co-opt some teen "lingo"—she was frozen, staring at the new girl. Who was most definitely not phlegm-like. Not ugly. Not a loser.

No, from the BCBG shoes to the Marc Jacobs bag to the Ella Moss top, this girl was definitely a contender. Long, silky black hair, every strand perfectly in place (Harper unconsciously raised a hand to her own wild curls). A delicate china-doll face with just a hint of makeup to bring out her deep green eyes and high cheekbones.

And the clothes . . . Harper squelched a stab of envy, thinking of the pile of rejects still lying on her bedroom floor. The winning ensemble, hip-hugging jeans and a white backless top (the better to show off her deep tan) had seemed a good choice in the morning, but although she'd driven two hours to Ludlow this summer to find the Diesel knockoffs, she could hardly call them haute couture. Faux couture, maybe. No one around here could tell the difference. But this girl—in a red silk printed halter and matching red Max Mara skirt, an outfit Harper was sure she'd spotted in last month's *Cosmo*—this girl looked like she could.

Trying her best not to imagine what the arrival of this cooler-than-thou girl might do to her carefully maintained social status, Harper took a deep breath and began the tour. She led Kaia (what kind of a name was that, anyway?) down the hall, furiously searching for something to say that would make her sound more sophisticated than the small-town hick that Kaia was sure to be expecting.

But, wit and charm failing her when she needed them the most, Harper settled for the obvious.

"So, where are you from?"

"Oh, around." Kaia looked bored. "We have an apartment in New York—and my mother keeps a place in the country. Of course, some years I'm away at school. . . ."

Boarding school? Harper fought to maintain a neutral expression—just because the new girl was the epitome of urban rich cool and looked as if she'd just walked off a movie screen was no reason to panic.

And maybe . . .

Maybe Little Miss Perfect would actually be an asset. There had to be a way.

"Boarding school?" Harper asked, trying to sound as if she cared—though not too much, of course. "So what happened?"

"Which school?" asked Kaia, smirking. "This last time? Long story. Let's just say that if you're going to be sneaking two guys out your window, it's best to check first that the headmistress isn't spending the evening in the quad, watching a meteor shower. It's also probably best if the guys aren't carrying a stash of pot—the other half of which is in your dorm room."

Harper bit back a smile. If nothing else, this was going to be interesting.

"So as punishment, they exiled you to no-man's-land?"

"Yeah, my dad lives out here. Tough love, right? I guess they figured there'd be no trouble for me to get into out in the middle of nowhere." Kaia frowned and scanned the empty corridor. "Obviously, they were right."

It was true. Haven High wasn't much to look at— and appearances weren't deceiving. The squat building, erected in the late sixties, had been ahead of its time, its designers embracing the riot-proof concrete bunker style of architecture that grew so popular in the next decade and then deservedly vanished from sight. It was an ugly and impersonal structure, painted long ago in shades of rust and mud—also, conveniently, the school colors (although the powers that be preferred to refer to them as orange and brown). Built to accommodate a town swelled by baby boomers, the small school now housed an even smaller student body, and the dilapidated hallway in which Kaia and Harper stood was largely empty.

The girls fell silent for a moment, contemplating the peeling paint, the faint scent of cleaning fluid mixed with mashed potatoes drifting over from the cafeteria. The year to come. At the moment, neither was too thrilled by the prospect.

"So, Harper Grace," Kaia began, breaking the awkward moment. "I don't suppose that's any relation to Grace, California, my oh-so-fabulous new hometown?"

"You got it." Harper allowed herself a modest smile. She did love being great-great-great-granddaddy's little girl. "Grace Mines, Grace Library, Grace, CA. There used to be a Grace High School, too, but it burned down in the fifties."

Kaia failed to look impressed—or even particularly interested. But Harper persevered.

"This used to be a mining town, you know. My great-great-great-grandfather was like a king around here. Graces ran the mine all the way until it closed in the forties."

"Uh-huh."

Of course, Harper didn't mention the fact that a few years after the mine ran dry, the family bank account had done the same. Being a Grace somehow didn't seem to mean as much these days when the only family business was a dry cleaning shop on North Hampton Street. But at least she had the name.

Not that Kaia seemed to care.

What was the point of trying to impress this girl, anyway? She'd find out soon enough that Harper was as good as it got around here. When that happened, she'd come crawling back—in the meantime, why bother trying?

With that, Harper reverted to autopilot tour guide mode.

"And this is the gym," she explained, directing Kaia's attention to the wall moldings. "Refurbished in 1979, it can hold over one hundred people . . ."

You think you're bored now, Kaia? she thought. *You ain't seen nothing yet.*

"She said *what*?" Miranda's eyes widened.

Harper grinned. She so loved a good story, and

Miranda was such an appreciative audience—suitably shocked and awed in all the right places. Not that that was why Harper kept her around, of course . . . but it didn't hurt.

"You heard me. I asked her why she'd been kicked out of her swanky boarding school and that's what she told me." Feigning sudden disinterest in Kaia's sleazy past, Harper idly picked up one of the beakers of solution sitting on the lab table in front of her—but, thinking better of it, quickly set it down again. As if she'd been paying attention to what they were supposed to be doing with all this stuff.

Miranda let out a long, low whistle. "Do you think it's true?"

Harper shrugged. "Who knows. To be honest, she looked like she'd lie about her own name if she thought it would get a rise out of people. You know the type."

Miranda arched an eyebrow but said nothing.

"What?" Harper asked.

Miranda looked at her pointedly.

"Please. As if she is anything like me, In her dreams, maybe. You should have seen her, sauntering around like she owns the place, acting like I'm going to collapse in awe of her Marc Jacobs bag."

"*Marc Jacobs?*"

"Oh God, chill out." The shock and awe were suddenly getting a little old. "It was a bag. Probably a fake. You can always tell."

But Miranda wouldn't be put off the scent. "So why do you think that—"

"Girls, a little less conversation, a little more science, please?"

Mrs. Bonner, a short, all-too-perky blonde who liked to wear her unnecessary white lab coat even on trips to the grocery store (and Harper and Miranda could vouch for this, having once spotted the white-smocked figure ferrying a case of Budweiser out of the Shop 'n' Save), shot them a warning look and continued pacing around the room.

They were supposed to be titrating their solvent—or dissolving their titration, or something along those lines, Harper couldn't remember. Yet another reason, come to think of it, that it was useful to keep Miranda around. That and the fact that they'd been best friends since the third grade, when Mikey Mandel had knocked over Miranda's carefully constructed LEGO tower and Harper had punched him in the stomach. Mikey wasn't too happy—and Miranda had stuck by her side through all the hair-pulling, pinching, wrestling, and screaming that followed, through the unsuccessful lying and excuses when they'd been caught by the recess monitor, through the long hours they'd spent sitting out in the hall "thinking about their actions." Nine years later, Miranda had grown (if not as many inches as she'd hoped) from a shy, scrawny tomboy into a smart, snarky girl with a killer smile and the quickest wit in the West, and she was still loyally cleaning up Harper's messes—or, when that failed, readily plunging after her into the mud. Mikey Mandel, on the other hand, had grown into a serious stud: six foot four, football team's star running back, scruffy hair, smoldering eyes, never without a smiling blonde on his arm—and he was still a prick.

"I can't believe she's actually making us do a *lab* on the first day of school," Harper said, searching the photocopied packet of instructions for some hint of what she was supposed to do with the multicolored liquids staring her down from atop the table. "It's inhuman."

Miranda carefully suspended their beaker of solution over the lit Bunsen burner. "Who ever said the Bonner was human?"

It was true—they'd had her for science three years in a row (nothing ever changed at Haven High), and in all that time she'd yet to show up with new hair, new shoes, or a new lab coat—and who could imagine what lay beneath the glorified white sheet? Their very own Frankenstein's Monster, for all Harper knew. Maybe their science teacher was just some student's award-winning science project. She stifled a laugh at the thought.

"What?" hissed Miranda, flashing her a look of caution as the teacher circled toward them again. They bent intently over their flasks and beakers, feigning enthusiasm in the scientific process. The two girls at the next table squealed with joy as they measured their solvent—just as they'd predicted, to the millimeter. Woo-hoo.

"Great job, Einstein," Harper grumbled to the nearest squealer, a loser in a polo shirt and dark-rimmed glasses whom she recognized vaguely from homeroom. Probably on the math team. Or the chess "squad." "Can you invent a chemical solution that will make us care?"

The girl and her equally geeky lab partner studiously ignored her—but at least they shut up. Harper knew she probably shouldn't alienate anyone who might later be persuaded to do her work for her (since she knew from experience that doing these labs herself was basically a no-go), but it was all just too tempting. Especially given the mood she was in: shitty.

"So, is she going to be here all year?" Miranda whispered, once Bonner was a safe distance away.

"Who? Marie Curie over there? I hope not. I've already got a headache."

"No, the new girl—Kaia? How long's she staying?"

Harper shrugged. She was already sorry she'd ever started this conversation—she didn't want to talk about the new girl anymore, especially since this was shaping up to be the start of a yearlong conversation.

"It's a little stuffy in here, don't you think?" she asked, dodging Miranda's question.

"What? I guess. So?"

"So maybe it's time we get a little fresh air." Before Miranda could stop her, Harper crumpled up a piece of paper, dipped it into the Bunsen burner's flame for a moment, and then surreptitiously tossed the fiery ball into their trash can.

"What the hell are you doing?" Miranda hissed.

Harper ignored her, and instead watched with delight as flames began to lick at the edges of the squat trash can, slowly consuming the crumpled paper. It was mesmerizing.

"Fire!" Harper finally shouted.

On cue, the girls next to her began squealing in horror, and one slammed her fist into the emergency sprinkler button that hung next to each lab table.

That was all it took.

The room began to rain.

The smoke alarm blared.

And chaos broke out as the roomful of students scrambled to get their stuff together and escape the downpour, pushing and shoving each other out of the way, only a couple of them craning their necks to search for the fire, which had very quickly gone out. Mrs. Bonner raced back and forth across the room, herding students out of danger but clearly more concerned about making sure that her precious chemicals and lab equipment stayed safe, sound, and dry.

Laughing, water pouring down her face, Harper pulled Miranda out of the classroom and down the hall. They ran for an exit together and ducked into the parking lot, finally sinking down behind a row of parked cars, convulsing with laughter on the warm concrete.

"I can't believe you just did that," Miranda gasped, half annoyed and half amazed. "I'm totally soaked."

Harper grinned lazily and, catlike, stretched her body out and preened in the sun.

"You'll dry. And now instead of titrating and distilling and blah, blah, blah, we can spend the rest of the hour talking about the important things in life."

"Like?"

"I don't know. Guys? What we're going to do this weekend? Whether any of your cigarettes are still dry enough to smoke?"

Sighing, Miranda pulled out her pack—only slightly wet on one corner—and tossed it to Harper.

"I don't want to rain on your parade, but did you even stop to consider what would happen if you'd gotten caught? Or if, I don't know, you'd *set the school on fire*?"

"Rand, it was a *double period*." Harper spoke slowly and loudly, Miranda needed a little help trying to wrap her brain around the basics. "We would have been stuck in there *forever*."

"Oh, please." Miranda began digging through her soggy backpack, assessing the damage: Spanish notebook: dry. Sort of. Paperback *Hamlet* for AP English: soaked. Emergency repair kit (mascara, cover-up, extra-strength safety pins, etc.): mercifully intact. "If you'd waited, we would have been out in an hour."

Harper took a long drag on the cigarette and took a moment to consider that.

"We're seniors now," she said finally. "We've waited long enough."

Boring.

It had taken the girl—Harper—an endless fifty minutes to guide Kaia through the school, fifty minutes of her life she would never get back. And the rest of the morning had been more of the same. People she didn't want to meet, telling her things she didn't want to know. As if the mundane details of anything in this tedious town could be anything less than tedious.

Anything but boring.

Boring.

Boring.

The word had been beating a steady tattoo in her head ever since she'd arrived in this one-horse (or in this case, she supposed, one-Walmart) town. The whole place had the feel of a different century, except for the tacky tourist strip of Route 66 running through the town center—*there* time seemed frozen in a particularly bad year of the 1970s.

She'd plodded through three hours of the school day and knew pretty much all that she needed to know about her new life in Grace—as in, there wouldn't be much of one.

Now here she was, standing in line in a cafeteria—a *cafeteria*, a smelly, cramped room painted hospital green, with long metal tables bolted to the floor, cranky old women in hairnets doling out lumps of food, hordes of dull-eyed students who at least deserved credit for not all outweighing an elephant, if they'd been eating this greasy crap their entire lives. Who knew places like this actually existed?

Kaia's schooltime meals had varied. There was the gourmet health food in the regal boarding school refectory, with its vaulted ceilings and centuries-old oak tables. And of course the Upper West Side takeout cuisine grabbed to go during lunch periods—well, any and all periods—at her city prep school. (Prep school had been before and after boarding school—getting kicked out was easy when you had plenty of money and connections to kick you into somewhere else. How was Kaia supposed to know she would only have so many opportunities to vacillate between frying pan and fire before getting thrown off the stove altogether?) Even the lunches the maid had occasionally put together for her—or, years ago, the lunches her mother had packed before she'd decided that mothering was too last season—even those had been better than this slop.

But that was then, this was now.

This was life in Grace: dry heat, neon, decrepit gas stations, incompetent teachers, grease, dust, *cafeterias*. This was her life.

She was stuck. Stranded. A world away from everyone and everything she'd ever known.

At least it was also a world away from her mother.

"Kaia, over here!"

Kaia turned lazily to see the mind-numbing tour guide, Harper, waving in her direction. She stuck on a smile. No reason to burn any bridges—not yet, at least. Besides, no way was she eating alone.

"*My friends* wanted you to come have lunch with us," Harper said.

Kaia noticed, but didn't mention, the pronoun plainly missing from Harper's halfhearted invitation. She followed Harper obediently out of the dingy cafeteria and into the cramped "quad" behind it, where students were apparently allowed to eat—if they could find a place to perch amidst the broken tables and scattered garbage. Kaia wrinkled her nose—this whole school should be declared a toxic-waste site. Students included.

"Everyone, this is Kaia Sellers," Harper said with a sarcastic flourish of her hands, once they'd found the right table.

Mmm . . . maybe not *all* the students. "Everyone" apparently included two tasty guys who looked as if they'd just walked out of an Abercrombie ad. They were sprawled on the wooden benches along with a few other apparent A-listers—even mahogany-filled dining halls have tables set aside for the social elite, and as a lifelong member of that class, Kaia could spot the signs from a mile away. The table was on the outskirts of the quad, far from the lunch-room monitor who poked her head outside every once in a while to make sure no one was smoking, drinking, or destroying school property.

But even physically on the margins, the group was still somehow at the center of everything—attention, conversation, focus. These kids were loved, they were hated—but most of all, they were watched. Kaia had found her place.

"This is Miranda Stevens." Harper stood next to Kaia but had carefully angled her body away, so that she could keep a close watch on her but didn't have to make any direct eye contact.

One of the girls, apparently Miranda, stepped forward to shake Kaia's hand. Scarecrow thin; limp, dull hair pulled back into geeky braids; some unfortunate fashion choices—the white T-shirt under the imitation Chanel jacket just wasn't doing it. *But cute*, Kaia thought. She'd do.

"And I'm Beth," the other girl, blond and beautiful—if you liked that farmer's daughter thing—waved from the other end of the table, where she was tucked under the arm of Abercrombie Number One. "Welcome to Haven High. I'm sure you—"

"And this is Adam and Kane," Harper interrupted, stepping around to the other side of the table and placing a possessive hand on each of their backs.

Adam was an all-American boy, with blond hair, a square jaw, an honest face, a dark blue T-shirt that no doubt hid washboard abs but revealed astonishingly thick biceps—no surprise, then, that he would be dating the farmer's daughter.

He kept one arm tightly around the blond girl, but reached out the other to shake Kaia's hand. His fingers were warm, his grasp firm—she held it just a second too long.

Kane, on the other hand—there was nothing honest about him. The same muscles (they definitely didn't make them like this in New York), the same striking good looks, but she could tell from his hooded eyes, from the smirk playing across his lips, from his unabashed and appreciative appraisal of her body as he rose to greet her, that he was playing in a different league. Maybe playing a different game.

Again Kaia extended a hand; instead of shaking it, Kane gently turned it face down, then raised it to his lips and gave it a light kiss.

"Charmed," he said, and somehow it worked.

Both boys grinned at her, and Kaia could feel their gazes traveling down her long neck and lingering at the point where her silver pendant disappeared into the darkness of her low-cut V-neck. *Boys and cleavage*, she thought. *It never fails.*

She noticed Harper noticing the boys' glances—and saw the girl's eyes narrow.

Who knows—maybe she could have a little fun here after all. . . .

It was a perverse rule of nature: The first day of school always lasted forever. Temporal distortion not covered by the theory of relativity: One hour of first-day time roughly equivalent to half an eternity of normal time. Endless minutes of staring out the window, cursing the wasted daylight, all that time *not* getting a tan, *not* drinking a frozen strawberry margarita, *not* listening to cheesy eighties music and complaining there was never anything to do while secretly delighting in the Madonna sing-along. Outside was suddenly Eden—inside, sweating through sixth period and watching the decrepit clock tick off the minutes, surely nothing less than the seventh circle of Hell.

But this year, waiting through the day presented, at least for some, a special torture. They weren't waiting for the final bell, they were waiting for the final period: advanced French.

Normally a snoozefest with 150-year-old Madame Marshak (who, in the best tradition of hatefully eccentric high school French teachers, remained convinced of her essential Frenchness, despite her Houston birth certificate and unmistakable Texan twang). But this year Marshak had finally gone on to greener pastures—her sister's house in Buffalo. Although given her advanced age and penchant for driving around tipsy after too much cheap French wine, it seemed likely that Buffalo would be only a brief layover on the way to her final destination.

Regardless, there was a new *professeur* in town—the first new teacher Haven High had seen in years.

He was young.

He was British.

And, if freshman gossip was to be believed—for he'd

already made an appearance in third period's French for annoying beginners—he was hot.

Seriously hot.

There was only one advanced French class, which meant that Beth, Harper, and now Kaia would be stuck in the small room together all year long.

Beth sat toward the front and flipped through her organizer, trying to figure out how she was going to fit in homework, editing the school newspaper, applying to colleges, babysitting her little brothers, and working a part-time job without going insane. And, oh yeah, without letting her boyfriend forget what she looked like.

Harper, ensconced as usual in the back row, lazily examined her nails and decided that it was definitely time for a manicure. And, come to think of it, maybe a pedicure. And a haircut. Not that there was a decent salon anywhere in town, but at Betty's off of Green Street, they did a slightly better than half-assed job, and threw in a ten-minute head and shoulder massage for free. Which was an appealing thought—it was only the first day of school and already she could use a serious de-stressing.

Kaia slipped into the classroom just before the bell—Haven High stuck its language classes down in the basement, and she'd already stumbled across a decrepit boiler room and overstuffed janitor's closet before finally finding her way here.

She took the only seat that was left, on the aisle next to a boy who smelled like rotten fruit. A fitting end to the day. Or *un fin parfait pour le jour*, as her new French teacher would say. Wherever he was. "Advanced" French. Such a waste of her time, Kaia thought, considering she'd spent half of last summer on the Riviera, gossiping with the château's staff like a native. Such a joke. Such a—

Such an unexpected treat. If the man who had just appeared in the doorway, flashed the class a rakish smile, ran a hand through his adorably floppy hair, and strode to the front of the room was actually their teacher, life at Haven High was suddenly looking up.

For the rumors were right.

This guy was hot.

Seriously hot.

Just like a movie star, Beth sighed to herself as he grabbed a piece of chalk and wrote his name on the board in quick, loping script.

Jack Powell.

"Hola! Me llamo Jack Powell. Cómo está?" he asked, as the class stared blankly back at him. "Okay, and if you understood any of that, you're probably in the wrong place and you should get out. As for the rest of you, *bienvenue* and welcome to French 4."

Hot and British, Harper mused. *Tasty—Tom Hardy*

meets Jonathan Rhys Meyers. So what the hell is he doing here?

"As you probably know, I'm new around here," Powell admitted, taking off his sports jacket and perching casually on the edge of his desk. "So I'm sure this class is going to have some surprises to offer all of us."

You have no idea, Kaia thought. She had never expected to find someone like him in this shitty town. But now that opportunity had knocked, it seemed only polite to open the door and invite him in.

chapter three

"ADAM, I TOLD YOU. NOT YET." BETH REACHED OUT a hand toward him, but he pulled away, rolling over on his side. It was still strange for her to see him there, in the bed she'd slept in since she was a child. It was a child's room, really—ruffled bedspread, white wooden furniture with light blue trim, so much pink that it was embarrassing. If she'd had her way, the room would be sophisticated and sparse, with only a dark mahogany desk, some Ansel Adams prints on the wall, and a crowded bookshelf in the corner. But these days her parents had neither the money nor the patience for interior decorating, so her seventeen-year-old self was forever trapped in the pink pleated land of her eight-year-old self's dreams. There was even a stuffed animal, the only thing in the room she didn't hate—though at the moment, poor Snuffy the Turtle was crushed beneath Adam's half-naked body. *One of these things is not like the other*, she thought crazily, the Sesame Street lyric wandering through her mind as she sought frantically for something to say that would make Adam understand. Was this really her life? "I'm just not ready."

"I know, and I'm not trying to rush you," he said with his back to her, a petulant tone creeping into his voice. "I'm *not*—it's just that . . ."

Beth sat up and pulled on her pale pink bra, struggling to fasten the clasp behind her. It was past five and her mother would be home soon. Now was not the time for yet another round of this conversation.

"Look, Adam, you know it's not that I don't love you, it's not that I don't want to . . ." God, how she wanted to.

"What, then?" He rolled back to face her, pulling her close. "What's stopping us? I know you wanted to wait but . . . what are we waiting for?"

If only she knew the answer. If only she could put into words the terror she felt when she let her fantasies get away from her and imagined throwing herself at him, losing herself to the moment, and—but her imagination took her only so far. That's when the fear set in.

And however handsome he looked lying there, one arm stretched out over his head and a lock of hair falling over his deep, dark eyes, however much she may have wanted him—all of him—she just couldn't do it. Not yet. Not like this.

It hadn't always been like this, the pressure, the silent give-and-take, worrying about what she wanted and what he wanted and what happened next. No, in the beginning, it had been simple. She had hated him.

Totally hated him, and everything he stood for—which as far as she was concerned, was sports, sex, and beer. She'd hated the way the whole school thought he walked on water, just because he could swim quickly across a pool every fall, could drop a ball into a hoop every winter, just because he was tall, and chiseled, and had a smile that warmed you like the sun. She'd hated his stupid jock clothes, his stupid jock jokes—most of all, his stupid jock friends. All so arrogant, acting like Beth and her friends were expected to bow and curtsy every time they swept down the hall—and the girls hanging on them were even worse, simpering and giggling, desperately trying to keep their jock's attention, or at least to win favor with Harper and her gang, the female counterpart to all this athletic royalty.

When she'd been stuck with Adam as a lab partner last year in bio, all her friends had been jealous—but Beth had just sighed, figuring she'd have to do all the work. She'd been right—put a scalpel in his hands and a pickled frog in front of him, and Adam was as helpless as she would be if plopped down in the middle of a basketball court, facing down the WNBA all-star team. She'd been right about that—but not much else.

He wasn't arrogant, he wasn't stupid, he wasn't an asshole or a dumb jock. By October he was just . . . Adam. Sweet, funny, adorable—and he would stop at nothing until she went out with him. For whatever reason—well, basically for the reason that he'd flirted with or dated half the school, and she didn't particularly want to be his next randomly selected conquest—she refused. And refused again.

It hadn't stopped him. He'd started slipping notes in her locker, leaving flowers for her at her seat in lab—he wouldn't give up. Then came the day he'd waited for her at her locker after school, greeting her with a giddy smile and a goofy wave. Before she knew it, he was down on one knee.

"Marry me?" he'd asked, pulling a giant plastic ring out of his pocket. It was a bright blue flower, about the size of her palm. It was ludicrous—and irresistible.

"Get up!" she'd urged him through her giggles, blushing furiously as a crowd began to gather.

"Not until you give me a chance." He'd seemed

oblivious to the curiosity-seekers. Or maybe he was just used to being the center of attention.

"I'm not marrying you, idiot." She was losing the battle against laughter. He stayed in position.

"Okay then, we'll start slow. One date—one chance. Then I'll never bother you again."

How could she say no?

He'd been her first kiss, her first boyfriend, her first love, her first—everything. And everything had been perfect. Until now—when she wanted him more than ever, which only made things worse. Everything that had been easy between them, all the effortless conversation, the casual kisses, the laughter—it was all weighed down by the silence of what they couldn't say. Everything on the surface was still so right—but beneath that, Beth feared, there was something brittle, something fragile. Something wrong.

She leaned over and kissed him gently on the forehead and once on the lips, then hopped out of bed to gather up the clothes they'd strewn haphazardly across her bedroom.

"Up 'n' Adam," she chirped, hoping her voice wasn't shaking. She tossed a balled-up T-shirt toward him. "You know my mother will be home any minute, and if she finds us up here . . ."

Silently, Adam got out of bed and pulled on his clothes. The quiet minutes dragged on for an eternity, until Beth was afraid he would leave without saying another word. But before he did, he came up and put his arms around her, pulling her into a tight embrace. Beth buried her head in his chest, reveling in the soft, familiar scent of his cologne and trying her best to fight back the tears.

"You know I love you," he whispered. He released her, then tipped her chin up, forcing her to meet his eyes. "You know I love you," he said again, his lips only a breath away. "And you know I'll wait."

Beth nodded. She knew he loved her, and she knew he would wait—but for how long?

Kane surveyed the tacky surroundings in disgust. Magazine clippings from the fifties papered the walls, fake plastic records dangled from the ceiling, and a giant neon jukebox blasted out oldies while bored waitresses plodded back and forth between the crowded booths and the crowded kitchen, snapping their gum and pretending they didn't desperately wish they were somewhere, anywhere, else.

"Remind me again why we keep coming back here?" he asked.

Harper hit an imaginary *Jeopardy!* buzzer.

"What is 'the only diner in town'?" she reminded him. She took another spoonful of her ice-cream sundae and moaned with pleasure. "Besides, who could deny the appeal of a restaurant with a motto like that?" She tapped a

perfectly manicured finger on top of the fluorescent menu:
LIFE IS SHORT—EAT DESSERT FIRST.

"Good point," Kane admitted, scooping off a good chunk of her ice cream, complete with cherry—he'd finished his own sundae within minutes of its arrival.

"Hands off!" Harper laughed, smacking his spoon away. "Sure you don't want some, Miranda?" she asked, pushing the giant bowl across the table toward her friend. Miranda squirmed back, waving it away.

"Some of us actually want to have room for dinner," she pointed out.

"Oh, come on, Stevens, live a little," Kane encouraged her, grabbing a spoon and digging in once again. "Be a rebel—I know you've got some bad girl blood in there somewhere."

Miranda hesitantly took a small bite of the ice cream, flushing as his deep chocolate eyes paused on her and a slow, satisfied smile lit up his face.

"Atta girl. I knew you had it in you."

Is he flirting *with me?* she wondered.

If only.

Miranda had known Kane for almost as long as she'd known Harper a few minutes short of forever. She doubted that he remembered the time they'd spent a third grade recess playing dominoes together, or the knight in shining armor moment when he'd tossed her a towel after an embarrassing "wardrobe malfunction" at Shayna Hernandez's eighth grade pool party. In fact, she doubted that he would even remember her name—or at least admit to doing so—if she wasn't usually joined at the hip with Harper, one of the only people that Kane didn't find to be a yawn a minute. But whatever the reason that put him across the table from her so often, she was grateful. And sometimes wondered whether this wasn't perhaps the year that he'd get sick of the bimbos and finally notice her.

Maybe the next time her bikini top popped off, Kane wouldn't be so quick with the towel. . . .

"Earth to Stevens." His voice punctured her reverie. "Dreaming about my hot bod again? You girls just can't help yourselves, can you?"

Miranda snorted, hoping her face wasn't too red. "As if."

Did she sound believably casual—but not so disgusted that he would think it inconceivable that she'd been thinking about his tightly toned forearms?

Miranda knew there was a middle ground somewhere between obsessed stalker and mortal enemy, but she'd never had much luck finding it. (This likely explained why all her carefully constructed flirty banter, designed to make junior high crush Rob Schwartz realize she was interested, but not *too* interested, had instead left the JV quarterback with the unshakeable conviction that she hated him.)

She'd gotten a little better since then—but not much.

Beth and Adam were late.

They came into the diner arm in arm, whispering to each other. Harper waved to get their attention, then quickly looked away. It was too sickening to watch.

"Where've you guys been?" Kane asked with a leer when they arrived at the table. "As if I have to ask."

Beth tucked her hair behind her ears, blushing, and Adam began to stammer out something about lost keys and car trouble and—

"Oh, just sit down," Harper interrupted. "We waited for you to order dinner, and we're starving, so let's just get to it."

"Spoken with your usual grace and accuracy," Kane said. "I second the motion."

Beth and Adam squeezed into the booth next to Miranda, smushing her up against the window since the bench was meant for only two people. But Harper chose not to say anything about it—the way things were going, Beth would probably just smile politely and offer to spend the rest of the night perched on Adam's lap, to save room. She was just *so* accommodating. And, Harper had to admit, beautiful. She'd changed out of her first-day-of-school outfit (standard Beth: classic-cut jeans, black T-shirt, gold hoop earrings, bland and forgettable) into a backless turquoise sundress that matched her eyes and perfectly set off her sun-drenched hair. And Harper wasn't the only one to appreciate it. As Beth leaned forward to order her food, Adam reached over and began slowly rubbing her bare back; Harper couldn't pull her eyes away from his hand, lightly playing its way up and down Beth's skin. She could almost feel its warm pressure on her own.

Harper shook her head violently to knock the fantasy away, and then waved them all to be quiet. There was a reason she'd invited them out tonight—aside from the understandable need for large amounts of grease and sugar after the long first day of school. And, since she was losing her appetite by the minute watching the lovebirds fawn, it was probably time to get started.

"Okay, now that you're *all* here"—she tried not to glare at Beth—"here's the deal. We've got two weeks until the annual lame back-to-school formal, right?"

Kane groaned. "Don't remind me. What a joke."

Harper ignored him and continued. "And two weeks until the annual top secret after-party, organized by a select group of seniors."

"Kerry Stanton and those girls did it last year, right?" Beth asked. "Wonder who they tapped for this year."

Harper gave her a withering stare. Was the girl an idiot?

"Kerry e-mailed me this afternoon," Harper explained with a self-satisfied grin. "Looks like I'm up."

"You?" Miranda asked, grinning. "Awesome."

"Actually—us."

Adam held up his hands in protest. "Hold up, Harper— look, we're all impressed that you're now officially the coolest of the cool and all, but if you think you're roping me into some kind of *dance* committee . . ."

"God, it's not a dance, Adam. It's a party. A secret, illicit, just-for-seniors party?" She smiled winningly. "And I know you *all* want to help out, get on the inside track, be adored by the masses—"

"Not to mention, get first dibs on the best beer and the comfiest mattresses," Kane pointed out. "Sign me up."

Harper smacked him and was about to launch back into her spiel when the diner door opened, and in walked Kaia. On anyone else, her Little Black Dress would have looked ridiculously out of place amidst the neon and trucker chic, but Kaia seemed oblivious of context, striding forward with purpose and grace. She looked completely at ease, though Harper could tell, just from the little things—the single finger she'd used to push open the door as if afraid of the germs, the delicate steps she took as if expecting at any moment to splash her kitten heel into a puddle of mustard—that she was not.

"Are you kidding me?" Harper muttered to herself. "Maybe she won't see—"

"Kaia, over here!" Beth chirped, waving the new girl over. "I invited her to come along," she explained to the table. "I thought it would be nice—you know, she doesn't know anyone, and—what?" she asked, irritated, as the boys laughed, while Miranda and Harper just rolled their eyes. "What is it?"

"It was a nice thing to do," Adam assured her, laying a hand on hers. "I'm sure she appreciated it."

"I know *I* do," Kane added, quickly shutting up as Kaia approached.

"Am I too late?" Kaia asked as she arrived at the table, eyeing the empty ice-cream dishes.

"No, we haven't even ordered yet," Kane reassured her, shifting over to make room for her (now Harper, too, was smushed against the window—and if there was going to be a male body pressed up against her like this, Kane's was really *not* the one she would have chosen). "Don't worry, Grace here just likes to eat dessert first."

"Why am I not surprised?" Kaia asked, and while her tone was light and pleasant, Harper could feel the girl's icy eyes boring through her.

"So, about this party . . ." Miranda began, trying to defuse the tension.

Harper kicked her under the table, but it was too late.

"Party?" Kaia asked. "Sounds like I'm just in time."

"We're all going to help Harper organize this party thing in a couple of weeks," Adam explained.

What was with the "we"? Harper wondered. He hadn't sounded so enthused a moment ago. Before *she* walked in.

"Not all of us," Beth added, her eyes darting away. "Sorry, Harper, I wish I could help, but I'm way too busy already."

"What are you talking about?" Adam asked. He whirled to face her, his mouth crinkling into a frown.

"You know, I have a bunch of after-school meetings, and this new job, and my brothers to take care of, and—"

"Can't you just make the time? We never get to do anything like this *together*," he complained, running a hand through his hair in frustration. He took her hand in his, but she quickly pulled it away.

"No, I can't just *make* time—it's not that easy. And anyway—" Beth suddenly realized that the whole table was eagerly watching their back-and-forth. "Can we just talk about this later?" she requested in a more measured tone.

"Fine. Whatever," Adam said sulkily. "I guess Kaia can take your spot."

"I'm sure Kaia's way too busy for that sort of thing," Harper quickly interrupted. "Places to go, people to do, you know how it is."

"Harper!" Adam turned toward her, shocked.

"What? She's a big-city girl—why would she want to waste her time on small-town shit like this?"

"Uh, she is sitting right here, you know," Kaia pointed out. "Though apparently you'd prefer it if I weren't. Excuse me." And, perfectly composed, she stood up and glided toward the door.

"What are you doing?" Adam hissed. "Why are you acting like this?"

"Whatever, she said it herself this morning," Harper told him. She raised her voice so that more of the restaurant—specifically, those who were putting on a big show of leaving in a petty snit—could hear her. "All she cares about are drugs and sex."

"Which should give the two of you a lot in common," Adam retorted, and pushed himself away from the table, following Kaia out of the restaurant.

Harper sucked in her breath sharply, and the rest of them stared at her in stunned silence. It was a pretty rare sight to see perpetually good-natured Adam turn ugly—and an even rarer one to see Harper as the target of his attack. Harper squirmed under their gazes and chewed nervously on the inside of her cheek. Picking a fight with Adam wasn't part of tonight's plans—but then again, having Kaia tag along with the whole party planning thing wasn't either. There had been a brief, blessed moment, just after Beth had refused to play, when Harper imagined what it might be like working side by side with Adam—long hours, private strategy sessions, laughter, flirting, and then one day, maybe, she would make her move. Or—even better—he would make his. One moment of possibility. And then Kaia had ruined everything.

Adam soon led Kaia back into the restaurant, his hand held lightly on her back as he guided her down the aisle and back to the table. As Kaia whispered something in his ear and Adam burst into quiet laughter, Harper was hit with a bizarre flash of déjà vu. Hadn't this scene just happened, with a different starlet playing the role of female ingenue? She wondered if Beth, too, had picked up on the instant replay—then again, Miss Manners really had no one to blame but herself, since she was the one who'd invited the wolf to come have dinner with the lambs.

Not that Harper had any intention of playing the lamb in this little romantic grudge match.

Adam and Kaia sat down again, and Harper—after a stern look from Adam—grudgingly apologized. They ate in relative peace, but when the burgers, fries, and Miranda's salad were gone, no one was in the mood for a second round of desserts.

As they rose to leave, Adam pulled Harper aside, and they walked slowly, out of earshot of the rest of the group.

"I'm sorry," he said quietly. "For what I said earlier."

"Don't worry about it," Harper told him, not quite meeting his eyes.

"No, I was totally out of line—it's just, I'm just a little edgy these days." They had reached the door, and Adam held it open and swept her through with exaggerated chivalry. She paused in the doorway and looked up at him, his face only inches away. If she stood on her toes, she'd be close enough to . . . well, it was close. She could smell his cologne, a cool, fresh scent that smelled like rain. Like Adam.

"Seriously, don't worry about it." Harper swallowed her pain and her anger and forced a smile, then gave him a quick kiss on the cheek. "I swear—all is forgiven."

She glared at Kaia's back, a few steps ahead.

Forgiven—but not forgotten.

Kaia took one last disgusted look at the Nifty Fifties Diner before following the "gang" into the parking lot. This town was pathetic. It was like being trapped in the Vegas stage version of a *Glee* episode—disgustingly earnest teenagers with boring middle-America issues, prancing around on a set lifted from a Travel Channel rundown of America's Tackiest Tourist Traps. At least there was some good scenery. All it needed was the tone-deaf sound track. Exhibit A: Adam Morgan.

"You need a ride, Kaia?" he asked, taking Beth's hand as they headed toward his car, a maroon Chevrolet with a dented fender and a discolored side panel that seemed lifted from a different car.

Kaia, who had parked her father's Beamer around the corner, figured she could find a way to retrieve it in the morning.

"Actually, I was just about to ask," Kaia answered, smiling at Adam. "I got a ride here from my dad, but he's out for the night—are you sure it's not too much trouble? I live pretty far out."

Beth laughed and jabbed her boyfriend in the arm good-naturedly. "Are you kidding? Adam loves to drive, don't you? I think he secretly wishes I lived out in the middle of nowhere so that he'd have more chances to take his prized possession for a real ride."

Kaia grinned naughtily at the thought of taking Adam for "a real ride," but she kept her mouth shut—it was just too easy. Besides, she'd already committed herself to play-ing the wounded good girl role. Her little chat with Adam earlier had convinced her that he was just burning for a chance to play knight in shining armor to some fragile princess. And Kaia was happy to accommodate him— which meant the knee-jerk sex kitten comments would just have to go unspoken.

"Great," she said, trying her best not to wrinkle her

nose at the sight of Adam's Chevy. It looked even more wretched close up, like a junk heap molded into the shape of a car, held together with duct tape. Prized possession? It didn't speak very well for his taste—of course, from what she'd seen so far, neither did Beth. But she was willing to give him the benefit of the doubt.

She looked over her shoulder at Kane, who was climbing into a vintage silver Camaro. And he was just as hot as Adam, though he lacked the adorable Southern accent. But the guy was obviously a total player—and thus not nearly as much fun to play with. No, she decided, climbing into the backseat and pulling the door shut behind her, Adam it is. At least for now.

Beth and Adam chattered together in the front while Kaia sat in silence, watching the dark streets fly by.

"You want to come back to my place?" Adam asked. "My mom's probably out for the night. . . ."

There was a long pause, and Beth looked over her shoulder and glanced at Kaia. "I've got a lot of work to do," she said eventually. "And, you know, curfew."

"I just thought that—"

"Why don't you drop me off first," Beth cut him off. "I'm on the way."

Trouble in paradise? Kaia wondered. Interesting.

Adam grunted and turned off onto a side street. He pulled up in front of a squat ranch house, sandwiched between a row of identically impersonal boxes. A tricycle lay on its side in the middle of the small front lawn, which looked as if it hadn't seen a lawn mower in years. The cramped patch of overgrown weeds was the perfect companion to the house itself, with its peeling paint job and rusted aluminum siding. Home sweet home.

Adam turned off the car and unfastened his seat belt, but Beth stopped him with a quick kiss.

"You don't have to walk me in," she whispered. "I'll just see you tomorrow." She kissed him again, this time long and hard, and then got out of the car and raced up the front walkway, a narrow path of loose gravel and chipped cement. She paused in the doorway, fumbling in her purse for the key, then, finally, pulled open the door and slipped into the house, the slim beam of light cut off as she closed the door behind her.

Adam was still for a moment, watching her figure disappear into the darkness. Then he twisted around in his seat and grinned at Kaia.

"Why don't you come sit up here?" he suggested, patting the seat next to him.

Perfect. Kaia hopped out of the car and switched into the front seat. As she fastened her seat belt, she lightly brushed his hand, which rested on the gearshift—he tensed, almost imperceptibly, and she knew he'd felt the same electric charge of excitement that she had at the touch.

She ignored it, however, and began playing with the radio stations, searching in vain for something that was neither country-and-western nor fire-and-brimstone.

"Not much to listen to out here, is there?" Kaia complained, as Adam started the car and pulled back out onto the road. She flicked off the stereo. "Not much to do, either."

"No," he admitted. "But it's a good town. Good people, you know?"

Could this guy be any more of a small-town cliché? She didn't know they *made* them like this in real life.

"Anyway," he continued awkwardly, "I'm sorry again about before, in the diner—Harper's just, well . . ."

"An acquired taste?" Kaia suggested, faking a smile.

"I guess you could say that," Adam admitted. "See, the thing you've got to understand about Harper is . . ." His voice faded off, and he squinted his eyes in concentration, trying to find the right words.

"Her bark is worse than her bite?" Kaia offered.

Adam laughed ruefully and shook his head. "No, I'd watch out for her bite, too."

Good to know, Kaia thought. "Then what?" she persisted. "I mean, you seem like such a nice, genuine guy, and I guess I'm just surprised that you're . . . that not all of your friends are . . . I'm just a little surprised." Kaia guessed there was no particularly polite way to say, *So, your friend is an überbitch*. Hopefully she'd made her point without doing major damage to her mission.

"Look, I know Harper can be kind of—"

"Harsh?"

"Kind of a bitch, basically," Adam acknowledged. Kaia suppressed her laughter—good to know he wasn't totally blind. "It's not something I love about her," Adam continued with a sigh. "But the thing about Harper is, well, things come pretty easy for her. She gets bored—and you can see why."

"Bored? In this town? *No*," Kaia drawled sarcastically. How could you be bored when the bowling alley was open 24/7?

"No, it's not just that," Adam clarified. "It's not just that it's a small town. It's Harper—she just—doesn't belong here, somehow. She's better than this place." He shook his head ruefully. "And the problem is, she knows it."

"It sounds like you—" But Kaia cut herself off almost as soon as she began. No reason to put ideas in his head. If he was too dense to figure it out for himself, she certainly wasn't going to help him along.

"I what?" he asked, confused.

"Nothing." Kaia paused, watching the dark shadows of parked cars, deserted buildings, flat, arid land speed by. The emptiness was endless. "Have a lot of respect for her, that's all," she finished feebly.

"Well, I've known her a long time," he explained, pulling onto the empty highway. "She was the first friend I made when I moved here. I trust her—and whatever else she's done, she's never betrayed that. She's the same with Miranda. When Harper decides you're worthy of her time, she's actually the best friend you could have. Loyal as a pit bull."

"Which would explain both the barking and the biting," Kaia pointed out.

He laughed. "Exactly."

They were both quiet for a moment, and Kaia realized that this was the most she'd ever heard Adam speak. He hadn't said much during dinner, and even when Beth was in the car, he'd mostly been listening to her prattle on about her day. The strong, silent type, Kaia decided. Likes listening better than talking—so maybe she should give him something to listen to.

"Well, pit bull or not, you don't have to worry about me," she assured him. "I can handle myself. You have to be tough when you . . ." She let her voice trail off and looked down at her hands. Would he take the bait?

"When you what?" he asked, sounding concerned.

Score.

"It's just—you know, it's hard, bouncing from school to school, always being the new kid, knowing that neither of your parents want you around. . . ."

Amazing how truth can sometimes be more effective than fiction.

Kaia let her voice tremble, just a bit. "And people assume things about you, you know, treat you in a certain way, like you're this person, this person who has nothing to do with who you really are. . . ."

Adam took one hand off the wheel and rested it on her shoulder; Kaia suppressed a grin.

"Hey, we're not all like that," he assured her.

Kaia laughed, shakily.

"Listen to me, 'poor little rich girl.' And I don't even know you." She wiped an eye, hoping he wouldn't notice the lack of a tear.

"Can we just . . . just forget I said anything?" she asked.

Adam nodded—but he kept a firm hand on her shoulder.

They drove in silence down the empty highway for several miles, until Kaia pointed to the shadowy silhouette of a mailbox, the only sign of civilization along the dark stretch of road.

"Turn up here, I think," she said, and the car swung left, up a long gravel pathway, arriving at the foot of a large house of glass and steel.

"Whoa," Adam murmured softly. "Unbelievable."

The house—more of an estate, really—gleamed in the moonlight. Its sleek modernity would have been utterly out of place amidst the age-encrusted remnants in the

Grace town center, but out here on the fringe, the elegant beast seemed a perfect fit with the harsh aesthetics of the dessert landscape. Stark steel beams, giant windows, a jig-saw puzzle of smooth surfaces—it was like no house he'd ever seen.

"This is where you live?" he asked in a hushed voice.

"Like I said, 'poor little rich girl,'" Kaia quipped.

Adam turned off the car and hopped out to open Kaia's door for her.

A total gentleman.

"Listen, Kaia," he said as they walked up the long, narrow path toward her door. "Obviously we don't know each other that well yet, but I just want you to know—if you ever need anyone to talk to, you know, I'm around."

Brushing away another fake tear, Kaia threw her arms around Adam and hugged him tightly to her.

What a body.

"Thank you," she whispered into his ear, making sure to graze his cheek with her moist lips. "You'll never know how much that means to me."

She let herself into the house, pausing in the doorway to watch him walk back to the car. Even his silhouette had sex appeal.

This is almost too easy to be worth my time, she thought. Almost.

❧   ❧   ❧

By the time Adam got home, it was too late to call Beth—and besides, what would he say? "In case I didn't make it clear to you before, I'd really like to sleep with you—and even though I am the perfect PC boyfriend and will stand by you no matter what and don't—I swear to you, *don't*—just want you for sex, I think it's natural for me to want that, too, especially since I'm probably the only eighteen-year-old homecoming king virgin this side of the Mississippi"?

Yeah, that would go over really well.

He sounded like one of those Neanderthals in the teen after-school specials they played on local access TV and occasionally showed as a precautionary measure in health class: "But gee, honey, I have these urges . . ."

No, best just to wait it out.

It hadn't always been like this, of course. Back in the beginning, she couldn't get enough of him—they couldn't get enough of each other. He would come over to her house after school and they would try to do homework together, and after a few minutes she would tire of aimlessly flipping through the pages of her history textbook, and he would give up on furiously writing and erasing and rewriting wrong answers to the same trig problem over and over again, and that would be it. He would look up, she would look up, their eyes would meet, and they would be on each other, kissing, stroking, fumbling with buttons and bra straps, desperate to drink each other in, to find every one of their bodies' hidden secrets, to touch, to meld. Sometimes all it took was an accidental touch—sitting across a table from each other, his hand would brush against hers, and it was like a stroke of lightning, a bolt of charge between them, and he would have to have her. And it wasn't just him. There were times . . . that day last spring in the empty hallway when he'd given her a quick peck on the cheek before going off to practice. He'd turned to leave, and she grabbed the back of his shirt collar, pulled him back to her, back into her arms. Then Beth—practical Beth, shy Beth, tentative Beth—had pushed him up against the wall and dug her body into him, sucking on his lips and kneading her fingers into his muscles. Not caring who saw. In the beginning it had been like that.

Not in the *very* beginning, of course. At first they'd done nothing but talk. Which, to be honest, was the exact opposite of what he was used to. They talked and talked— on their first date, they talked through dinner, through dessert, late into the night, until Beth realized her curfew had long since run out and, like Cinderella, she fled into the night. He'd never really *talked* to a girl before (except Harper, and that didn't count), but then he'd never met a girl like Beth, who really listened. Who really seemed to want to know him—not the all-star jock, not the homecoming king, but *him*. On their second date they'd talked even more. About everything—families, school, religion, what they loved, what they wanted. They'd talked, and talked, and that was all. As he walked her to her door, he'd hesitantly taken her hand, and she'd let him. They'd stood in the doorway, her hand warm in his, and he'd slowly lifted his other hand to her face, touched her chin, but before he could lean in, close his eyes, bring his lips to hers, she'd pulled back. Jerked her hand away and slipped inside the house, without a word.

It was on the third date—the date he'd figured would never happen after she'd run away from him on date number two—that he knew. They'd stood in the park, looking up at the stars—Mars and Venus would be spectacularly bright that night, she had told him. And with any other girl, that would just be a tactic, a ruse to get him somewhere dark and alone. But Beth just wanted to show him the stars. They'd stood close together, his arm brushing hers, their necks craned toward the sky.

"It's so beautiful," she'd said in a hushed voice.

"Yes," he'd whispered. But he was looking at her. He put a hand on her waist, another on the back of her head, on her soft blond hair, and drew her face toward his. And their lips met, their bodies came together. She'd been so hesitant, so scared and tense, almost pulling away. Then she took a deep breath—he could feel her chest rise and fall in his arms—and her arms wrapped around him, her fingers running through his hair and caressing his neck. When they finally broke away from each other, she didn't move away, but stayed close to him, her arms loosely wrapped around his shoulders. At first he'd thought she was crying—but she was laughing.

"I had no idea," she'd told him, when he asked why. "All this time, and I just—I had no idea."

But she wouldn't explain, just kissed him again.

That was the beginning of everything. They had still talked, all the time, for hours, but they talked in quiet voices, their lips inches apart, their bodies wound together. It seemed like it would last forever—but here they were, or rather, here he was, alone.

It was all different now, now that there was this *thing* in their way that they wouldn't, or couldn't, talk about. And that was the problem. It wasn't about what he wanted or what she didn't want—it was about what neither of them could say. She was tense again, scared, hesitant, but this time there was no endless conversation, no soul baring. After all they'd had together, she wasn't turning to him, and he was afraid to push—afraid that this time, if she ran away, she might not come back.

He stripped down to his boxers, fell into bed, and, as his tired mind began to wander, pictured himself back in bed with Beth, curled up tight against her warm body.

Except—

Except that Beth didn't have long black hair that cascaded down her back like a shimmering river, or eyes of deep green that you could lose yourself in for days. Glistening, full red lips and a mischievous smile. And she didn't cling to him, didn't lean on him—didn't need him.

But someone did.

chapter four

THEY DECIDED TO MEET THAT WEEK TO DISCUSS
logistics for the party. An anti–Dance Committee committee. Kaia had offered her place—though it was a
fifteen-minute drive out of town, on a deserted stretch of
broken-down highway, it had plenty of space and came
with a guarantee of no parental supervision. And by Grace
standards—both Grace the town, whose mining elite had
had neither the time nor the inclination to build grand
estates even when there was money to do so, and Grace
the family, whose four-bedroom house, a holdover from
the good ol' days, may have been on the right side of the
tracks but was in dire need of a fresh paint job and a new

roof—it was a palace. Five bedrooms, three bathrooms, maid's quarters, a shiny stainless steel kitchen that would have been at home on the Food Network—and the crowning glory, a capacious living room that took up half of the ground floor and was walled by floor-to-ceiling windows that overlooked the wide desert expanse. Kaia's father had flown in an architect and designer from Manhattan, and the two had guaranteed that every detail—from the moldings to the banister of the spiral staircase, from the towels in the pool house to the sterling silver cocktail shaker on the fully stocked bar—worked in concert, creating a pristine world in which everything had its place. (Everything except Kaia, of course, who hadn't been prescreened and carefully selected for her ability to match the wallpaper— and, mainly out of spite, never used a coaster.)

Pool table, hot tub, open bar, an inside glimpse into the lifestyles of the very rich if not so famous? It was an offer even Harper couldn't refuse.

After all the oohing and aahing had ended—quicker than might be expected, since Adam had already seen the place from the outside and he'd had plenty of time to imagine what wonders the inside might hold; Kane's excitement was rarely roused by anything he couldn't smoke, drink, or grope; Harper would rather have died than admit even a fraction of the awe and envy that struck her as she stepped through the doorway, and

Miranda loyally followed Harper's lead—they got down to work. Almost.

"So, what's this I hear about a hot tub?" Kane asked, sauntering through the large living room and pausing before one of the oversize windows that looked out over the pool deck.

Harper cleared her throat in exasperation and waved her notebook in the air. "Forget the hot tub, Kane—we've got work to do. Remember?"

Kane spun around to face the room, a slow grin creeping across his face. "Yeah, yeah, work before play," he allowed. "But . . ." He strode to the edge of the room and squeezed himself behind the mahogany bar. "Rum and Cokes before work—don't you think?" He cocked an eyebrow in Kaia's direction—the closest Kane ever got to asking permission.

"Be my guest," she said, shrugging. "That's what it's there for."

"Harper?" Kane asked, brandishing an empty glass at her and temptingly dangling a bottle of rum over its rim.

Harper sighed and tossed her notebook down on one of the leather couches. "Okay. Fill 'er up."

She was only human, after all.

Delighting in his favorite role, Kane began to dole out the drinks—vodka cranberry for Miranda, beer for Adam, dry martini for Kaia, and, of course, rum and

Coke for Harper. Finally, Kane poured himself a glass of single-malt scotch, then stepped out from behind the bar and suggested they get started. He was already getting bored.

"So Beth's definitely not coming?" Miranda asked, catching Harper's look and trying not to laugh as her eyes practically rolled out of their sockets.

Adam shook his head. "She's got some meeting for the school paper," he said, frowning. "She told me to say she was sorry she couldn't help out, though."

"Now, how could I begrudge her when she's devoting her time to the worthy cause of Haven High investigative journalism?" Harper asked.

Miranda and Kaia snorted in sync.

"I'm on the paper," Miranda commented. "There was no meeting scheduled for today."

"Some one-on-one thing with her and the new adviser," Adam explained. "To discuss the 'new direction' or something."

"One-on-one with Jack Powell? Lucky bitch," Miranda sighed. "I guess there's some benefit to being editor in chief after all."

"Hear that, Adam? Looks like you've got some competition." Kane smirked. "And from what I hear, you and James Bond aren't even playing in the same league."

"Whatever," Adam growled. "Can we just get started?"

70

Harper perched on an ottoman at the end of the room and pulled out a checklist. She loved being in charge, all eyes on her. (And she was studiously ignoring the fact that two pairs of those eyes kept darting glances over to a certain raven-haired beauty at the other end of the room who'd splayed herself out along a black leather couch like a particularly flexible cat.)

But even though Harper was in charge and thus had a power trip to keep her awake, and even though they were planning what Harper was determined would be the best—or at least most entertaining and depraved—after-party yet, the meeting was boring. As all meetings inevitably are.

Logistics, list making, blah, blah, blah.

It was hard to keep her mind on topic—and neither the rum and Coke nor Adam's distracting grin were much of a help.

Decisions, decisions.

Miranda would handle music.

Kane—unsurprisingly—volunteered to take care of alcohol and "miscellaneous substances."

Adam, son of the area's most successful—and most absentee—real estate developer, would scout locations.

And Kaia would help, because, "Wow, what a great way to get a better sense of the town!"

Harper thought she might throw up.

✒︎ ✒︎ ✒︎

Mission eventually accomplished, an afternoon's worth of diversions beckoned.

"What do you say, guys?" Kaia asked, rising from her sprawl and flinging open the glass doors that led out to the deck. "Should I turn on the hot tub?"

Kane, who—bored out of his mind—had been moving at half speed all afternoon, sprang off the couch and tore off his shirt.

"Just show me the way," he said, grinning.

Miranda smiled at the sight of his bare chest, then blushed and quickly darted her head around to make sure no one had noticed. Harper may have been right about Kaia. She might be a "skanky, superficial bitch" (Miranda, for one, felt it was slightly too soon to tell, but she wasn't about to get in the way when Harper went into battle mode), but there was now at least one reason to be thankful for her arrival in town. Actually, plenty of reasons—Kane's six-pack abs, his bulging biceps, his rippling back muscles, and the adorable indentation that dipped beneath his waist-band. . . . Miranda said a silent prayer of thanks and followed Kane, Kaia, and the rest of the group outside, where a large Jacuzzi was embedded in the hardwood deck.

"My father's midlife crisis has been very expensive for him," Kaia explained, "and very fun for me." She flipped on the jets.

Stripping down to his fitted black boxer-briefs, Kane eased himself into the steaming water with a satisfied moan, as the rest of his friends looked on in envy and amusement.

"Now *this* is what I call a meeting," Kane murmured to himself, raising his glass and toasting the empty air. He closed his eyes and leaned his head back on the marble lip of the hot tub, taking deep, measured breaths, shutting out the world.

Kaia turned to Harper and Miranda, beckoning them toward the door back into the house. "Girls, I have plenty of bikinis upstairs, if you—oh," she stopped herself, giving Harper a none-too-subtle once-over. "Actually, I guess none of my suits would fit *you*, Harper," she said loudly. "Sorry."

Miranda sucked in her breath. Most guys ranked Harper's delicately curvy body somewhere between Jennifer Lopez and Beyoncé. But curves were curves—something that the willowy Penelope Cruz clone Kaia distinctly lacked. And *not* in a bad way.

Harper visibly tensed, and Miranda waited, as if watching a wild animal poised before potential prey—would she recoil, or attack?

After a measured pause, Harper did neither.

Instead, she merely smiled gracefully—and pulled off her shirt.

"No problem," she assured Kaia sweetly. "I think I can take care of myself."

And, stripped down to a satin black bra and matching panties (the latest from Victoria's Secret—mail order, of course, since the only underwear within a decent drive of town came from the Walmart off Route 53), Harper strolled slowly across the deck toward the hot tub.

Kane favored her with a long, low whistle.

"Looking good, Grace," he crowed as she slid into the churning water and took a spot beside him. Even Adam, still fully clothed and pressed against the wall of the deck, flushed a bit and gave her an appreciative smile. Harper shot a triumphant glance at Kaia and then let herself slip deeper into the water, finally submerging herself completely. She burst through the surface, face dripping, hair glistening, and then leaned back against the edge, her slender neck in perfect position to be pummeled by the massage jets, her long, bare legs swung over Kane's lap.

Kaia just shook her head. "Miranda?" she asked. "How about you?"

Miranda looked longingly at the hot tub—and, more to the point, Kane's supine figure stretched out along its width, his head now leaned back, eyes closed once again, arms splayed out along the edge. The Greek god of cocky laziness.

But consider her options:

Borrowing a suit from Kaia—who towered over her by a foot and differed in several other, far more crucial, measurements as well.

Or the Harper approach. Except that Miranda's underwear of choice today was baby blue with yellow polka dots and, in fact, recently purchased from that Walmart off Route 53. As would likely be immediately clear.

Add to this the fact that, much as she was enjoying the chance to examine and memorize every tiny detail of Kane's mostly naked body, there was no way she was going to give him the same opportunity. He was taut perfection; she was, drawing from her always at-the-ready mental list of imperfections, stomach fat and arm flab and thigh cellulite and—well, suffice it to say, she was amply flawed.

"No, thanks," she simply said to Kaia. "I think I'll just sit on the side and gawk at all this partial nudity. Teen depravity, et cetera."

"Yeah, I'm quite the turn-on, aren't I?" Kane called to her, eyes still closed.

"You know I can barely keep myself from tearing off those boxers," Miranda called out sarcastically, pulling off her shoes. If he only knew. She sat on the edge of the hot tub, dangling her bare legs in the steaming water, fighting the urge to lift one leg and begin lightly running her toes up and down his tantalizingly close bare skin. Instead, she flicked a foot sharply in his direction, splashing him with a torrent of hot water. "Somehow I think I'll manage to restrain myself."

Kane opened his eyes, lifted his head, and, steadily holding her gaze, wiped the drops of water off his face. He squinted at her, then shook his head and let it gently drop back down. "Do your best," he warned her in a low voice, "but I'm irresistible—one of these days, Stevens, you're not going to be able to stop yourself from tearing off all those clothes and jumping in."

"Don't hold your breath," Miranda said sharply, hoping that he was right, that someday she'd find the nerve.

But today?

Not gonna happen.

"Hey, how's your meeting going?" Adam pressed himself against the back wall of the deck, the only spot he'd been able to find with good reception. He cupped a hand over the mouthpiece of the cell phone to prevent the splashing and cackling from the hot tub a few feet away from drowning out his low voice. "Is it over yet?"

"No, we've still got a ways to go," Beth told him. "We're going to be here for a while."

"That sucks." He pictured her in the sparse newspaper office—really a spacious former supply room that Beth had commandeered her sophomore year to serve as the headquarters of the *Haven Gazette*. Despite the old editions hung proudly on the bulletin board, the short row of outdated computers lining the wall, and the ever-present stack of reporter's notebooks and old tape recorders available for loan, the room still looked—and smelled—like exactly what it was: a dark, dank basement cave. A flickering overhead light, a fraying couch probably infested by termites, a tiny window that looked out onto a ventilation shaft—Adam couldn't stand to spend more than five minutes there, but Beth loved it. She said it made her feel like a "real" journalist.

"No, it's actually really great," Beth protested, her bright smile so present in her sunny voice that he could almost see it. "Working with Mr. Powell is going to be so much better than last year with Donovan. He actually wants to *listen* to my ideas. In fact, you'll never guess . . ."

Adam sighed good-naturedly as Beth began to chatter about her plans for the paper. He hated how busy she always was, but he loved her earnestness, her passion. The way she threw herself into what she loved.

He grinned—the way she threw herself at him sometimes didn't hurt either.

"Anyway, I think we might work through dinner," she finished apologetically.

"What? I thought we were having dinner together," he complained, annoyed as quickly as, a moment ago, he'd been aroused.

"I know, I know, I'm sorry—I was just about to call you and—"

He stole a glance at the hot tub, where Kane was now flailing his arms wildly as Harper and Kaia struggled to knock him off balance and submerge him under the water. Kaia let loose a laughing shriek as Kane grabbed her wet, squirming body and tossed it away from him with a loud splash. Adam shook his head in exasperation. Kane was basically beating them off with a stick, and meanwhile Adam was getting stood up by his own girlfriend. It was more than frustrating, it was humiliating. "Beth, we practically haven't seen each other all week!"

"I know." She lowered her voice into a sexy whisper. "Look, I promise I'll make it up to you. This weekend we'll—oh, wait, hold on."

Adam waited, his annoyance mounting. In the background he could hear distant voices and the familiar melody of Beth's laughter.

Finally: "Sorry, Ad, Mr. Powell needs to go over something with me and the sooner we get through this, the sooner I can get out of here."

Adam made a noncommittal sound. It was better, he knew, to say nothing than to voice the bitter thoughts pounding through his brain.

"So we're okay then?" she asked, sounding worried.

And so he gave in, as always unable to resist the sound of her voice.

"Of course we're okay. Go show him how brilliant you are."

"Thanks!" she chirped. "Talk to you tonight."

"Love you," he told her.

But she'd already hung up.

Adam sighed and stuffed the phone into his backpack. Now what?

He supposed he could go home and sulk, have dinner with his mother—or, more likely, order a pizza with the guilt money his mother had left before leaving on some date with the flavor of the week. Watch TV, wait for a phone call that might never come.

Or . . .

Kane was once again stretched out in the water, letting the jets pummel his upper back and lazily tipping the last few drops of his drink into his mouth. Harper, looking—he had to admit—totally hot, was flicking water on a squealing Miranda.

And Kaia was sporting a barely-there white bikini, which, set off against her perfect tan, made her look like a *Sports Illustrated* swimsuit model. She floated against the side of the Jacuzzi, her chest to the wall and her chin propped up over the edge on her delicate, slender arms. Her hair fanned out behind her, floating atop the water like a cloud of india ink. She was staring right at him.

And that was *definitely* what his mother's trashy romance novels dubbed a "come hither" smile.

Enough was enough. Adam began peeling off his clothes, hoping he wouldn't have to take too much shit for the cartoon hearts that decorated his boxers (last year's Valentine's Day gift from Beth). He could already imagine how good that water was going to feel as he slid in, right between Harper and Kaia.

So, yeah, he'd been stood up—but was he supposed to complain about getting to spend the evening surrounded by beautiful half-naked women?

Maybe the whole thing was, in the end, for the best.

A hot tub, after all, is a terrible thing to waste.

"Sorry about that," Beth said, snapping the phone shut and slipping it back into her bag. She turned back to the table, where a pile of old *Haven Gazette*s lay haphazardly in front of her, all flipped open to the articles she had deemed the best—and worst—of the lot. They were conducting a systematic investigation of everything that was right and wrong about the school paper, and at the rate things were going, it was going to take all night.

"I hope I'm not keeping you from something important," Mr. Powell told her, looking concerned.

He looked so—dashing was the only word for it—when

he was concerned. Who knew that there were real-life British people who looked like they came out of a Jane Austen novel? Or, more accurately, a James McAvoy–Christian Bale Hollywood remake of a Jane Austen novel. But here he was, sitting only a couple of feet away, poring through the old newspapers along with her, actually *listening* when she talked, actually seeming to care what she had to say. Not that it was easy for her to make much sense, not when she couldn't take her eyes off the curly brown lock of hair that kept slipping over his left eye no matter how many times he impatiently flicked it away. She wanted to reach out and smooth his unruly curls, straighten the silk tie that was loosely knotted at a rakish angle . . . she just wanted to touch him and assure herself that he was real.

"What?" she asked, suddenly realizing that he had asked her something and was, apparently, waiting for a response.

"I said, if you've got somewhere else to be . . . ," he repeated.

"No, don't worry about it," Beth assured him quickly. "*This* is the most important thing right now." She tossed one of the old editions of the paper away from her in disdain. "It's like I've been saying, I really want to make this paper *something*. I want us to publish regularly and investigate stories and challenge people's preconceptions—I want it to be more than just a few pieces of paper that the kids laugh at and then use as a place mat on a monthly basis. And I think that—"

"Whoa, whoa," Powell cut in, laughing. "You're preaching to the choir here. Aren't I ordering us some food so we can get to work and stay at work on this thing? Trust me, you've sold me."

"Sorry," Beth said, blushing. It was easy to get carried away—she'd never had a teacher like Mr. Powell, so young and energetic and—well, she didn't even know that they *made* teachers like Mr. Powell.

"I hope I'm not keeping *you* from something important," she said, suddenly realizing that a guy—man—like that probably had a number of better things to do.

He laughed again and began ticking off Grace's social limitations on his fingers. "Let's see. I'm new in town, don't know anyone, and from what I've been able to tell, tonight's social options range from Wet T-Shirt Night at the local bar to Bingo Night at the local church."

Beth sighed quietly in relief and tried her best not to picture Mr. Powell parading across a makeshift stage wearing only a clingy wet T-shirt and a pair of boxers. Her best was far from good enough.

"I suppose you should be very honored I'm willing to pass it all up for you," he continued. "So, what'll it be? Chinese? Indian? Thai?"

Beth rolled her eyes.

"You *are* new in town," she scoffed. "The only place that delivers around here is Guido's Pizza Shoppe—where the pizza's guaranteed to come in fifteen minutes or 'whenever the hell Guido feels like bringing it.'"

"Sounds like a real customer-friendly operation," he said. "I'll take it. A medium cheese should cover us, I think—do you know the number?"

"Yeah, it's in my phone." Beth pulled it out and made the call. "Thanks again for working with me on this, Mr. Powell," she told him once Guido had answered and, with a surly growl, put her on hold.

"It's just wonderful to have a student who's so engaged," he told her, briefly placing a hand on her shoulder. "I'm here for whatever you need."

Beth flushed with pleasure. "Thanks, Mr. Powell," she mumbled, dipping her head and tucking her hair behind her ears.

"I should be thanking *you*—you're saving me from Wet T-Shirt night, after all." He winked at her, then turned back to their stack of work, all business once again. "Oh, and Beth?" he asked, after they'd spent a quiet moment sorting through the papers.

"Yes?" she looked up and, despite the temptation to dart her eyes around the room lest he read her expression and the embarrassing thoughts that lay behind it, met his gaze.

"It seems like we're going to be spending a lot of time together this year, working pretty closely and all—so at least when we're out of the classroom, why don't you just call me Jack."

chapter five

"REMIND ME AGAIN WHY I EVER AGREE TO DRIVE YOU anywhere?" Adam asked, bemused, as Harper flung herself into the car, still bleary from sleep and clutching a cup of coffee as if it were a life preserver. Two weeks into the school year, and dragging herself out of bed each morning still took every ounce of willpower she had. Some mornings—the ones where she showed up at school two hours late with a forged note about a lingering migraine or unavoidable dentist appointment—it took more.

"Because you love me?" she suggested sweetly, buckling herself in. "Because you can't get enough of me?"

"Because I'm an idiot who keeps forgetting that you're incapable of being on time?"

Harper gave Adam an affectionate slug on the shoulder.

"Just drive, Jeeves," she instructed him. "Or do you want us to be late?"

Adam shifted the car into gear and took off toward the school, while Harper played absentmindedly with the radio. It only got AM stations—but given the overall state of the car, with its clanging exhaust, its nonexistent suspension system, the front doors that would never open, and the back doors that would never quite close, Harper was always pleasantly surprised when the pile of junk managed to make it from point A to point B. A fully functioning radio seemed too much to ask.

Not that she would ever insult Bertha (the car was named after a golden retriever that Adam had been forced to abandon when he and his mother moved here from South Carolina so many years ago)—at least not in front of Adam. He was just a little . . . sensitive when it came to the car, which he had lovingly restored. (It was now only half as much of a piece of shit as it had been, which was saying very little.) But, ugly as the Chevy was, it got her where she needed to go, which was more than she could say for her family's Volvo. Her parents' car never broke down, it had an FM radio and an untarnished paint job—and she wasn't allowed to touch it.

Adam had been giving her rides to school ever since tenth grade, when, courtesy of an early birthday and a generous mother, he'd gotten both a license and a car long before Harper had been able to even imagine a life liberated from parental chauffeuring and bicycles. Now that she didn't get to spend much one-on-one time with him anymore, she'd come to look forward to these rides to a ludicrous degree. (Especially now that she was waging her thus-far-unsuccessful campaign for his affections, a depressing thought she preferred not to dwell on this early in the morning.)

"So, any exciting plans for tonight?" she asked as they sped through the streets of Grace, and all the sepia-toned hot spots whizzed by —bar, pool hall, gas station, liquor shop, bar. Any quaintness the main drag may have had in the past had leached out over the decades. It was hard to be quaint when all you had to work with was neon, bankruptcy, and decay. "Hot date?"

Adam shook his head ruefully.

"Yeah, hot date with my TV. Beth has another newspaper meeting this afternoon, and tonight she's got some job interview." He sighed and rolled open his window, letting a rush of arid air sweep into the stuffy car. "Dating someone lazier might have been a little less brutal on my social life."

Tell me about it, Harper thought. Once he kicked Little

Miss Do-It-All to the curb, Harper (Little Miss Have-It-All?) would be only too happy to remind him of the joys of slacking off.

But all she said aloud was, "I'm sure if she loves you, she'll make time for you." Sweetly. If not sincerely.

Adam had always been the one guy in her life who didn't really appreciate the Harper Grace Bitch on Wheels show—maybe because he was also the only one who saw it for the act it was. Or at least that was his take on things, and she was perfectly happy to keep him in the dark about the "real" Harper Grace. If he wanted to think the hard shell covered a soft center of sugar and spice and everything nice, so much the better.

"Yeah, well, in the meantime, I'm in for the night," he complained.

Harper was about to suggest an alternative, when—

"Or maybe I'll give Kaia a call. She's been wanting to go take a look at some spots for the party. Could be fun."

Harper gritted her teeth. She'd remained silent on the subject for a week now, saying nothing when Adam invited Kaia to come sit with them at lunch, forcing a smile when he had driven her off on a tour of the "sights," grinning and bearing it every time Kaia accidentally-on-purpose brushed up against him with her fingers, her shoulder, or, increasingly often, her chest. She'd waited for Beth to do her dirty work for her—but Beth was apparently too busy to notice that her carefully trained lapdog was sniffing around someone else's yard, so maybe she'd waited long enough.

"Adam, don't you think Beth might get a little jealous of you taking some other girl out for the night?" she suggested hesitantly.

"Who, Kaia?" he glanced at her briefly in surprise, then turned his eyes back to the road. "It's not like that. Beth knows that—besides, don't you want us to find a place? It's your party, I'd think you would be a little grateful."

So defensive—what was the deal with that?

"It's not that," she protested. "I just don't want you getting too involved with her. I . . ."

Hate her?

Despise her?

Loathe her with every fiber of existence?

". . . don't trust her."

"You don't even know her!" Adam exploded. "People always do that, and it's not like they know what the hell they're talking about."

"What people? Always do what? What the hell are *you* talking about?"

Adam tightened his lips into a thin and narrow line and, although they were stopped at a light, refused to turn his head and face her. He stared straight ahead, his shoulders tense, his voice hard. "I just—I think you should give someone the benefit of the doubt for once, Harper."

"And what's that supposed to mean?"

"You can be kind of hard on people," he stammered. "And Kaia—I just think Kaia could use a break."

"Oh, please!" Harper burst into harsh laughter. "That girl's entire life has been a break."

"What do you know about it?" he retorted.

"More than you, apparently." She threw up her hands in disgust, then brought one down to rest lightly on his shoulder. "Adam, are you really this naive?"

"Apparently I am," he said stonily, shrugging her off. He turned up the radio, the pounding rock beat drowning out whatever Harper might have said in response.

They drove the rest of the way in very loud, very angry silence.

"I don't know what his problem is," Harper complained. "It's bad enough having to watch him tag along after Beth like a lonely puppy, but if that bitch gets her claws into him . . ."

"Jesus, Harper, dial it down a notch," Miranda said, lighting her friend's cigarette. "Do I have to start making catfight hisses or something?"

"I just can't stand her," Harper growled. She raised the cigarette to her mouth and inhaled deeply, then flopped back onto the freshly cut grass, breathing in the summery smell and enjoying the cool touch of the tiny stalks against her bare neck. She closed her eyes and took a few deep breaths, watching her chest rise and fall, and tried to find somewhere to bury all of her anger toward Kaia, toward Beth, toward everything. When that didn't work, she ripped a few clumps of grass out of the ground, pretending they were strands of Kaia's glossy hair. "This year isn't starting out the way I expected it to," she sighed.

"Yeah, yeah, tell me about it." Miranda let herself fall back onto the grass next to her friend and stared up at the wide expanse of cloudless sky. It was a warm day, not—as was usually the case—blisteringly hot, just warm. If you closed your eyes and held perfectly still, you could almost feel a cool breeze brushing past, the air smelling crisp and clean—a nice change from the traditional Grace bouquet: smog and asphalt. It felt almost like rain, although Miranda knew that the desert rain, if it came at all this year, would arrive as a dirty gray drizzle for a few days in January. Still, there was something sweet and fresh in the air, something that felt almost like fall. Or what she imagined fall might be like. Weather like this should be enough to make you forget everything—the bitchy new girl, the math class they were cutting, the SATs, college applications, and their many, many guy problems.

But maybe that was asking too much of the weather.

"Harper?" she began hesitantly, hoping that her friend wouldn't laugh when she heard why Miranda had coaxed her into spending this period smoking in the football field rather than sitting blankly through a lecture on binomials. "I've got a secret."

Harper shifted onto her side to face Miranda. "Spill it—you know I must know *everything*," she ordered eagerly.

"It's Kane," Miranda told her, avoiding Harper's eyes and instead looking over her shoulder into the distance; she could just barely make out a few small figures scurrying back and forth through the glass corridor that joined the classroom building with the cafeteria and gym. She took a deep breath, forcing herself to continue, trying to convince herself that Harper would understand. "I kind of, I mean, I think I . . ."

Trying to get the words out made her realize how stupid the thought was. What would *he* ever want with *her*? But if you can't tell your best friend your most embarrassing secrets, who can you tell . . . right?

"Well, do you think he might ever want to go out some time?" Miranda finally spit out, all in one breath. "I mean, with me?" she clarified quietly.

Harper sat straight up and peered down at Miranda incredulously.

"*That's* your big secret? You have a crush on Kane?

Duh." She flopped back down again. "I thought you had something *interesting* to tell me."

"You knew?" Miranda froze, a cavernous hole opening in the pit of her stomach, her heart beating wildly in her ears.

Harper rolled her eyes in exasperation. "Rand, I'm your best friend," she pointed out. "Plus, and more importantly, I'm not blind. Of course I knew. I've just been waiting for you to break the news." She laughed. "Big secret. Right."

Miranda had to remind herself to breathe. If Harper had figured it out—if it was so obvious . . .

"Uh . . . do you think that—does everyone know?" she asked in a small voice.

Meaning, of course, does *he* know?

"No, no, I'm sure they don't," Harper instantly assured her, realizing she'd sent her friend into total crisis mode. "But what's the big deal, anyway? He's got to know eventually. I mean, are you picturing ramming your tongue down his throat and then taking a time-out to say, 'But don't get me wrong, Kane, I just like you as a friend'?"

"Harper!" A bright red blush spread across Miranda's face—and, judging from the warm tingling she felt from the top of her head to her fingertips and toes—it didn't stop there.

"What?" Harper grinned and stuck her tongue out at Miranda. "You know you want to."

Miranda said nothing, just closed her eyes and began massaging her temples as Harper dissolved into laughter. This could go on all afternoon.

"Okay, okay," Harper choked out through her giggles. "I'll stop, I promise. But seriously, maybe you should just go for it. Tell him."

"Like you've told Adam?" That was sure to shut her up in a hurry.

"Point taken." But Harper was stymied only for a moment. "Okay, Plan B. We—by which I mean I, in my capacity as best friend and master planner—figure out a way to get the two of you together."

"You really think he'd go for me?" Miranda asked dubiously.

"He'd be crazy not to."

"Um, great, but you're my best friend—you have to say that," Miranda pointed out. "Now let's talk real-world possibilities."

"Real-world, serious answer, I think it could happen," Harper assured her, without a hint of humor. "And I'm going to make it happen. *Someone's* love life should work out this year, and since mine may be screwed beyond repair, looks like it's your lucky day."

"Can you imagine? Me and Kane." Miranda sighed. She could—and often did—imagine it pretty well.

"Personally, it's not clear to me what you see in the

guy," Harper replied. "I mean, I love him and all, but he's kind of an asshole."

"But—"

Harper held up a hand to stop her. "Hey, if it's what you want, it's what I want. I swear to do whatever I can to make him *your* asshole."

"You swear?"

Harper gazed at her solemnly for a moment, then placed her right hand over her heart and held her left hand up in midair, as if swearing in as a courtroom witness.

"Cross my heart and hope to die, may all my hair fall out if I lie," she said in a loud and deep voice, biting the inside of her cheek to keep herself from laughing.

Miranda giggled at the sound of the oath they'd repeated to each other so frequently as kids, when a bad hair day had seemed like the worst punishment the world could dish out.

"Hair swear?" she asked Harper with mock solemnity, extending her right pinkie finger. "Are you sure?"

"Hair swear," Harper repeated, linking her pinkie with Miranda. "You and Kane—it's a done deal."

And they shook on it.

It had become a routine. Every Wednesday, Adam would meet Beth after her English class and they would sneak off to have lunch together, a private picnic in a secluded dusty knoll just off the main quad. They'd discovered it the year before—full of overgrown weeds and bordered by a rusted wire fence on one side and a concrete slab on the other, it wasn't the most romantic spot in the world. But what it lacked in ambience, it more than made up for in convenience and privacy. Some weeks, their Wednesday picnic was really the only time Adam got to see Beth, got her full attention. Other days she might have lunch in the yearbook office, or he would have lunch with the guys on the swim, basketball, or lacrosse team (depending on the season). Then she would have to babysit after school, he would have practice, she had dinner with the folks, he had pizza on the leather recliner while watching History Channel Nazis—sometimes it seemed their busy schedules were conspiring to break them up, but Wednesdays? Those were sacred. Untouchable.

They would sprawl atop an old picnic blanket and lay out a spread blessedly devoid of cafeteria food: bread, cheese, fresh fruit. Beth was too nervous to bring any wine or beer onto school grounds, despite the fact that as far as they knew, their private hideaway had never been discovered—but to keep him from whining about the lack of illicit substances, she usually showed up with a Tupperware container filled with homemade brownies or freshly baked banana bread. It was a fine compromise. They would eat, they would talk, they would kiss—and then the bell would ring and they would go back to their crowded and busy lives.

As soon as he arrived outside the classroom, Adam caught sight of Beth amidst the wave of students pouring out. He raised his hand to wave hello, then quickly lowered it again, taking a moment just to watch from a distance as she chatted with her friends, tossing her head back and laughing, her blond hair swinging, her arms whirling through the air as she made some passionate point. Sometimes he still couldn't believe she was all his.

Soon her friends had taken off down the hallway, and Beth stood alone in front of the door, digging through her bag for something and waiting for her boyfriend to show up. As quietly as he could, Adam crept up behind her and gently laid his hands on her waist, whirling her around and into his arms before she'd even realized he was there.

"Hi," she whispered, giving him a soft kiss. "I've been waiting to do that all day."

"I know what you mean," he agreed, and kissed her again, then pulled her into a warm embrace. He breathed in deeply, burying his face in her hair.

It always smelled so good—like lilacs, she'd told him once, but that didn't mean much to him. All he knew was that it smelled sweet and pure—and that it brushed against his face like a fresh summer breeze.

Not that you'd ever catch him saying any of that corny shit out loud, of course.

"You look great today, you know that?" he said instead, stepping back a foot so he could take a good, long look.

Adam had long ago learned that greeting a girl with a kiss and a compliment was a sure ticket for success (you didn't get to be homecoming king by being oblivious). But Beth made it easy. She was a beautiful girl, and today—unusual for her—she was wearing a light coating of makeup that made her lashes look luxurious and her lips shimmery and moist. And the light blue miniskirt—the incredibly *short* light blue miniskirt—perfectly matched her sparkling eyes. It showed off a few other high-quality attributes, as well.

"*Really* good," Adam repeated, kissing her again.

"Thanks," she said, pleased. She twirled around, modeling the look.

"What's the special occasion?" he asked. "Did your meeting get cancelled? Is our date back on?"

Beth quickly looked away.

"No—no, I still have to go. I just felt like getting a little dressed up today, that's all."

"Good choice," he told her, then was quick to add, "Not that you don't always look beautiful, of course."

"Nice save," she said, laughing. "Flattery will get you everywhere."

She leaned in to give him another kiss, a soft, deep kiss, then nibbled on his lip for a moment and pulled back, giving him a long, appraising look.

"In fact," she continued, her hand tracing its way down the curve of his back and pausing just below the waistband of his jeans, "I wish we could just skip lunch, cut out of here, and I could take you home right now."

It sounded like a good idea to Adam, but he knew better than to suggest it—Beth had never cut a day of school in her life. Even if her hand was continuing its investigations and her other hand had begun twirling its way through his unruly hair, lightly tickling the nape of his neck. It was maddening. Maybe this *was* the right moment to suggest . . .

"Speaking of—you know." He waggled his eyebrows and gave her an exaggeratedly lascivious leer, "turns out my mother's going out of town next week. So I'll have the place all to myself, and I figured . . ."

His arms still around her, he could feel Beth tense up.

"You figured what?" she asked coolly.

"Well, I know you've got issues with, you know, you're always afraid that we're going to get, you know, interrupted—and I thought maybe if we had some alone time, that we could—that you would—"

"That I would what?" she hissed, glancing around at the crowd of students still milling around them. "That I would forget all about my stupid 'issues' and just give you what you want?" She pushed him away.

"Hey, I just thought—"

"I'm sure you did. I'm sure it's all you ever think about—but why don't you think about what *I* want, for once?"

"That's not fair, Beth," Adam protested. How had the conversation gotten away from him so quickly? "I'm *always* thinking about what you want. Why are you getting so uptight about this?" He lowered his voice. "If *that's* all I wanted, it's not like I couldn't find it somewhere else."

Crap.

He knew as soon as the words were out of his mouth that it had been the wrong thing to say. The absolute worst possible choice. But if he hadn't, the blood rising to Beth's face, the thin, angry line her lips made pressed together, and the haste with which she was backing away from him would all have been a pretty decent tip-off.

"If that's how you feel—"

"I'm sorry!" he pleaded hastily. "Come on, please, can we talk about this? Can we just have lunch and talk about this?"

"I'm not hungry anymore. But don't worry, I'm sure you can find *someone else*. Someone less *uptight*." She spit out the words and stalked away.

"I don't want someone else—I want you," Adam said plaintively.

But there was no one left to hear him.

By the end of the day Beth had pretty much calmed down—though every time she thought of Adam, her muscles tensed and her breath quickened, the anger surging through her once again. She couldn't decide—was she angrier at him or at herself? Either way, she was doing her best to keep her mind on something else.

Like, say, Mr. Powell.

Jack.

Okay, so it wasn't a total coincidence that she'd labored for an hour over her hair (silky, straight, and hanging free, with two thin braids pulled around from the front and tied together with a light blue ribbon), experimented with some new makeup, and donned her cutest miniskirt on the day of her one-on-one meeting with the newspaper adviser.

"Deep in thought already?" Mr. Powell asked, stepping into the tiny newspaper office. "Hope I haven't missed any strokes of genius."

Beth laughed and blushed.

"No, Mr. Powell." He gave her a stern look. "I mean, *Jack*, don't worry, the genius is waiting for you."

"Well, then, wait no longer. Your inspiration has arrived! Let's get to work." He sat down next to her and began talking animatedly about his—no, *their*—plans.

They were supposed to be putting together a new layout for the paper, figuring out which fonts and photo borders they wanted to use, where to stick the comic strips and the lunch menus. They were supposed to be debating how large the headlines should be and whether the column "A Day in the Life of a Cheerleader" really belonged in the sports section. *Supposed* to be, but Beth wasn't having too much luck with the whole concentration thing. She sat in front of the computer, an old Mac that she had persuaded the school to donate to the floundering newspaper, even though it could barely run the design program they used for the layout. Mr. Powell stood behind her, close enough that she could smell his cologne—something mysterious and European—close enough that she could feel his presence without having to turn around. And then there were the moments when she needed him to look closely at something on the screen, and he would lean down, sometimes placing his hands on her shoulders for balance, and peer over her shoulder, his stubbly cheek only inches from hers. He would stare at the screen, and she, out of the corner of her eye, would stare at his angular profile, wishing the moment would never end.

Beth knew she was being silly, that despite all the joking around, despite the whole first-name-basis thing, despite the fact that last time they had ended up talking together for hours, not just about the newspaper or French class, but about politics, movies, *life*—despite all that, he was a teacher and she was a student. He was an adult—worldly, cosmopolitan, brilliant, handsome—and she was just a kid. Nothing would ever actually *happen*. Of course not. So there was no reason whatsoever to feel guilty about having a little crush—or occasionally wishing that her boyfriend would be a little more like Mr. Powell and a little less like, well, Adam.

Besides, it's not like she was some pathetic twelve-year-old drawing hearts around his name in her notebook or dreaming about how good their names sounded together (although "Beth Powell" did have a nice ring to it . . .).

Okay, so she was being ridiculous. Utterly ridiculous. She should forget about the whole stupid thing, focus on her work, on the newspaper, on her *real* relationship. She should stop wasting so much mental real estate on juvenile fantasies.

But still, she thought, crossing one leg over the other in what she admittedly hoped was a seductive shift in position, she was glad she'd worn the miniskirt today.

After all, it never hurt to look your best. . . .

chapter six

THERE MUST HAVE BEEN SOMETHING IN THE AIR.

Harper stared down at her French quiz, the letters swimming on the page, as she struggled to focus on the *subjonctif* tense instead of on Adam.

She'd been having just a little problem with that all day long.

She'd seen him the night before, shooting hoops in his driveway.

No shirt on.

God, she wanted him.

She had been about to go to sleep when she heard the rhythmic pounding of the ball on the cement pavement—

and when she looked out the window, there he was, barely visible in the dim light of the full moon.

Racing back and forth across the driveway, his muscles straining with the effort, his hair wild, his movements fluid, one sculpted pose melting into the next.

So lean and taut, so graceful. His large, warm hands, his supple fingers massaging the ball.

She liked to imagine those fingers grazing her body, climbing through her tangles of hair, stroking her legs. Too bad it was only her imagination; too bad his fingers were, for the moment, taken. Just like the rest of his body, from his thick calf muscles to his tight pecs to the light sprinkling of freckles across his nose.

Her memory was far from photographic, but when it came to the minutiae of Adam's body, in all its curves and spots and ripples, she had total recall.

Harper forced herself to scrawl down a couple of answers and then laid her pen down and closed her eyes for a moment, imagining the warm pressure of his arms wrapped around her, his lips kissing their way down her neck, her shoulder, her breasts. . . .

Her body was tingling, and she raised a hand to her breastbone, lightly grazing her fingers across the bare skin.

If only . . .

❦ ❦ ❦

If only she would just trust him. If only she would just get over whatever it was that—

No.

Adam shook his head. It's not that sex was all he wanted. He wasn't that kind of guy. (Not that Beth seemed to notice.)

But he was a *guy*, for God's sake. He was eighteen, he loved his girlfriend—was it so wrong that he wanted to be with her?

Did it bother him that all his friends just assumed that he and Beth were sleeping together? That they would probably laugh him out of the locker room if they knew the truth? That half the cheerleading team would be happy to jump him and tear off his clothes—and yet he was still a virgin?

Okay, yeah, maybe a little.

Enough that he couldn't look at Beth without thinking of sex.

Hell, he couldn't even *think* of Beth without thinking of sex—and sex was the last thing he wanted to be thinking about while sitting in history class staring blankly at his middle-aged teacher and her poorly bleached mustache. But he couldn't stop himself. It was like he was fourteen again—totally out of control.

It wasn't a status thing, it wasn't about his reputation. He loved her, and he *wanted* her—those slim arms wrapped around him, her lithe body tangled up in his, her hair splayed out on his bed. He wanted her—all of her.

And she wanted him, too—he could tell. So what was holding her back?

She didn't trust him. That was obvious. And completely unjustified. He was absolutely, totally devoted to her. And if he thought about other girls sometimes, well, that was normal too, right?

No harm, no foul.

Unless it's just *one* other girl, a small voice in his head pointed out, and Kaia's flawless figure suddenly sprang, unbidden, into his mind.

Now *there* was a girl who knew what she wanted and went for it.

His dream Kaia smiled mischievously.

"I want *you*," she said silently to him, licking her lips and peeling off her damp, clinging shirt.

With horror, Adam realized that he—or at least, his body—wanted her, too. He shifted around in his seat and surreptitiously pulled a notebook onto his lap to cover up, a move he hadn't had to make since the hormonal nightmare that was eighth grade.

And in his mind's eye, the dream Kaia tilted her head back and laughed, chest heaving. And then she went back to the task at hand: stripping off her clothes.

It was just a fantasy, right?

No harm in that.

✎ ✎ ✎

Just a fantasy, Beth told herself. *No harm in that.* She'd whipped through her quiz in a few minutes and was now left with nothing to do but stare at the front of the classroom, where Jack Powell was relaxing, feet kicked up on the desk and hands clasped behind his head. *What was he thinking about*, she wondered. *Parisian cafes? African safaris?*

When they'd last met, he told her all about his travels around the world, and it set her mind on fire. And his voice—she could listen to those words spilling over her, the impeccably crafted sentences and delicious accent, for hours. For days.

She pictured the two of them sitting across a breakfast table from each other, exchanging sections of the *New York Times* (she'd once seen this in a movie, and it had since seemed to her the epitome of sophisticated romance). Or maybe they'd be working their way through a crossword puzzle together . . . in bed.

Beth blushed furiously, and Mr. Powell looked up, as if he'd somehow sensed that she was picturing what he looked like beneath his chambray shirt and khakis. Their eyes met, and he grinned at her and winked.

God, she loved that smile.

Kane always had a hint of a smile on his face. It was one of the things Miranda loved about him. And that perpetual smirk in his voice—as if all of life was a joke, and only he knew the punch line.

Which, Miranda supposed, was enough to make most people think he was a jerk. And he was. Cocky, pampered, self-centered, lazy, a confirmed believer in "never walk when you can ride" and "never do today what you can put off until tomorrow."

But it was all part of his charm.

She loved watching him in class, the way he leaned back in his chair and propped his feet up on the rim of the seat in front of him, as if he were kicking back in an armchair after a long day's work, rather than suffering through forty-seven minutes of American history. Sometimes he scrawled something on the single piece of paper atop his desk, sometimes he tipped his head back and closed his eyes—occasionally, he even sat up straight and looked at the teacher, though the smoldering disdain never left his eyes. And the cocky smile never left his face.

He was a jerk, all right. A slimy asshole who sailed through life on his good looks, who probably, if asked, would tell you he had never truly cared about anything or anyone but himself. And he would probably be telling the truth—or at least he'd think he was.

But Miranda wasn't fooled. She'd watched Kane for years now. Laughed at his jokes, insulted his attitude, admired his effortless skill at almost everything—noticed the way, every once in a while and only when they weren't looking, he would actually be there for his friends. They didn't see it, they weren't looking for it; but Miranda paid attention. She was an A-plus, Phi Beta Kappa student of Kane Studies—and she was convinced that beneath the smirking curl of his lip and the chiseled abs and the perfect tan, there was something else. Something real.

You just had to be willing to look.

Long and hard.

Looking for love was hard work.

There was Ilana: all body, no brains.

Shayna: all brains, no body (but a great sound system—and more than five hundred channels).

Julia: all boobs, no ass.

And, of course, Katie: all mouth. Which wasn't necessarily a bad thing. But even that got old.

Sometimes Kane felt like Goldilocks (a tall, good-looking, straight male version of Goldilocks, of course)—nothing he tried out ever quite measured up.

Not that he didn't love the variety—forget too hot, too cold, too tall, too short. It was all a beautiful rainbow of possibility as far as he was concerned, and he had no complaints.

Okay, he had one: He was bored. Even more bored than usual.

LUST

Whatever happened to the thrill of the chase, the lust for victory? That was the problem, actually. Most of these bimbos didn't give chase—just head.

Of course, there was one girl who might present quite the interesting challenge. One girl he'd been waiting a long time to get a taste of.

That blond hair, those blue eyes, all that innocence crying out for a little corruption.

There were, of course, a few stumbling blocks in his path.

His supposed best friend being a not inconsequential one.

Her supposed love for said friend being another.

So it wouldn't be easy. Kane smiled. He was done with easy. Easy was boring.

Difficult? Challenging? Messy and emotional and violent and dirty?

That was more his speed.

That was *fun*.

It's all fun and games until someone gets hurt—and then, Kaia thought with a grin, that's when the *real* fun starts. Now that things with Adam had been set in motion, it was really only a matter of time—which meant it was time to start thinking about what would come next. Adam was, after all, just a diversion. He couldn't be expected to hold her attention for long.

No, she had her sights set on a much bigger fish.

An older, more sophisticated, *British* fish.

She glanced up at the front of the classroom where Jack Powell had stretched himself out in his chair. He looked bored out of his mind.

She knew the feeling.

And she decided that it was time to answer both their prayers.

She knew every girl in the room was thinking the same thing, every girl *wanted* the same thing—she could see it in their hungry eyes, hear it in the way they tittered as he brushed past them on his way to the front of the room. But it didn't matter what they wanted. Because of all of them, Kaia was the only one who had the nerve to act. These pathetic small-town girls could fantasize about him, long for him, *want* him all they liked—but that's all it would ever be. A silly fantasy. As far as Kaia was concerned, fantasizing was a waste of her time—when you saw something you wanted, you took it.

She looked down at the quiz in front of her. Still blank. *Subjonctif?* She snorted. *Give me a break*, she thought. As if she hadn't covered this stuff in tenth grade. This place was so backward.

She grabbed her pen, thought for a moment, and then began to write: large, deliberate letters, the words spanning across the width of the page.

VOULEZ-VOUS COUCHER AVEC MOI?

(*En anglais:* "Would you like to sleep with me?")

A little hackneyed, perhaps, a little cliché—but he'd get the message.

Kaia, after all, didn't believe in being subtle.

She believed in getting the job done.

chapter seven

HARPER PICKED UP THE PHONE ON THE SECOND ring. Thanks to caller ID she knew it was him, and—irrationally—felt the need to smooth down her hair and do a quick mirror check before saying hello. As if he would be able to somehow hear her beauty through the phone. Ridiculous, she knew. But still—every little bit helped.

"Adam, what's up?" she greeted him, lying back on her bed and relishing the sound of his musical voice in her ear.

"Great news—I think I may have found a spot for the party. I just need to drive over and check it out."

It was just what she'd been hoping to hear. She and

Miranda had already spent hours assembling playlists, and Kane had promised them that the drinks, courtesy of his older brother—and a number of mysterious other "connections"—were a done deal. But all the beer and hip-hop in the world wouldn't be enough to make this party work if they didn't find somewhere to hold it, and so far every possibility—the golf course, the gravel pit on the edge of town, some kid's dingy basement—had been a major bust.

Harper knew she should have been somewhat worried, but she had other priorities right now, and one of them—the only one, really—involved getting some quality alone time with Adam. So if he'd found some suitably large, deserted outpost with ample facilities for drinking, dancing, and doing . . . whatever, it seemed only right that in her capacity as leader of this little party squad, she help him with his final investigations. And whatever else he might need help with, of course.

"Cool," she said, as nonchalantly as she could. "Do you want me to—"

"Kaia and I are heading over tomorrow afternoon," he added.

Oh.

She should have known. Since when did Adam go anywhere without Kaia by his side? She shut her eyes tight and tried not to picture the two of them creeping through a deserted building together, hand in hand. She supposed that she should be able to assure herself that Adam was too much of a stand-up guy to ever cheat on his girlfriend—but it was a little late to make that case, given that she'd spent the last couple of months convincing herself that, under the right circumstances and with the right girl (read: Harper), he'd have no trouble doing exactly that.

"So, should we all meet tomorrow night?" Adam continued, after it was clear that Harper wasn't going to be squealing in enthusiasm any time soon. "Hopefully, we'll have some good news."

We. Great.

Harper sighed quietly and sat up in bed, scrolling through her calendar on her phone. Saturday night was free and clear—plenty of time for sitting around, staring at Adam, or aiming death glares (or at least some finely honed sarcasm) at the girls who kept standing in her way.

"I don't know," she hedged. "I've got this thing . . . but I guess I can move it." Not for the first time, Harper gave thanks that video phone technology had never really caught on. Adam always claimed he could tell when she was lying, something about the way she narrowed her eyes or played with her left earlobe. She didn't really buy it— but still, better safe than sorry.

"Are you sure?" he asked. "I don't want to deprive some lonely guy out there his long-awaited chance to—"

"Shut up," she said irritably. "First of all, this is more important. Second of all, there is no lonely guy—I don't do desperate. Third of all," she added, figuring it couldn't hurt to appear a little in demand, "he can wait."

"If you're sure . . ."

"Positive," she assured him, wondering how it was that she'd become the one talking *him* into this little shindig, given that it was really the last place she wanted to be. "How about eight?" she suggested, trying to muster up some fake enthusiasm.

There was a pause.

"Maybe a little earlier?" he requested. "I have to be out of there by nine—I promised Beth I'd go give her some moral support at the diner. It's her first night of work."

"Beth's working at the diner?" Harper asked incredulously. "*Our* diner?" She smirked, imagining the preppy princess decked out in the Nifty Fifties tacky costume (pink tank tops and poofy fluorescent-green skirts with crinolines underneath), smeared with ketchup and barbecue sauce and smelling like stale pickles. This day was looking up.

"Yeah, her last job wasn't really paying enough," Adam confided. "You know, her family . . ." His voice trailed off, but he didn't really need to continue. Grace was a small town, and even before Adam and Beth had started dating, Harper had known exactly how that story ended. "Her family . . ." was packed like sardines into a tiny ranch house in a squalid development one step up from the trailer park. Her parents worked three jobs between the two of them and still struggled to buy new clothes every year for their swiftly growing twin sons. Her family's one car, a fifteen-year-old station wagon, broke down more days than it ran. Beth's family, in essence, worked on a simple principle: Ask not what your family can do for you, but what you can do for your family. It seemed that Beth was stepping up to the plate once again—and Harper supposed that she should dig down inside herself and find a little sympathy, or at least a little respect.

On the other hand, there were a lot of things she *should* do. "Should" didn't have much of a hold over her these days. "Could" was, after all, so much richer in possibility.

"So I think it's a great idea!" Harper enthused, as a plan began to form in her mind and a dark smile crept across her face.

"What idea?" Adam asked, confused.

"*Your* idea, genius. Moral support—we'll just have our meeting at the diner, and then we can all cheer her on. It'll be such a great surprise." As in: *Surprise! Devoted boyfriend that I am, I brought along all my friends to watch you serve and clean and grovel for tips, and basically humiliate yourself in front of everyone you know on your first day of work. Don't you love me, baby?*

Plus, added bonus, Harper realized: A new locale for the meeting would guarantee a nonrepeat of the hot tub incident. Party planning in an empty mansion with plenty of drinks and a giant hot tub had seemed like a good idea at the time—but Harper still shuddered at the memory of the half-naked Kaia rubbing herself all over Adam. *Oh, you look so tense—do you want a massage?* Please, who knew people still used that line? (And why hadn't she thought of it first?) It was a mistake she'd vowed never to make again.

"I don't know," Adam said doubtfully. "She might not want us all there—not on her first day and all."

"Hey, we're her friends, aren't we?" Harper wheedled, hoping he would take the bait. "Come on, you're a guy, what do you know about what she wants? Speaking as a girl, I can assure you that she'll be totally grateful."

"You think?"

Eyes narrowed, Harper smiled.

"Trust me."

Late Saturday afternoon, Adam pulled the car into the empty parking lot and the two of them stared up at the dark, abandoned building that loomed before them.

"It's perfect," Kaia breathed.

And it was. The old Cedar Creek Motel (no creek in sight, of course—only a moldy drainage pipe and a dirty concrete pit that had once served as the "swim at your own not insignificant risk" pool), was covered in dust and exuded a stale aura of hollow disrepair. A tilted sign with cracked neon tubing hanging over the entrance hailed the wreck as GRACE'S FINEST LODGING, complete with REAL COLOR TV and 100% REFRIGERATED AIR. The two-story motel, a fifty-room complex on the outskirts of town, had once been painted a proud flamingo pink, standing as a boldly fluorescent oasis amidst the desert wasteland; now the grayish husk of a building, sallow weeds nipping at its foundations, effort-lessly faded into its environment, an overgrown concrete cactus. Unlike the empty, gutted storefronts that littered the main streets of Grace, the Creek stood whole and complete—no boarded-up windows, no graffiti covering its walls, no garbage strewn across its empty parking lot. But it had been abandoned for months.

Not surprising—Grace didn't have much of a tourist trade. There was no reason to pull off the interstate and drive twenty miles down a bumpy local road, just to stay in a dilapidated no-tell motel. Tourists had better things to do with their time—and those truckers who did pass through town usually took one look at the Creek and decided they'd be better off sleeping in the cab of their trucks.

Kaia and Adam approached the lobby door—locked, but not boarded up—and Adam pulled out the set of keys he'd snagged from his mother's real estate office. She'd been trying to unload the place for months with, unsurprisingly, no luck.

They stepped inside—and the normal, in-color, living, breathing world outside disappeared.

"It's like a ghost town in here," Kaia whispered in wonder. "As if everyone just picked up and left one day, just disappeared—and no one's touched it since."

And it did seem as if the lobby had sat frozen in time since the day the motel's owners had skipped town, a few steps ahead of the bankers trying to collect on a year's worth of missed mortgage payments. A thick layer of dust covered everything, but the furniture, the dingy carpeting, and the vintage seventies wallpaper were all still intact. Preserved. And waiting.

"No one wants to spend the money to clear it out," Adam explained, stepping behind the reception desk and smearing a track through the thick layer of dust with his index finger. Even the reservation book (no newfangled computer system for this motel) still lay open atop the desk, he marveled. He flicked the light switch on the wall behind him—nothing. No electricity, but that wasn't a problem; the afternoon sun filtered in through the lobby's small windows. It was dim and shadowy, but they would be able to see. "They're just waiting for someone to buy it," he explained to Kaia, enjoying, as he often did when he was with her, the unusual sensation of being an expert; she knew so much, but nothing about the West, about life in a small town, about anything that mattered—really, she needed him. And she seemed to know it. "Then the new owners will figure out what to do with all this stuff," he continued, gesturing toward the vinyl chairs and wood-paneled coffee table to their right. "Or maybe they'll just tear it down. Cool, huh?"

"I think it's creepy," Kaia said in a hushed voice, pressing close to him.

Adam had grown up amidst the ruins of Grace's past—playing spies in the empty shells of old factories, hunting for buried treasure around the abandoned mines. But he put a comforting hand on Kaia's back—of course she wouldn't be used to that kind of thing, he reminded himself.

"Come on," he said, leading her through the dark lobby. "Let's take a look. It's perfectly safe."

She stayed by his side, and they crept down the hallway, explorers in a lost world. Not that there was much to explore. The surprisingly spacious lobby, a narrow hall with peeling orange wallpaper and a long stretch of numbered bedroom doors, a cramped staircase leading up to an identical hallway on the second floor (though here the wallpaper was green and purple—or had been, until all the colors faded to gray). And that was about it.

"This is the place," Adam said with confidence, as they surveyed the "courtyard," a paved area by the empty pool with some plastic tables and chaise lounges—he could already picture the scene, drunken seniors spilling outside, dancing in the moonlight, hooking up in the shadows. It was perfect. "It's on the edge of town, so no one will notice us here, it's big, it's dark—this is the place."

"We should check out a room first, before we decide, don't you think?" Kaia asked.

"Aren't you scared?" Adam teased. "Ghosts of truckers past, and all?"

"I think I can handle it," Kaia said with a smile. "Just stay close."

They chose a room on the first floor, at the end of the hall. Adam pulled out his mother's skeleton key and turned it in the lock (Cedar Creek was a bit behind the motel curve—the electronic key card craze had passed them by). They stepped inside.

The room was musty and dark, and just as frozen in time as the rest of the building. But it was a motel room nonetheless—bathroom, chair, TV—and queen-size bed.

What more did you need?

"I have to admit," Kaia began, "it looks—aaah! What the hell was that?" She squealed and threw her arms around Adam as a grayish white streak raced across the floor and disappeared into the far wall.

"Did you see that?" she asked between rapid, panicked breaths.

"It's just a mouse," he assured her. "No big deal."

"It practically ran over my foot!" Her arms still around him, she squeezed tighter.

"Hey, it's okay. It's gone now." He rubbed her back for a moment until her chest stopped heaving and her muscles unclenched. "It's okay now," he repeated. She closed her eyes and slumped against him, leaning her head against his chest. He stared at the wall over her shoulder, trying to focus on the complicated pattern of flowered diamonds, on the large spiderweb dangling from the upper right-hand corner of the ceiling, on the critique his swim coach had given him yesterday after a subpar performance in the butterfly heat. On anything but the body quivering in his arms.

Kaia looked up at him, his face only inches from hers.

"Good thing you were here," she said softly. "I'm terrified of mice—but with you here, somehow I feel so safe."

Adam blushed and mumbled something incomprehensible.

"It's funny," Kaia said, leaning closer and tightening her grip. "I've only known you for a few weeks, but I just feel so close to you. Sometimes I think . . ." Her voice faded away, and then she tipped her face toward him and closed the narrow gap between them, pressing her lips to his.

For a moment he responded, pressing his body to hers, pulling her tight, his lips opening slightly, his tongue gently running along her lower lip, tasting her—

And then he pushed her away.

"What are you doing?" he asked harshly.

A look of surprise and what might have been anger flickered across her face. And then she crumbled.

"I—I'm sorry," she whimpered. "I don't know what I was—you brought me here, and we're all alone, and then you brought me to the bedroom, and—"

"We're scouting locations for a *party*," he yelled, backing away from her. Overreacting. (Had he been sending out some kind of messages? Hadn't he, in fact, kissed her back? But he cut off that line of thinking before it could go any further. He couldn't afford to go any further.)

"I know, I'm sorry—I told you, I don't know what I was thinking. I just—got carried away."

She raised her hands to her face and turned away from him.

"I'm so embarrassed," she said in a muffled voice. "I'm sorry."

Adam instinctively reached out a hand to comfort her, to still her shuddering shoulders, and then, on second thought, let it drop to his side.

"No, I'm sorry," he said stiffly. "Don't be embarrassed. If I—if I gave you some kind of wrong idea, I'm—it's just, you know. Beth. And I—"

"Can we just go?" Kaia asked, turning around again, her eyes dry. "I think we should just go now."

The awkward pause lasted all the way out of the building, across the parking lot, and throughout the interminable ride back into town.

Kaia leaned her cheek against the cool glass of the car window and sighed, remembering when seducing a guy meant slipping into some sexy lingerie, crawling into his bed, and waiting for him to come home and get his surprise. Either that or, if she was feeling lazy, just grabbing the nearest hot guy and pulling him into a lip-lock. No questions asked.

Things were so much simpler on the East Coast.

Okay, so seducing Mr. All America was somewhat more interesting—but it was also turning out to be a lot more work.

She darted her eyes to the left, admiring his profile; he sat rigidly in the driver's seat, hands at ten o'clock and two o'clock on the wheel, eyes resolutely focused on the road. This guy had by-the-book written all over him. Well, that's why she'd picked him, right? She liked a challenge. And even if his heart was still totally committed to Beth, she now had some concrete evidence that his body was less than hopelessly devoted. No, his body seemed to have some ideas of its own.

They hadn't spoken since pulling out of the motel parking lot, and Kaia had plenty of quiet time to plan her next move. She just wasn't sure what it should be. She'd come so close back there, with the ridiculous mouse scare—and damsel in distress had certainly seemed the right way to go. But she was getting a little tired of waiting around for him to sweep her onto his white horse and off into the sunset; maybe it was time to be a little less subtle.

Adam parked the car in the diner lot and hopped out. Kaia waited a moment, and when it became clear that he wasn't planning on opening her door for her (as he usually did), she got out as well. They walked together toward the entrance, Adam careful to keep at least a foot of space between them. Kaia could feel the guilt coming off him in waves, and she made sure to compose her face into the perfect combination of embarrassment, rejection, and vulnerability.

Just to rub it in.

Before they stepped inside the restaurant (undeserving as it was of the name), he pulled her aside, grasping her wrist to get her to stop—then dropping it quickly as if the touch of her skin had burned.

"Listen, Kaia, I'm really sorry—again—if I sent you

the wrong signals or something," he stammered, rubbing his temples and looking down at his feet. "I don't want you to feel like, well—" He paused and finally looked up, meeting her eyes. "I'm sorry," he finished lamely.

"Don't worry about it," she assured him. "It's totally okay. I'm okay."

But she averted her eyes and let her voice waver, and she knew he didn't quite believe her.

Good.

"Here they are," Adam said in a light and brittle voice. He waved frantically toward the silver Camaro pulling into the lot. Harper and Miranda hopped out and jogged toward them, Kane loping behind at a more leisurely pace.

"Well?" Harper asked, before anyone had a chance to say hello. "Did you find a place?"

"Impatient much? Wait until we sit down," Adam told her, visibly relaxing now that it was no longer just the two of them. Kaia suspected that with all the excitement, Adam had almost forgotten their original reason for visiting the motel, or the triumph he'd felt when declaring it the perfect spot. He caught her eye, and the tips of his ears turned a bright red—was he thinking not of the motel's ample party space or conveniently out-of-the-way location, but of the feel of her skin beneath his wandering hands, the touch of her warm breath on his face? She gave him a cryptic half smile—and he quickly looked away.

The group crowded inside and grabbed a booth next to the jukebox. Kaia would have sacrificed a few quarters to save herself from the tedious Ricky Martin song currently booming through the speakers positioned over every table, but she'd taken a quick look at the playlist last time she was there. If you weren't a Taylor Swift fan and didn't want to groove to the sweet sounds of Carly Rae Jepsen or the Beach Boys, there wasn't much there. Kaia grimaced, wondering how much she'd have to pay to get them to turn the music *off*.

As the rest of the "gang" bantered back and forth, Kaia quickly scanned the menu, reconfirming for herself that there wasn't a thing on it she wanted to eat. She certainly wasn't going for the "Sushi Special," the mere thought of which filled her with nausea. (They were three hours from the nearest ocean and no freshwater in sight; the fish on the menu might very well have been, as advertised, the "catch of the day"—but *which* day? And in which year?) She did her best to suppress a sudden pang of homesickness—there was a little place in the West Village that served thirty different kinds of sushi, all better than anything you could get in Japan (which she knew from personal experience). She and her friends had made it a policy to stop there at least once a week—and the secluded park just down the street made the perfect spot for a picnic, as she and an incredibly hot NYU student had discovered one night. He'd satisfied her craving for sushi, and she'd satisfied his for something equally fresh and spicy. One of those perfect New York nights. It all seemed a very long time ago—and very far away.

Thankfully, before she could spiral downward into a cesspool of nostalgia and self-pity, the waitress showed up to take their order—and the shock of it was enough to slam Kaia back into the present. She was surprised enough by the quick service, but she was even more surprised that the waitress, beneath the tacky spangled tank top and gaudy makeup, was Beth.

Beth, her hair pulled up into a high side ponytail and garish blue eye shadow smeared across her lids, looked even more surprised to see them. And not in a good way. She fumbled with the small notebook she used for taking orders and dropped her pen; as she was bending down to pick it up, she came within a few centimeters of smashing her head into the edge of the table. Finally, she stood again and waved a feeble hello, trying to smooth down the wisps of blond hair that had escaped from her ponytail and shifting her weight back and forth from one foot to the other.

"Hey, honey!" Adam said giddily, oblivious to his beloved's disarray. "Look—I brought everyone down to cheer you on. How's the first day going?"

"Yes, tell us, Beth," Harper added. "We're all eager to hear about your adventures in food service."

Beth flushed and shot a nervous glance over her shoulder, where a rotund middle-aged man was giving her the fish eye from behind the counter. Kaia guessed he must be the manager, or perhaps the owner—either way, she shuddered at the thought of his greasy hands coming anywhere near her food. Good thing she hadn't really been planning to eat.

"I—uh, hey guys," Beth said finally, with a weak smile. "Adam, why didn't you *tell* me that everyone was coming?" she added, glaring at her boyfriend.

Kaia could easily pick up on the thinly disguised hostility in her voice. The people across the restaurant probably picked up on the hostility in her voice. But Adam, unfortunately for his peace of mind and fortunately for everyone else's entertainment, did not. (Was he still too shaken from the afternoon's events to participate in normal human interaction? Kaia hated to give herself too much credit . . . but on the other hand, she knew she was pretty damn good.)

"I wanted to surprise you, Beth," Adam said, grinning.

"Well, you definitely did," she acknowledged through a gritted smile.

Before she could say anything else, the greasy manager guy with the bad comb-over strolled by.

"Back to work, Manning," he ordered Beth. "You're on a shift, not a date."

"Yes, Mr. White," Beth said meekly. "I was just about to take their order."

"That's a good little girl," he smarmed, nodding his head sharply.

Beth blinked her eyes furiously for a moment, then whipped out her notebook and drew back her lips in a poor imitation of a smile.

"So, uh, what can I get for you all?" she asked in a coolly professional voice.

"How about the secret of where I can find an outfit like that for myself?" Kaia asked sarcastically, gesturing to Beth's bright green poodle skirt. "It's just stunning."

Everyone laughed, including—Kaia was pleased to note—Adam. A bit of the frustration of the afternoon slipped away, and Kaia suddenly realized this dinner might be a lot more pleasant than she'd thought. Good-bye damsel in distress, hello other woman.

After they'd downed their drinks and scraped the bottom of their ice-cream sundaes, everyone left—except Adam, who waited dutifully for Beth to finish up her shift. He liked watching her work—she was so efficient, every move measured and practiced, as if she'd been behind the counter for years, rather than hours. As the restaurant emptied out, he followed along behind her as she wiped down the tables and collected the bills from a few final lingering customers, trying to keep her company, but she refused to give him more than one- or two-word responses to his steady stream of chatter.

"Can you just let me finish this up?" she finally said sharply, as he traced his hand down her back. She shrugged him off. "You don't have to wait around for me—just go home if you want."

"No way," Adam protested. "Of course I'm waiting." They'd planned a night out on the town to celebrate her new job—and although the options open at this hour ranged from a stale cup of coffee at the imitation Starbucks to a greasy slice of pizza at Guido's, he was determined to give her a stellar night and make the most of the little time he was finally getting to spend with her.

Not to mention, make up for whatever it was she thought he'd done. (And to make up for what he *had* done—though Beth could never find out about that.)

Her shift ended at eleven, and she disappeared into the back to clean up and change. Adam fidgeted as he waited, fiddling with the jukebox, studiously ignoring her manager's glare, and reading the newspaper headlines and vintage movie posters hanging on the wall. *Revenge of the Forty Foot Woman*, read one. *Her love will move mountains . . . and her wrath will crush cities.* Adam shivered—he could relate.

Beth eventually reemerged and, hesitating for a moment, made her way toward the door, gesturing to Adam that he should follow her.

"Hey, you did great!" Adam said, hurrying over and throwing his arms around her. Maybe if he ignored the tension, it would just go away. "How was it?"

Beth extricated herself from his grasp.

"It was fine," she snapped. "No thanks to you."

Here it came. Adam ran a hand through his hair and sighed. "What are you talking about?"

"Let's just get out of here," she muttered, brushing past and stalking out of the restaurant. She walked briskly to the beat-up Chevy, one of the only cars left in the lot, and stood silently, arms crossed, waiting for him to unlock the doors.

"So, where to?" he asked, opening her door for her. She climbed past him without a word and tossed her backpack into the backseat. "Coffee? Ice cream? Beer? All three?"

"You know what?" she said irritably. "Just take me home."

Adam climbed into the car and slammed the door behind him, feeling an immediate spasm of guilt—after all, it wasn't poor Bertha's fault that Beth was throwing some sort of PMS shit fit. The old car couldn't take too many more fights like this.

"What's your problem?" he asked, hostility seeping into his voice. He put the key into the ignition, but paused before turning the key. Better to finish this. Now. "I'm trying to be nice here," he pointed out. "I thought we were celebrating. And you're being a total—" He stopped himself just in time.

"What? I'm being a total what?"

"Forget it," he said in a softer voice. "Seriously, what's wrong?"

"What's wrong? What's wrong?" she screeched, her voice rising in decibels with every word. "What's wrong is that I was just totally humiliated in front of all of our supposed friends, and you just sat there and watched. No— no, better, you helped!" A few tears leaked out of her eyes, and she angrily wiped them away.

"What are you talking about?" he asked helplessly. "I was trying to be supportive. We all were."

"Yeah, thanks so much for the support," she drawled. "You bring them all here, without asking me, without even telling me—like it's not bad enough it's my first day at a new job, I have to *serve* my *friends*. Did it ever occur to you that might be a little embarrassing for me?"

"Look, I'm sorry, I didn't—you should have said something," he stammered.

"Said something?" she asked, her voice choked with emotion. "When? When you didn't tell me you were bringing them? Or when Kaia was making a fool out of me and they were all laughing at me? When *you* were laughing at me?"

Adam looked down—there was too much pain in her voice, in her eyes.

"Should I have said something when Kaia dumped her milkshake on the floor and I had to get down on my hands and knees and clean up her mess? Adam, how could you not know that would be horrible for me?" she pleaded. "How could you, of all people, not understand that?"

"That's not fair," he protested, holding his hands in front of him as if to stem the torrent of accusations. "First of all, that milkshake thing was an accident—"

"That's all you've got to say?" she asked incredulously. "You're defending *her*? I'm sitting here telling you all this, and I've had the worst night ever, and—and all you can do is tell me I'm being too hard on *Kaia*?" She shrugged and turned away from him. "I guess it's good to know where your loyalties lie," she told him in a muffled voice.

"What are you even talking about? I'm so loyal to you that I—" He cut himself off. Somehow, he didn't think it would help his case to point out the temptation he'd valiantly resisted this afternoon. But his anger rose, throbbing beneath the surface, as he thought about the beautiful girl he'd pushed out of his arms, about everything he had given up, was still giving up, all for Beth. And did he get any credit for that? Any gratitude or understanding? *Anything?*

"You know what?" she asked, when it became clear he was never going to finish his thought. "That's not even the point. I just can't believe you thought this was a good idea. I mean, it's like you don't even know me at all. How is that even possible?"

"If this is the way you're going to be, maybe I don't *want* to know you!" he shouted back, his temper finally snapping.

She burst into tears—but he was far too angry to care.

Harper was tired. Tired of the whole hidden unrequited love thing, tired of being consumed by bitterness and jealousy and paranoia, tired of feeling bested by other girls—blonder girls, bitchier girls, lamer girls, and most of all, tired of sitting around waiting for something to happen.

She wasn't that kind of girl.

Not usually, at least. And not tonight.

So after the meeting in the diner (and Harper had at least derived a measure of pleasure from watching Beth twist in the wind, as Adam cluelessly dug himself into a deeper and deeper hole), Harper had decided she needed a break. A vacation from this unsettling and ineffective good girl version of herself that was trying to forge some kind of honest emotional bond with her oldest friend. A return, if brief, to reality.

Enter Derek.

Derek was blond, built, brainless—and had been chasing after her for months. A few dates with him had been all she needed to deem him more irritating than nails scraping on a blackboard, but tonight? Tonight he had seemed just what she needed.

So here she was, an hour after her unabashed booty call, tangled up in his idiotic arms. It hadn't taken much. She'd washed off the diner grease, slipped into a red camisole and black faux leather skirt, applied a fresh coat of makeup, and been more than ready to go fifteen minutes later when his black SUV pulled up to her house and honked until she emerged from the front door. Derek had, of course, been all over her the moment she stepped into the car—or, as he preferred to speak of it, his "love machine"—but after a few slobbery kisses, she'd suggested they stop off for a drink. If she was going to make it through a night with Derek, sober just wasn't going to cut it. (Though she knew from experience that drunk was an equally unwise way to go; when dealing with Derek "Magic Fingers" Cooper, it was best to keep your wits about you. Moderation, that was key.)

So—one drink. One long drive down a dark road, hiphop blasting from the speakers, Derek keeping one hand on the wheel and the other massaging the contours of her inner thigh. Harper let her hand creep across into his lap, returning the favor—after all, he was incredibly hot, and with the music blaring, it was too loud for him to say anything dumb that would spoil the pretty picture.

Ten minutes more and they were there. "Lover's Lane"—in this case, a quiet stretch of back road with plenty of cactus tree cover and open space for the picnic blanket Derek "just happened" to have in his trunk. They lay on the scratchy blanket and groped each other, with plenty of heavy petting and heavy breathing. Soon Harper was sprawled out on her back, wearing nothing but a pair of violet satin panties. She was also bored out of her mind.

"You're so hot," Derek said, stroking her breast with his meaty hand and then leaning in to plant a slobbery kiss on it. "I mean, *really* hot," he added, coming up for air.

"Mmm-hmm," Harper agreed as she shifted position, searching for a comfortable spot on the gravelly, uneven ground. No luck. She shivered—September wasn't such a great time to be out at night with no clothes on, she supposed. On the other hand, she thought, her mind wandering as Derek kissed (or, judging from the feel, licked) a path across her chest, at least the stars were beautiful. She'd never been one for star-gazing, but she needed *something* to do.

"You're hot too," she added mechanically, after it

became clear that Derek was waiting for something of the sort. *And is that the Big Dipper?* she wondered idly.

It had been like this for the whole tedious, predictable night. Sure, at first it had been good to be reminded of how desirable she was, but it had gotten old. Fast. Or maybe she was the one getting old—because, for whatever reason, she just couldn't get into things. In the past, she would at least have had a little fun before drifting into boredom. Put her brain to sleep and let her body run on autopilot. But now, it was like she couldn't stop herself from thinking.

And thinking and Derek? Not a match made in heaven.

Not that he wasn't a pretty perfect physical specimen, Harper conceded, running her tongue along the outline of his ear and then kissing her way down his neck. She'd give him that.

No, she wouldn't be lying here naked in an abandoned field on a ratty blanket with some guy who couldn't cut it on the A-list. Ripped chest, deep blue eyes, cut biceps, adorable dimples on his face (and butt)—he certainly wasn't getting through life on his wits.

"Did anyone ever tell you that you look just like Lara Croft?" he asked, rolling over on his side and gazing at her with an adoring look that made her cringe.

"Who?" If, in the heat of passion, he was comparing her to some ex-girlfriend, he was even dumber than she'd thought.

"You know, Lara Croft. Tomb Raider." Derek paused in his inch-by-inch examination of her body. "It's kind of lame, not as good as Madden NFL or Grand Theft Auto—but dude, she's hot." He went back to work. The guy was industrious. "Mmm, not as hot as you, babe."

Okay, Harper decided, enough was enough. Seriously— video game chick? Even an ex-girlfriend would have been better than *that*.

Harper abruptly pulled away from Derek and began collecting her rumpled clothes from where they'd fallen during his hasty scramble to strip her bare.

"I'm a little tired, Derek," she said, squeezing into her strapless bra and pulling her top over her head. "Can we head home now?"

"But I told you, I've got protection," he protested, confused. He tugged lamely at her shirt, trying to pull it off again; she wriggled out of his reach. "We were just getting started!"

"Well, now you can get started getting dressed," she informed him, throwing his pants in his face. "Because I promise you this—it's not going to happen."

chapter eight

IT HAD BEEN TWO DAYS.

Beth and Adam still weren't speaking to each other—
and Beth was desperate.

Which was the only possible explanation for her call.
A last, the very last, resort.

And after all, there was no one else. She hated to admit
it, but after getting together with Adam, she'd drifted
away from most of her girlfriends. There was nowhere
else to turn.

Desperation sucked.

"Hey, Harper, it's . . . Beth," she said timidly, once

the other girl had answered the phone. And they began to chat. Awkwardly pushing through all possible areas of small talk (big surprise, there weren't too many), Harper at least had the grace not to ask, "Yeah, but what do you really want?" though Beth was sure it was at the forefront of her mind. And why not? When had she ever called Harper "just to chat"?

As Harper prattled on about something that had happened to Mr. Greenfield's toupee during third period, Beth asked herself again whether she really wanted to have this conversation. Whether she could actually bring herself to have it out loud. She shuffled through some papers on her desk, began doodling on the back of one—nothing but meaningless scribbles, but it passed the time and calmed her down. Finally, she glanced over at the bed, which she'd neglected to make that morning. The sheets and comforter were tangled and strewn haphazardly across its surface; it seemed a bigger mess than one person could possibly have made on her own, even tossing and turning all night, as she had. It was the bed that convinced her; she didn't want to be on her own there, not forever.

"Harper, can I ask you something?" she interrupted. Harper was *still* talking, laughing about whatever it was she'd just divulged, but she broke off immediately, sensing the tension in Beth's voice.

"Of course."

"Well . . ." Beth had no idea how to begin. "You and I have spent a lot of time together, but we don't really know each other that well, I mean, I guess we're not really *friends*. . . ."

"Don't be ridiculous," Harper said quickly. "Anyone important to Adam is a part of my life. You know how *close* we are."

Beth felt a quick stab of pain at the words—yes, of course she knew how *close* Adam and Harper were. Hadn't she suffered through hours of conversation about how wonderful Harper was? What a great friend she was? How misunderstood she was? Like she needed a reminder that her boyfriend considered some other girl his best friend, maybe his soul mate. (He'd never said it aloud . . . but then, Beth had never had the nerve to ask, not wanting to hear the answer.) Platonic soul mate, she reminded herself—and, after all, why else had she picked up the phone?

"You do know him better than anyone else—probably better than I do," Beth admitted, gritting her teeth. "That's kind of why I wanted to talk to you."

There was a long pause.

"Well," Beth began again, "maybe it's been obvious that Adam and I haven't been getting along all that well lately."

"Really?" Harper's voice oozed concern. "I hadn't noticed—what's wrong?"

"It's been a lot of little things, I guess—but, I mean,

there's this one big thing hanging over us. And I think— no, I know, that's the real problem."

"What?"

"You'll laugh."

Of course she would laugh. Harper went out with a different guy every week, and Beth was sure she wasn't pushing any of them away with some half-articulated excuse that she only half believed herself. Not that she wanted to be like Harper. Of course not. She didn't even *like* Harper. But all the more reason not to want the other girl to laugh at her, hold it over her for the rest of the year, spread it around the school that Beth was . . . well, Beth was sure Harper would find an appropriately cutting description.

Maybe this had all been a big mistake.

"I swear, I won't laugh," Harper promised.

"You will," Beth countered.

"Beth, I promise you," Harper said seriously, "you can tell me anything. If you have a problem, I really want to help."

On the other hand, she sounded so sincere—and Beth was so desperate.

"It's sex," Beth said finally. "I've never—well, it would be my first time, and I'm not sure I—"

"You haven't slept together yet?" Harper asked incredulously.

"You probably think that's pathetic, don't you?" Beth held her breath and waited for the inevitable.

"No, no, of course not," Harper said hastily. "You just caught me off guard, that's all. I always assumed . . . but there's nothing wrong with it."

Beth sighed in relief. Maybe she could confide in Harper after all. This thing had been eating away at her for too long, and it would be so good to actually talk to someone about it. Even Harper . . .

"I don't know what's wrong with me," Beth explained. "It's not that I don't want to. I *do*. Or at least, I think I do. But every time we get close, I just freeze up. And he thinks it's because I don't trust him, but it's not that—it's just that . . ."

"You're not ready," Harper prompted.

Beth sighed again.

"I guess so. I mean, I guess I'm not." Why was it so easy for Harper to grasp, but still so hard to make Adam understand? It's not like she'd made some hard-and-fast rule for herself, no sex until college or something. And it's not like she thought there was something wrong with the girls in her class who were doing it—even the ones who were doing it a lot. She had just always thought of herself as someone who would wait. Until she was really in love, until she was old enough—it had all seemed pretty simple and straightforward in the abstract. But now? With Adam? Now she wasn't so sure—what did it mean to be "really" in love? When would she be "old enough"? What did it mean to be "ready"—and would she even know when she was? Would it be when she wasn't scared anymore? When sex didn't seem like such a big deal that might change everything, ruin everything? What if that time never came, and *this* was what it felt like to be ready? After all, when she was with him, part of her always felt ready, more than ready—eager. Hungry for more. It was just that the other part of her, the part that said no, wait, not now, not yet—that part was stronger. And that was the part that stayed with her when she got out of bed. That was the part she had to trust—right?

"So, have you two talked about this?" Harper asked.

"It seems like it's all we ever talk about anymore," Beth admitted. "And he says he understands, but it's like there's always all this tension between us. We're always fighting about something—but it seems like, somehow, it's always about this. I'm just afraid . . ."

"What?"

Beth had never put the fear into words before, although it was always with her, simmering just beneath the surface. Somehow saying it out loud made it just a bit more real, a bit more dangerous. But it had to be said.

"Sometimes I'm afraid that he's going to break up with me," she said quietly. "Find someone else who's not so—someone who *is* ready."

"Beth," Harper said in a grave voice. "Like you said, I know Adam. He would never do that. He loves you."

"You don't understand, Harper," Beth said plaintively, and suddenly all of the concerns she'd bottled up over the last few weeks came spilling out. "There's something off, and lately it's like, everywhere I turn, he's with Kaia. What if she—and he—I don't know. Maybe I should just—do it, you know? What am I waiting for?"

"You're waiting until you're ready," Harper reminded her.

"But how will I even know when I am?"

"Trust me, when it's time, you'll know," Harper promised.

"And in the meantime?" Beth asked, already knowing the answer.

"In the meantime, you wait," Harper explained. "And if he loves you, he'll wait too. I promise."

"Thanks, Harper." Beth was grateful, but unconvinced. "Listen, don't tell anyone about this, okay? Especially Adam. I'd be so embarrassed and—"

"You don't even have to say it," Harper assured her. "My lips are sealed."

"Miranda, you'll never *believe* what I just found out!" Harper squealed into the phone.

Talk about the light at the end of the tunnel. So

the perfect little relationship was missing one thing? Meaning—unless something had happened last year that she didn't know about (unlikely)—Adam, too, was still a virgin. Unbelievable.

She laughed and laughed.

If he loves you, he'll wait, she mused. *Yeah, right.*

Miranda hung up the phone feeling strangely optimistic. Harper seemed convinced that Beth's impenetrable virginity was a sign that the relationship could never last. Miranda wasn't so sure—and as Harper was tossing out the insults, Miranda silently wished that she wouldn't be so quick to forget Miranda's own virginity. But Harper's buoyant tone had swept her beyond all doubt or annoyance. And the feeling of hope was contagious. So contagious, in fact, that when Harper suggested that Miranda call Kane and ask him to the upcoming formal, it actually hadn't sounded like an insane idea.

That was then, this was now. And now her phone was staring her down like a cellular firing squad.

Miranda took a deep breath, gulped down an Altoid (though the minty fresh breath did little for her confidence level), and brought up his number on the phone. She couldn't overthink this, Harper had pointed out. She just needed to suck it up and do it. Whatever happened, at least she would know she tried. Right?

At least she'd know she had some balls.

Miranda hit talk and waited, with mounting panic, as the phone rang and rang.

"Hey, Kane, it's Miranda," she said when he finally picked up. She tried to make her voice slightly low and husky, aiming for perky but not too perky, casual but intense, sexy but not sex starved—but most likely, it just came across as lame.

"Oh, hey, what's up?" He sounded vaguely surprised to hear from her—small wonder, since in all their years of semifriendship she'd never called him (the number was in the phone only as a concrete manifestation of her pathetic wishful thinking).

"So how's your weekend going?" she asked, trying her best to sound nonchalant even as her stomach clenched and her heart thudded rapidly in her ears. She'd always prided herself on her clever banter, but all remnants of wit flew out of her mind now that his voice was on the other end of the line, and the moment of truth—or, potentially, of abject humiliation—crept inescapably closer with every passing second of small talk.

"Better now." She could almost hear the smirk in his voice, and she knew that his deep brown eyes were twinkling beneath an ironically raised eyebrow. She'd memorized his face, and the minute movements it made, well enough that she could close her eyes and see him peering back at her. Which, on a ten-point scale, upped her nervousness level to about a thousand.

Is he flirting with me? she wondered as always—or was this just the only way Kane knew how to talk to people? After all, he also "flirted" with the old woman who ran the cash register in the cafeteria, and occasionally the bald guy with the unnecessary hairnet who ladled out the food from behind the counter. Maybe he just couldn't help himself.

"I'm glad I could bring a little ray of light into your dark and lonely life," she told him, an electric thrill running through her when she scored a laugh.

"So what's up?" he asked, chuckling. "Or did you just miss the sound of my voice?"

"You wish. No, I'm calling because—" Miranda stopped, the words choking in her throat.

Because I want to ask you to the dance.

Because I want to know whether you had a date yet for the dance.

Because I want to come over there and rip off all of your clothes.

"Because, uh, I was wondering if, I mean, do you have—"

"Spit it out, I've got a hot date coming over," he joked. Probably it was a joke.

"Do you have—do you know which chapter we were supposed to read for Setlow's class?" God, she hated herself sometimes. It was an asinine excuse for calling him, which, she supposed, was appropriate, since it had been asinine to call in the first place. She looked down at herself in disgust, at the oversized T-shirt and boxers she'd thrown on after dinner, her lying-around-and-watching-TV outfit. Or, the way things were going, more like her boring, frumpy, destined-to-grow-up-into-an-old-maid-and-die-fat-and-alone outfit. A fate Miranda supposed she deserved, since she apparently didn't have the nerve to do anything about it.

"You called *me* to check up on the homework?" Kane asked incredulously. "Stevens, are you feeling okay? Taken any recreational drugs lately?"

She laughed shakily. At least he'd bought it. She didn't know whether to be angry at herself for chickening out, or grateful that whatever insanity had convinced her he might be interested had subsided before she could make a complete fool of herself.

"Miranda, you still with me?" he asked, when she didn't respond.

"No, yeah, you're right. I don't know what I was thinking. It was stupid. I'd better go," she babbled, all in one ragged breath, and cut off the call before he could say anything else.

Stupid was right.

Adam sat in his empty living room, staring at the darkened screen of the TV. The phone rested on his lap, as it had for the last half hour, ever since he'd flipped off the TV in disgust, midway through some crappy sitcom. He'd picked up the phone, determined to make things right. And then he'd put it down. He'd gone through the pointless routine again and again, even dialed part of the number a few times, but couldn't bring himself to finish.

He wanted to apologize to Beth, of course he did. But he didn't know what to say. He still wasn't quite sure what he was apologizing for, to be honest, or even whether he was the one who should be apologizing in the first place. His mother often claimed that the man was *always* the one who should be apologizing—and that was certainly his father's way. Adam Morgan Sr. had apologized and apologized, but it was, Adam supposed, never enough. At least it hadn't been enough to stop his mother from throwing plates at his father's head, or sneaking a gulp from an ever-present bottle of scotch when she thought her young son wasn't looking. Adam resolved—not for the first time—that there was no way he would ever model his relationship after his parents' short-lived marriage. Better to die alone than go down that path.

Still, Adam reasoned, he'd obviously done something wrong. Hurt Beth in some way. And hurting someone he loved was the last thing he'd ever wanted to do.

He picked up the phone. Dialed the familiar number. Listened to it ring.

"Hello?"

He opened his mouth, closed it again.

Hung up.

chapter nine

HARPER HAD GYM FIRST PERIOD THE NEXT MORN-
ing. Though this was normally, and with little competition, the bane of her week, she was actually looking forward to it this time—it would give her just the opportunity
she needed. Kane was stuck in gym too—killing time on
the basketball courts while the girls paraded lazily around
the tiny track. The geniuses behind Haven High's physical
education program had a somewhat lackadaisical attitude
when it came to female participation. The guys had a rigidly determined schedule: football one week, soccer the
next, running sprints the week after that. If the girls, on

the other hand, chose to opt out of the period—or because of their periods—and do some "power walking" around the track instead, that was fine.

Harper knew it was sexist and offensive and she should probably lead a schoolwide campaign to remedy the problem . . . but since she hated gym even more than she loved muckraking, she had little incentive to do so. Besides, sexism sometimes came in handy—this morning, for instance. As she stood in the middle of the ragged field with the rest of the girls, waiting for the teacher to explain the morning's paltry athletic task, she figured she'd soon have no problem sneaking off, grabbing Kane, and doing Miranda's dirty work for her.

It was no surprise that Miranda had chickened out the night before. The only surprise was that Miranda had even entertained the idea of asking Kane out in the first place. Harper had only suggested it as a joke, an empty dare. She'd never expected Miranda to actually buy into the idea.

Small wonder that she hadn't followed through.

"Kane," Harper called to him, once she'd made it safely over to the courts. She poked her face through the chain-link fence and waggled her fingers at him. "Over here! I need you for a minute."

Kane tossed in an effortless layup that swished through the net, and then jogged over to join her.

"What's up, lover?" he asked, his familiar smirk already painted across his face. (Kane's motto: Never leave home without it.) Only Kane could still look debonair in a Haven High gym uniform—bright orange T-shirt and ungainly brown shorts. Harper wasn't too thrilled to be seen out in public in the female version, especially by the entire guys' gym class, but sometimes you had to make sacrifices for your best friend. Plus, the T-shirt was a couple of sizes too small and she knew that despite the hideous color, it showed off more than a few of her best attributes. Kane, for one, blatantly sizing her up, didn't seem to mind.

"Who are you taking to the stupid dance next week?" she asked, skipping the small talk.

"Ah, I don't know if I'm even going," he told her, shrugging. "I'm sick of the girls here—great asses but no spines." He paused for a moment, then widened his eyes in a purposely exaggerated look of surprise. "Why, Grace, was that just your clumsy way of asking me out? I'm flattered, I'm flabbergasted, I'm—"

"An idiot, I know," she cut in. "Now shut up." She took a quick look around, making sure no one could overhear them. While a few of Kane's cronies had stopped shooting hoops and were clustered together on the court looking over at the two of them, they were safely out of earshot. "Look, I think you should ask Miranda."

Kane burst into laughter.

"And why the hell would I do that?"

Harper smacked him on the shoulder.

"What's wrong with you?" she asked irritably. "Why wouldn't you do that?"

"Harper, it's *Miranda*," he protested.

She stared blankly at him.

"I mean, she's great and all—smart, fun—"

"Beautiful, witty, a great dancer," Harper continued.

"Yeah, whatever—but it's still Miranda." He rolled his eyes, but Harper just looked at him, her face betraying no expression. "As in 'Miranda, can I copy your math homework?'" he continued. "Or 'Miranda, what's a seven-letter word for sarcastic?', not 'Miranda, how I love to lick whipped cream off your breasts.'"

Harper took a quick step back.

"Please, please tell me you've never actually said those words to a girl," she begged him.

"*Woman*, actually," he bragged.

"God, you're pathetic. And now that image is burned into my brain. Thanks."

He just smiled at her, the picture of innocence.

"So you can see why I'm not going to ask her, right, Grace?" He paused, and then a glimmer of understanding dawned on his face. "Why'd you ask, anyway—does she have a little crush on me or something?"

He started to laugh again, but she cut him off quickly.

"As if she'd go for an idiot like you—no, I was trying to do *you* a favor," Harper said, thinking fast. "I figured you've probably had your fill of bimbos by now. Obviously, I was wrong." And she began to walk away. Even pretending to jog around a track would be better than this.

"Harper, wait!" he called after her. "I've actually been meaning to talk to you on exactly that topic," he said conspiratorially once she'd turned back around.

"Bimbos?" she asked, raising an eyebrow.

"Being fed up with them. I've got my eye on someone new, and I think you're just the girl to help me get her."

"The great Kane Geary—actually admitting he needs someone's help?" Harper was still disgusted—but also intrigued. "And who is this unapproachable goddess?"

"Beth." Kane had the grace to look at least slightly abashed.

"Oh, Jesus Christ," Harper swore. What was it about the Bland One that made her so irresistible? "Why would I want to help you with that?" she asked in a more measured voice. "Adam's one of my best friends—and, incidentally, I thought he was one of yours, too. I'm supposed to help you steal his girlfriend?"

Now it was Kane's turn to raise an eyebrow.

"Come on, Harper, I think we both know why you'd

have an interest in breaking up Ken and Barbie—do you really need me to say it out loud?"

Harper feigned ignorance, said nothing.

"I've seen the way you look at him, Grace. I know you want this as much as I do—and there's no one else I'd rather have on my side. Who's more devious than you?"

"Flattering as that is . . ." Harper murmured, her mind spinning through options at a furious speed. Kane and Beth . . . It was true that there was only one person at Haven High more devious than Harper: Kane himself. If he'd targeted Beth as his next conquest—and if the two of them worked together . . .

And then she remembered Miranda. And the promise she'd made.

"Sorry, Kane." And she was—more than she could allow herself to let on. "Much as I'd like to take part in your sordid little plot, I think I'll sit this one out. I do have a *few* principles, you know."

Kane looked skeptical. Even more so than usual.

"Doesn't sound like the Harper I know." He shrugged. "Well, I'll still be here when you change your mind. And trust me, Grace: You will."

"He said he doesn't really see you that way."

The words were still echoing through Miranda's

mind. She pressed herself against the locked door of the bathroom stall, trying to slow her panicky breathing.

Harper seemed to think there was still hope, that Kane just needed to see the light—that he thought Miranda was smart, beautiful, funny, etc.

Whatever.

Miranda knew the truth and—she should just admit it to herself—she'd known it all along. Kane could never be interested in someone like her. She was too pale, too bland, too ugly—too everything. And, on the other hand, just not enough.

Harper Grace's loyal sidekick. Everyone's best pal. Good for a joke—and not much else.

Miranda had nodded calmly when Harper sat her down at lunch and gave her the bad news, then said, with a wry smile, "Well, his loss, right?"

That was her thing, after all. Living on the surface, never taking things too hard, never letting bad news knock her off stride, the voice of reason and moderation to Harper's nonstop drama. Always neurotic, but always staying just a few feet back from the edge. Harper was the one who lived life on the brink. Miranda just watched.

She'd lasted ten minutes. One minute of deliberate deep breathing as Harper told her the bad news, and one minute of concerted effort to keep her face perfectly still and the tears from falling as Harper tried to console her. Two minutes of laughing it off, to convince Harper that consolation was uncalled for. Five minutes of forced gaiety when a group of girls sat down with them and began gossiping about homework and music videos and what they were planning to wear to the dance next week. And one minute of torture, as she pushed the food back and forth on her tray, blood thumping in her ears loudly enough to drown out the chatter swirling around her, the claustrophobic panic boiling within her threatening to burst out. Almost one minute too many, and that's when she'd left—just in time.

She'd pushed herself back from the table, walked slowly out of the cafeteria, and raced down the hallway to the nearest girls' bathroom. It was only after she'd brushed past the two skater punks smoking by the sinks and slammed herself inside one of the stalls that she'd allowed herself to burst into silent tears.

Chest heaving, she berated herself for getting her hopes up, for thinking she had a chance. Not with a guy like that.

Lester Lawrence, captain of the chess team, who'd sent her one love letter, written in iambic pentameter, every week for a year? Vince Weiss, who'd taken her to the Starview Theater's annual showing of *It's a Wonderful Life*, spent the first hour trying to devour her with his large, saliva-covered lips and the second hour trying, unsuccessfully, to pick his gum out of her hair?

That was her league. That was her life.

Miranda felt her stomach churning and regretted the two brownies she'd scarfed down in the cafeteria, a chocolate chaser for the fries and meat loaf. Harper always lost her appetite when she was nervous or upset, but Miranda had no such luck. No crisis was too small, no emotional tailspin too shallow that Miranda's appetite didn't decide her woes deserved a piece of cake.

Because when you're truly upset, she thought bitterly, *turning yourself into a fat, ugly blob is just what you need to make yourself feel better.*

She sagged against the cool wall of the stall and noticed, among the graffiti advising "Lacey" to "suck this" and suggesting that all guys were either "dicks," "pigs," or, in a nice display of creativity, "bottom-dwelling, scum-sucking creatures of darkness," a new warning etched into the plastic: "Remember, girls: This is a no purging zone! :)"

Skinny, sanctimonious bitch, Miranda thought.

It was the smiley face that really got her—she could imagine the girl's perky voice warning of the evils of eating disorders and the benefits of a healthy diet. As if she, whoever she was, knew anything about—well, anything.

With a grim smile, Miranda pulled out her thickest black pen and scribbled over the "no" in "no purging zone."

Then she leaned over the toilet, stuck her finger down her throat, and made it official.

chapter ten

THE WORDS WERE COMPLETELY INNOCENT: "KAIA,
can I see you after class for a moment, please?"

But the tone told Kaia all she needed to know—
specifically, that Jack Powell had finally gotten around to
grading those pop quizzes. And had thus finally discovered
her little invitation. Took him long enough.

She stayed in her seat as the rest of the class filtered out
of the room, alleviating her boredom and excising some
nervous energy by mentally rating the girls who filed past
her. Too fat, too short, too thin, too gawky, too geeky—
no, not too much competition at all, Kaia decided. There

was Harper, of course, undeniably gorgeous, if in a seedy, film noir kind of way; but from what Kaia had observed, Harper had too many other things on her mind to think about screwing their French teacher. Her forbidden fruit grew on a different tree. Still, the sultry brunette shot her a curious look as she stepped out of the room. Probably wondering whether to be pleased that Kaia was—to all outward appearances—getting into some kind of trouble, or dismayed because she had snagged some one-on-one face time with Haven High's Most Wanted.

When the room had emptied out, Kaia finally stood and walked slowly to the front of the room, where Jack Powell maintained his customary position, arms crossed behind his head and legs propped up on the desktop. A perpetual five o'clock shadow only added to his good looks; it gave a much-needed edge to his boyish charm. And Kaia was all about edge.

"What can I do for you, Mr. Powell?" she asked, sitting down across from him and watching his eyes follow her leg line up from her low heels to the high slit in her snug-fitting skirt. It was always nice to be appreciated. "Or should I just take this as a yes?"

Powell looked taken aback, then leaned forward in his chair and grinned.

"Well, you're bold, I'll give you that," he told her. He pulled out a piece of paper from the top drawer of his desk—Kaia recognized her telltale scrawl across the page.

"I'm sure you can guess why I've asked you here, Kaia," he began.

Oh, she could guess all right—although the classroom was a bit public for her tastes.

"Well, I didn't think it was to work on my pronunciation skills."

Powell laughed. "No, you've demonstrated quite a— proficiency in the subject matter," he admitted. "I want to talk to you about what you wrote here," he said, tapping the page with his index finger. "I'm flattered, Kaia, I really am."

"As you should be." She smiled to let him know she was joking. Sort of.

"But this sort of thing, teacher-student—it can't happen."

She leaned in, giving him easy visual access down the dark crevasse of her cleavage, if he wanted it—which, she could tell, he did.

"Oh, it *can* happen, Mr. Powell," she assured him. "Trust me, I've seen it."

"Okay, then," he said, folding the quiz in half and methodically tearing it into small pieces, letting them filter through his fingers and drift down into the trash can. "It *won't* happen. Don't be embarrassed," he added quickly. "It's very common that a student develops a crush on a teacher, especially since you're new here. I'm sure it's been a little tough for you to adjust. I can empathize."

"Mr. Powell," she interrupted him coolly, "I think you've got the wrong idea. This is not some sweet schoolgirl crush. I'm not in love with you, nor do I dream of marrying you someday and bearing your British schoolteacher children."

"I didn't say—"

"What I'm offering you is a simple physical relationship with a very attractive woman," she informed him. "So if we're going to talk about this, let's do it adult to adult, instead of pretending I'm some kind of blushing virginal teenybopper. Because I'm not."

"That much is obvious." His voice hardened, the genial warmth replaced by a sliver of ice. "You want to be treated as an adult?" he asked, offering a condescending smile. "I make it a policy not to get involved with my students—but even if that were not the case, I wouldn't touch you, Ms. Sellers. Not if you paid me. You're trouble dressed up in a miniskirt, and I'd have to be blind not to see it."

She tried to interrupt, but he cut her off.

"Blind and stupid—which must be what you think of me if you imagined this little Lolita act was actually going to work."

"Mr. Powell, I—" Kaia broke off in midsentence. For once, she was speechless.

He sat up straight and smiled at her, but the smile never touched his eyes.

"Play all the games you want with the boys your own age, Kaia, and have fun." He folded his arms on the desk and leaned toward her, their faces now separated by only a few inches of frosty air. "But trust me—I'm way out of your league."

Kaia left the classroom fuming . . . but intrigued. This new and improved Jack Powell was even sexier than the old one. Who didn't prefer Colin Farrell to Colin Firth? No, this cold, calculating front was definitely hot. And promising.

After all, any teacher willing to speak to a student like that clearly had a somewhat flexible understanding of standard school policy—whatever he may have said, she knew he'd be up for bending the rules. It was just a matter of getting him to bend in the right way.

But she still needed something to keep her entertained in the meantime. Down but not out, she decided to take Mr. Powell's advice and pick on a boy her own size.

So, onward to the boys' locker room. (Where else?)

By her calculations, the swim team should be just about finished with their practice—which meant that Adam, who, despite his halfhearted commitment to the sport, was too much of a stand-up guy to ever skip a practice—should be on his way in. Hot, wet, and mostly naked. Perfect.

She burst through the door, and the locker room echoed with enraged shouts of flustered jocks as they whipped towels around themselves and ran from Kaia's prying eyes.

"Get out of here!"

"What gives!"

"Hey, baby, you want some of this?"

"Trust me, boys, I've seen it all before," she said calmly as they shouted her down. And while that was true, it didn't mean that she couldn't appreciate a repeat performance. Once again, she marveled at the caliber of male bodies this tiny town had produced.

She threaded her way through the crowd of flesh, searching for Adam, finally spotting him on the edge of the sea of muscles.

Those orange bikini briefs didn't leave much to the imagination.

"What the hell are you doing here, Kaia?" he asked when she stopped just in front of him and stared him down. "Is something wrong?"

"Nothing's wrong," she said sweetly. "I just wanted to see you." *All* of you, she could have added—but it seemed redundant.

"It couldn't have waited?" he asked, wrapping a towel around himself protectively and slowly inching away from her.

"I'm tired of waiting," she explained, taking his hand and threading her fingers through his. He pulled away and shot a quick look behind her, where the rest of the guys on the swim team were toweling off and throwing clothes onto their wet and sticky bodies as quickly as possible. Each was keeping a close eye on the live-action soap opera.

"What are you talking about?" he hissed, dropping the towel and pulling on a pair of jeans over his sopping briefs. He grabbed the rest of his clothes and ushered her over to a—relatively—more private area behind a bank of lockers. "Tired of waiting for what?"

"For this," she said, and grabbed his face and kissed him, sucking in the taste of his soft lower lip before he harshly shoved her away.

"Kaia, what the fuck . . . ?"

"What? You didn't enjoy that? You didn't *want* that?" she challenged him.

"Can you please lower your voice?" he whispered frantically. He peered around the edge of the locker—the room had pretty much emptied out, but a few swimmers still lingered, hoping for some excitement.

"Can you get out of here, guys?" he called out. "Come on, help me out here!"

He turned back to Kaia.

"What are you trying to do to me?" he asked in a low

and urgent voice. He suddenly looked down and, realizing his chest was still bare, quickly pulled on a T-shirt, the thin white cotton clinging to his wet body. "It's going to get back to Beth that you came looking for me here. She'll freak."

"To be honest, Adam, I don't really care," Kaia explained patiently. "And I'm not sure why you do, either."

"Kaia, I'm *in love* with her," he shouted in frustration. "You know that. You said you understood. That the whole thing, that other thing, was a mistake, that—"

"Forget what I said," she cut in. Now she knew she'd done the right thing, shucking the good girl act and coming after him hard and fast. Being soft and subtle, giving him time to think and regret before he acted, would never have worked. She needed him to stop thinking and start *acting*. And for that, he needed to know exactly what was on the table—exactly what he would be passing up.

"It wasn't a mistake," she informed him. "When we were in that motel, I wanted you. Just like I want you now." She placed a hand on the waistband of his jeans, then let it slide slowly downward. "And you can't tell me you don't want me, too."

He shoved her away. Hard. She slammed into the lockers behind her with a crash. The shock of impact was mirrored on his face when he saw how hard he'd pushed her. But he shook it off, letting anger sweep over him again—and she was glad of it. Finally, some real, deep emotion breaking through that placid surface. Some passion. Kaia knew what that meant—it was only a matter of time. She couldn't suppress the smile.

He saw the look on her face and shook his head violently, backing away.

"Forget it, Kaia," he snapped, stuffing his belongings into his backpack as quickly as he could. "It doesn't matter what you want, or what you think I want. It can't happen. It *won't* happen."

It was the second time in an hour that Kaia had heard those words. This was getting old—but once again, Kaia was certain: He may have *said* no. But he *meant* soon.

Adam slammed through the door of the locker room, with Kaia close behind him. This whole situation was maddening. Okay—flattering, too, but also completely out of control. *Kaia* was out of control. And word was sure to get back to Beth and—

Uh-oh.

Looks like word wouldn't have to.

Beth was standing in the hall outside the locker room, facing the door, so Adam got a good look at her face as he walked out—the tentative smile when she saw him, twisted into a grimace of disgust a moment later as Kaia emerged, the front of her shirt still soaking wet from when she'd pressed herself up against Adam's bare and dripping chest.

"See you later, Adam!" Kaia said pleasantly, as the couple stared at each other in silence. She smiled sweetly at Beth, then turned back to him. "Thanks *so* much for your help in there." And she strode away down the hall.

Adam stopped in the doorway, as if half considering a retreat back into the locker room. Maybe if he went inside, came out again, the world would give him a do-over, and he and Beth could start afresh.

Unfortunately, Beth didn't look like she was much in the mood for fresh starts. She stood a few feet away, pressed against the brick wall as if she needed it for support. Her hands were clasped in front of her, in a loose and relaxed pose betrayed by the tension in her frozen face. She wore a light gray, short-sleeved sweater that he'd never seen before. It was the soft color of mist, the same gray that flecked her clear blue eyes. Her eyes, he noticed, were glassy, unshed tears pooling at the lids. She looked very angry—and very beautiful.

"Beth," he finally said. "Uh, what are you doing here?"

"I came to find you," she said mechanically, staring off in the direction Kaia had gone. "I was going to apologize. One of the guys told me you were still in there. So I waited."

Thanks a lot, guys, Adam thought. That was some team loyalty for you.

"I'm glad you did," he said hesitantly, taking a step toward her and gently grasping her hand. "I wanted to talk to you, too."

The contact seemed to shake her out of her state of shock—she whipped her hand away.

"I said I *was* going to apologize," she corrected him. "Past tense. That was before I . . . interrupted you." She looked away. "I guess you weren't expecting to see me here."

"What's that supposed to mean?"

"You know what it means." She swiped a hand quickly across her eyes and finally met his gaze. Her lower lip was trembling—and she looked at him as if he were a mysteriously familiar stranger, someone she'd once known, long ago. "God, Adam, in public? In the locker room? What were you thinking? Did you think I wouldn't find out?"

"You don't even know what you're talking about!" he protested. The best defense, after all, was a good offense. Not that he had anything to be defensive about. He hadn't *done* anything—was it his fault that Kaia kept chasing after him? Wasn't the point that he kept turning her away? Didn't that, in fact, make him a *better* boyfriend? What more did she want from him?

"What do you think happened in there?" he snapped, losing his patience. "You think I threw her down and *did* her? Right there on the floor in front of half the swim team? Do you even want to know what really happened? Maybe you'd rather just assume the worst." He heard the words coming out as if someone else had spoken them— surely it hadn't been him. Surely he wouldn't say something so hurtful to someone he loved. Surely he wasn't that kind of guy.

"What's the point in asking if you're just going to lie to me?" Beth asked, furiously blinking back tears. "I see the way you look at her—I know you think she can give you what you want. Fine—go get it." She whirled around, as if to leave, but he grabbed her arm and tugged her back around. She wasn't walking away, not this time. All of this, the constant fights over nothing, the tears, the silent treatment, it had to end. They had to actually deal with this— which meant she was, for once, going to have to stick around.

"I'm so sick of you making everything about sex," he spit out, totally exasperated. How many times could they have the same conversation?

"Me? What about you? You—"

"No, *you*," he argued. "This is not about sex, or Kaia, and you know it." And he tried to force the image of her clinging to his wet body, of her lips on his, of her arms wrapped around him, out of his head. "This is about *you*. About you not trusting me. Not trusting us."

Beth's face softened, and for a moment Adam thought

he'd gotten through to her. Then she shook her head.

"No. No!" She flung his arm off and pushed him away. "You can't turn this around on me—this is about *you* acting like a jerk. This is about *you* skulking around in a boys' locker room with another girl. This is about *you* wanting—" Her voice broke. "Wanting what you can't have and acting like it's all my fault."

"Beth . . ."

"Of course I don't trust us," she said dully, sounding suddenly exhausted. "Right now, us sucks."

She walked away—and this time, he let her go.

"Thanks for the heartfelt apology!" he called after her, punching the wall in frustration. The stinging pain in his knuckles only made him angrier.

This was his reward for doing the right thing? For resisting temptation? He might as well have thrown Kaia down on the locker room floor, torn her clothes off, satisfied his every pornographic desire—why the hell not, if that's what Beth was going to believe either way?

He'd been there for her, he'd thrown himself into this relationship, he'd done everything he could for her—and she couldn't even be bothered to ask him for the truth. She couldn't be bothered to stick around for a damn conversation.

And you know what?

Good riddance.

chapter eleven

SHE'D NEVER KNOWN A KNEE COULD BE SO SEXY.

But there it was. Under the table. An inch away.

She could feel his leg there next to hers, could imagine moving hers over just a bit, just an inch, pressing their legs together. And that's not all she could imagine. He was so close—she could just slip her foot out of her shoe, slide her toes up his calf, trace a gentle design across his skin. She could reach out, take his hand in hers beneath the table, massage his fingertips and then press him against her body, so hungry for his touch. . . .

"Harper? What are you thinking about?"

Adam's warm voice startled her out of her frozen

reverie. And thank God for small favors—if she didn't stop obsessing over her stupid fantasies, she might miss the chance to turn them into reality. And that's what this was—her chance.

"Harper?" he repeated, sounding concerned. "What's up?"

"Nothing—don't worry about it," she assured him.

"Are you sure?"

"No, I'm fine, it's nothing," she said again. "Besides, I'm supposed to be cheering *you* up. What are you thinking about? As if I have to ask . . ." Beth, of course. It was always Beth. Whether they were in the gazing-into-each-other's-eyes-there's-only-two-of-us-in-the-whole-world mode, or in the I-may-never-speak-to-you-again mode (as, happily, they were tonight), Harper knew that the Blond One was never far from his thoughts.

But Adam just laughed. "No, I'm not thinking about her, Harper, I swear—I'm just enjoying the music. Thanks again for dragging me out tonight."

It had been a brilliant idea—after all, who knew how long Beth would be stupid enough to stay away sulking, leaving Adam on the open market? Opportunities like this didn't come along very often and didn't last for very long—so Harper was planning to take full advantage of this one while she had it. Seize the day, right? She looked around at the grungy bar, the local band that was—just

barely—cranking out something that bore a distant relation to music, and sighed. If only she didn't have to seize
the day in such seedy surroundings. Though she had to
admit, what with the darkness, the haze of smoke, the
music (sort of), the place had possibilities. . . .

Of course, a *true* friend probably wouldn't take
advantage of Adam's postfight instability, wouldn't do
her best to talk him out of a relationship he clearly
wanted to stay in (not that she planned to stick with
talking)—on the other hand, Harper reminded herself,
wasn't it her duty as a true friend to help him see the
error of his ways?

"You know I'm always here for you, Adam," she said,
hoping he would hear the emotion in her voice, would, for
once, realize what all her loyalty, all her attention, all her
efforts really meant.

"It's true, Harper—you're really a great friend."

And that was Adam—hopelessly oblivious, as always.

But so painfully perfect, in every other way.

She closed her eyes for a moment, imagining what it
might be like to open them to a different world, one in
which Adam was sitting across the table gazing at her in
that way, that tender awestruck way that had always been
reserved for Beth. If she could just get him to really *look*
at her, to see what he was missing. She raised a hand to
her neck, let her fingers play their way down the bare skin

until they reached her silky neckline—if she opened her eyes, would she catch him sneaking a forbidden glance, wondering what lay beneath?

She opened her eyes.

And the answer was no.

He wasn't even looking in her direction—he'd turned toward the door, toward a gaggle of girls from their school who had just walked in. Toward Kaia. Of course.

And there went her perfect night, her golden opportunity.

Kaia spotted them, raised an arm in greeting, and treated Adam to a long, slow smile. Harper just sneered. And waited.

Adam paused for a moment, nodded briefly in acknowledgment—and then turned away.

Harper breathed a sigh of relief, and only then realized that she'd been holding her breath, tensed and ready for rejection. But Adam was still there, and Kaia— one eyebrow raised in—surprise? Skepticism? Disbelief? Whatever—Kaia sat down across the bar.

Good. And you'd better stay there, Harper thought. She resisted the impulse to make some snide comment about her nemesis—or about the fact that Adam seemed suddenly to have abandoned his Siamese twin act and was actually allowing some space to intrude between him and his illicit beloved.

No reason to ruin a perfect moment—even for the perfect snark.

Besides, the important thing was that he was staying away. Whatever the reason, Kaia had lost this round— she was across the bar and Harper was here, across from Adam.

Across from his deep blue eyes and luscious smile and biceps that could—

"Harper, there's—there's something I need to talk to you about."

That's it—no more gazing, no more dreaming, she told herself sternly. *Must stay focused. Listen.* Even though he was looking at her so intently—was, unbelievably, leaning in close and laying his hand on top of hers. Even though it was hard not to lose herself in the electrifying contact and in fantasies of where this might be going. . . . No. Must focus. Pay attention. Hope.

"You've always said I could talk to you about anything," he began hesitantly.

Harper just nodded, afraid, for once, to speak.

"Well . . . you know that Beth and I have been really happy together, that I think she's wonderful. . . ."

His voice trailed off, and Harper nodded again, impatiently. There was only so much of this she could listen to, and if the evening was about to devolve into yet another monologue about Beth's million-and-one divine attributes, she was going to need a *lot* more to drink.

"And I mean, she is wonderful," he continued, "but . . ."

But? That was more like it.

"Well, this last week I've just been—"

"Harper! Harper! Over here!"

Oh God, not now.

Distracted by the shrill voice, Adam broke off what he was saying, and they both looked up to see a pale, skinny girl waving frantically from a few tables away.

"Harper! Look, we're here too!"

A ditzy blond sophomore who'd decided last spring to make Harper her role model, life trainer, and personal guru, whether Harper liked it or not.

It wasn't enough that the girl followed her around so much at school that Harper had dubbed her "Mini-Me"? She had to follow Harper *here*, too? Had to ruin what might have been her perfect night?

"Just ignore her," she urged Adam. "What were you about to say?"

Adam paused, then laughed nervously. "You know what? Forget it."

"But—"

"No, you go talk to your friends—I'm heading off to the bathroom." He grinned. "You'll still be around when I get back, though, right?"

"I don't know, Adam." Harper looked pointedly at the

next table over, where a middle-aged guy with too much stomach and too few teeth was chugging his beer, soggy cigarette lodged firmly in the corner of his mouth. "Lots of hot prospects around here—once you disappear, who knows who I'll find. . . ."

He laughed, and Harper forced herself to join in. But as soon as he turned away, her face turned to ice. What if, when Adam came back, he'd lost his nerve, and never said whatever it was he'd been about to tell her? She couldn't believe that one loser with bad timing had just torpedoed her moment—and here came Mini-Me now, dragging along her equally bland best friend, aka Mini-She.

Both apparently gluttons for punishment.

"Hey, Harper, didn't you see us over there? I can't believe that you're here too!" Mini-Me gushed.

"Isn't the band great?" Mini-She asked excitedly.

"Yeah, and the lead singer is so hot—don't you think?" Mini-Me added.

Harper looked up onstage, where scruffy Reed Sawyer, stoner, sixth-year senior, wannabe badass, all-around burnout—and lead singer of the Blind Monkeys—was torturing a guitar with only slightly less incompetence than the rest of his band of losers.

"I think love must be blind *and* deaf," Harper drawled.

The girls looked back at her blankly.

Harper was undecided. Despite their utter cluelessness

and stalker tendencies, she rarely went out of her way to torture these girls—not out of pity or virtue, but because they were embarrassingly easy targets. On the other hand, as demonstrated by tonight's disaster, her tolerance had apparently been a hideous mistake. . . .

"Hey, you know who else is here?" Mini-Me asked.

"Lady Gaga?" Harper guessed.

"No way—but how cool would that be?!" Mini-Me said. Apparently she'd been absent the day sarcasm genes were handed out. "No—*Kaia's* here! And you should see what she's wearing—she says it's from *Dolce and Gabbana.*"

"*So* cool," Mini-She sighed appreciatively.

Harper rolled her eyes, taking only minimal joy in the fact that her little friends had apparently intruded on the new girl's night too. The last thing she needed right now was a Kaia lovefest. Enough was enough.

"You know, the scene here is getting kind of lame," Harper confided. "I think pretty soon I'm going to head out to this party I heard about. You should—oh wait, no, they probably wouldn't let you in."

"What?"

"Where?"

"A party?"

Good, she'd hooked them. Now, to reel them in. "Yeah, some college guys who haven't gone back to school yet," she continued. "They're set up in this old warehouse along the highway."

"No way!" Mini-Me said breathlessly. "So . . . think we could come with you?"

"Well . . . I probably shouldn't even have told you about it." The girls looked crestfallen. "But since I have . . ." She pretended to stop and think for a moment, and then, "Hey, why not? If I give you the password, they should let you in."

Harper wrote down an address and "password" on a napkin and surreptitiously passed it to the girls. "You shouldn't wait for me, though—I have to stick around here for a while to take care of Adam." She leaned in and lowered her voice. "Don't tell anyone, but he and Beth had another fight."

There, that should get the gossip chain started and hopefully put a nice shiny nail in the coffin of that relationship.

"But you know what," Harper said, smiling at her own bright idea, "why don't you invite Kaia along? I'm sure she'd love to see what a good party looks like around here—and she certainly won't want to spend the rest of her night in this dump."

"Thanks, Harper, that's a great idea," Mini-Me enthused. "You're really the best, you know that?"

Harper just smiled. "Actually, I do."

The girls took off, and Harper watched them as they

LUST

headed back to their table and collected their stuff. Looked like they were taking the bait. She felt a momentary twinge of guilt at the thought of them wandering through a dark and empty warehouse wondering where the frat boys were and where the keg was hidden—but Harper didn't believe in rewarding stupidity with leniency. And at least this way they would learn their lesson.

Maybe.

Now if only they could drag Kaia along with them. She peered through the crowd to check out Kaia's table—but Kaia was gone. Home for the night? It seemed unlikely that such a wild party girl—or so she claimed—would have given up on the nightlife so early, pathetic as it was. More likely, she was off somewhere looking for trouble.

Speaking of which . . . Adam had been gone forever, and the bathroom just wasn't that far away.

So where was he?

"You know you want me," Kaia whispered, her breath hot and moist against his ear.

Adam said nothing, but didn't—couldn't—push her away.

He'd pushed her away in the motel room—and she'd come back.

He'd pushed her away in the locker room—and she'd come back.

He'd pushed her away when she accosted him outside the bathroom—and yet she was still here. Still had her arms wrapped around him.

He was so tired of pushing.

And she was so beautiful.

It amazed him—how Kaia and Beth could be so different, how Kaia could be the opposite of almost everything he loved about Beth (and he did love her, he reminded himself, reassured himself). Kaia was hard where Beth was soft, confident where Beth was shy, determined where Beth was so easily deterred. Kaia's jet black hair, her sparkling green eyes, her icy beauty—they were nothing like the silky blond comfort he found in Beth's arms.

So different, and yet—

And yet he wanted them both so much.

But Beth would never forgive him.

"Beth would never have to know," she whispered, as if she'd read his thoughts.

Or had he spoken them aloud?

Adam no longer knew. Kaia's perfume washed over him, mixing with the smoky air, and he was suffocating, he was dizzy, he was lost in the pounding of the music, the vibrations running through the floor, through their bodies, the thunderous bass. He was lost in the sight of her swollen lips, her wide eyes, her body pressing against his in the darkness.

He thought of Beth, of the look on her face when she'd walked away from him outside the school, of the sound of her voice through her tears, telling him she didn't trust him, could never trust him. He thought of what Beth would think, what she would do if she saw him here with Kaia. Thought of proving her wrong, thought of proving her right—

And then, as Kaia's hands tightened around his waist, as his chest pressed against hers, as her tongue slipped past his lips—he wasn't thinking about Beth anymore.

She should never have gone looking for him.

That was all Harper could think, the only words her mind could muster as she stood frozen, staring at the two of them. Together. Wrapped in each other's arms.

Harper wanted to say something—wanted to spit out a venomous one-liner that would make them leap apart in shame. She wanted to shoot them both a murderous look, then shrug her shoulders, spin on her heel, and walk off in disgust.

A perfect exit.

Classy.

Cool.

Unconcerned.

But she had no words—she'd lost the power to speak, to stalk away. It was all she could do to keep standing, breathing . . . watching.

And so, paralyzed, half-hidden by the darkness—not that either of them would have noticed her had she been lit up by a spotlight—she stayed, wanting nothing more than to turn away. But couldn't.

Couldn't stop watching him, his hands running through her hair, his lips pressed against hers, her hands running up and down his back, then their hands clasped, their fingers intertwined—Kaia's hands, Kaia's fingers, Kaia's lips where she had always dreamed that hers would, should be. . . .

No.

Harper took a deep breath and forced herself to turn her back on the couple, on her best friend, on what the night could have been. Turned away.

She would not cry. No matter what, she would not cry—and she would not stay.

She pushed her way through the smoky bar and threw herself out into the cool desert night.

Let him wonder where she'd gone.

Let him find his own ride home.

And—she knew he would.

Hating her, hating him—hating herself for being so weak, for being so pathetic, for not being able to hate him at all—not even now, when the two of them, together, all over each other, was all she could see, Harper walked aimlessly down the empty street.

She was shaking, but she didn't feel the cold—could feel nothing, except the painful, empty hole in the pit of her stomach. Her bare hand, which had so recently been warmed by his touch. And finally, after a few blocks and a few deep breaths, the rage. The hot blaze of anger—and the cool certainty that this was not over, that this was not a fight she was prepared to lose.

Adam would be hers . . . and Kaia would be sorry.

They went back to the abandoned motel. Of course.

Adam felt like he was watching the scene happen to someone else. That couldn't be him, clutching Kaia's hand, following her down the long and dusty hallways and into one of the cramped, dark rooms. It must be someone else giving in to her warm touch, the soft pressure of her hands forcing him down onto the mattress. It couldn't be him.

All his willpower had drifted away, all the excitement and energy that had surged through him in the club as he finally let himself go and ran his hands over her body, as she nibbled his earlobe and whispered, "Let's get out of here"—all that had seeped away. This wasn't a crime committed in the heat of passion—it was a crime of omission, a failure to stop the chain of events that had started in the bar, that had brought him here.

But who could stop an avalanche? Who could stop a train wreck?

Inevitability.

That was the word he was groping for. Everything had taken on a strange tinge of inevitability, as if everything that had happened in the last few weeks, everything since he'd first seen her, first taken her hand in his, had led directly to this moment. To Kaia.

She stood before him and, with a sultry smile, pulled off her halter top, revealing the black lace bra that lay beneath.

Then off went the shimmering silver skirt.

Off went the lace.

She crawled into bed beside him.

"Your turn," she whispered, and began unbuttoning his jeans.

A warm heat flushed through him and he felt his lost passion returning—and along with it, his doubt.

"Kaia," he said softly, allowing her to pull his T-shirt over his head, to kiss her way across his bare chest as his hands, as if of their own accord, massaged the soft contours of her body. "Kaia, I'm not sure we should . . ."

"Shh," she whispered, stopping him with a kiss. "Don't worry, I'll be gentle."

And off went the boxers.

chapter twelve

THE PHONE RANG AND RANG, BUT THERE WAS NO answer. As the voice mail kicked in again, Adam hung up in disgust. He'd left too many messages, and his voice was beginning to take on a distinct tinge of desperation. But where was she?

(*Screening your calls*, his inner voice whispered. He ignored it.)

He needed to talk to her, needed to see her—and for what? He didn't even know. When he'd woken up this morning, the whole thing, the foggy memory of their bodies wrapped together, of their feverish wrestling, thrusting, caressing, moaning—it had all seemed like a dream.

But it had happened.

And it could never happen again—except that there was nothing he wanted more than to see her, to touch her, to feel her hands all over him.

Guilt burned through him every time he thought about what he'd done, and he thought about it constantly. And maybe the pain of guilt was worth it.

He decided to go outside, shoot some hoops, burn off some nervous energy. His mother had yet to return home from her own escapades the night before, and the house was too empty, too quiet. He didn't want to face anyone else—not now that he had a secret that was weighing down on him so heavily. Besides, normal human interaction might bring him back down to Earth, penetrate the haze that seemed to lay over him, that gave every moment a heightened clarity, every sensation a powerful charge. He felt different, somehow, and he wasn't ready to share the feeling—or to lose it. He didn't want to be alone with his thoughts, though—well, more than anything, he wanted to be alone with his thoughts and his fantasies, but that seemed too dangerous. Because the more he thought, the more he wanted.

He changed into a ratty T-shirt and some running shorts, grabbed the ball out of the garage, and jogged over to the driveway. It was a blisteringly hot day, the heat billowing up in waves from the black concrete.

Good. Maybe he could sweat out this disease that Kaia had infected him with, this bottomless craving for her body, for the feel of her skin against him. He needed to stop thinking about her, to stop thinking at all, to just focus on the feeling of his muscles straining in exertion, his feet pounding the ground, his hands on the ball, sending it flying toward the basket. He would lose himself in the moment.

He brought the phone outside with him, though. Just in case.

Adam didn't know how long he was out there, dribbling, racing back and forth across the length of the driveway, trying to force himself into an oblivion of exhaustion. It almost worked. Finally he stopped, out of breath and every muscle screaming. He bent forward, letting his arms dangle freely toward the ground, then straightened up and dumped a bottle of water over his head.

And there was the phone, lying on the ground, taunting him with its silence. He wrestled with himself, then slammed the ball into the pavement in frustration. It bounced with a resounding thud; Adam scooped it up with one hand—with the other he picked up the phone. He flipped it open, just in case he'd been so in the zone that he'd missed a call. But he hadn't.

And then, as he shuffled up the walkway toward his front door, it rang in his hands. Startled, Adam fumbled it for a moment, almost dropped it—dropped the ball instead—and finally got a look at the caller.

Beth.

She'd been calling all weekend.

He silenced the ringer, ignoring the tension creeping through his body.

For now, at least, what was there to say?

The phone rang and rang, but Harper didn't even bother to see who it was, much less consider answering it.

It would be Miranda, of course, as it had been the last twenty times, calling to see where she'd disappeared to, wondering what had happened Friday night. Harper's mouth twisted into a sour grin—maybe Miranda was imagining her and Adam holed away in the bedroom together, an isolated lovers' tryst. Right.

The first few calls, she'd raced to the phone, expecting it to be Adam, begging for forgiveness. Not that she would have answered, she reminded herself—but there would have been a certain satisfaction in listening to his voice mail, groveling for mercy.

Saturday had passed, and most of Sunday—and the call had never come.

She would like to think that he was in his bedroom even now, staring out the window at her house, too racked with guilt to call her, too afraid of what her response might be. Agonizing over whether he'd thrown away a twelve-year friendship for a one-night stand.

Somehow, she doubted it.

She knew all she had to do was pick up the phone and Miranda would appear, complete with the requisite care package of trashy chick flicks and a bottle of Absolut. Miranda had a secret stash hidden in an old suitcase under her bed for moments just like this. She could easily have slipped a couple of bottles out of the house and spent the weekend over at Harper's, under the guise of keeping Harper company while her parents were out of town. She knew she should have called Miranda at some point, regardless, as the two of them had arranged to meet at the Cedar Creek Motel earlier that day to supervise the team of sophomores that Harper had suckered into cleaning the place. (They'd been sworn to secrecy about the location but offered admittance to the party—*if* their Lysol and vacuuming efforts were deemed up to snuff.) Too bad. Miranda would just have to take care of it alone or leave the sophomores to fend for themselves. She'd be pissed off, but Harper knew she would understand—there were plenty of extenuating circumstances.

And Harper just wanted to be alone. Her mother had dragged her father off for a weekend of "antiquing"—both he and Harper knew this was code for "digging through unwanted, flea-infested crap at roadside junk sales," but neither had much desire to puncture Amanda Grace's illusions. Harper's mother spent her time in a world of her own making, one that was infinitely richer, more elegant, more high society, more *appropriate* than the dirty present, in which the Grace family, once lords of the manor, now struggled to keep their heads above water.

But Harper was trapped in the harsh reality of the present: an empty house, empty hours to fill. As the phone began to ring again, Harper moaned and pulled one of the couch pillows over her head to drown out the noise. She'd been self-medicating with vodka and cookie dough, but forty-eight hours of that had only left her with a persistent thudding headache and periodic waves of nausea. In a few hours she would crawl into bed, hide under the covers, and pass out, trying not to think about waking up Monday morning and facing the world.

Struggle with a smile, she thought. It was her mother's cardinal rule. Do whatever you need to do—but never let them see you cry.

Kaia shut off her phone.

She was sick of seeing Adam's name pop up what seemed like every five minutes—and face it, it's not like anyone else would be trying to call.

She shuffled down to the kitchen to snag another pint of Ben & Jerry's. When she'd arrived in town a few weeks ago, the refrigerator and freezer had been completely empty, the sparkling stainless steel kitchen with its state-of-the-art appliances virtually unused. Typical bachelor pad. Even though the bachelor in question was a fifty-two-year-old defense contractor with two ex-wives and a seventeen-year-old daughter. Kaia didn't know what her father had been eating—it's not like there were a lot of takeout options in town, and she somehow didn't see Keith Sellers pulling his BMW sedan into the Nifty Fifties lot on a regular basis.

Since she'd arrived, she'd had the cook stock up on her favorite foods—at least the ones that could be purchased nearby or shipped in—and, after so many years of nonstop restaurant cuisine, she had to admit that night after night of home-cooked meals was actually a welcome change. Even if she did usually eat her gourmet food spread out on a TV table in the den—the dining room was too large and impersonal for one. And one was the most she ever got.

Anyway, she'd sent the cook home for the weekend, and instead of her usual diet of whole grains, soy, and fresh greens, she was treating herself to a couple of days of soggy pizza and Ben & Jerry's. Why not? Hadn't she accomplished her mission? Didn't she deserve a little reward?

Kaia scooped some Chubby Hubby into a ceramic bowl (ecru colored, to match the walls) and squeezed some chocolate sauce on top. Perfect. Grabbing a spoon, she headed back into the living room and settled onto the couch, just in time for the beginning of a "very special" Lifetime movie. Like all Lifetime movies, it was a cautionary tale of teen pregnancy or anorexia or domestic violence or something—Kaia didn't really care. She just liked to watch all the fucked-up people sort out their problems in such reliably melodramatic ways. And it helped kill the time.

"You're grounded!" her father had shouted in exasperation when she'd strolled in the door a little before dawn.

She'd just smirked. Grounded? As if that were a punishment in a place like this—as if there were anywhere else in this town she'd rather be than on her couch, watching shitty movies. Grace was nothing but tedium. Which her father might have known if he'd spent more than five minutes with her since she'd come to town. But no—he'd swooped home on the *one* night she was out until dawn, freaked out, grounded her, then disappeared before she woke up the next morning. Off he went on another "business trip," along with his omnipresent personal assistant, who, conveniently, looked like a low-rent Playboy bunny.

As if the maid was really going to enforce the whole grounding thing if Kaia decided to leave the house. In fact, Kaia realized, it would almost be worth the trouble of venturing out, just to force the confrontation. . . .

Almost, but not quite.

No, on Monday morning she'd go back to work, so to speak—continue her pursuit of Jack Powell, enjoy the taste of her conquest over Adam, sit back to watch the chaos that would inevitably ensue. And if anyone asked, she would describe a whirlwind jaunt to Manhattan, a jet-setting weekend filled with star-studded parties and risqué encounters—much like the weekend she was sure all her East Coast "friends" were currently sleeping off. Not that any of them would bother to tell her about it—or take a break from the high life and visit her in exile.

But no one had to know that. She turned up the volume on the TV—it was anorexia this time, with an "all star cast" featuring some guy from *The Vampire Diaries* and that woman from *Pretty Little Liars* (she showed up in 70 percent of all Lifetime movies—and Kaia would know).

It was a guilty pleasure, Kaia acknowledged, scarfing down another spoonful of her ice cream. Embarrassing, yes—but all in all not such a bad way to spend a weekend.

chapter thirteen

BY MONDAY, ADAM HAD LESS OF A GRIP THAN EVER on what he wanted to say to Kaia—he just knew that he needed to talk to her, needed to see her, needed it more with every passing minute. The guilt of what they'd done was crushing him; he'd managed to avoid Beth all day long, but his luck couldn't last forever. Even so, his nightmarish visions of what might happen were far less vivid than his impassioned memories of what *had* happened, and . . .

And basically, he was completely confused.

"Kaia!" he called, finally spotting her glossy black hair in the crowd as the final bell echoed through the halls. "Kaia, wait up a minute!" He jogged to catch up with her, breaking into a bright smile as she turned to face him. She was wearing a form-fitting black shirt that laced up the front and jeans so tight they could have been painted on. The indecision and complexities of a moment ago seemed to melt away.

"Adam." She sighed. "What is it?"

"Where were you all weekend?" he asked, hoping not to sound too desperate. He was, he reminded himself, a superstar on this campus. He was beloved by the masses, adored by throngs of girls. He shouldn't need to be chasing one through the halls, even if she was so beautiful it hurt, even if her touch made him forget that there'd ever been anyone else. *No* girl was worth humiliating himself. And yet—he heard the panic creeping into his voice. And couldn't stop it. "Didn't you get my messages?"

"I was away," she said shortly. "Back in New York. So what did you want?"

"I wanted—" Adam broke off. What did he want? That was the whole problem, wasn't it? He wanted her, of course, right here, right now. But didn't he also want to be with Beth, his sweet, innocent girlfriend? Other than the awkwardly mumbled hellos exchanged at their neighboring lockers, they hadn't spoken in almost a week, which was the longest time in months he'd gone without hearing from her. And he missed her, he did— but it was hard to remember that when his eyes, without his permission, remained riveted on Kaia's deep red lips.

He pulled her out of the path of the crowd and into a small alcove behind the lockers and lowered his voice. He'd just make it up as he went along.

"I wanted to talk to you," he said urgently.

"So you got me. Talk about what?"

About what? What else?

"About, you know, about what we *did*," he whispered, darting his head around to make sure no one could overhear. "About what we're going to do about it."

About whether we're going to do it again.

"What's there to *do* about it?" she asked, sounding mystified. "Or to talk about? We did it, and"—she touched his cheek briefly, gently—"it was great. But, you know, it's done. What do you want from me?"

Adam was stunned. "I just thought we could—well, you'd said—and when we were at the motel—I just thought you wanted—"

Kaia laughed—it was a musical sound, lighter and more spontaneous than anything he'd seen her say or do in the short time they'd known each other. That was the difference, he suddenly realized: This was real—and everything else had all been calculated.

"Oh, Adam," she said, her voice dripping with a patronizing sympathy. "What? Did you think we were going to *date* or something? Were you thinking this was going to be a *relationship*?" She pronounced the word as if it tasted rotten coming out of her mouth.

Then she laughed again, and Adam finally got it. He may have been slow, but he wasn't stupid.

"Whatever," he said brusquely. "I just wanted to be sure that you didn't get the wrong idea. I'm with Beth, you know. I love her." The familiar phrase sounded unconvincing, even to him. Especially to him.

"I know you do," Kaia assured him, grinning brightly now. "So you must be pretty terrified that she'll find out about this, hmm?" She gave him a cryptic look. "But hey, who would tell her?"

Shit. Adam had never before understood what it would feel like to have one's heart leap into one's throat. Now he knew. It felt like your chest was an empty shell about to collapse in on itself. It felt like strong hands had wrapped themselves around your neck, squeezing like a vise, choking the air out of you. He saw it clearly now, every step of her—what, her plan? Seduction. Betrayal. All that, just to get him into bed? Or to make him feel like a fool? Or was the true prize whatever was about to come next, all hell breaking loose when Beth learned the truth? Would anyone really go to so much effort, just to cause themselves a little pleasure—or someone else so much pain?

"Kaia," he said warningly, "you wouldn't—"

Who, me? she mimed, the picture of innocence.

"I'm hurt," she said aloud. "Don't you know me at all by now?" She gave him a quick peck on the cheek and skipped off down the hallway. "You know you can trust me!" she called over her shoulder.

He was so totally screwed.

"So which one do you like better?"

Silence.

"Beth? Beth? You still with me?"

Beth stared at the newspaper layout sheets with the same blank gaze she'd been aiming at the world for days. Ever since she'd caught Adam with Kaia outside the locker room, ever since she'd blown up at him and run away, she'd been a little bit lost. The first couple of days hadn't been so bad, as she'd been riding a wave of anger that swept away any lingering doubts or concerns. She'd avoided him in the hallways, she'd ditched out on their date—and, while working behind the counter at the diner, she'd pretended the tomatoes and onions were his head and spent a pleasant hour chopping him to pieces, over and over again.

But after that—well, she was still mad, but she was a little mad at herself, too. She was ready to kiss and make up—but Adam, it seemed, was too busy to take her calls. She'd spent all weekend trying to track him down, stealing a few minutes from her shift to sneak off with her phone;

LUST

bribing her little brothers into shutting up long enough to make a phone call; taking breaks every ten minutes from her stacks of homework to check her phone, see if he'd called. No.

Maybe this was it, she'd decided after a fitful night of sleep. She'd screwed up the best thing she had in her life—though, if he was willing to let go that easily, maybe it wasn't something worth fighting for after all.

"What?" Beth suddenly realized that Jack Powell, sitting across from her in the newspaper office, was holding up two layout sheets in front of her and waiting for some kind of response. Too bad she had no idea what he had asked. "Oh, sorry—uh, yeah, that looks fine."

Jack Powell laid the sheets down on the desk and turned in his chair to look at Beth head-on.

"Beth, is everything okay?" he asked with concern. "You've been a little out of it all afternoon—if there's somewhere else you'd rather be . . . ?"

"No!" she cried in alarm. Sitting here with Mr. Powell, she felt almost secure again, almost calm, for the first time in days. Yes, she was still thinking about Adam constantly, working through their fight again and again, trying to see where everything had gone so wrong—but somehow, having Jack there, droning on in his delicious voice about column space or layouts or whatever, made everything seem a little more manageable. Today he was wearing a stylish button-down shirt with colorful vertical stripes running down its length—it made him look years younger. Good thing he's not, Beth pointed out to herself, or sitting in this small, dark room with him, facing him across the table, their heads leaning in together, their hands brushing past each other to dig through the piles of papers—it would be a whole different story. One her boyfriend wouldn't like very much.

Then she remembered she might not have a boyfriend anymore, and the thought hit her with a stinging pain that brought tears to her eyes. She took a few deep breaths and looked away from Mr. Powell for a moment, calming herself down.

"No," she finally repeated in a steadier voice. "There's really nowhere I'd rather be. I just—I'm just having a little trouble concentrating today. That's all."

"Well, that's obvious," he said sympathetically. "Here's a radical idea—want to talk about it?"

Beth cringed. Talk about her love life with a teacher? A teacher she just happened to have an absurdly large crush on? Didn't seem like the best idea.

"I know it's weird, since I'm your teacher," he said, reading her mind. He placed a tentative hand on hers. "But Beth, I'd really like to be your friend, too."

Maybe it was the warmth in his voice, or the soft pressure of his hand, but something inside of Beth just broke.

"It's my boyfriend," she said, choking back the tears.

Powell nodded encouragingly. "Things have been weird lately, and we're fighting all the time, and now he's not speaking to me and I just—"

She broke off and buried her face in her arms, hiding the humiliating tears.

She felt a gentle hand on her back and, instinctively, tensed up.

"Beth," he said firmly. "Beth, sit up, look at me—you don't have to be embarrassed."

She reluctantly straightened and faced him. He pulled a light blue handkerchief out of his pocket and offered it to her—even in her dismay, she could appreciate the chivalry. She blew into it noisily, wiped the tears away from her eyes, then sat still, taking some deep breaths and twisting the soft cloth nervously in her hands.

"I think I may have ruined everything," she murmured, knowing from the look in his eyes that he understood.

Jack Powell shook his head.

"Beth, Beth, Beth, it's not you, it's him. I promise you that."

"How do you know?"

"Difficult as it may be to imagine, I was a teenage boy once. Trust me, we're all idiots."

Distraught as she was, Beth managed a small smile.

"No, I'm sure whoever this boy is," he continued, "whatever the problem is, he's being an idiot. He's just a boy. But you, Beth," he paused, looking her up and down appraisingly. "You're a woman. A beautiful, intelligent, kindhearted *woman*."

Beth flushed furiously, and her eyes darted around the room; she was unsure where to look, what to do, faced with words like that from a man like him.

"He can't give you what you need, Beth," he told her, slowly running a hand through her long blond hair. She wanted to pull away but didn't. "You need maturity, understanding, passion," he continued. "This guy doesn't deserve you."

She looked down at the table, but then he said her name again and when she looked up, his handsome face was right there, inches from hers and moving closer, and his hands were on her, drawing her in, and then their lips met and he held her to him.

"Oh, Beth," he murmured, and his lips were on her again, his tongue pushing its way into her mouth before she knew what was happening, exploring the moist, dark spaces inside of her, his hands running up and down her back—

She pushed him away, hard, jumped out of her seat and began backing toward the door.

"What are you—? Mr. Powell, what . . . ?"

But she knew what. And she wanted to throw up, wanted to scrub the taste of him out of her mouth, wanted to fly at him, pound his chest with her fists, tear at his face

with her nails, knock that bemused look off his poison-
ously handsome face. But instead she just stood in the
doorway, unable to take a step forward—or back.

He started toward her. "Beth, I'm sorry, calm down,
just sit down for a moment," he pleaded.

He held his arms out from his sides, a conciliatory
gesture, and gave her a weak half smile—it grew wider as
she remained unmoving, then took a hesitant step toward
him. He looked so stricken and apologetic, and after all,
hadn't he just done exactly what she'd been dreaming of
him doing all these weeks? Maybe, Beth realized, horrified, she'd sent out some kind of signal, had drawn him in,
overwhelmed his common sense—maybe she was the one
who'd ruined everything.

"Come back in," he repeated, "and we'll talk about it.
Everything will be fine."

More talk. But that's how it had all started—and after
what had just happened, what was she supposed to say?

Beth shook her head, tears streaming freely down her
face. She opened her mouth as if to speak, then closed it
again.

And ran out of the room.

Kaia pressed herself into the shadows, shaking with anger.

Beth, blinded by tears, ran by without seeing her. Kaia
would deal with her later.

For now: Jack Powell. The asshole, the liar.

After blowing off Adam, she'd come to take another after-hours crack at the French teacher, hoping to convince him that rules were made to be broken.

But apparently, he already knew that.

She stood outside his doorway and watched as he took a few halfhearted steps after Beth, then sighed and slumped back down into his chair. He tapped an index finger rhythmically against his lips, looked up at the empty doorway, and then checked his watch—as if wondering whether she would come back, and how long he should choose to wait.

Don't hold your breath, Kaia thought, shivering in disgust as the image of him lunging at Beth flashed through her mind. The girl (who'd obviously been mooning over Powell for weeks) was clearly either too wimpy or too stupid to take him up on the offer.

Kaia could see what he'd been thinking, of course. A girl like Beth would be easy to push around—she wasn't "trouble in a miniskirt." He'd probably guessed that she would jump at the chance to play his dutiful concubine for the year, rescuing him from boredom and then sweetly and quietly disappearing when the time came.

Kaia almost laughed—apparently, he'd guessed wrong. She was about to enter the room and blast Powell for spurning her, taunt him with what she knew. Then she stopped, considering his stooped figure—chin resting on his fists, staring into the distance, maybe wondering how to clean up the mess he'd made for himself if it ever came to light. If.

Kaia guessed that he was probably congratulating himself for picking a girl like Beth, who would likely lack the backbone needed to get him into any trouble. He probably figured that by steering clear of Kaia, by refusing to indulge in any "inappropriate fraternization" with the troublemaker, he would at least be safe on that front. At least he'd dodged that bullet.

Kaia shook her head in pity, and this time, she did laugh.

Sorry, Mr. Powell. Wrong again.

They ran into each other at their lockers—they were next to each other, of course. Midway through last year, Adam had bribed some sophomore to switch with him so that he and Beth could be side by side. Sometimes Beth slipped little love notes in through the ventilation cracks at the top, and once in a while, Adam had even thought to make a romantic gesture of his own. On Valentine's Day he had papered the inside of her locker with cut-out construction paper hearts and left a bouquet of roses waiting for her. It had always been a good thing, having the same home base to come back to, an easy meeting point, a safe refuge in the busy chaos of the day. But having neighboring lockers also meant there was no escape, and so here they were, side by side, at the worst possible time.

Still wet from swim practice and still steaming from his run-in with Kaia, Adam slammed his locker open and grabbed his bag, accidentally knocking down the photo of Beth he'd taped to the inside of the door on the first day of school. A spasm of guilt shot through him, and he snatched the picture off the ground, trying to stick it back up, but it was no use. The tape was too dried out, and he was forced to lay the picture atop a pile of junk; he swore to himself that he'd bring in more tape the next day and make things right. He'd make everything right.

He slammed the door shut, giving it a kick for good measure, and cursed Kaia under his breath, not for the first time.

The soulless, manipulative bitch.

And he'd let her ruin his life.

Enter Beth.

Tearful, replaying the moment in her mind again and again, and yet still unable to believe it had actually happened.

And had she wanted it to happen?

Asked for it to happen?

He saw her first—and had almost enough time to shrink away. But not quite.

"Beth!" he said forcefully. "I've been looking for you all day."

"Adam?" Beth, who had walked right past him without noticing and began slowly spinning the combination lock on her locker, looked up hesitantly. It was as if she didn't recognize him, didn't quite believe he was real. Maybe because she'd already been imagining him standing there, because right now there was no one in the world she wanted to see more—or less.

She closed her eyes and took a moment of silence to shut out the world and regroup—but when she opened them, he was still there, waiting.

"Adam, I, uh . . ." her voice trailed off. What was she supposed to do, forget about their fight, tell him the truth about what had just happened, send him off to beat up Jack Powell and then get thrown out of school? And, of course, he'd never look at her the same way again. The Beth he knew didn't go around seducing teachers—no, if she was going to make this work, she had to remain the girl he'd fallen in love with, and that girl was innocent, trustworthy, and above all, loyal. She didn't need anyone other than her boyfriend, even in her fantasies.

And that's who I am, she reminded herself. *I* am *that girl*.

"I'm sorry," he finally said, breaking the silence.

"I want to apologize," she sputtered at the same time. And that was all it took.

They spoke at once, the words spilling out hesitantly, their words overlapping, their voices growing in speed and strength as they decided where they were going, drowning each other out in their eagerness to get there.

"No, I'm sorry, I don't know what I was thinking."

"I've been horrible."

"I should have called—"

"I just wanted to say—"

"I missed you—"

"I love you—"

They stammered, and babbled, and then, finally, they embraced.

Adam held her tight, breathing in the fresh, clean scent of her hair. Thinking, *She can never find out.*

Beth dug her fingers into his flesh, wishing she would never have to let go. Deciding, *He can never know.*

They stayed like that, frozen in the empty hallway, for several long minutes, leaning on each other. Two minds with a single, desperate thought: *This time, I'll make it work. This time, I have to.*

She was lying in bed, stumbling haplessly through her math homework, when she heard it. His car, pulling into the driveway, a loud rumbling and clinking that could belong to no one but Bertha the beat-up Chevy. She would know it anywhere.

Harper flipped the book shut and leaped to her feet, creeping over to the window—there was nothing wrong with taking a quick look at him, she told herself. Just because she wasn't speaking to him (not that he'd seemed to notice—it probably didn't even count as the silent treatment if she hadn't actually seen him face-to-face yet and had the chance to snub him) didn't mean she couldn't watch from afar, just to see what he was doing. Who he was with.

The car pulled to a stop and Adam jumped out, walked slowly around to the passenger's side, and held the door open. A blond head appeared, and he put his arm around her waist.

Harper couldn't actually make out the girl's face from her perch, but who needed to? She should have guessed this would happen. Adam and Beth walked together up the pathway toward the front door, his hand still resting on her back, her head against his shoulder. Harper couldn't bring herself to look away. He unlocked his front door, but they paused before stepping inside—Adam cradled Beth's face in his hands and turned it up toward him. And they kissed.

That was more than enough.

Harper shut her blinds in disgust and flung herself back down on the bed. This was getting ridiculous. First she had to watch Adam getting it on with Kaia in public, right in front of her—on *her* date, no less. Then, just when she'd finally decided to embrace the silver lining (i.e., the imminent demise of Beth and Adam's lovers' paradise), he pulls into his driveway and heads inside with Little Miss Perfect herself in tow.

Was Adam hooking up with everyone in town but Harper?

It was beginning to feel that way.

chapter fourteen

"REMEMBER WHEN WE USED TO PLAY GI JOES OUT here?" Adam asked lazily, lying back on the large flat rock and staring up at the stars.

So he hadn't apologized. So what? After a few days Harper's anger had burned down to a low simmer, and with Beth back in the picture and Kaia up to God knows what, Harper didn't have time to waste sulking in a corner. If she was going to win Adam, she was going to have to get in the game. *Besides*, she thought, looking fondly over at her oldest friend, lying next to her on the cool granite, *it was Adam*. Too dense to realize he'd done something wrong, so what was even the point in making him feel guilty? Especially when he called out of the blue with a mysterious request to meet him outside, at *their* place, to talk about some "stuff." When he needed her, she was there—that's just how it worked.

"I remember when *I* used to play GI Joes while *you* spent most of your time with my Barbie collection," Harper teased him.

"Hey, Barbie was hot!" Adam protested.

Harper rolled her eyes. "Right, and *that's* why you used to beg me to let you dress her up and drive her around in the Barbie Corvette." She propped herself up slightly to give him a close look at her skeptical expression. "You just keep telling yourself that."

"I slept with her, Harper."

She froze, still facing him, and it took every ounce of strength she had to keep her face still. No eyes widening in shock or horror, no mouth turning down in disappointment, no tears or telltale blushing—she just looked at him steadily and concentrated on remembering to breathe.

"Who, Barbie?" she asked, narrowly managing to keep her voice light. She let some of the tension leach out of her muscles and sank back onto the smooth surface of the rock.

"Kaia. I'm serious, Harper. I slept with her." He made a strange keening noise, half between a groan and a yelp. "What the hell am I supposed to do now?"

Get yourself checked out for STDs?

But Harper bit back the comment and was glad for the darkness—it gave her a place to hide.

So he'd slept with her. At least now she knew.

Though she wished she didn't.

"So that's why we're out here?" Harper asked. Though she'd suspected as much. The rock bridged the boundary line between their two small backyards and had been a favorite spot for years—it was here that he'd told her, just after moving to town, that his parents were divorced, here that she'd confessed her seventh-grade terror of having no friends, here that, at twelve, they'd shared their first kiss. It was where they ran to when they needed to run away, where their most terrible secrets lived. It was their place, the only thing in the world they truly owned—and they owned it together.

But they hadn't needed their rock in a long time.

"Well, what do you want to do?" she asked simply.

"That's all you're going to say?" He rubbed his eyes furiously, like a little boy trying to rub out his tears. "Don't you want to tell me what a disgusting pig I am, or something?"

"I think I'll let Beth have that honor, if she ever finds out." And Harper almost immediately began sifting through her options—maybe she could play this to her advantage after all. If she could find the right angle, if little Bethie heard the news in just the right way . . .

"Oh God," Adam gasped, his voice filled with horror. "Do you think she will? What am I saying, of course she will. And then . . ."

"Adam, chill out," Harper advised, trying to keep her voice steady. "She probably won't find out—I'm obviously not going to tell her, Kaia has no reason to tell her—and I assume *you're* not going to tell her?"

Though the spineless brat would probably take about five seconds to forgive you, Harper thought with disgust.

"God, no. Unless—should I? Harper, I'm so screwed up. I don't know what I'm doing."

"So, like I said, what do you *want* to do?" Harper repeated. "Ball's in your court, Ad."

She shivered. It was a cold night, a brisk wind blowing through the yard, and she was dressed in only cords and a lacy tank top. Before she could even say anything—not that she would have said anything, nothing could have forced her to interrupt *this* train of thought—Adam pulled off his sweatshirt and tossed it to her. Beneath it, she noticed, he was wearing a vintage Transformers T-shirt she'd bought him for his birthday last year.

"What I want?" he mused, as Harper zipped herself into the cozy red fleece. "I want to go back to the beginning of the year and start over, do everything different."

"Not an option," she pointed out. "Try again."

He was silent for a moment, and Harper wondered

whether it was time for her to take a harder line. If he didn't know what he wanted, well, maybe she should just enlighten him.

"Remember when I kissed you out here?" he asked suddenly.

"Barely," she said casually, hoping he couldn't hear the heartbeat pounding in her ears. "Our braces got stuck together and you accidentally stuck your tongue up my nose—but other than that, it was a success."

They laughed quietly together.

"Everything was easier then," Adam finally said softly, his voice almost carried away on the wind. "I miss it—you and me, just having fun, being together."

"We hated it," Harper reminded him. "We were bored out of our minds. We just wanted to grow up."

Adam sighed. "Yeah, and look where that got us."

Harper watched his silhouette in the moonlight and then, because it felt right, and because she wasn't scared anymore, she took his hand. His fingers curled around hers, and she squeezed his hand gently. He gave her a quick squeeze back. They lay together on the rock, side by side, connected. She hadn't felt so close to him in a long time. This was it. This was her moment.

"Adam, maybe—maybe it's not supposed to be so hard," she suggested hesitantly. "Maybe being with Beth should be *easy*. Maybe if it's not—well, maybe you don't really want to be with her. Maybe you want—"

He pulled his hand away from hers and sat up.

"That's not what I was saying at all, Harper," he said hotly. But the sudden anger, the quick retort—maybe, Harper realized, he knew she was right. "I *love* her," he insisted. "It's not supposed to be easy."

"I know . . . but this?" she pushed. "Fighting all the time? Sleeping with someone else? You have to admit—it doesn't really sound like a good, healthy relationship."

"So we're going through a bad time," he protested—and from the look on his face, she wondered if she'd gone a step too far. "You don't just walk away when things are tough."

"Adam, I just—"

"Or maybe that's what *you* do," he said scornfully, leaping off the rock. "And maybe that's why you're always alone. You're so used to being alone, I don't even think you realize it—but maybe if you did, you wouldn't even care." He turned his back on her and walked inside.

Harper lay on the rock, perfectly still, watching the stars and listening to the silence of the night. She pulled Adam's sweatshirt tightly around her and breathed in the smell of him, still lingering on the soft fleece.

She did know, better than anyone. And she cared.

There are times when a girl just needs to be alone.

This was not one of them.

Harper hit the call button and waited impatiently for Miranda to pick up the phone. Finally, on the fourth ring, just when she'd almost given up hope, salvation arrived.

"911, Miranda," she said by way of greeting. "This is an emergency situation. We're going out."

"Harper, I've got a test tomorrow, I've got to study, I—"

Harper wasn't listening. She was too busy digging through her closet, searching. She needed the perfect outfit for a feel-good, look-better night on the town. And there it was. Spangled halter top—green, to match her eyes; skintight miniskirt—black, to match her mood. The strappy silver stiletto heels she never got the chance to wear. And a black beaded choker, to dress her naked neck. She pulled her hair back into a loose, low chignon, making sure that a few curly tendrils hung down over her eyes. It was a definite look. A little sweet, a little sassy; slightly slutty, but not too skanky. Basically—hot. Maybe a little out of place in the low-rent nightlife options Grace provided her, but if she got whistled at by some drunken trucker or hit on by a Hell's Angel, well, so much the better. It would be a reminder that plenty of people out there wanted her—more than half the high school, for one (99 percent of the male half, with a few alterna-females thrown in for good measure, or so she'd been told). And tonight, she could use all the reminders she could get.

Miranda was still babbling on about a test, and some bio lab that needed to be written up.

"Miranda, listen to me," Harper cut in impatiently. "SOS. Seriously, drop what you're doing—we're going out."

It took some persuading, some wheedling, and eventually a promise from Harper that she would treat Miranda to a manicure in time for the formal that weekend and would finish arranging all the playlists for the after-party on her own. Still, Miranda hedged—it was late, she was tired, she was in her pajamas, her parents would be suspicious. . . .

But Harper was nothing if not persistent—and Miranda was nothing if not loyal, and so, finally, she hung up the phone and answered the call.

As far as their parents were concerned, Harper was sleeping at Miranda's house and Miranda was sleeping at Harper's. All thanks to a supposed late-night cram session for an imaginary chem test. (Harper's parents foolishly thought that Miranda was a good influence, and as far as Miranda's mother was concerned, Harper was the golden child. It was almost too easy.) Later they'd sneak into Harper's house to get some sleep, knowing that her parents, always up and out by five a.m., would never know they'd been there.

As for the night's *real* entertainment, they settled on the Barnstormer, a seedy ribs joint on the north side of town that attracted a reliable clientele of truckers, motorcyclists, and a few regulars, who, by the time they passed through the red wooden doors, were already too drunk to pass along any information about their station in life (or possibly even to remember it themselves).

It was dark, smoky, and crowded, the perfect place to lose yourself and your problems. A sober observer would have spotted Harper and Miranda immediately—the two young girls, dressed to kill, were several decades younger and several layers of dirt cleaner than the majority of patrons. But by eleven p.m. on Rodeo Night, the only sober observers available were the waitresses, who, spending most of their time fending off wandering hands and cleaning up patches of vomit, had little inclination to bother the two girls from the slightly less wrong side of the tracks.

Feeling cloaked by a powerful haze of invisibility, they grabbed a small table in the dark recesses of the bar and, carefully avoiding any sticky spots, flagged down a waitress. Their order:

Two baskets of chicken wings.

One basket of ribs.

Two pitchers of beer.

It was going to be that kind of night.

As the twangs of country-and-western music blared in the background, Harper and Miranda spilled out their problems to each other, becoming increasingly incoherent and increasingly convinced that their problems could be easily solved by the elimination of all men from the face of the Earth. But, it seemed, nothing short of that would help.

A few years ago, the owner of the Barnstormer—a quietly practical middle-aged woman who had moved to Grace after the sudden death of her husband and concluded that the only money to be found in a town like this was in providing its population with food, drinks, or women (she'd hit the trifecta)—had hung a large piece of drift-wood over the inside entrance. The red paint scrawled across it offered a legend to all who passed beneath: EAT TILL IT HURTS, DRINK TILL IT FEELS BETTER.

By midnight Harper and Miranda had done both.

Long years of practice had taught Harper and Miranda that the quickest way to feel better was to remind themselves that other people were so much worse. And Rodeo Night at the Barnstormer provided them plenty of opportunity.

"Check out the guy in the cowboy boots," Miranda crowed, almost spitting out her mouthful of beer.

"Which one?" Harper asked, rolling her eyes. "They're *all* wearing cowboy boots."

"Yeah, but most of them are wearing a little bit more than that," Miranda pointed out, nodding her head to the right, where an overweight, middle-aged guy had stripped off his shirt and climbed atop the bar, gyrating and bouncing in time to the Tim McGraw jukebox beat and the hoots of the crowd.

They dissolved into laughter. This town was filled with enough losers to cheer them up well into the next decade.

"How about the Lone Ranger over there?" Harper snorted, pointing in the direction of an old man decked out in a fifties cowboy costume, complete with mask and capgun.

"God, we have got to get out of this town before we turn into one of them," Miranda declared. She grabbed the last barbecue wing and stuffed it into her mouth, then downed the rest of her beer.

"Tell me about it," Harper agreed, finishing her own. They poured themselves more from the pitcher and sloppily toasted, clinking their overflowing glasses.

"To us!" Miranda crowed.

"To getting the hell out of this place!" Harper added.

"To living fabulous lives—"

"Without shitty guys dragging us down!"

"To being wild and crazy—"

"And independent, on our own—"

"Together!" Miranda finished triumphantly.

And they drank up.

Beth had stayed home from school that day. She'd told her mother she was sick, and her mother had no reason not to believe her. For why would Bethie lie?

She'd spent the day in bed, and it was almost as if she were sick—she was immobilized. Normally unable to sit still for more than a few minutes at a time, her mind always on fire thinking of the next task to be done, the next mission to accomplish, she'd spent the entire day tucked neatly under her covers staring aimlessly at the TV and flipping between channels.

Talk show.

Soap opera.

Dora the Explorer.

Soap opera.

It was all the same to her.

She knew she couldn't hide in her room forever, battering herself with accusations and regrets, if only's and what if's.

If only I hadn't gone to the meeting.

If only I hadn't flirted with him.

If only I'd known what he wanted from me.

What if I wanted it too?

She'd have to leave her sanctuary someday. She'd have to face her life, face him, and soon.

Just not today.

There was a knock on her door.

"Beth? Honey?" Without waiting for Beth to respond, her mother opened the door a few inches and poked her head through the gap. "How are you feeling, sweetheart?"

Her face was filled with concern, and Beth felt a momentary stab of guilt for lying, but beneath that, a warm glow of pleasure—her mother was usually too busy to remember that Beth existed, much less worry about how she was doing. In fact, Beth realized, this was the first time in months that her mother had even set foot inside her room.

"I'm okay, I guess," she said listlessly, not bothering to look away from the TV.

"Are you feeling up for a visitor?" her mother asked, glancing over her shoulder into the hallway.

Beth sat up in bed and looked over at the clock. It was almost eleven—who would be visiting her? Usually she wasn't even allowed to have guests in the house this late—her parents were afraid it would wake up the twins.

"I know it's late," her mother added, "but he says he brought you your homework, so I thought just this once it would be okay."

He?

Beth nodded weakly, and her mother swung open the door all the way—revealing Adam, standing in the hallway with his hands behind his back and an adorable smile on his face.

As her mother disappeared and Adam came into the room, Beth panicked briefly, running her hands through her tangled hair and looking down at her ragged pajamas—she'd been in bed all day, hadn't brushed her teeth in hours or brushed her hair since yesterday. She was a total mess, and for a second, she was tempted to hide under the covers until he went away, but then he came and sat down on the bed next to her and all she could think was: He came. For me.

"Claire already called to give me all the homework," she told him—and then realized that she hadn't even thanked him for coming. She'd only just gotten him back, and now, if her scarecrow appearance didn't send him screaming in the other direction, her rudeness probably would.

"I know she did," he said, before she could say anything else.

"Then why—?"

"I wanted to give you something," he told her, brushing a lock of hair off her forehead. "Well, two things, actually. First, this."

He leaned down and kissed her softly on the lips—and if her parents hadn't been on the other side of the paper-thin walls, Beth would have been tempted to wrap her arms around him and throw him down onto the bed beside her. But instead, she just kissed him back gently, breathing deeply. He tasted like cinnamon, and she knew it was probably because he'd just finished a pack of the cinnamon-flavored gum he was addicted to. And she loved that she knew things like that about him. No matter how bad things got, she still knew him. And he knew her, better than anyone else.

"That's not all," he said, pulling away. She wrapped her fingers through his, and he squeezed her hand gently, and with his other hand unzipped his backpack, pulled something out, and presented it to her.

It was a red rose, beautiful and perfect. And it was threaded through a pink plastic flower ring—an exact match to the one he'd given her so long ago, just before their first date.

Beth laughed, and it felt like the first time she'd laughed in years.

"I'm still not marrying you, idiot," she giggled. But she took the giant ring and slipped it onto her finger.

"I thought we'd start slow," he said, just as he had all those months ago. "One date."

"What are you talking about?" she asked, inhaling the sweet fragrance of the rose. It was almost overpowering.

"Come to the formal with me," he asked.

Beth shook her head in confusion. "I'm already going with you," she reminded him. "You asked me weeks ago." She'd been saving up to buy a new dress, actually, but then they'd been fighting so much and had stopped speaking and eventually wasting all that money on a dress she might not get to wear hadn't seemed like such a great idea. But now, looking into his earnest blue eyes, now she couldn't think of anything she wanted to do more than look beautiful for him. To turn back time and forget about everything that had happened this month—*everything*. This weekend, this dance, it would be just the fresh start they needed.

"A lot's happened since then," Adam explained. "I've been an asshole since then," he added.

"No, it wasn't you, it was just—"

"Let me finish," he interrupted quietly. "I've been a jerk, and now I know it, and I just want us to start over again, fresh. Just pretend the last few weeks never happened. So, Ms. Manning, will you do me the great honor of going to the dance with me?" He pulled the rose from her fingers and played its petals gently across her lips.

"Well, I'll have to think about it for a second," she began with a frown. His face crumpled, and she rewarded him with a bright grin. "Of course I'll go with you." She moved the rose out of the way and put her arms around him, cradling his face in her hands. She pulled his face toward her and kissed him, wishing that she could freeze this moment, that they really could pretend that the last few weeks had never happened and that the future would never come. That there would be no more arguments, that the tension that crackled between them would just disappear and things would be sweet and easy again, like they were tonight. And, she realized, she knew how to make that happen.

"I love you, Adam," she whispered, her lips still just barely touching his.

"You too, Beth. Only you."

And even though it was late and her mother could burst into the room at any minute, Beth kissed him again. The moment couldn't last forever—but she wasn't ready to let it end.

chapter fifteen

MIRANDA WASN'T FAT.

She knew that much, at least.

After all, she wasn't *crazy*, she told herself, looking in the mirror. No double chins or rolls of fat—she certainly wasn't one of those girls who looked like a skeleton but imagined a blimp. She knew what she saw.

And what she saw wasn't much.

Short—an inch above freakish but only barely within the "cute" zone. Dull reddish hair. Pale, washed-out skin. Thick ankles (which she hadn't even noticed until her mother had oh-so-kindly pointed them out to her and helpfully suggested she steer clear of skirts). Bulky thighs.

Somehow, sometime, the lithe, slim body she'd had when she was younger—the one she'd never noticed until one of her mother's friends commented in envious awe on how she could "eat like an elephant and look like a giraffe"— had disappeared.

Now, she was just—medium. Bland. She knew that under other circumstances, in other, bigger towns, she wouldn't be best friends with the school's alpha girl; the A-list wouldn't notice her.

But in this life, in this town, she was best friends with Harper—which is why she'd gone along with the drunken suggestion that they ditch their dates for the stupid formal and go on their own. Prove to the world that they didn't need guys, that they'd have more fun without some testosterone-charged idiots pawing at them all night.

She twirled once more in front of the mirror, her gauzy black dress flaring out as she spun.

The other night at the Barnstormer, filled with alcoholic courage, spending the dance on the sidelines with Harper, watching a roomful of glamorous, dewy-eyed couples spin around the auditorium had sounded perfect.

Funny—in the sober light of day (or rather, in the sober half-light of twilight, awaiting her ride)—it was starting to sound slightly less than perfect. Asinine. Insane. Pretty much the worst idea she'd ever heard.

But unless she wanted to take her father as a date, it was

too late to do anything about it. She ran a brush through her hair one last time and quickly put on another layer of lip gloss. Her ride wasn't due for another twenty minutes, but she was done getting ready. Her parents—who had no idea there even *was* a dance—were out for the night. Miranda hadn't wanted to suffer through them fawning all over her, pinching her cheeks and taking pictures—or even worse, suffer through them ignoring the whole thing and going out anyway. Better not to risk it. So the house was empty, she had plenty of time to kill—and there was a bottle of gin in the cabinet next to the sink that had her name on it.

She had a feeling she was going to need it.

When Kane had suggested that she and Miranda ride over to the dance with him, he hadn't mentioned anything about the car—a limo. Sort of. It had a big backseat, all right, and a chauffeur up front, just like a real limo—but that was where the similarities ended. Kane's chariot of choice was a garish pink 1960s convertible, roughly the size of a boat, that made Harper feel like she was riding around inside a giant bottle of Pepto-Bismol. He also hadn't mentioned anything about his date. And that, as it turned out, was a much bigger problem.

"What are *you* doing here?" Harper sneered as she climbed into the car and took a seat—right across from Kaia.

"Nice manners," Kane chided her. "Didn't I mention it the other day? Kaia's my date." He slung an arm around the ice queen, who was draped in a shimmery Anna Sui gown the color of emeralds. Even Harper had to admit that it was stunning—though not out loud.

"Whatever, let's just get going and pick up Miranda," she snapped. "We're late."

"Aren't you going to say anything about our ride?" Kane asked. He gestured around the spacious backseat of the vintage convertible. "Limos are so—junior high prom. At least this has some style."

"What do I think?" Harper mused, glancing disdainfully at the velour seats—hot pink to match the exterior. She raised a hand to her hair, which had been carefully smoothed back into an elaborate upsweep—thanks to the lack of a roof on the rose monstrosity, she'd probably arrive at the dance looking like she had a bird's nest on top of her head. "I think I like your taste in cars about as much as I like your taste in women."

"Classy, Harper, real classy," Kane told her scornfully. Kaia, who had yet to say a word, just smiled and slid a hand onto Kane's inner thigh. She leaned over and, eyes never leaving Harper's face, whispered something in his ear.

Kane's eyes widened, and they both laughed.

"My thoughts exactly," he said, and began kissing her

neck. As his hand grazed Kaia's breast and her lips found his, Harper recoiled in disgust.

Classy, Kane, real classy, she thought. It was going to be a long night.

Adam always looked handsome in a tux. With his broad chest and chiseled features, he looked like a film star from the fifties, full of glamour and chivalry, ready to sweep her away on some elegant adventure. He gently pinned on a small corsage—a delicate white rose—and she wondered how her eye ever could have strayed to someone else. Much less a teacher.

All the stupid fighting—she'd come so close to losing him. Beth shivered at the thought.

"Are you cold?" he asked, tucking her silver wrap around her shoulders and rubbing his warm hand up and down her back.

Inside the house everything had been so loud. Her brothers running circles around them. Her parents hopping up and down, snapping pictures and fawning over Beth as if they'd never seen her in a dress before. But out here on her front step, it was quiet and dark. Just the two of them.

"I'm fine," she assured him. "Let's get going." She was eager to get to the dance—and through the dance—because she had a surprise waiting for Adam at the end of the night. The sooner it came, the less time she'd have to worry about it.

She'd never ridden in a limousine before, and when she saw the long black car waiting outside her tiny house, she stopped and closed her eyes, savoring the moment. Then Adam took her hand and they walked down the path together to the curb, where their carriage awaited. It was such a romantic, regal procession, under such a bright, starry sky.

Beth felt like a princess—and she knew it was going to be a perfect night.

"Have I told you how beautiful you look tonight?" Adam asked, handing her a glass of champagne and leaning back against the seat of the limo. It had set him back a hundred bucks, but it was worth it for the look on Beth's face. He owed her so much—she could never know how much.

"Only a couple hundred times or so," Beth laughed, tucking a tendril of hair behind her ears and blushing. "But keep going, please."

"Ravishingly beautiful. Awe-inspiringly beautiful," he told her, moving closer. "The most beautiful thing I've ever seen. More beautiful than—"

She kissed him, and he drank in the intoxicating feel of her.

It wasn't just a line. She really was more beautiful than

he'd ever seen her—the pale blue of her dress matched the deep ocean of her eyes, and its silky material hugged her body, revealing curves that he hadn't even realized she had. Her corn-silk blond hair, usually loose and flowing over her shoulders, was swept up into a loose bun, long tendrils framing her delicate face. And the way she was smiling—it was radiant, almost mysterious, as if she had some secret happy thought hidden away in the recesses of her mind. She was glowing—and looking at him as if he was the one who'd made her glow. Even the way she held her glass, her long, slender fingers curling around the narrow stem—even that was soft, elegant, perfect.

She was perfect. And every time she looked at him with her loving, trusting eyes, he had to look away in shame. After all, every word out of his mouth was a lie, just pretty phrases designed to hide the truth. He could mean them all he wanted—and he did—but it wouldn't change things. It wouldn't change the one thing he could never say.

"Are you okay, Ad?" she asked, and he realized he'd been staring at her.

He smiled.

"Just thinking of what a great night we're going to have together," he told her. Another lie.

More lies piled up by the minute, and his skin crawled with the fear that everything was going to come apart.

LUST

Especially tonight—when he and Kaia, and worse, Beth and Kaia, were bound to come face-to-face.

"It's going to be a wonderful night," Beth sighed, leaning her head on his shoulder. "It's going to be perfect."

Adam slugged back his glass of champagne and poured himself another—anything to get him through the night.

Perfect?

Unlikely.

Miranda jumped out of the car almost before it pulled to a full stop—it had been all she could do to restrain herself from jumping out miles ago, at full speed. Between Harper and Kaia's intermittent sniping and Kane and Kaia's apparent inability to keep their hands off each other, the fifteen-minute ride had felt like an eternity.

Now that they were finally here, she just wanted to get out and away as quickly as possible—and if she managed to avoid being seen emerging from Kane's hot pink cotton candy machine, that would also be a perk. Though the way her luck was running, it seemed unlikely. Speaking of incognito—

"Harper!" It was Harper's hideously annoying sophomore clone.

"Miranda!" And her equally annoying sidekick.

"Kane and Kaia!" they chorused. "Hiiiii!"

It was too late to escape. The two girls, dressed in

243

identical satin slip dresses (Mini-Me in lavender, Mini-She in eggshell blue) tottered up to them on shaky heels. Their dates, two pimply sophomores who, in matching crew cuts and rented tuxedos, looked as identical to each other as the Minis (one was blond, one was brunet—they were otherwise interchangeable), trudged dutifully behind them.

Kaia, Harper, and Miranda each nodded wearily at the fan club—Kane couldn't even be bothered to do that much.

"Kaia, your dress is gorgeous," Mini-Me gushed. "Where'd you get it?"

"Bitches-R-Us?" Harper suggested.

"Anna Sui, actually." Kaia glared at Harper. "Where'd you get yours, Walmart?"

"That's where I got mine, too!" Mini-She cried. She linked arms with Harper and leaned toward her conspiratorially. "So, Harper," she asked in a low voice, "where's your date?"

"Oh, Harper and Miranda came together," Kaia simpered. "Isn't that adorable?"

Now it was Harper's turn to glare. She extricated herself from the sophomore and moved quickly over to Miranda's side.

"Are you guys, like, a couple now?" Mini-Me asked, eyes agog.

"No, no," Miranda said hastily. God, this was just what

she'd been afraid of. Worse, even. "We're just—I—"

"We told our dates to go screw themselves," Harper jumped in. She glanced at Kaia. "Not *everyone's* self-esteem is dependent on testosterone."

"Looking for some testosterone?" Kane asked, suddenly paying attention. "Why didn't you say so?"

He grabbed Kaia and swooped her down into a dramatic dip, kissing her as her hair grazed the ground. The sophomores giggled and Harper and Miranda just shook their heads until finally he pulled her up and took her hand.

"Well, milady, shall we away?"

And they walked inside, Mini-Me, Mini-She, and their unfortunate dates in hot pursuit.

"Suck it up, Rand," Harper said as Miranda's eyes followed Kane's figure into the gym. "You know he could care less about her—he's just trying to be an asshole."

"He's doing a pretty good job of it," Miranda admitted.

"Now see, that's what I've been trying to tell you," Harper pointed out. She grabbed Miranda's arm and pulled her forward. "Come on, let's go find some real men. You ready for this?"

Miranda nodded and followed silently. *Here we go*, she thought gloomily. *Ready—or not.*

chapter sixteen

THE HIGH SCHOOL GYM HAD BEEN TRANSFORMED. A diligent team of party planners (culled from a joint task force of student council members, cheerleaders, and some devoted PTA moms) had hung enough multicolored leaves, paper lanterns, and WELCOME BACK banners to turn the place into an autumnal paradise. Could you even tell that beneath all those decorations lay a dirty, smelly, multipurpose room that, in two days, would once again be filled with sweaty students and the occasional fistfight?

In a minute.

It even smelled the same, Adam mused, looking around in disdain at the tacky setup. He supposed all this crap was some girl's idea of romantic—he was just glad it wasn't anyone he had to date.

"Is her back turned?" Kane asked Adam, who was supposed to be on the lookout for the nearest chaperone. They stood in a back corner, just under the bleachers—the exact spot that, if the teachers had any sense at all, they'd be watching around the clock. Where else would you go to make trouble? Fortunately for would-be troublemakers, common sense was commonly absent among the Haven High faculty—or at least, those unsavvy enough to get themselves roped into chaperoning a school dance.

"Yeah, you're clear," Adam assured him. "Not that she'd see you." (Dolores Martin, the school librarian, was about 140 years old and hadn't been able to see more than ten feet ahead of her since the Nixon administration.) "What are you up to, anyway?"

"I told you, it's a surprise," Kane said mysteriously. "I've equipped everyone else, but I had to improvise." He pointed toward one of the guys from the swim team, who was gulping from a plastic bottle.

"Vitamin water?" Adam asked, peering at the bottle.

"Yeah, new flavor—kiwi strawberry with a little something extra."

"Extra?"

"Vodka can be very healthy for you, you know," Kane confided with a laugh. "But for you, my friend, something special. A little more risk—but a lot more style." He pulled a tiny silver flask from inside his jacket and surreptitiously passed it to Adam. "Just don't get caught."

Adam fumbled the flask for a moment, then pushed it back toward Kane. He could see it now—the laser beam eyes of his AP history teacher spotting a glint of silver coming out of his pocket. Getting pulled out of Beth's arms and hauled off the dance floor in front of everyone. Thrown out, disgraced. Beth would certainly never forgive him for ruining her night over something so stupid. No, he had enough to worry about already.

"Doesn't seem like a great idea," Adam explained, as Kane shook his head and slipped the flask into one of his outer pockets. "Especially the way my luck is going. Last thing I need is to get suspended for getting drunk on school property or something."

"Your call," Kane said ruefully. "Well, I guess a man in love doesn't need any other forms of intoxication. Speaking of which, I better go collect my date before your beloved tells her too many lies about me. Or worse"—he raised his eyebrows—"the truth."

Adam followed Kane's gaze across the room and, with alarm, saw Beth and Kaia in a corner, deep in conversation.

His heart missed a couple of hundred beats.

"Uh, you're right, we better go break that up," he

stammered. Kane started off, but Adam grabbed him and pulled him back.

"Changed my mind," he whispered, slipping the flask out of Kane's pocket and, checking to make sure no one was watching, downing half its contents.

He felt better already.

"So what did you need to tell me?" Beth asked impatiently, glancing across the room at Adam. She held back a smile as she thought about what they'd be doing later tonight. If he only knew. She just wanted to be with him—and away from Kaia, who'd pinned her in a corner for some mysteriously urgent reason that had evaporated as soon as she'd gotten Beth alone.

"Have I told you how great you look tonight?" Kaia asked sweetly.

"Thanks. Can you just tell me what was so important?" The DJ had just started a slow song. "Take My Breath Away"—a little cheesy, maybe, but one of Beth's favorites. She wanted to be swaying back and forth to the melody, eyes closed, head on Adam's shoulder. Not here.

"What? Oh, that was nothing. I mean, I thought you might want to know that Adam—" Kaia cut herself off with a sigh. "Oh . . . Check out Mr. Powell—doesn't he look hot tonight in his tux?"

"What about Adam?" Beth persisted. The last thing

she wanted to think about was Jack Powell, or how good he looked in his tux. Which, despite her best efforts, she'd already noticed.

"Oh, we can finish this later. Maybe you want to go talk to Mr. Powell?" Kaia asked innocently. "I won't mind—I know how *close* you two are."

For the moment Beth forgot about Adam and whatever secret was about to be revealed and studied Kaia closely. Did she—could she possibly—know?

"We're not close," she said coolly, deciding, or at least desperately hoping, that Kaia didn't know what she was saying. "And if you ask me, he's not a very good teacher. Working with him on the newspaper sucks."

"That's not what I heard," Kaia said with a sly grin.

"What are you talking about?" Beth asked in a hushed voice. All her breath had slipped away.

But before Kaia could answer, Kane snuck up behind her and grabbed her waist, twirling her around. A moment later, Beth felt Adam's strong hands around her as he lifted her off the ground and swung her into his arms. She hoped he couldn't feel her trembling.

"So what's going on over here?" Kane asked, once the girls had stopped squealing.

"Trust me," Kaia said, looking directly at Adam. "You don't want to know."

✍   ✍   ✍

Lucky break that Powell was chaperoning the dance.

Luckier still that he was standing amidst a small circle of other teachers. Kaia knew that no self-respecting chaperone could turn down an innocent request to dance with one of his students—at least, not without having a lot of explaining to do.

Kaia excused herself and strode over to the cluster of teachers. Powell, seeing her approach, was already preparing his getaway.

"Mr. Powell!" she exclaimed. "You look so handsome in your tuxedo! Think you could spare me a dance?"

He glared at her, then smiled for the sake of the group.

"Oh, Kaia, I'm not much of a dancer—you know, two left feet and all."

"Go for it, Jack," urged Mr. Holcomb, from the English department.

"Yes, 'cut a rug,'" the librarian added.

The group began to laugh as Kaia led a reluctant Mr. Powell onto the floor. She knew what they were thinking: *How adorable, a little crush.* Well, let them think what they wanted—she knew what she was doing.

Kaia looped her arms around his neck, and his hands found a spot on her waist—he held her rigidly, carefully keeping a half foot of space between them.

"Did I not make myself clear before, Ms. Sellers?" The amiable facade was gone. Good. "You and me? It's never going to happen. And certainly not in the middle of a crowded dance floor with the whole school looking on."

"Oh, I know, Mr. Powell," she said, lowering her eyes and giving him an exaggeratedly chastened look. "After all, it's your policy not to mix business with pleasure, right?"

"I don't consort with students, yes, if that's what you mean," he said stiffly.

"And I don't consort with *liars*," Kaia hissed.

He stopped dancing and pushed her away.

"What's that supposed to mean?" But some of the steely certainty had faded from his voice.

She put her arms around him again.

"Better keep dancing, and keep smiling, Mr. Powell—you don't want your friends over there thinking we're having a lovers' spat." She gave a friendly wave to the group of teachers smiling and cheering them on from the sidelines.

"I'll ask you again, what are you talking about?" he repeated, smiling through gritted teeth.

"I'm talking about your nonexistent policy, Mr. Powell. I'm talking about your loose relationship with the truth and your looser one with the rules." She moved in closer and lowered her voice to a whisper. "I'm talking about you and Beth—I *saw* you."

"I'm quite sure I don't know what you mean," Powell protested. His face had gone white. "There was nothing to see."

"Right," Kaia said sarcastically. "I hope that's not the poker face you're planning to use when you talk to the principal, or the school board, or hey, the police—"

His fingers tightened on her waist.

"That's right, the police," Kaia said. "Small town like this, full of all those family values, I imagine they don't look too kindly on this sort of thing. Teacher preying on innocent students. We're just children, really. . . ."

"You don't want to screw with me, Kaia," he warned her in a low, ominous voice.

"Not anymore," she said lightly, shaking her head. "No, you chose someone else for that—and I can live with it. I just hope that *you* can."

And, waving again in the direction of Powell's fellow teachers, she squeezed in close to Jack Powell and slammed her lips to his, jamming her tongue into his mouth before he knew what was happening, and then, with a less than gentle nibble on his lip, she pushed him away.

"See you around, Mr. Powell—you can count on it."

Beth, Adam, Miranda, and Harper witnessed the scene from the sidelines with a mixture of shock, awe, and horror (in different proportions, depending on the witness).

"That girl is unbelievable," Harper gasped. "What the hell is she thinking?"

"Unbelievable is right," Adam repeated, sounding

almost impressed. Beth looked at him sharply, and his eyes shot down to the ground, avoiding her gaze. In his pocket, his hand tightened around the now-empty flask.

"Bet you wish you had the nerve to do that, Beth," Miranda laughed. "I know I do."

Beth stammered and blushed and mumbled something about nothing, and finally Harper cut in.

"Oh, please, Beth's not that pathetic, and neither are you, Miranda. She practically jumped down his throat—it was embarrassing to watch! What was that you were saying about her being so sad and misunderstood, Adam?"

Now it was Adam's turn to stammer nonsensically.

"It's really, uh, none of our business," he finally said, turning away from the dance floor, where Mr. Powell was still standing alone and motionless, only barely visible through the swirling wall of dancers.

"You're totally right," Beth added with relief. "Let's just dance."

"Definitely." He clasped her by the hand and led her quickly onto the dance floor, leaving Harper and Miranda behind in disbelief.

"None of our business?" Miranda asked. "Since when does that stop us? Is this a new policy I wasn't told about?"

"I guess we both missed the memo," Harper said in disgust. "Look at them." She gestured weakly toward Beth and Adam, who were slowly swaying in each other's arms, despite the fast-paced rock song blaring through the speakers. "He can't keep his hands off her for a minute."

"This dance sucks," Miranda said.

"Tell me about it."

They stood together at the edge of the action, watching dozens of couples swirling around the floor. That was the problem with scoping for hot guys at school formals. The inspirational girl-power-themed episodes of bad TV shows notwithstanding, the fact was that all the normal guys showed up to these things with dates. So unless you were ready to break up a matched pair and leave some unfortunate girl drying the tearstains on her dress under the bathroom hand blower (not that Harper hadn't left her share of those in her wake), you were shit out of luck. No, instead you were stuck with prizes like Lester Lawrence, decked out in a sky-blue tux and ruffled Hawaiian shirt, and his gang of losers. Miranda was sure any one of them would be happy to dance with her. Great.

And then, like Prince Charming, appearing as if by magic out of the mist: Kane.

He strode purposefully toward them, with Kaia nowhere in sight.

"You ladies look bored," he said. "How about a dance?"

For a moment Miranda, who figured any drugs harder than pot weren't worth the dead brain cells, finally understood what people were always talking about, that rush of ecstasy, a shot of pure joy exploding out of you, so powerful that it shut out the world for a moment, threatened to sweep you away.

But it was just for a moment.

Because when she came down to earth, Kane's words still ringing in her ears (familiar words, as he'd uttered them so often in the G-rated portion of her fantasies), she realized that his arm was outstretched to Harper. Of course.

Harper took his hand and headed toward the dance floor, shooting Miranda an apologetic look over her shoulder. There was nothing to apologize for, of course. This was just the way it worked.

Couples danced, the band played, Lester Lawrence talked to the pet grasshopper in his pocket, and Miranda stood on the fringes of it all.

Alone.

That's life, right? *C'est la vie.*

Kane swung her around the dance floor, moving effort-lessly in time with the music, now a slow R&B groove. He danced with ease, skill, and grace—the same way he did everything else. (If Kane couldn't do it well, he didn't do it at all.)

"Having a good time, Grace?" he asked.

"Not particularly." There was no point in putting on a brave face, since she was sure he couldn't care less. "How about you? Enjoying your date with our very own Lolita?" She spotted Kaia on the sidelines, fending off a crowd of curiosity seekers—Mini-Me, she was pleased to see, among them. Harper supposed she should be a bit dismayed that her own personal fan club seemed to be redevoting itself to Kaia-worship, as it was just another sign of the rich bitch encroaching on her territory. But somehow, she just couldn't work up the energy—besides, having the sophomore squad chase after her was, in the end, far more punishment than reward.

"I'm enjoying myself very much, thanks," Kane replied. "Of course, not as much as *him*." He swung her around, bringing her face-to-face with Adam and Beth, arms draped loosely around each other, swaying in the middle of the dance floor, clearly in a world of their own. Their eyes were closed, and Beth's head rested on Adam's broad shoulder. He ran his hands slowly up and down her back.

Harper felt sick. She looked away—right into Kane's disgustingly knowing grin.

"Jealous?"

Harper said nothing.

"Just letting you know, my offer still stands. You and me, the anti-Cupids. Just say the word."

Harper stole another glance at the happy couple. Adam was now running his fingers through her long blond hair.

God, it was tempting.

"Mind if I cut in?"

Harper breathed a sigh of relief—Kaia's icy voice had never been more welcome. "He is *my* date, after all," Kaia pointed out snottily.

Harper let her hands drop and stepped away.

"My pleasure—he's all yours." She walked away—but not quickly enough that she didn't overhear Kaia's parting shot.

"It's so sweet of you to keep Harper company, Kane," she oozed. "You know, since she couldn't find a date of her own."

Harper resisted the temptation to turn back and slap her—and the marginally more powerful temptation to take another look (or extended, longing stare) at Adam. Instead she kept her eyes focused on Miranda, lingering next to a large bowl of pretzels and looking forlorn; she focused on Miranda and, about ten feet behind her, the exit.

It was time to get the hell out.

When the going gets tough, the tough get stoned. Which is exactly what Harper and Miranda proceeded to do.

They stopped off at the after-party (Harper: "After all, we planned the damn thing") but after ascertaining that all the details were in place—beer, music, lanterns, illicit acts featuring Haven High's elite—they ditched out. (Harper: "Just a bunch of losers getting laid.") Kane had roped scuzzy Reed Sawyer into supervising things so that the rest of them could focus on their night of debauchery—all it took was a dime bag of weed and a six-pack; apparently Reed didn't have anything better to do anyway. A burnout like him certainly wouldn't be caught dead at a school dance—and there was no way he would have made it onto the invite list under any other circumstances, but Harper supposed that climbing his way up the Haven High social ladder wasn't too high on his list of priorities. *Getting* high? Yes. Scoring some kind of record deal for his posse of talentless losers? Probably. But that was about it. Trust Kane to find a guy like that.

He lay sprawled on one of the motel's musty sofas and lazily watched the chaos swirl around him. Harper wasn't sure exactly what "supervising" was supposed to entail— yes, he'd turned on the music and made sure that the kegs were tapped and flowing, but if someone tried to make off with the stereo or burn the place down, would this guy be willing or able to do anything about it? Harper highly doubted it—but at the moment, she didn't really care.

Besides, back at Miranda's place, the parents were out, the pot was ample, the beer didn't come from a keg, and there were no unidentifiable fluids or condom packages littering the floor. Nor was there anyone they didn't want to talk to—which, at the moment, included pretty much everyone except for each other.

It took an hour for the one taxi company in town to dispatch a driver—but it was well worth the wait. (It was also worth it not to have to ride away from the party in the hot pink monstrosity that had carried them to the dance.)

"Did you see Lauren's dress?" Miranda asked once they were safely ensconced in her bedroom. She exhaled a puff of smoke and flopped back onto her bed.

"How could I miss it? It was practically fluorescent!" Harper cackled, taking the joint from Miranda and inhaling deeply. She was sitting on the floor, leaning against the bed and rubbing her bare feet against the soft plush of Miranda's rug. The best part of going to a formal was always the hour before getting ready and the hour afterward rehashing the night—so who cared if they'd pretty much skipped the middle? "And how about the way Peter King kept drooling every time I walked by?"

"Peter the Perv? Didn't he get thrown out of school last year for trying to install that camera in the girls' locker room?" Miranda asked with a laugh, almost choking on a kernel of popcorn.

"He's b-a-a-a-a-ack," Harper sang out.

"Hey, at least you didn't have Lawrence Lester and the bug thugs chasing after you all night," Miranda complained.

"Lester Lawrence," Harper corrected her sternly. "Lester and Miranda Lawrence—has a nice ring to it, don't you think?"

"Shut up!" Miranda slammed a pillow into Harper's face and they both dissolved into giggles. There were a lot of kids in their high school, and most of them sucked—if they tried hard enough, this could keep them going all night long.

chapter seventeen

"DUDE, GREAT PARTY!" ADAM SAID, STUMBLING through the doorway of the motel. Beth caught him just before he fell.

"Yeah, great," she echoed weakly, taking in the cloud of smoke, stench of beer, pumping music, and scattered couples making out in the darkened corners.

Adam high-fived Kane. "Your brother manage to score us the kegs?"

"You know it," Kane assured him.

"Awesome—point me to it, liquor-man."

"Adam," Beth began tentatively, "don't you think maybe you've had enough?"

He brushed her off and charged ahead. "No such thing!" he called back, before disappearing into the darkness.

Beth froze in the lobby, not sure what to do. A few tinted paper lanterns hung from the ceiling, casting an eerie, shadowy pall over everything. There was no electricity, and they'd decided against candles (nice ambience but overwhelming likelihood of disaster), so they were stuck with the dim reddish lighting of the battery-powered lanterns and the few shafts of moonlight filtering in through the lobby windows.

She and Adam had been one of the last couples to leave the dance, so all the seniors on the secret invite list had already showed up—the place was packed, but in the darkness, Beth couldn't pick out any familiar faces. There were only strangers, blank bodies bouncing in time with the music or squeezed in together on one of the couches, ignoring the crowd. She was so tired, and so alone.

And she'd been feeling that way for hours—despite glimpses of sobriety and sweet moments of romance, Adam had spent the end of the night in a vodka haze, laughing it up with his friends while Beth stood awkwardly on the fringes, with only Kaia to talk to. And so, with no one to talk to at all.

Now she was on the fringes again, with Adam nowhere to be seen. She felt invisible, and yet totally exposed. As if everyone in the room was watching her, knowing with certainty that she didn't belong. And indeed, if it weren't for the Adam connection, she never would have been there—all of her old friends were probably home in bed, or sitting up in Lara Tanner's basement eating ice cream and watching old black-and-white movies. Much as she wished she was with them, she just didn't belong there anymore—too bad she didn't seem to belong here, either.

She looked around in vain for someone she knew, someone she could talk to—even Kaia, at this point, would have been a relief. But it was as if the moment they'd stepped through the door together, everyone else had been pulled off into some kind of vortex. Vanished. And here she was, alone.

She supposed this wasn't the kind of party where you made small talk, anyway. It was the kind where you passed out on one of the dusty couches, or threw yourself into a sweaty mass of dancers—or you did what she'd come here to do.

She could always go home, she guessed. Call a taxi, get out of here, escape. Forget this night had ever happened, forget about the supposed fresh start, about what she'd been planning to do. Save it for some other time.

The place was a skanky mess.

Adam had morphed into a drunken idiot.

But Beth had waited long enough to know that perfection wasn't coming—tonight was just going to have to do.

And maybe finding the keg first wasn't such a bad idea.

"Think we can go somewhere a bit more . . . private?" Kaia whispered to Kane, running a hand down the small of his back.

"Say no more."

They threaded their way through the crowd in the lobby, away from the flickering light and the echoing music. Up the stairs, down a long, dark, narrow hallway, ignoring the shadowy shapes pressed against the walls, the bodies writhing together. Into a small, dark room at the end of the hall, the faded drapes drawn, allowing a slash of moonlight to cut through the room. It lit Kaia's hands as she slowly unbuttoned Kane's shirt. Their bodies remained in shadow, figures silhouetted against the night.

"Not quite the penthouse suite," Kane admitted ruefully, his fingers expertly unhooking her bra as they stumbled together toward the bed.

"Not quite." Kaia lay back and pulled him down on top of her, pressing herself against his tight body, relishing the heavy weight bearing down on her. "But it'll do." And so would Kane. He wasn't the catch he imagined himself to be—but he was hot, he was cocky, and, most importantly, he was there. Sometimes Kaia needed a challenge—but sometimes she just needed a break.

She pulled him toward her, closed her eyes, and let herself go.

Along with copious amounts of alcohol, Kane had also supplied the party with two wooden barrels filled with condoms, positioned considerately just inside the door.

As Adam blundered off in search of more to drink, Beth had surreptitiously grabbed one and slipped it into her purse—and then, on second thought, she'd grabbed a handful more.

Now, an hour further into the night, her bold act was beginning to seem like a total waste. They were still down in the lobby amidst a group of Adam's drunken teammates; Beth's head was throbbing, and as Adam regaled a cluster of admirers with a story of last year's basketball triumph, he leaned against her heavily, as if without her support he would drop to the ground.

"Adam, let's take off," she whispered urgently, when he finally stopped talking.

"You wanna go home?" he slurred. "Party's just starting. Right, guys?"

The "guys," whose shunted-aside dates all looked about as nonplussed as Beth felt, let out a hearty cheer of support.

"Not home," she explained in a low voice. *"Upstairs."*

"She wants to go upstairs!" he crowed to the crowd. "Lez go, honey. You want me, you got me."

Irritated and humiliated—but knowing how hard it had been to prepare herself for this night and determined to finally go through with it—Beth allowed Adam to shepherd her into the dark bowels of the hotel, where they finally found an unoccupied room and slipped inside.

"Beth," he said, seeming to sober up a bit now that he was away from the noise and the people and the stench of beer, "I feel like shit. Maybe we should just head home."

"I don't think you want to go home yet, Adam. This is your lucky day," she said, trying to sound more brazen than she felt. Beth had never had to make a first move in her life, and she had no idea what to do. But how hard could it be? All guys ever wanted was sex, any time, all the time, right? So she just needed to let him know that a new option had been added to the menu, and hopefully he'd do the rest.

"I want you, Adam," she said in what she hoped was a sexy voice. "Now."

She pushed him down on the bed, and he landed with a thud, knocking his head against the wooden headboard.

Oops.

"Jesus, are you trying to kill me?" he shouted, rubbing the back of his head.

"I'm sorry, I'm sorry." She hopped into the bed, kissing the bruise gently. "This isn't going the way I wanted it to."

"What isn't?" he asked in confusion.

"This. Tonight. Right now," she told him, kissing him again, more urgently.

"What's right now?"

Why couldn't he just *get* it? Why was he making this so hard for her?

"Right now is when—when I tell you that I'm finally ready," Beth admitted. She bit the inside of her cheek and nervously waited for him to say something. Who knows—maybe he didn't even want her anymore. Maybe that's what all this had been about.

He sat up, couldn't see her face in the darkness, but reached out a hand to touch her cheek, as if trying to read her expression.

"Ready? For . . . ?"

She nodded, and then realized he couldn't see her. "Yes."

"Now?"

"Yes." And she kissed him, and he kissed her back, eagerly, hungrily, and they rolled over on the bed together, drinking each other in, their bodies lost in each other, and then—they stopped.

Beth tensed, her back clenched and her muscles stiffening, as they always did, just before she reached the point of no return. He pulled away, and she lay on her back, breathing quickly, glad it was too dark for him to see the tears that were leaking from her tightly closed eyes.

"Beth?" came his warm voice in the darkness. "Beth, are you sure you're ready for this?"

No.

No.

"Yes."

She groped for her purse on the night table, pulled out one of the condoms, and tossed it to him.

"I mean, we're in love, right?" she asked. "I love you, you love me, we're adults. This is the right thing to do." It came out sounding like a question.

There was a long pause, and then, "Yeah, we're in love," he agreed. And he sounded almost sure.

"I just—I just need a minute," she promised him. "Then I'll be ready."

He reached over and found her hand, and she clenched it tightly, and they lay side by side on the musty bed. She stared up at the cracked ceiling and breathed deeply, in and out, picturing his body lying next to hers, so close, and how it would be to have him inside of her, to be with him, to lose herself in him. To finally let herself go.

She tried to unclench her muscles, reminded herself that she loved him, she wanted him—and she did, so much that it terrified her. For if she let that wave of emotion, of pleasure, sweep her away, how would she ever find her way back?

Breathe in.

Breathe out.

She had to do this, and she had to do it now—because one thing she knew, one thing was certain: She didn't want to lose him.

"I'm ready," she whispered to herself. "Adam? I'm ready," she said louder.

There was no response, and his hand was still.

"Adam?"

She rolled over on her side, kissed his cheek, his lips, then propped herself up, her face suspended a few inches from his. His still, peaceful face. Eyes closed. Breath slow and even.

And then—a snore.

Beth flopped down again on her back, next to him.

Unbelievable.

She had been dressed like a fairy-tale princess—and was trapped in the wrong story. In her story, Prince Charming decorated the room with a thousand candles, took her in his arms, and sweetly, gently, took her away with him. In her story, a handsome boy and a beautiful girl danced the night away at the ball and swept off into the sunset. They swore their everlasting love to each other. They lived happily ever after.

Not this story. Not this night.

In this story, the wrong story, she lay atop a grungy bedspread, a hard and creaky mattress, in a slimy motel room, groping in the darkness and ignoring the moans and thuds seeping through the paper-thin walls.

In this story, Prince Charming was a drunken clod who passed out and left her alone.

Beth lay very still, listening to his even breathing and trying to forget the night, though it hadn't yet ended. The hours stretched ahead of her, a desert of time. So much for her perfect night; so much for her fairy tale.

This is not the way it was supposed to be, Beth thought, closing her eyes and wishing for sleep. *This is not the way it was supposed to be.*

This is not the way it was supposed to be, Harper thought, scuffing her weary feet against the pavement. She'd left Miranda's house elated, the alcohol and pot and laughter fusing into the perfect painkiller.

But over the long walk home, strappy heels in hand, her mood had changed.

When she reached her house, she took a few steps up the stone walkway to the front door, then stopped. Her parents, as always, thought she was sleeping at Miranda's, so it's not like they were waiting up. There was no reason to go inside—not yet. She veered around the house and found her way into the backyard. She clambered up to the flat top of her rock—their rock—and shivered in the chilly night breeze.

Somehow, everything had gone wrong.

It was her senior year. It was the night of the party. Her party. She wasn't supposed to spend the night rolling joints with Miranda—she was supposed to be with Adam, happy, in love. Not bitter, not alone.

It was only a few weeks into the school year, and everything, *everything* was wrong.

And there was no way in hell that she was going to take it anymore.

She was Harper Grace. Alone and pathetic, jealous and bitter were not her style. *Tears* were not her style, she reminded herself. She angrily wiped them away, then sat up and pulled out her cell phone. Pulled up a familiar contact, then began composing her text message.

She hesitated for a moment, hand hovering over the keys, thinking about the night she'd just spent with Miranda, the loyal friend who stayed with her through everything, who always rescued her, who always got her through.

She thought about a promise she'd made, a promise that she'd meant.

And then she thought about Adam—about Adam and Kaia, the embrace she still saw every time she closed her eyes. About Adam and Beth, who were probably together right now, hand in hand, body on body, flesh against flesh.

There are some things more important than friendship, Harper decided. Some things more important than promises.

And, hoping she was right, she hit send.

Kane was likely busy right now, she knew, but sometime tomorrow he'd wake up, slough off his hangover, and read her message: IF OFFER IS STILL OPEN—I'M IN.

seven deadly sins

ENVY

For Grandma

When Envy breeds unkind division:
There comes the ruin, there begins confusion.
—William Shakespeare, *Henry VI, Part I*

You can't always get what you want.
—The Rolling Stones

chapter one

BETH LOVED TO TRACE HER FINGERS ALONG THE
gently curved line of Adam's back. It was her favorite part,
this moment, this quiet pause just after they'd finished
rolling around beneath the covers (careful not to go too
far or to mention the fact that, as always, they stopped just
before they did). And just before the inevitable. The tension. The bitter look. The fighting.

No, it was worth it to lie there for a moment, watching the rise and fall of Adam's back as he sprawled on his
stomach, spent. Easy to prop herself up and admire his
lean, muscled form, to marvel, for the thousandth time,
that he was hers, that she was in his bed, that she could

lean forward and softly touch her lips to his bare back, that her body still glowed, warm and tingling where he'd last touched her. Better to lie still, breathe deep, enjoy the light streaming through the windows, warming her bare skin, and feel close to him, like their bodies were connected, like they were one. It was always her favorite moment—and it never lasted.

"So, are you still working at the diner tonight?" he asked in a carefully casual tone, stretching and rolling over onto his back.

"Unfortunately." She kissed him again. "You know I'd rather be with you, but . . ."

"I know," he said quickly. Sourly. "Duty calls."

"But maybe I can come over again after school tomorrow?" she asked hopefully. Her voice sounded falsely cheerful, brittle, even to her. But maybe she was imagining that. Maybe he wouldn't notice.

"Can't. Swim meet," he said. "But we're on for Saturday, right?" He sat up in bed and began looking around for his clothes, which had been tossed aside hastily a couple hours before.

"Definitely. Right after that SAT prep meeting." Beth's chest tightened at the thought of it, the test that would define her future. She had only a few weeks left to study, which meant she didn't have the time to waste on a stupid school-sponsored practice test and prep session that would surely fail to teach her anything she didn't already know. But, like all school-sponsored wastes of time, it was mandatory.

"Great," Adam said shortly, pulling a T-shirt over his head. It was pale blue—the same shade as his clear, sparkling eyes.

"Wait!" She sat up and grabbed his wrist, pulling him back to the bed, back to her. She didn't know what to say to him, didn't know how to get back that feeling of closeness that, these days, disappeared every time one of them spoke. It used to be so easy, so comfortable, and now it was like their relationship was some fragile piece of glass. If one of them said the wrong thing, spoke too loudly or too long, it would shatter. So they were careful. They were polite.

They were strangers.

Was it because she'd been so jealous of him and Kaia, the new girl who looked like a model and sounded—to her, at least—like a phone-sex operator? Because she had refused to trust him, no matter how many times he'd assured her that nothing, *nothing* would ever happen? Or was it because of what had happened with her and Mr. Powell, the hot French teacher who'd taken such an intense interest in the school newspaper, and an even more intense interest in Beth, its editor in chief? Was it because of the unexpected, unending kiss Powell had suddenly planted on her, a kiss she'd never asked for, that she'd fled from, that she'd said nothing about—but that maybe, deep down, she'd wanted?

Whatever it was, she wanted it to just go away. She wished that she and Adam could somehow find their way back to normal, if only she knew where to start.

"What are you thinking, blue eyes?" he asked, half in and half out of the bed—and his clothes.

She could tell him, and they could talk about it, about everything. Finally, an actual conversation—open, honest, painful. Real. And maybe they could finally try to fix things.

Or not.

"I'm thinking I'm not due at work for another hour," she told him, and threw her arms around his neck, drawing him to her. "I'm thinking that this shirt has got to go."

He obediently pulled it over his head and tossed it back on the floor, then lunged toward her and swept her into his arms. It wasn't open or honest, and it wouldn't fix anything. But it was easy. And right now, easy was all she could handle.

In most towns the Nifty Fifties Diner, with its rancid burgers, temperamental jukebox, tacky decor, and rude waitresses, would have quickly become an empty shell, housing a few lonely patrons whose taste buds had long

ENVY

since abandoned them. Empty on weekends, scorned by
the breakfast crew, it would, by all rights, have lasted
about six months before the owners shut its doors and
got the hell out of town. But this wasn't most towns. This
was Grace, California, where haute cuisine meant ordering from the booth rather than at the counter, and even
MacDonald's feared to tread. In Grace you took what you
could get, and pretty much all you could get was the Nifty
Fifties Diner, wilted french fries, surly service, and all.

Which is why every day after school, a crowd of bored
teens crowded its way into the diner's rusty orange booths.
But it wasn't just the desperation that drove them to it.
Harper Grace (formerly of Grace Mines; Grace Library;
Grace, California—currently of Grace Dry Cleaning on
North Hampton Street) had been known to favor the
place with her presence. And after all, the masses concluded, if Harper Grace and her crew deigned to eat there,
it must have some redeeming quality.

As far as Harper was concerned, it had one and only
one: It was there.

Actually, make that two, she thought, snagging a fry off
Miranda's plate. As usual, her best friend had eaten about
one-tenth of her order and spent the past hour pushing
the rest of the food around on her plate.

One: The diner was there.

Two: Everyone in it cared less about the food than

about watching Harper's every move. It was just like school . . . only without all the boring parts. Popularity without the homework.

And she so loved the attention.

"Think Beth is working today?" Miranda asked, looking around for the blond bombshell they both loved to hate.

"Who knows?" Harper asked, rolling her eyes. "Who cares?"

Miranda laughed. "Be nice, Harper," she warned, but Harper knew she didn't really mean it. For one thing, Harper Grace hadn't clawed her way up the school's social ladder by being nice. For another, rule number one of their friendship was that Harper said aloud all the bitchy thoughts Miranda was too polite to voice. Why mess with tradition?

"What, would you prefer she be here hovering over us with that stupid smile?" Harper gave Miranda her best Beth Manning grin and affected a high and fluttery voice. "'Hey guys! Can I get you anything? Water? Coffee? My backbone? Don't worry, I won't be needing it.'"

"You're right," Miranda admitted with a sly smile. "Much better she be off somewhere with Adam. Better making out with him than bothering us."

And at that, all traces of joy vanished from Harper's face.

"I'm eating here, Rand," she complained. "Can we keep the vomit-inducing comments to a minimum?"

Miranda shook her head in apology. "I'm sorry, it just slipped out. I'm a little off today."

"Yeah, what's the deal with that, Rand? I know why *I'm* climbing the walls," Harper whined, the image of a blissful Beth and Adam popping, unbidden, into her head. There had been a moment, back at the beginning of the school year, when she'd thought she had a chance. Especially when, in a moment of weakness, Adam had turned his back on true love—and slept with someone else. Just two little problems with that scenario. First, the "someone else" wasn't Harper. Second, Beth had no idea that her perfect boyfriend had cheated on her. The golden couple was still going strong, and Harper was still out in the cold.

She noticed everything, every look, every touch that passed between Adam and the girl he thought he loved. Every day, it seemed, Harper was treated to an endless series of disgusting displays, her days at school transformed into a constant reminder of what she wanted and couldn't have. And, since Adam lived next door, his bedroom window facing hers, her nights weren't much of an improvement. Needless to say, these days she was a little off her game.

"Yeah, I know why my life sucks," Harper said bitterly. "What's wrong with yours?"

"I can't stop thinking about him," Miranda admitted.

"Kane?" Harper's heart sank. Miranda hadn't mentioned the local lothario in days, and Harper had hoped that this little chapter was over. No such luck, apparently.

"I know, I know, he's out of my league," Miranda complained.

"No, you know that's not true," Harper assured her. But it was a halfhearted protest. Kane Geary was handsome, cocky, a consummate asshole—and had privately confirmed for Harper that the Miranda thing was a no go. He had his sights set on someone else. It hadn't come as a huge surprise. Miranda was many things—smart, caustic, funny, and at least a seven or eight on the ten point scale—but she wasn't some gorgeous bimbo who would strip down to her thong in a wink of Kane's eye. And as far as Kane was concerned, that pretty much took her out of the running.

"No, it's true. He's out of my league," Miranda insisted. "But I've been thinking." She grinned, and her voice took on the same "can do" bravado it had had back in fifth grade when she'd convinced Harper they should start their very own babysitters club. Harper issued a silent groan. That plan hadn't worked either.

"It's time for a New Miranda Stevens," she continued. (Harper could hear the capital *N* in her voice.)

"Uh, do I get a vote?" Harper asked, raising her hand

in protest. "Because I like the old Miranda."

"Are you six feet tall with dark brown eyes, washboard abs, and a killer smile?"

Harper rolled her eyes.

"Then no," Miranda confirmed. "You don't get a vote. So here's what I'm thinking. . . ."

Harper sighed as Miranda began to outline a self-improvement strategy that included hair, makeup, fashion, body, and personality makeovers, and so much detail Harper was surprised it wasn't accompanied by a PowerPoint presentation. Was she supposed to tell her best friend to give it up, that Kane would never be interested in her? Or that the "someone else" Kane was after was Beth? Was she supposed to admit that she'd secretly agreed to help Kane get Beth, if he would help her get Adam? Should she tell her best friend in the world that she'd basically screwed her over and made a pact with the devil, that all was fair in love and war, and Miranda would just have to deal?

Yeah, that would go over really well.

"So, are you in?" Miranda asked.

"What?" Harper could tell by the self-satisfied grin on Miranda's face that while she'd been zoned out in guilt land, the lengthy presentation had finally come to a close.

"Will you help? With the New Miranda?"

"I told you, I kind of like the old one," Harper hedged.

"Harper! Have you been listening to anything I've said? I need to do this if I'm ever going to get Kane to notice me—and you *swore* you'd help me get together with him."

"I remember," Harper said. And she did. The promise echoed in her ears every time she saw Miranda, and it faded just as quickly every time she saw Beth wrap her tentacles around Adam. She needed Kane's help on this one—more, apparently, than she needed Miranda's trust.

Though maybe if she played things right, she could get both.

"Besides," Miranda wheedled, "you're my best friend. This is what you're here for. If I can't count on you, who can I count on?"

Good question.

"Where are we going?" Heather giggled. At least, he thought her name was Heather.

"Shh. I told you, it's a surprise!" Kane whispered as they crept down the empty halls of the high school, deserted now that the last of the after-school meetings had disbanded and all the teachers had climbed into their dismal cars and driven home to their dismal lives. Kane supposed that there were those who wouldn't see the point of sneaking *into* school—but some people just didn't have any vision.

"What if we get caught?" Heather whispered.

Kane grinned and gave her a quick peck on the lips. It was a sexy whisper, nothing like the shrill screeching that passed for her regular voice. She had an amazing body, a passable face, but that voice—it could make your ears bleed. Kane suspected that after today's little adventure, it would be time to show Heather the door. Unless he wanted to make illegal trespassing a constant theme of their dating life. Which, come to think of it, had some possibility. . . .

"We won't get caught," he promised her. "And if we do, I'll take all the blame."

She giggled again. "My hero."

They stopped abruptly in front of an unmarked door and Kane pulled out a key similar to the one he'd used to get them into the building.

"Where did you—?"

He put a finger to her lips, then silenced her with another kiss.

"The master never reveals his secrets," he explained. "Don't ask—just enjoy." He pushed open the doors and ushered her down the stairs to the dark and deserted boiler room. Heather clung to him in fear and admiration as he made his way around the room by memory, setting up the candles and mohair blanket he'd brought along.

"Voilà!" he finally said in triumph. Soft candlelight lit

up the room. It was a romantic getaway, of sorts—and it was clearly enough for Heather.

For all the Heathers of the world, Kane thought. It always was. And he was getting a little tired of it. He'd always looked down on the guys at school with steady girlfriends, *relationships*. Suckers, he'd thought. Tying themselves down to one girl, being responsible, being trapped, and for what? A guaranteed date on Valentine's Day? A constant ego boost? A steady source of blow jobs?

Kane had all that already. And without all the whining, complaining, and demanding that seemed to come along with having a girlfriend.

On the other hand, lately, when he looked at Adam and Beth together, when he saw the way she looked at him, held him, Kane wondered. Was he missing out? Was it possible that Adam had stumbled onto something better? Kane didn't believe there was anything out there better than the life he'd crafted for himself. But he had to be sure, because if there was, he would do whatever was in his power to have it.

In the meantime he'd have no trouble finding something, or someone, to occupy his time. . . .

Heather wrapped her body around him, running her fingers through his hair.

"You're amazing," she whispered, kissing his ear, his neck, his chest.

Kane let her pull his shirt over his head and watched in appreciation as her pert breasts, tucked into a red satin bra, made an appearance, accompanied by a tan, taut stomach and slender, perfect legs. Then she pressed against him again, her hands massaging their way down his back—and he had other things to appreciate.

"You're totally amazing," she repeated.

"Yeah—I know."

Kaia took a long sip of her vodka tonic and stretched out along the shallow bench of the Jacuzzi, her long, jet black hair fanned out along the marble edge. She closed her eyes and moaned in appreciation as the jets pummeled her muscles and all of her stress melted away into the steaming water.

Not that she had much to be stressed about. Stress required caring what happened, wanting something, worrying about something, *doing* something—and none of that posed much of a problem in the lame exercise in small-town boredom that passed for her life these days. No, any stress she'd had was left behind in New York, along with her friends, her boyfriends, her uncaring bitch of a mother, and her Saks Fifth Avenue credit card. All this apathy was probably doing wonders for her complexion—too bad there was no one around to see.

"Need a refill, Ms. Sellers?" the maid asked cautiously.

"No thanks, Alicia," Kaia said sweetly. It was useful to be nice—sometimes—to the help. After all, she didn't think her father—if he ever came back from his latest business trip—would appreciate hearing that she'd drunk her way through half his liquor cabinet. Right now it was her and Alicia's little secret, and Kaia intended it to stay that way.

It was a good thing, too, because if it weren't for the Jacuzzi and the booze, and the satellite TV, she'd go crazy out here.

Ever since her mother had shipped her out to the middle of nowhere, claiming that a year at her father's house in the desert would do wonders for her character, life had become one long, uninterrupted stretch of tedium. While her mother was taking full advantage of her new childless state, whoring around New York's spas, sales, and singles bars like a middle-aged Kardashian sister, Kaia was stuck here in this scorching hot ghost town, making nice with the low-rent losers who made up the local teen scene. She'd caught only the occasional glimpse of her father, who'd claimed he was delighted to have her, then promptly left town, returning to his desert McMansion and his delinquent daughter for a few hours each week before getting the hell out again.

Kaia couldn't blame him. If she had the cash, she'd head for the hills (or better, L.A., only a six-hour drive away) and never look back.

But Daddy Dearest had sliced through all her credit cards, so she was stuck. Now that she'd proven to herself that she could bed the two hottest guys in school—and for such a small and pathetic school, they were pretty damn hot—she was fresh out of ideas. Adam Morgan, with all of his supposed virtue and loyalty, hadn't been much of a challenge, but the payoff had been fun, though not as much fun as watching his puppy dog face crumble when she'd blown him off a heartbeat later. Kane, on the other hand, had been no challenge at all, but that's not to say he didn't have his merits. . . .

But now it was only October, and she was already bored. Again. What next? Storm the "popular crowd" and get voted homecoming queen? Rededicate herself to last month's quest of screwing—and then screwing over—the dashing French teacher who seemed to think he was too good for her? Snag one of her father's credit cards and get the hell back to New York?

Kaia let her head sink under the water for a moment and then burst back above the surface, the cool desert air stinging her dripping face. She was too blissfully comfortable right now to worry about tomorrow, or the next day. She was sure that eventually she'd manage to find herself some interesting trouble.

She always did.

✿   ✿   ✿

Adam brushed Beth's blond hair out of her face and gave her a soft kiss on the forehead. This time when he climbed out of bed and began to hunt around for his clothes, she made no move to pull him back down. It was too bad; things were so much easier when they were kissing instead of talking.

Then he didn't have to worry about all the things he wasn't allowed to say, things that kept threatening to spill from his lips. Things like, say, "I slept with Kaia." Every time he opened his mouth, he feared the confession would pop out. Part of him just wanted it out in the open. Anything to be free of all this crushing guilt.

And, of course, when they were in the midst of hooking up, they were also relieved of the burden of not talking about the reason they always *stopped* hooking up. It was the only time they could, for once, ignore their biggest problem: sex—or the lack thereof.

It had been bad enough this summer, when it seemed like he couldn't say anything right, when Beth assumed sex was all he wanted and seemed to silently hate him for it. Almost as much as he hated himself . . . because sometimes it felt like sex was all he wanted. But ever since the dance at the beginning of the school year, things had, on the surface, been much better—and beneath the surface, where it counted, much, much worse.

It was all a little hazy for him, but from what he could

piece together from his drunken, fragmented memory of the night, Beth had decided that she was ready to sleep with him—and he'd passed out. When he awoke, sometime early the next morning, she was staring at him in disgust and wouldn't say a word.

They hadn't talked about it then, or the next day, or any time afterward. She had never brought it up. And he had never apologized.

And now sex, such a hot topic before, was off limits. Taboo. He never asked what had happened to her being "ready," or when she might be again. Certainly never mentioned that he now knew what sex was like—and how much he wanted more of it. Sometimes he envied Kane, who could get any girl he wanted and could get anything out of her. Not that he would ever give up what he had with Beth, but sometimes he wished he could just take a break. Slip into a parallel universe where he was single. Free.

"So, it's looking like the swim team might make it to the championships this year," he said, trying to wipe such thoughts from his mind and searching for a neutral subject. Making it work with Beth meant *not* dwelling on what he couldn't have. What he shouldn't even want. "We're having a pretty strong season."

"I know," she said with a rueful smile. "I wish I could make it to your meet tomorrow."

"It's okay," he assured her, looking away. "I know you're busy." Last year Beth had come to all of his swim meets and basketball games, and cheered him on from the sidelines. This year she'd been too busy to make it to any of them. And he'd tried to pretend he didn't care.

"If we do make it to the championships," he began tentatively, "I think a bunch of kids from school will probably come along, sort of a cheering section, and maybe—"

"I'd love to go!" Beth cried. She hopped out of bed and gave him a quick hug before pulling on her denim skirt and a light pink tank top. "I mean, if you want me to be there. . . ."

"Of course I do," he said hastily, giving her a soft kiss. "I've missed my good-luck charm. And it'd be fun to be there together. Good for . . . us, you know?"

"Speaking of us, Adam, I think we should—well, we haven't really . . ." Her voice trailed off.

"What?" he prompted her gently, not really sure he wanted to hear the answer.

"Uh, I just think I should get going," she said, her voice suddenly brisk and cheerful. "I want to get in some studying before work."

"You have a test tomorrow?" It seemed unlikely. Usually when there was a test imminent, he knew it. It was generally pretty hard to miss—Beth had flashcards, study sessions, not to mention an endless litany of concerns about failing out of school—culminating, each time, in the inevitable A.

"No, for the SATs—you know, life-altering event only a few weeks away?" she reminded him.

"Plenty of time for that later," he scoffed, pulling her toward him. She pushed him away. Sometimes their relationship felt like an endless tug of war. He pulled her in one direction, and something within her kept pulling in the other.

"This is my future—*our* future—that we're talking about here," she said passionately. "It's *important*."

"I know, I know," he said, trying to reassure her.

"You are coming on Saturday, right?" she asked, suddenly suspicious. "You know this thing is mandatory, right?"

"I know, you don't have to remind me a million times," he complained, turning away from her. "I'm not an idiot."

"I just wish you'd take these things a little more seriously," she whined. "You're always—"

"What?" He tensed. Along with sex, they usually tried not to discuss the future—neither wanted to acknowledge that they were headed in two very different directions.

"Nothing." She came up behind him and put her arms around him, massaging his chest and kissing his neck. "Let's just forget it," she mumbled, her lips against his skin.

It worked for him.

It was the worst possible timing.

Harper pulled into the driveway, and there they were, a few yards away, wrapped in each other's arms. Couldn't they ever just give it a rest?

"Hey, Harper!" Adam called to her in his lilting Southern accent. It was the one thing he'd held on to from an early childhood in South Carolina. Adam hated it, as he hated any reminder of his distant past. But to Harper, his voice was like a song, sweet and intoxicating. "Come over and say hello!"

"Can't, busy, gotta—you know," she babbled, waving back as she raced for her front door.

Awkward postcoital convo with the love of her life and the love of his? No thanks.

Besides, they'd already forgotten her existence and gotten back to the serious business of groping each other. Harper shook her head in disgust and slammed through the doorway. When Adam had confessed to Harper—his oldest and most trustworthy friend—that he'd cheated on Beth, Harper had been sure that their relationship wouldn't last the week. But the incident had proved nothing more than a hiccup, a tiny bump in the path of disgustingly true love. In fact, if their nonstop PDAs were any indication, he and Beth were going stronger than ever. It killed Harper to know that, with a few carefully chosen words, she could destroy their happiness. She could drive Beth away—but Adam would never forgive her.

Ignorance is bliss, Beth—right?

As for Adam, he'd never mentioned Kaia after that, and now, once again, all he could talk about was his perfect, wonderful Beth.

Screw that. Harper was done waiting around for Adam to wake up and discover he was with the wrong girl. Harper the passive good girl (if she'd ever existed) was gone. Harper the scheming bitch was back in action.

And finally, she had the beginnings of an idea. . . .

chapter two

SATURDAY MORNING, HAVEN HIGH, ROOM 232. THE disgruntled seniors, all forty-eight of them, filtered into the room, spitting out variations on the same theme.

It was Saturday.

It was early

And in a just world, they would all be at home in bed.

No one wanted to be there.

Not Kane, bleary-eyed and hungover from last night's revelry, who thought studying was for saps and that SAT prep courses, even the lame one-time freebie offered by their tiny public school, should be reserved for those too stupid to score well on their own.

Not Adam, who'd decided he didn't need the SATs or college—not when he was planning to stay in Grace until the day he died.

Not Beth, for whom every minute wasted in the classroom listening to the teacher drone on was a minute she wasn't able to spend shut up in her room poring over Princeton Review books and searching for the magic strategy that would guarantee her a perfect score. (And the fact that the class was led by Mr. Powell, that she could feel his eyes boring into her even as she stared resolutely down at her desk? It didn't help.)

And certainly not Jack Powell, who, as the newest hire, had been compelled to "volunteer" for the Saturday class. Sacrifice his morning. Stare down Beth and pray she wouldn't grow a spine (or a mouth). Avoid the penetrating gaze of Kaia, whose very unwelcome and very public lip-lock with him in the middle of a school dance had left him the focus of hallway gossip, faculty lounge whispering, strict administrative scrutiny—and temporary probation.

No, Jack Powell would rather be at home and in bed too. Jack Powell would, in fact, rather be strapped into a dentist's chair getting a root canal.

But no one had asked him.

"Okay kids, quiet down," he called out in his clipped British accent. He was only too aware of its charm—he'd made girls swoon all up and down the eastern seaboard, and it wasn't surprising that the upper crust London inflection had an even greater effect out in this desert wasteland. "I know you don't want to be here."

Shouts of agreement.

Join the club, he thought, with more than a trace of bitterness. If his former colleagues could see him now, stranded in the middle of nowhere, policing these deadbeats-in-training. None of them knew how good they had it. He hadn't known himself, until he'd ended up in this godforsaken corner of the world. And the worst part was, he had no one to blame but himself.

"Well, let's make it quick and painless, then." He began to distribute a practice test—at least that would keep them busy for an hour or so.

He looked around at the roomful of students with a flicker of pity. *They don't pay me enough to work on Saturdays*, he reminded himself, *but hell, these suckers have to be here for nothing*.

Two hours later Beth staggered out of the school, feeling like she'd just emerged, not entirely unscathed, from an emotional car wreck. Sitting through French class with Powell was bad enough. Especially with the whole school buzzing about Kaia's kiss at the dance: Debate still raged as to whether Kaia had thrown herself at the clueless young teacher—or whether the dashing Jack Powell was, in fact, carrying on a not-so-secret affair with his hottest student and God knew who else. Beth flushed every time the subject came up and just hoped no one could read the truth that was, she feared, written all over her red cheeks and tortured frown.

She still couldn't believe that she'd been stupid enough to trust him. Yes, he was the new sponsor of the newspaper and she was its editor in chief—at the time it had made sense that he'd want to spend a series of long, intimate afternoons together, going over logistics—but it had been more than that, right from the start, hadn't it? "Call me Jack," he'd suggested—she shuddered at the memory. She had trusted him, believed in him, confided in him, until that final day. When it turned out that all he wanted was—

"Beth, wake up!"

That was the trouble with zoning out—it made it a lot harder to avoid the people you didn't want to see. People like Harper Grace. Haven High's resident alpha girl: best dressed, best coiffed, best bitch. And, oh yeah, Adam's best friend.

"Hey, Harper," Beth greeted her, hoping her grin didn't seem too fake.

She didn't like Harper, didn't trust Harper—but since she'd drifted away from her real girlfriends a few months into the relationship with Adam, she also didn't have too many other options.

Harper pulled her away from the crowd of students milling across the school grounds and gave her a conspiratorial grin.

"So, I've been meaning to ask you," she said softly. "How are things going with you and Adam?"

"Uh . . . okay," Beth responded guardedly.

"No," Harper leaned in even closer. "I mean with, you know, that *problem* you were having."

"I'm not sure what you mean." But Beth had a sinking feeling that she did. She'd made the mistake of confessing her fears about sex, and about her relationship, to Harper. The conversation hadn't been a total nightmare, but she wasn't looking for an instant replay anytime soon.

"I've been so concerned about you," Harper said, linking her arm through Beth's. "I mean, I just feel so terrible for you, with all your issues."

Beth pulled her arm away but forced herself to do it with a smile. Adam was always urging her to see the good in Harper, and so for his sake she'd tried, and failed, and tried again. She was still working on it—the least she could do in the meantime was be polite.

"So . . . you two still haven't . . . ?" Harper prodded.

"That's really none of your business," Beth snapped.

Harper looked at her appraisingly. Beth squirmed under the scrutiny of her gaze.

"Mmm-hmm, that's what I thought," Harper said finally, nodding her head.

"Look, I really have to go," Beth told her, pulling away, wishing that a hole would open up and swallow her before their little chat could go any further.

"No, no, I almost forgot why I wanted to talk to you in the first place," Harper said, once again threading her arm through Beth's as if they were the best of friends. As if they were anything. "So, listen, you aced that practice test, right?"

Beth darted her eyes toward the ground and reddened slightly.

"I guess. . . . Why?"

"We knew it!" Harper said triumphantly.

"We?"

"Me—and Kane. Look, he'd kill me if he knew I was telling you this, but Kane's not too hot on standardized tests. He's a smart guy, but he just freezes up. Have you heard that rumor, how they give you six hundred points just for writing your name?"

"Uh-huh," she mumbled dubiously.

"Well, let's just say Kane's going to need it."

Beth snuck a glance over at the Greek god of Haven High, preening for a couple of blondes from the cheerleading team. Beth wasn't surprised to hear he was lagging behind. From what she'd seen of Kane (another one of

Adam's friends whose "good side" was impossibly difficult to find), his definition of a hard day's work involved vodka, girls, and plenty of naps. Still, it didn't seem like her business—or her problem.

"Why are you telling me this, Harper?" she asked, again pulling her arm away.

"Kane doesn't want to be stuck in this deadbeat town any more than the rest of us," Harper explained. "Which means college. Which means decent SAT scores. Which means . . . he needs your help."

"Me?" Beth wrinkled her face in surprise—but a warm rush of pride began to spread through her. That they were desperate, and they'd come to her, needed her . . .

"You," Harper confirmed. "He wants you to tutor him."

"Then why isn't he asking me himself?"

Harper laughed and shrugged. "You know guys, they're idiots. He's just embarrassed. Kane can be a little shy sometimes, you know?"

"Kane?" Beth repeated in disbelief. She looked back toward the entrance of the school, where Kane had hoisted one of the cheerleaders into his arms and was now spinning her around as she squealed in mock dismay. He didn't look shy to her. Arrogant, maybe. Sleazy. Impressed with his own existence. All of the above. But shy?

"I'm not really going to have that much time," she cautioned Harper. "I don't know if—"

"Beth, he *needs* you," Harper pleaded. "Really, you're his only hope. He told me he knew you were the only one who'd be able to help him."

"Really?" When she was eleven, Beth had found a three-legged jackrabbit lying in her backyard and, with her father's help, had nursed it back to health. She'd never been able to say no to desperation—and today was no different. "Well, I guess if he needs me . . ."

"Great!" Harper tore a piece of paper from her notebook and scrawled something on it before handing it to Beth. "Here's his number. I'll tell him you're going to call ASAP."

And she skipped away before Beth had a chance to change her mind.

Mission accomplished—and so easily that it was difficult to feel too proud of herself.

But Harper managed.

"You are going to love me," she crowed into her cell once Kane answered the phone.

"Not unless you're waiting for me in the parking lot with some black coffee and a Playboy bunny," Kane retorted. "Otherwise, I'm kind of busy right now."

"Yeah, I can see that." Harper, about a hundred yards away, sneered at the sight of his adoring harem. Had these girls no respect for themselves?

Stupid question.

"What do you mean, you can see?" Kane looked up from the nearest buxom brunette and began scanning the parking lot.

"On your left, loser boy." Harper waved lazily until he spotted her. "And you're not too busy for this. Trust me."

She ended the call and watched as Kane grudgingly kissed the girls good-bye and jogged over.

"This better be good," he grumbled once he'd reached her. "I've been bored long enough for one day. I need to go out and wash off the stench of all this educational earnestness with some good old-fashioned debauchery."

"What you need is to go home and study for the SATs," Harper countered.

"The SATs?" he asked incredulously.

She nodded.

"The SATs that are three weeks away?"

She nodded again.

"The SATs that I couldn't give a shit about?"

"You got it."

"Harper, you know that practice test in there? I scored above a seven hundred on every section. You know what that means?" He spoke slowly and patiently, as if she would soon be taking her own test—English as a second language. "It means I'm not studying today, tomorrow— hell, I may never study again."

Harper gave him a gentle pat on the back and shook her head sadly. "No, you're going home and cracking the books. Right now, and tomorrow, and the next day. You're going to make the library your new best friend."

"And why would I want to do that?" he sneered.

Harper grinned, and jerked a thumb across the parking lot toward Beth, who was climbing into Adam's rusty maroon Chevrolet.

"Meet your new tutor."

Kane's eyes widened. "You didn't!"

"Oh, I did."

Harper laid out her vision for him—long, late nights huddled together over the books; frequent breaks for coffee, pizza, and intimate getting-to-know-you sessions; close quarters; moonlit strolls; high stress, low inhibitions—when Harper Grace made a deal, she delivered. And even Kane had to admit that she had just delivered Beth to his doorstep, complete with gift wrap and ruffled bow.

"And while I'm sweeping Beth off her feet with my charm and feigned stupidity, I assume you'll be . . . taking care of Adam?"

Harper allowed herself a moment to enjoy a second vision: Adam, sitting at home, bored, lonely, angry, jealous, and primed for . . . well, anything.

"A girl's gotta do what a girl's gotta do," she said sweetly.

Kane laughed and slung an arm around her shoulders.

"And I have no doubt, Grace," he assured her, "that you're just the girl to do it."

Having finished eavesdropping on the pathetic scheming out in the parking lot, Kaia headed back inside the school to take care of some unfinished business. Watching Harper and Kane haplessly put together their juvenile little plot had inspired her—why should they be the only ones having any fun?

She tugged down her silk tank top and hitched up her blue miniskirt so that her perfect (and worth every cent) cleavage and Pilates-sculpted thighs had maximum visibility. Then she stepped inside the classroom. Jack Powell may have thought he could avoid her forever, but his time had just run out.

"Hey, Mr. Powell," she whispered, leaning against the door frame and aiming an unmistakable look in his direction, familiar to any adult-movie fan as a silent "Hey, big guy, throw me down and do me right here on the floor" invitation. It was intended to be ironic. Partly. "Long time, no see."

"I see you every day in class, Ms. Sellers," he said. She shivered at the sound of his voice. "And trust me, that's quite enough."

He turned his back on her. Big mistake.

Kaia closed the door and crossed the empty classroom, shedding the cheesy sex-me-up grin as she went. It seemed Mr. Powell was still playing hard to get—and she was beginning to enjoy his game. She laid a light hand on the small of his back, saying, "I see *you* every day in French—but I'm not sure you're really seeing me."

He whirled around to face her and backed away.

"What kind of game are you playing?" he hissed. "Isn't it enough for you that I'm on probation after your little stunt at the dance? It was all I could do to talk them out of firing me."

"Hey, don't look at me, I'm the victim here," Kaia countered. "According to Mr. Hemp, at least." Kaia had been reprimanded for her "flagrant disregard of Mr. Powell's personal space" and had been sentenced to six weeks' worth of meetings with the school psychologist, who, she suspected, had received his pseudo degree off the Internet, if not purchased it at Shrinks "R" Us. She would have preferred a prison term.

"Victim?" He snorted. "I'm warning you, Kaia, if you're trying to spread some kind of—if you think you can set me up—"

"Chill out, Jack." She flashed an insouciant grin. "I think you got my message. This time I come in peace. I want to call a truce."

"A truce?" he repeated dubiously. "So this means

you're going to stop throwing yourself at me and end this apparent quest to get me fired?"

"Provisional yes to the latter, definite no to the former." She leaned forward to give him a quick peck on the lips, but he twisted his face away, and instead her lips brushed his coarse stubble. Good enough. "You want me, Mr. Powell. You just don't know it yet. But you will."

"I want you to get out of here," he said coldly, "and make sure that no one sees you go. And then I want you to drop French and do me the favor of pretending I don't exist. Or at least letting me pretend that about you. Let's start now."

He sat down at the desk and began shuffling through a stack of papers, pointedly refusing to look at her.

Kaia stood before him, hands on her hips, shaking her head and clucking her tongue against the roof of her mouth, like a mother reprimanding her young.

"Mr. Powell, I thought we'd already established that if I want to, I can make life here very unpleasant for you. You said it yourself—I can be trouble. You're right. I don't think you want to be rude to me."

Silence. And more paper shuffling.

"Okay," Kaia agreed, heading for the door. "You're lucky I'm in a 'make love, not war' mood . . . for now."

After escaping the SAT session, Beth and Adam treated themselves to an impromptu picnic in Dwyer Park (complete with brownish tufts of grass, brownish decaying picket fence, and brownish pond—as desert oases went, it ranked somewhere between Palm Springs and a garbage dump). Once they'd gotten everything set up, Adam ran off to grab them some soda from the nearby drugstore. Beth's phone rang as soon as he was gone.

It was Kane. She'd left a message for him just after leaving the school, so she wasn't surprised to see his name pop up on her phone. Still, it was strange—he'd never called her before. And if he had, she probably wouldn't have picked up the phone.

They only spoke for a few minutes, just enough time to agree on the tutoring and pick a time for their first meeting. But the conversation wasn't nearly as awkward as she'd feared—and weirdly, Beth found herself almost looking forward to their first encounter.

She put the phone away with a quizzical frown. Kane had seemed so genuine, so earnest, so pleasant, so . . . totally un-Kane-like. He'd limited himself to only two sarcastic comments and one sexual innuendo. For a five-minute conversation, it had to be a personal best. And even stranger—he actually seemed to want her help. He seemed to want to do well, whatever it would take.

Kane? Working? Had she walked out of the school this morning and into some alternate universe?

The Kane she knew—though, granted, she didn't

know him very well and had never wanted to change that—thought hard work meant applying a little extra torque when opening a stuck bottle lid. And even that was only worth it if the bottle contained some kind of alcoholic beverage or was handed to him by a weak and soon to be very grateful cheerleader. Back before she and Adam had gotten together, Kane had chased after her, as he did every girl—for about a day. She'd blown him off, and he'd disappeared. Kane didn't believe in making an effort.

She shook her head. This time he really must be desperate.

"Who was on the phone?" Adam asked, sitting down on the worn quilt that served as their picnic blanket and passing her a deliciously cool bottle of Coke.

"Your best friend, actually." Searching for a relief from the searing, dry heat of the afternoon, she pressed the bottle against her forehead, enjoying the icy chill that ran down her spine.

"Harper?" he asked, confused.

Beth flinched. She respected Adam's friendship with the beautiful girl next door, but she didn't have to like it.

"No, your other best friend—you remember Kane, don't you?"

Adam shook his head in disgust. "What, is he trying to track me down? Dude, I never should have told him I was going out with you today."

"Actually, he was looking for me," Beth said, smacking him lightly with an annoyance that was only half for show.

"You? Why would he be calling you?"

"People have been known to want to talk to me," she informed him, irritation mounting.

"I know, I know," Adam murmured, kissing her on the forehead. "You're in high demand. In fact," he added, kissing his way down her nose and landing on her lips, "I want you right now."

"He wants my help," Beth explained, somewhat mollified. "With studying for the SATs."

"Kane? Studying?" Adam burst into laughter. "I don't think so. Seriously, what did he want?"

"I know, I thought it was weird too," Beth admitted. "But he seems to really want a tutor."

"And he asked *you*?"

"Why wouldn't he ask me?"

"I just meant—whatever," Adam stopped himself. "So he's had a personality overhaul and wants a tutor for the SATs. You're not going to do it, are you?"

"Of course I am—he's my friend," she reminded him. "Well . . . he's your friend. And he needs my help. Why wouldn't I do it?"

"Oh, I don't know, maybe because these days you're too busy to eat or sleep, not to mention see your boyfriend?" He kept his voice level and light, but Beth could feel the dangerous tension bubbling beneath the surface. There just didn't seem to be much she could do about it— and she couldn't stop herself from egging him on.

"Not all of us want to spend our lives lying around watching TV and drinking beer," she snapped, hating herself for it the moment she heard the words slip out of her mouth. "At least Kane cares about something and is willing to work hard to get it. How could I say no to that?"

"Fine," he grunted.

"Fine." And, after a moment, "We're starting tomorrow."

"What?" he yelped. "We've got plans for tomorrow!"

"I know," she said in a gentler voice. "I'm sorry—it's just, he wanted to get started right away, and he seemed so desperate . . ."

"You see? This is exactly what I'm talking about! How hard was it to find some time together this weekend, and now you're just . . . ?" He threw up his arms in disgust.

"Adam, stop." Beth took his hands in hers and clasped them to her chest. "I'm here, with you, now. Can't we just enjoy this?"

He didn't respond, but he left his hands in hers, and she felt a gentle pressure squeezing back. Beth looked around—the park was mostly empty, and they were partially hidden from view by a cluster of decrepit trees.

She brought his hands to her lips and kissed them

softly, then released them. He grazed his fingers across her cheekbones and cradled her face.

"How about if we stop talking about Kane for a while?" she suggested, lying back on the quilt and pulling him down beside her. He stroked her hair, and she breathed in the nearness of him, the familiar scent that somehow evoked both a cozy kitchen of fresh-baked bread and the wide expanse of a bright summer morning. "Why don't we just—"

"Stop talking *at all* for a while?" he finished for her, his hands slipping under her pale pink shirt and massaging her bare skin.

Beth sighed, feeling her tension slip away. It sounded like a plan.

chapter three

"HOW ABOUT THIS?" MIRANDA CREPT OUT OF THE dressing room and timidly spun around to display the newest ensemble—bright red pants that looked like they'd been painted on, paired with a black lace corset whose tackiness quotient would have made Christina Aguilera cringe.

Uh, no.

Harper sighed. Three hours into the total transformation shopping trip (step one on the road to a new and improved Miranda, whatever that was supposed to mean) and she was bored out of her mind. Shopping in Grace was never the most thrilling of experiences since the options consisted of three or four sorry stores in a local excuse for a strip mall, a large thrift shop (useless, since the middle-aged Grace matrons who made up its pool of suppliers couldn't really be counted on to supply the type of "vintage" threads recommended in last month's *Vogue*), and, of course, the Walmart out on Route 53 (the less said about that, the better).

No, Harper preferred to buy most of her clothes online—and Harper's parents preferred her not to buy clothes at all, as the meager profits from the family dry cleaning business rarely seemed to justify that kind of supposedly wasteful expenditure. Harper failed to see how a fur-lined J Crew raincoat or tan suede boots could be deemed wasteful—so what if the temperature never dipped below sixty degrees and it rained only eight inches a year? Sometimes fashion was its own excuse. Regardless, Harper had managed—just barely—to put together a wardrobe befitting her position in Haven High's social strata. It didn't mean that she wanted to spend a Sunday afternoon watching Miranda fork over Daddy's credit card in return for an armful of clothes she didn't need and would never wear—*especially* when phase one of Operation Anti-Cupid was in full effect and Adam was, even now, sitting home alone, ripe for the picking.

But Harper was still feeling nagging guilt about helping the love of Miranda's life pursue someone else. So here she was, figuring the least she could do was save her ever faithful sidekick from making a serious fashion faux pas.

After all, what are friends for?

"Well . . . I suppose Halloween is coming up," Harper finally said, and gave her a thumbs-down.

Miranda studied herself in the mirror from a number of angles before wrinkling her nose and sighing. "You're right, as usual." She disappeared back inside the dressing room. "Just a couple more things," she called out.

Harper checked her watch and then leaned back against the wall, pressing her weight against it as she slumped to the floor. Was this going to drag on forever?

"What about this?" Miranda asked, popping out of the dressing room, a hesitant smile creeping across her face. She had slipped into a snugly fitting suede skirt, paired with a gauzy green shirt that laced up the front, offering a glimpse of cleavage and leaving just enough to the imagination.

It was stylish, edgy, slightly daring—it was, in other words, totally Harper.

It looked okay on Miranda, Harper judged, but she could almost feel that suede wrapping around her legs and knew that shade of green would light her auburn hair on fire.

Miranda had seen it first, true. And, more importantly, Miranda was the one with the credit card. She was also the one with the identity crisis, Harper reminded herself. Harper was just along for the ride—she was supposed to sit by and watch, do the loyal and supportive friend thing. But Harper wasn't very good at being the sidekick—it was one of the reasons she and Miranda worked so well together. Their friendship only had room for one star, and usually Miranda was more than willing to let Harper bask in the spotlight while she waited in the wings.

"It's . . . it's not really you, Rand," Harper pointed out. And that much was true, at least. Miranda's fashion choices usually ran to white V-neck T-shirts and jeans, with the occasional brightly colored tank thrown in on days she was feeling a little wild.

"That's the idea," Miranda pointed out, her smile widening. She turned slowly in front of the mirror, craning her neck to try to get a glimpse of what she looked like from behind.

It was a contortion that Harper knew well, and she knew exactly what Miranda was looking for—or, rather, looking at.

"Is that the right size?" Harper asked innocently. "It looks a little tight across your . . . hips."

"You think?" Miranda asked, twisting herself around even farther. "It feels okay, but—oh God, it's my ass, isn't it? You can say it. All this brown just makes it look huge."

Harper bit her lip. "It's not huge, exactly."

That was also strictly the truth, Harper told herself. Though it's possible the message could have been delivered in a more confident tone. Miranda was only a few pounds beyond stick thin, but for some reason, when she looked in the mirror, all she saw was flab and cellulite. Harper hated to encourage her, but how could she just sit there and watch an outfit like that walk out of the store in someone else's bag?

"It's just . . ." She let her voice trail off and gave Miranda an apologetic smile.

"Ugh, I knew it," Miranda cried. "Look at me—I look like a tree! She flicked the low, loose green top with her index finger. "Big, thick trunk and a slutty green top. Great."

"You do not look like a tree," Harper assured her, half laughing and half kicking herself for getting Miranda started down this road. "It looks good, really," she insisted.

Too little, too late.

Miranda was already back inside the dressing room, and soon Harper saw the shirt and skirt drop to the floor. She looked at them longingly. She could always save up some money, come back in a few weeks—if they were still there. . . .

"I don't know what I was thinking," Miranda's disembodied voice complained from behind the curtain. "Sorry I wasted your time with this stupid trip."

She came out, in her own clothes, and extended a hand to Harper, hoisting her up off the ground. "Let's just get out of here."

"You're not getting *anything*?" Harper asked in disbelief. There went three hours of her life she'd never get back—and with nothing to show for it.

"Just this," Miranda sighed, holding up a shirt that was almost identical to the one she was wearing.

So—nothing to show for it except a pain in her ass from sitting on the floor and a white V-neck T-shirt that she didn't even get to take home with her. Not that she would have wanted it.

Miranda slung an arm around Harper's shoulder.

"Screw the shopping," she said, leading her friend out of the fitting area. "Let's go get some coffee. My treat."

Harper took one last longing glance at the pile of clothes dumped in the corner of her best friend's dressing room. Too bad she and Miranda couldn't be combined into a single person—with her body and Miranda's wallet, they'd be looking pretty damn good.

Harper slipped a hand into the pocket of her fake Diesel jeans, just in case a few crisp twenty-dollar bills had decided to magically appear.

Nope.

"Coffee it is," she agreed. "Definitely your treat."

Grace wasn't a Starbucks kind of town. Big shock. If you wanted coffee, you had two choices. You could drink the black sludge they dished out at the diner, or you could step inside an unassuming and unnamed hole in the wall in the center of town and drink the finest blends this side of the Mississippi. The neon sign out front said only HOT COFFEE. (Or rather, it read HO CO FE .) But if you were a local—and in Grace, who wasn't a local?—you knew it as Bourquin's, after its owner, an angry, rotund woman who went by Auntie Bourquin. No one knew her first name—and no one had the nerve to ask. Auntie Bourquin was slow and surly, and her establishment was cramped and not too clean—but the coffee was delicious, and the fresh baked goods that appeared every morning tasted like chocolate heaven.

Miranda, who was feeling worn, deflated, and ugly after her unsuccessful bout with the shopping gods, had every reason to hope that a steaming diet mochaccino and an oversize chocolate chip cookie (it was the constant and bitter irony of her life that feeling fat and ugly made her want to run for the cookie jar) would cheer her up. They didn't call it comfort food for nothing.

But comfort wasn't in the cards.

"Do you see what I see?" Miranda hissed to Harper as soon as they'd stepped inside the coffee shop. At Harper's clueless look, Miranda jerked her head toward the far wall, where Beth was huddled over a stack of notebooks, clearly studying her bland little heart out. Not a big surprise. The surprise was sitting across from her—and his name was Kane. She pulled Harper back out the door, hoping they hadn't been seen. "What's *he* doing with *her*?"

"Calm down, she's just tutoring him for the SATs," Harper said impatiently. "Can we please go back inside now?"

"*She's* tutoring him?" Miranda asked incredulously.

"What's the difference?"

Harper could be so dense sometimes. Miranda knew that when Kane looked at her, he didn't see some babe he was desperate to bed. She knew he probably didn't even see someone he was that eager to be friends with (fortunately for her, he was stuck with her by default—she and Harper were pretty much a package deal). But she'd always thought that he'd at least seen her as a brain. Who did he call when he needed to copy some homework? Who did he go to when he needed to cheat on a test?

Miranda, that's who. It had been her one thing, and she had always hoped that someday it might be her in. It was, if nothing else, a start.

So what had changed?

"The difference is, if he needed someone to tutor him, why didn't he just ask me?" Miranda asked, staring at the two of them through the window. They were laughing about something, and she saw Kane briefly touch Beth's arm. And she knew. "He's after her, isn't he?"

"Don't be ridiculous," Harper said quickly. "She's dating one of his best friends. Even Kane wouldn't stoop that low."

"But look at them in there," Miranda said dubiously.

"Miranda, if he were after her, I would know. I promise."

"I still don't understand what he's doing with her," she complained. "They're not even friends." And she wanted very much for it to stay that way. As far as she was concerned, she had one—and only one—advantage over the bimbos Kane constantly draped himself with. They were bimbos—and Miranda wasn't. So if he ever got tired of making conversation with beautiful airheads, if he ever wanted a real relationship with a real girl, where else would he look but his old friend Miranda? Or, at least, that was her secret hope. But it all depended on the fact that, aside from Harper, Miranda was the only girl of substance he really knew—until now. For all Beth's blandness, she was sharp, serious. Real. If he befriended tall, slim, beautiful Beth, if she was in his life when he finally stopped playing the field—then Miranda's last, best hope was dead.

"I'm sure it's nothing, Rand, really," Harper assured her. "Can we go in now?"

But Miranda shook her head and turned away without a word, walking back over to the car. Her appetite was gone.

They had spent two hours buried in books, digging their way through algebra equations and an endless list of synonyms for good and evil. And there was still so much more to do. Beth felt the familiar flutter of panic as she began to think about the massive number of practice questions she needed to get through and strategies she needed to memorize before the big test—but somehow, everything seemed a little less daunting than before. Maybe because, thanks to Kane, she was no longer alone. Maybe because he'd bought her a mug of chocolate milk and a fresh-baked chocolate chip cookie, the best in town. (It was a little juvenile, Beth knew, but her sweet tooth demanded daily chocolate intake, and nothing was better than a Bourquin's cookie dipped into a frosty glass of chocolate milk. Kane had been only too happy to oblige.) Maybe it was just Kane, sitting across the table from her, working, questioning, laughing—making the time fly by. They'd only had one afternoon together, but she could already tell that working with Kane was going to be nothing like she'd expected.

He was nothing like she'd expected, Beth mused, watching him up at the counter grabbing them both refills.

The Kane she knew was smug and self-absorbed, caustic and catty, and above all, lazy.

Not this Kane.

Not the guy who'd pulled out her chair for her when she'd sat down, who'd thanked her so profusely for spending the time to tutor him, and who'd been working diligently, without a break—or a single snide remark—for more than two hours.

No, this was a complete stranger to her. But she hoped he wouldn't be for long.

Adam flipped through the channels idly, too bored to watch anything for more than a few seconds. It was pretty slim pickings: a Food Network documentary on the secrets of cereal (hot stuff), a stupid political show . . . even ESPN was showing some kind of greatest hits montage of old golf shots, and who wanted to watch that? No one under the age of sixty-five. Adam would be willing to bet on it. And thanks to *Secrets of Las Vegas*, showing around the clock on the Travel Channel, he now knew exactly how and where to do so.

Just because Beth had stood him up was no reason to spend the day lying around on the couch, counting the cracks in the ceiling, he reminded himself. It's not like he didn't have plenty of other friends and plenty of other options. It was just that there didn't seem to be much of a point. Why go to all that effort just to do something he didn't particularly want to do? He *wanted* to spend some time with his girlfriend. Was there something wrong with that?

So he'd told the guys to leave him out of whatever half-assed activity they'd come up with for the afternoon (last he'd checked, it had been a tie between bowling and shooting rats down at the town dump—neither a big draw, as far as he was concerned). But half-assed activity or not, he was beginning to regret the decision. Even hunting rats might be better than lying on the couch nibbling stale pizza all day.

Lucky for him—and for the rats—the phone rang.

"I thought you might be a little bored," Harper said by way of a greeting.

She didn't know the half of it.

"I just ran into Kane and Beth at the coffee shop," she continued, "and figured you might need someone to play with."

Adam's stomach clenched, but he forced himself to ignore it. He also forced himself—and it took a significant mental and physical effort—not to request any details. So what if his girlfriend and his best friend were getting cozy over coffee while he played couch potato?

"She's tutoring him for the SATs," Adam explained gruffly.

"I heard that," Harper said in a perky voice. "It's so nice of her—I know how *busy* she always is. It's great that she made the time for him."

Drive the knife in a little deeper, why don't you, he thought, but struggled to keep his irritation in check. After all it's not like any of this was Harper's fault.

"You know Beth," he offered half-heartedly.

"She just can't say no," Harper agreed.

Interesting choice of words, Adam mused. Lately, it seemed that "no" was the only word in Beth's vocabulary. At least when it came to him. When it came to the questions that counted.

But that, too, wasn't Harper's fault.

"So I'm bored," he admitted. "What are you going to do about it?"

"Funny you should ask. . . ."

Freshly showered and changed from his ratty Lakers shirt and boxers into jeans and a slightly less ratty Red Sox shirt, Adam met Harper in his driveway, and they drove to the 8 Ball, a pool hall on the outskirts of town. The place was reliably empty on a Sunday afternoon, except for a few die-hard pool sharks and a deathly pale, spiky-haired bartender with a thick snake tattoo coiled around the length of his right arm. He waved at Harper as she came in, and Harper grinned back, giving him a sly wink.

"You *know* that guy?" Adam asked. But she'd already left his side, flitting over to the bar to order them a pitcher of beer. With a bemused shrug, he followed behind and slid into a seat at the bar next to her as she poured them both a mug of Pabst. It was crap, but it was also five dollars a pitcher—three on Sunday afternoons. The large wooden sign on the wall read CONSERVE WATER: DRINK BEER—and Adam was only too happy to oblige.

"So, you come here often?" he asked Harper, leering as if it were a pickup line.

"I get around," Harper, reminded him. Like everyone else she knew, Harper had a fake ID—not that you needed one in a place like Grace. It was one of those towns where everyone knew everyone else—which meant every bartender in town knew Harper and her friends were underage. Fortunately, it was also one of those towns where none of them cared.

"I just had no idea this was your kind of place," he admitted, raising his glass to her (once he'd managed to peel it off the mysteriously sticky tabletop).

"There's a lot you don't know about me," she pointed out, laughing. She downed her beer, then leaped up and tugged him toward one of the pool tables. "Come on, hotshot, time to show me your moves."

"I don't know . . . ," Adam hedged. Harper in competitive high gear wasn't a pleasant sight to see. (After losing a close game of Monopoly in third grade, she'd accused him of cheating, then stuffed two game pieces—the metal thimble and top hat—up his nose.)

"I'll go easy on you," she promised. "What—are you afraid of losing to a girl? Chicken?" She started clucking and flapping her arms, and soon the couple next to them— Adam assumed it was a couple, though he couldn't tell the man from the woman—turned to stare.

"Enough, woman!" he roared in mock anger, throwing his arms around her from behind in a tight bear hug. "You asked for it." He lifted her off the ground easily and carried her over to one of the pool tables. She squealed and kicked her feet in the air, but it was no use.

"I'll only let go if you promise to behave," he warned her, depositing her in front of one of the tables.

"As if I'd ever promise to do that," she giggled, and despite the fact that her arms were pinned to her sides, she began to tickle him—after years of practice, she knew exactly the right spots. Adam shivered with laughter and let go immediately, backing away. She smacked him affectionately on the butt and grabbed a pool cue.

"Enough playing around, mister. Let's get down to business."

Harper leaned over the pool table, drew the cue back, and, in a single, graceful sweep, knocked it into the cue ball, hitting it dead center. She paused, her chest grazing the soft green felt, her ass only a few inches away from Adam, who hovered behind her waiting for the shot and, she hoped, admiring the way she filled out her dark, snug jeans. The cue ball slammed into the eight ball and sent it skidding across the table into the far corner pocket, exactly as she'd planned.

Victory!

She spun to face Adam, who shook his head in rueful defeat.

"I give up, Harper," he said, throwing his arms up in surrender. "Three games in a row? You're clearly a better man than I."

"Let's not forget the two darts games in the middle," Harper pointed out. One of the things she loved about Adam was that he knew how to lose (of course, another thing she loved was that it was a skill he didn't need to use very often). "What can I say? I came, I saw, I conquered." And this was different from the rest of her life how? "You came close in that last game," she conceded, softening a bit.

"Yeah, real close," Adam said sarcastically, rolling one of his striped balls into a corner pocket. There were still four left on the table.

"What? Can I help it that I'm a natural?" Harper asked with a grin.

"Yeah, yeah, come on, champ—let me buy you a victory drink before I take you home."

He grabbed her hand and led her to the bar, and Harper took a deep breath, glad he was a step ahead and couldn't see the way her face lit up at the touch of his fingers on hers. They'd had such a long, amazing afternoon, laughing and bickering and horsing around. Not flirting—for how could you flirt with someone you'd known your whole life? Flirting required some air of mystery, the sense that you were hiding more than you were revealing, the possibility that a look, a word, a touch all meant more than you were willing to admit. With Adam, everything was transparent, every move anticipated and understood.

Not that she didn't have her secrets, of course. There was the small fact that she was hopelessly in love with him. The smaller fact that she was conspiring to send his girlfriend into the arms of another guy.

But when they were together, and things were going well, stuff like that disappeared. It was like she could stop hiding, stop strategizing, stop anticipating, and just be. Not "be herself," because who was the "real" Harper Grace after all? Who knew? Who cared? No, with Adam, she didn't have to worry about being herself—but she didn't have to be someone else, either, like she did for the losers at school. Being popular was like a 24/7 game of Let's Pretend. It didn't matter to them who she really was—all that mattered was who she needed to be. Who she *appeared* to be.

With Adam, it was different. *She* was different. She was, they were, Harper-and-Adam, a seamless organism different and somehow better than either one alone. And there were times, when she caught a look in his eye or felt the comfortable weight of his arm around her waist, that she knew he felt it too. She could read him like that. Completely.

They were, thus, way beyond flirting.

Unfortunately, the same could not be said for Chip, the scrawny bartender-cum-bouncer-cum-heavy-metal-wannabe-boy-toy grinning at her from behind the scratched-up bar. Chip was cute enough, and useful—one of the reasons she'd gotten so good at pool was that Chip could always be counted on for a few free drinks, making the 8 Ball a perfect late-night pit stop. Once, in a fit of alcoholic gratitude, she'd even agreed to a date. Big mistake. Now he couldn't stop leering at her, and unless she wanted to start paying for her beer, she couldn't afford not to flirt back. Besides, how painful could unadulterated adoration be? And if Adam happened to notice how easily she could turn a guy on? Well, so much the better.

When they reached the bar, Chip ignored Adam, who was attempting to order. Beer for Harper, soda for him—he was too conscientious to drive drunk. Such an adorably good boy. Chip eventually nodded absentmindedly in response to Adam's request, and filled a glass with beer, never taking his eyes off Harper.

"How you doin', beautiful?" he asked, grazing his fingers along hers as he handed her the glass. His eyes dipped down from her face to her cleavage, blatantly enough that even Adam noticed—she could tell by the way he stiffened next to her. She loved it. He was priming himself to defend her honor. Perfect.

"Better, now," Harper replied, taking a demure sip and smiling up at Chip through lowered eyes.

"You're looking better than ever, I'll tell you that much."

Harper flicked her hair away from her face and giggled. "I bet you say that to all the girls."

"Can I get that soda now?" Adam cut in.

Chip studiously ignored him. "So, when you gonna let me take you out again, gorgeous?"

"Sooner than you think," Harper said playfully, noting the horrified look Adam shot her. *When Prada goes on sale at Walmart* would have been a more accurate response— Harper shuddered, remembering the hot blast of Chip's garlicky breath on her neck—but that was no reason to spoil all the fun.

"Seriously, my soda?" Adam growled.

"Dude, tell your *friend* here to chill out," Chip complained. "What are you doing with him, anyway? Sweet piece of ass like you shouldn't be wasting your time with Joe Quarterback."

Adam jumped off his stool and took a menacing step toward the bar, where he loomed over the twerpy Chip, who, even in his pseudo-hip platform sneakers still looked about as tall as his name implied. "What did you call her?" Adam asked dangerously.

Chip seemed too stoned—or too stupid—to notice the tone. Harper smiled and sat back, ready to watch the show.

"What, you telling me you don't want to hit that?" Chip asked, gesturing toward Harper. "I know I did—and let me tell you, once isn't enough."

Adam opened his mouth and shut it again, whirling on Harper.

"Are you telling me that you and, and this—" He turned back to Chip, groping for the right words. Harper could have supplied a few choice ones, all accurate—pip-squeak, mouthbreather, pencil dick—but this was Adam's show.

"Look, asshole, say something like that about her again, and I'll—"

"Like what?" Chip sneered up at him. "Like what a luscious body she has? How good she looks in those jeans? Or how good she looks *out* of them?"

"That's it. We're getting out of here." Adam pulled

Harper off the stool with one hand and grabbed his wallet with the other. He tore out a five-dollar bill and threw it down on the bar.

Chip slid it back toward him roughly.

"Oh no, my treat."

"Take it," Adam growled, pushing it back toward him.

"I *said*, it's on me."

"You know what? Have it your way." Adam grabbed the bill back and lifted Harper's half-full glass of beer in a mock toast. "It's on you." And he dumped the beer on Chip's head, grabbing Harper and pulling her out of the bar before the dim-witted loser's reflexes had time to kick him into motion.

"What the hell did you just do in there, Ad?" Harper asked, gasping with laughter, once they were safely out in the parking lot. "I can never show my face in there again!"

"He was asking for it," Adam said, stone-faced. "And you!" He shook his head. "I know you've dated some losers in your time, but this guy?"

"Well, Chip's an idiot," Harper admitted, "but he's got a few other things going for him."

"Stop." Adam lightly covered her mouth with his hand. "Please, I don't want to hear it."

She batted her eyelashes up at him. "What? Jealous?"

"Oh, please," he scoffed. "Just get in the car."

She laughed, and did as he said. She didn't have to

press the point—because she knew she was right.

He'd fought for her honor.

He'd been jealous, jealous of the idea of her with another guy.

Which meant that somewhere in that thick and oblivious head of his was buried the knowledge that she really belonged to him. That somewhere beneath all those layers of puppy dog love for Beth and all that "just friends" bullshit he reserved for Harper, he wanted something more.

He wanted her.

She knew it.

He just needed a little push in the right direction. And he was about to get it.

chapter four

KAIA SKIPPED LUNCH ON MONDAY. IT WAS NO BIG loss. After a month in this hick-filled hellhole, she'd learned that the less Grace-produced food ingested, the better. Besides, Kaia had other things on her mind. One in particular.

He wasn't in his classroom, but she found him a few minutes later in the so-called "faculty lounge," really a dark, oversize closet with a few threadbare couches and a malfunctioning coffee machine.

Students weren't allowed in the room—it was to be a sanctuary for the underpaid burnouts whose snoozing students failed to see the applicability of algebra to a future career in tractor-pulling, or the ability of Shakespeare to improve their application to the beauty academy. Two years ago the teachers had gone on strike, demanding shorter hours, fewer students per class, more pay; they'd received a faculty lounge.

Kaia didn't know any of that, of course, but if she had, she wouldn't have cared.

She did know she wasn't supposed to go inside. The boldfaced NO STUDENTS sign on the door was a good tip-off. The sharp glare Mrs. Martin shot her as she scuttled out of the lounge was a better one. Teachers-only territory. No trespassing.

Kaia didn't care about that, either. She pushed through the door into the dark space, and there he was, Jack Powell—adorable, and alone.

At first he didn't see her. He was sprawled on one of the couches, reading by the dim light of a halogen lamp—the overhead lighting was about as much use as a half-dead flashlight when it came to lighting up the room, much less the page. He'd kicked his legs up on the makeshift coffee table and was poring over a thick hardcover, his face scrunched up in thought. He was completely absorbed, and failed to notice when the door swung open. It was left to Kaia to break his concentration.

"Greetings and salutations, Mr. Powell," she said in a low voice.

He looked up with an expression of absentminded bemusement; it disappeared as soon as he paired the voice with her face. He snapped the book shut in anger and quickly stood, backing away from her.

"Did I not make myself clear the last time we spoke, Ms. Sellers? Get out of here."

"Don't trust yourself alone with me?" she taunted him. "Worried about what you might do?"

"I'm not the one who's worried—thanks to you, I've got half the school thinking I want to play Humbert Humbert to your Lolita. But I'm sure you know that already, since it's exactly what you wanted."

"All I ever wanted was you, Mr. Powell," she said sweetly. "Didn't *I* make myself clear?"

"Crystal. Now, did anyone see you come in here?"

"Only Mrs. Martin," she admitted.

"Well, that's just great." He shook his head and raised his eyes to the ceiling in exasperation. "She'll have half the town ready to lynch me if she figures out we were in here together. You have to get out of here. Now."

"You're sounding a little desperate there, Mr. Powell—it's not very becoming." That was a lie, actually. The sharp edge of desperation in his voice made the whole hard-to-get act even sexier.

He paused and gave her a piercing look. It was the same intent gaze he'd given her in their very first encounter, just before explaining that even if she hadn't been "trouble dressed up in a miniskirt," he made it a policy not to get involved with students. That had been before she caught him trying to get "involved" with Beth, of course—it turned out the only students he stayed away from were the ones he saw as potential threats. She was too hot to handle, apparently—which was infuriating. And flattering.

"Kaia, you seem like a bright girl," he finally said. "Bright enough to know that you can make life here rather uncomfortable for me."

"I'm glad you noticed."

"So I'll assume you're bright enough to understand that *I* can make life rather uncomfortable for *you*," he pointed out. "I could, for one, fail you."

"I could say it was sexual harassment," she countered. "Retribution."

"I could say it was your word against mine."

"I could say that's attacking the victim."

"And I could say the same—so it would seem we're at an impasse."

"Why, Mr. Powell," she asked flirtatiously, "are you suggesting a truce?"

He slumped back down on the couch and began massaging his temples. "Kaia, I'm not the one who declared a war," he reminded her. "I'm suggesting you drop this whole thing, drop my class if you can, do whatever it takes for you to walk out this door and out of my life forever."

"You'd miss me," she chirped.

"I doubt it."

"What would you do for fun without me?"

"I suspect I'd find something else," he said wearily. "Something that didn't cause blinding headaches and nausea."

Any more of this sweet talk and she was going to get a cavity.

"Okay, I'll go," she allowed. "For now. But I should point out that when you say we're at an impasse, you're forgetting two things."

"Enlighten me."

"One." She ticked it off on one of her fingers. "You're right that it would be your word against mine, and maybe my word's not worth too much around here. But *Beth's* is. And something tells me she might have some interesting things to say on the subject."

He stood up again—but suddenly seemed slightly unsteady on his feet. "Is this your ham-handed way of threatening to blackmail me, Kaia?" It sounded tough, but she knew she'd shaken him. Good. Now they both understood that she had the upper hand.

"No—let's call it a demonstration of goodwill," she offered. "Because for the moment, I'm planning to keep my mouth shut. You're the only person who knows what I saw. And for the moment, I'm willing to keep it that way."

"And why, pray tell, is that?"

For one thing, she'd decided that this was the kind of information that could keep. Why use it now when she could get what she needed out of him first? She'd save this for when it counted. But an honest answer wouldn't do much to help her cause.

"Well, that would be point number two," she told him, ticking off a second finger. "I like you, Jack Powell. I think you've got a lot of . . . possibilities. So I'm going to keep quiet about Beth. I'm going to walk out of here and show you that I can be as discreet as any of the adoring goody-goody students I'm sure you've wooed into bed in the past—but I'm not giving up. I have a lot of patience when it comes to getting what I want."

"And what about what I want?" he asked drily.

"You don't need patience," she pointed out. "I'm right here. You just need to come and get me."

They'd needed somewhere out of the way, somewhere no one they knew would ever be or would ever think to look for them. The school library was an obvious choice. Huddled over a small table in the back (sandwiched in the stacks between self-help and pet grooming), Harper and Kane quickly got down to business.

"It's a good start, Grace, but we need to kick it into higher gear. Slow and steady's not going to win us the race on this one," Kane whispered.

Harper craned her neck around, once again making sure that no one she knew could overhear them. Her crowd wasn't much for the musty book zone, it was true—but a certain brainy Barbie clone had been known to stop by.

"I don't know, Kane—that relationship has a definite expiration date. And with Beth fawning all over you for the next two weeks, maybe . . ."

"Adam will have enough space to discover you're the best thing ever to happen to him?" Kane finished for her.

Harper blushed. That was, in fact, exactly what she'd been thinking. "Well, if you want to put it that way."

"Wake up, Harper," Kane said sharply, snapping his fingers in front of her face. "These two could go on like this indefinitely. They're both too noble to cut their losses. I know Adam, and he's going to stay in this to the bitter end, and Beth—"

"Couldn't stand on her own two feet if you nailed them to the floor and shoved a pole up her—"

"Hey, watch how you talk about my woman."

"*Your* woman?" She arched an impeccably plucked eyebrow. "Someone's getting a little ahead of himself."

"Exactly my point—I don't like waiting, and I didn't think you did either. Isn't that why we're in this thing?"

"Okay," she conceded. "So we've got the setup, Adam's already jealous—"

"And soon it will start to fester—," Kane added.

"Especially if we help it along a bit," Harper concluded. So not a problem. If there was one thing she could handle, it was feeding the flames of jealousy—hadn't she proved that well enough over the weekend? "But we need something else, something more dramatic, with a little flair."

"I couldn't agree more. But what?" Kane asked. They were right back to where they'd started. "That's the million-dollar question. And it has to be done right, with finesse—we don't want this to backfire."

"Are you thinking of something specific?"

"I'm just trying to ensure that we *both* get what we want," Kane explained, winking, "since, never let it be said I think only of myself . . ."

Harper raised both eyebrows this time.

"Okay, usually I do," he admitted. "But in this case, we're in it together—one for all, all for one, et cetera."

"Whatever, I'll believe it when I see it. I've known you for too long."

"Oh, you wound me!" he exclaimed. Mrs. Martin, the ancient and evil-eyed librarian, walked by and gave them a nasty look. The shut-up-or-get-out kind of look. Harper lowered her eyes and tried to muster a chaste and innocent smile. But Mrs. Martin, immune to the act, just scuttled on by.

"I'm supposed to trust you?" Harper asked, lowering her voice to a whisper. "When you're trying to steal your best friend's girlfriend?"

All traces of a smirk vanished from Kane's face, and he glared at her with hooded eyes.

"First of all, Grace, I don't believe in trust—which is why I don't believe in best friends. It's easier that way. And second of all, as for stealing his girlfriend . . ."

Harper leaned forward eagerly. She'd been wondering how Kane could justify his scheming, especially when he seemed to have no particular motivation for choosing Beth, of all the girls he could have pursued.

". . . let's just say—karma's a bitch."

"Care to elaborate?" Harper asked.

"No."

They stared at each other in silence for a moment, each daring the other to speak. Harper broke first.

"Fine—just get back to what you were saying," Harper urged him. "What kind of backfiring are you afraid of?"

"Well, we could pin something on Adam, like, say, he slept with someone else—believable enough, I guess," Kane said, his smirk returning. "Deep down, all guys are pigs."

Harper opened her mouth—then closed it again. She

couldn't betray Adam's confidence. At least not until she heard all of what Kane had to say.

"That could work," she mused.

He shook his head slowly but surely. "Not so much—think about it. Beth breaks up with Adam in a fit of anger, and Adam spends the rest of his life trying to win her back. And I don't think either of us wants to deal with that."

"Agreed," Harper said, her heart sinking. He was right—and she had nothing. Nothing that wouldn't turn Harper and Adam's potential relationship into collateral damage. "In fact, I think Adam needs to be the one to break it off," she concluded in spite of herself. "He feels betrayed, she feels unjustly wronged, they both want nothing to do with each other and go running into our arms."

"Sounds like the perfect plan. Except . . ." Kane sighed in exasperation. "We still need to figure out how to get from point A to point B."

"We'll figure it out," she comforted him. "In the meantime we continue to drive Adam out of his mind with jealousy?"

"You got it. And, hey, never underestimate the power of the Kane Geary charisma. For all I know, a couple more of these study 'dates' and she'll be begging *me* to hit the bedroom."

Harper balled up a piece of paper and tossed it at his big, fat head. "Leaving Adam ready and waiting for some sympathetic TLC from his beautiful next door neighbor?" she suggested sarcastically. "Unlikely."

"Hey, you never know—it could happen."

It's not like Miranda had no one to eat lunch with. No, she reassured herself, she had plenty of friends. Just because Harper had randomly decided to skip out on lunch didn't mean Miranda was adrift on some sea of loserdom. There were plenty of people she *could* sit with, plenty who would covet her presence at their table if only because the reflected beams of Harper's glory made Miranda glow with the light of borrowed popularity. But the prospect of pushing "food" around on her tray while listening to the stupid simpering of these so-called friends—without Harper across the table to exchange timely eye rolls with—was just too much for her to handle this afternoon. So instead, Miranda opted for a snack-machine lunch (granola bar and mini canister of Pringles) at the newspaper office, which had a door that locked and a couch that creaked noisily but had yet to collapse.

But first, a pit stop at the girls' bathroom. She stood in front of the mirror, touching up her makeup—and making a mental note that a makeup makeover would definitely have to be the next stop on her road to self-improvement. The peach frosted lip gloss and smoky gray eye shadow she'd picked out in tenth grade just wouldn't do. Her mother, though usually having more than enough to say on the subject of Miranda's appearance—and how to improve it—knew nothing about makeup herself. She'd been able to contribute very little to Miranda's education on the subject beyond such helpful pointers as "That blush makes you look like a whore."

The bathroom was surprisingly uncrowded for this time of day. A couple stoners lurked in the back corner, from the sound of it competing over who had more Phish bootlegs. A cluster of super-skinny bottle blondes—Miranda didn't recognize them, so figured they must be freshmen—hogged most of the mirror area, reapplying their hairspray and shimmery lipstick. From the short skirts to the perfect manicures to the cocky tilt of their heads, Miranda could tell they were jockeying for a place in the line of succession, ready to fill the power vacuum once Harper had graduated. *Cosmo* clones, Miranda thought disdainfully. They could look the part all they wanted, but they'd never have that spark, that something special Harper had that made people want to follow her to the ends of the earth (or at least to the end of good judgment). Harper was a leader. These girls— it was obvious—were sheep.

And yet . . .

And yet, she thought, looking from one perfectly sculpted and outfitted body to the next, wasn't this exactly the look she was craving?

Long, silky smooth hair that could bounce and blow in the wind—Miranda's hair was brittle, thin, and impossibly flat. Flawless complexions—Miranda had zits and freckles. Long, slim, tanned legs—Miranda's thunder thighs were albino pale.

The girls bustled out of the bathroom, chattering about who had hooked up that weekend and who was feeling fat. Big surprise—unanimous responses to both.

Miranda sighed and considered trying to score some pot off the stoners in the corner, anything to calm the rising tide of anxiety she suddenly felt at the daunting prospect of finding a way to turn herself into *that*. Not that she wanted to be vapid, of course. But beautiful? Stylish? *Skinny?* The kind of girl who screams "high maintenance" but which, it seemed, was all any worthwhile guy wanted?

Yes, please.

Haven High was a small school. Claustrophobically small, it sometimes seemed to Adam. But he'd done a decent job so far of avoiding Kaia. He hadn't spoken to her, in fact, since their last encounter. He still shuddered at the thought of it—the intense, mind-blowing sex in an abandoned motel, followed almost immediately by an utterly humiliating blow-off. What a loser he'd been. He saw that now. It was too late, of course—he'd done it, this huge, horrible thing that weighed on him, crushed him, and yet still flickered through his fantasies, taunting him with what he couldn't have yet still, in some deep part of him, wanted.

Beth had wondered why he suddenly stopped following Kaia around and inviting her out with the group, but she had no fond feelings for Kaia herself, so hadn't wondered very long or very loudly. And maybe she didn't want to know.

Still, it was a small school, and he'd been bound to bump into Kaia eventually. He just hadn't counted on a literal collision.

"Oh, sorry!" he exclaimed, after spinning away from his locker and slamming into someone rushing past him down the hall. Then—"Oh, it's you." Suddenly, the split-second collision became, in his mind, an embrace, as if he could still feel the ghostly touch of his body pressing against hers, their hands and chests and hips awkwardly rubbing against each other, her silky hair whipping across his face.

"And it's you, too," she pointed out. "Where've you been, stranger?"

"Far away from you, which I thought was how you wanted it." Her words to him at their last meeting echoed through his head. And the mocking laughter.

"Oh, Adam, I hope I didn't hurt your feelings." She placed a soft hand on his chest—he pushed it away. "I don't know what I'd do if I thought you hated me!"

"Give it up, Kaia," he said harshly. "I'm not falling for your crap again. Find someone new to screw over."

Kaia rolled her eyes. "Oh, right," she scoffed. "You're such the wounded victim, used and abused, right? You didn't seem to mind the screwing part so much."

"Shut up," he hissed, suddenly aware of the students swarming around them. Watching. Listening? "I thought we agreed you weren't going to tell anyone about that."

"Oh, calm down. My lips are sealed. Why would I do anything to get between you and your precious Beth?"

"I appreciate that, Kaia." He tried to ignore the disdainful edge to her voice. Kaia, he'd decided, was like a venomous snake—you just had to be very careful, stay very still, and wait her out until she got bored and went away.

"Of course," she added, smirking, "maybe I'm not the one you need to worry about."

"What's that supposed to mean?" he asked, against his better judgment.

"I saw your blushing rose getting cozy in the coffee shop with your supposed best friend the other day. Just thought you'd want to know."

"Old news," he said, affecting nonchalance. Ignoring the taste of bile. "She's tutoring him for the SATs. I know all about it. And it's completely innocent." And this he believed wholeheartedly, he told himself. He had to, right?

"So I heard. Such a sweet girl, to commit her time to helping him, when she's oh so busy. But totally innocent, of course," she assured him, voice dripping with false sincerity. "I'm sure you're right. Just another platonic extracurricular, like any other: yearbook, newspaper, party planning . . ."

She narrowed her gaze suggestively and Adam felt the tips of his ears turn red. It was, after all, planning a party that had brought Adam and Kaia together in the first place. A few weeks' worth of purely platonic meetings culminating in one night of illicit but extraordinary passion.

"I'm sure you have nothing to worry about, though," she said after a moment of silence. "I mean, you're in love, right? And that's what love is all about—trust."

Trust. Right.

If Beth's love for him proved as trustworthy as his love for her, they were in for some serious problems.

Job well done, Kaia congratulated herself. Adam had, of course, walked away from her in disgust, but she could see the beginnings of doubt in the nervous twist of his lip and the tiny rivulets of sweat that traced a path down the muscles of his neck. She'd gotten under his skin—again.

Kaia laughed to herself. It probably wasn't very nice of her to pick on Adam again. After all, he was such an easy mark, and clearly still smarting from their last encounter.

On the other hand, she considered, she'd given him a true gift—one that he'd certainly enjoyed enough at the time, no matter how much he may now claim she'd ruined his life. Didn't she deserve to have some fun too? And if it was fun at Beth Manning's expense, even better. Much as she tried, she couldn't forget the fact that Mr. Powell had chosen that simpering softie over her. Yes, it was clearly because he thought Kaia spelled trouble, while Beth would be easy prey. Powell was a predator; it was why she liked him so much. But still, there it was—he'd rejected her in favor of Beth, and while that was a lapse in judgment she was willing to forgive, Beth still needed to pay.

This time, she'd decided, there was no reason to go it alone. Not when such a good game was already afoot.

So she headed to the library. She'd spotted Harper heading in that direction at the beginning of lunch period, and she had a sneaking suspicion she'd find her huddled over a desk with Kane, hatching some pathetic plan. It was time to lend these small-town tricksters the wisdom of her experience.

Why?

Why the hell not?

She found them just as she'd imagined, heads together, arms waving animatedly, whispers flying. She crept up slowly behind Harper, finger to her lips, trusting Kane to keep his poker face, which he did, right up to the moment that Kaia tapped Harper on the shoulder and smiled angelically into her face, which reflected, in quick succession, surprise, guilt, and disgust. Harper settled on the latter, but Kaia kept up her icy smile.

"What do you want?" Harper hissed. "We're busy here."

"I don't mind if the lovely Kaia joins us," Kane said generously.

"Shut up, Kane." Harper glared at him, then turned back to Kaia. "Why are you still here?"

"What, is this where you tell me, 'This is an A, B conversation, and I should C my way out of it?'" Kaia sneered.

"I was leaning more toward, 'This is an X, Z conversation, so Y don't you just go away," Harper corrected her. "Or at least *I would* have been if this were 1998 and we were ten years old. What do you think this is, VH1's *Lamest Slang of the '90s?*"

"Well, your outfit does say 'retro gone wrong,'" Kaia pointed out, "but I guess you're not out of time, just out of taste. I can live with that."

"I'm supposed to take fashion tips from someone who makes Kim Kardashian look classy?" Harper scoffed.

Kane, whose eyes had been bouncing back and forth between the two as if he were following a heated Ping-Pong match, began to softly applaud. "Bring it on, ladies. When do we take out the mud wrestling pit?"

"Shut up, Kane," they snapped in unison.

He chuckled softly. "Okay, okay, I know when I'm not wanted." He checked his watch and stood up, collecting his books. "Besides," he gave Harper a meaningful look, "I've got to go meet someone. We're setting up a study 'date' for later. See ya."

Harper shot him a vicious, how-dare-you-leave-me-here-alone-with-*her* look, but he just grinned and disappeared.

"Such a studious guy all of a sudden," Kaia commented.

"Yeah, well, you know Kane, needs to win at all costs," Harper said uncomfortably. "Even if it means some hard work."

"It's going to be pretty damn hard to win at the rate you two are going," Kaia pointed out.

"What's that supposed to mean?"

Kaia laughed to herself. It would have been cute if it weren't so pathetic, this little show of ignorance and innocence. Harper was going to have to work on the poker face a bit if this whole thing was going to work.

"I think you know," Kaia said simply.

Harper sighed. "Kaia, it's a little early in the week for mind games, don't you think?"

"Look I didn't come here to fight, or play games," Kaia promised her, wishing they could just cut through the bullshit and skip to the part where they got something done. But, as she well knew, that's not how these things worked. And the bullshit was, in the end, half the fun. "At least, not with you."

"Then what?" Harper asked wearily.

"I know what you're up to," Kaia said, relishing the involuntary shudder that ran through Harper's body. "And I want to help."

"You know what we're up to? Are you talking in code now? What is this, a James Bond movie? What would we be 'up to'?"

"Do you really want me to spell it out for you? Adam, Beth, Operation Screw Over Your Supposed Best Friend—or, in your case, just screw him?"

Harper's face turned pale. "I don't know what you're talking about," she claimed in a strangled voice.

"Yeah, yeah, whatever you say. You're totally innocent, you're appalled I would even suggest it. Whatever." Kaia checked her watch. This was getting old. "Here's my point. I want to help—you two are playing out of your league, and I think you need some coaching from a pro. That's me."

"Just out of curiosity," and it was clear that Harper had plenty, "let's say Kane and I did have some unholy alliance—why would *you* want to help? And why would we trust you?"

"I'm helping because I'm bored, and because I hate to see a good opportunity go to waste. As for why you should trust me?" Kaia paused. It was a good question. One that deserved a reasonably honest answer. "You shouldn't. But you're going to anyway because you've got almost everything you need—will, motive, lack of scruples—but you're missing one key thing, and that's what I can supply."

"And what's that?" Harper asked skeptically.

"A plan."

chapter five

IT WAS HARPER'S POLICY NEVER TO HAVE TO DEPEND on someone. Especially not because she was desperate.

She was Harper Grace.

She didn't do desperate.

At least, not usually. Under normal circumstances she plowed through the world and everyone else got out of the way. Unless you were slow. Then you just got run over. She certainly didn't need anyone's help to do it. Of course, under normal circumstances she didn't usually betray one of her best friends for the purposes of seducing the other, but these circumstances were anything but normal, and with the fate of her love life hanging in the balance, speed was of the essence. Which meant that Harper, lacking scruples and strategy in equal amount, was desperate.

And desperate times called for desperate measures . . . right?

So when Kaia stood up from the cramped library table with an ultimatum: "Meet me after school and listen to what I have to say, or forget the whole thing," Harper had nodded. Finally, and fatefully, she had decided to give Kaia a chance.

But she wasn't about to do it anywhere near the school, where someone could see them together. Kaia's Eurotrash wardrobe, frozen beauty, and outlandish public liplock with Haven High's most eligible bachelor had won her a fair amount of notoriety, but it wasn't the kind that translated into social acceptance. She had a few followers, of course, but she was too high and mighty to inspire much loyalty, and most of the initial curiosity seekers had drifted away as Harper slowly but thoroughly put out word that the new girl was not to be touched. Someone like Kaia could have easily toppled Harper's carefully constructed high school hierarchy—so Harper did what she had to do to neutralize the threat.

When Harper spoke, people listened. And if they knew what was good for them, they obeyed.

She wasn't about to waste all that hard work by meeting with Kaia in a public place and letting the world think they were suddenly bosom buddies. Harper saw her friendship as a powerful gift, and Christmas for Kaia wasn't coming anytime soon.

So she needed a place where no one—*no one*—would recognize her, where no one she knew would ever deign to set foot. Hence: the Cactus Cantina. A greasy Tex-Mex bar with Cheez Whiz nachos and double-shot margaritas, the Cactus was good for inducing a heart attack or drinking yourself into oblivion, but little else.

Harper was already seated (albeit gingerly—she had no interest in letting any part of her body touch the mysterious sticky patches that dotted the booth) when Kaia arrived. So she got a good look at the cover girl's face when she walked in the door. It wasn't pretty. Or, rather—this being Kaia—it was spectacularly pretty. But it was prettiness scrunched up into a grimace of horror and reticence, her whole body telegraphing a single message: Dear God, don't make me go in there. Please.

She stood in the door for a moment, half in, half out, and a shaft of light sliced into the darkness, sending up a groan of discomfort from the bowels of the bar.

"Yer in or yer out, senorita," the bartender with the fake Zapata mustache called to Kaia. She flinched at the scraping sound of his voice. "Make up your mind, *por favor!*"

Harper waited and watched. It was the first test of

Kaia's commitment to the cause—and, to her credit, she passed.

"Was *this* really necessary?" she asked Harper, sitting down across from her.

"What?" Harper tried her best to look comfortable, though not *too* comfortable, as if this world were foreign but unintimidating—and especially as if she weren't planning to take a shower the moment she got out of there to wash the stench out of her hair. The goal had been to throw Kaia off balance, to make sure she was out of her element—a plan which, by all appearances, had worked like a charm. Harper would just have to deal, and keep her own squirming and scowling to a minimum.

"This *place*," Kaia said, waving her arms in elaboration, as if to encompass the cardboard lizards and cacti papering the walls, the tinny salsa soundtrack, and the seedy denizens all in one sweep. "Or is this just your thing?"

Harper shrugged, affecting unconcern. "You're the one who thinks Kane and I have this dirty little plan," she pointed out. "I would think you'd understand the need to be a little discreet."

"Whatever." Kaia grabbed a napkin and gingerly flicked away the mysteriously colored crumbs littering her side of the table. "I take it we're getting right down to business?"

"I'm done with small talk if you are."

"Good." She leaned forward, and Harper was once again taken by her perfect form and poise, even in a place like this. And that rust-colored asymmetrical shirt? It was unmistakably a Betsey Johnson original. Harper closed her eyes for a moment and, with a sharp pang of envy, briefly considered what it would be like to have Kaia's life—but she couldn't even begin to imagine.

"Here's how I see it," Kaia continued. "You want Adam. Kane—for whatever reason—wants Beth. You teamed up to split them up, and you're ready and waiting for them to fall, heartbroken and sobbing, into your arms. How am I doing so far?"

Harper was disgusted with herself. Some secret plan. What a joke. And it sounded even more pathetic coming out of Kaia's mouth. But she played it off. She had to.

"So far you haven't told me anything I don't know," she complained.

"I'll take that to mean, 'Why, yes, Kaia, that's the situation exactly. Please enlighten me as to how to make my dreams come true.'"

"I'm listening."

"So you've got Beth tutoring Kane—a nice move, incidentally, but Adam's too much of a wuss to break up with her just because he's jealous. He'd never trust his own instincts on that one—and princess Beth isn't going to fall on Kane unless you push her."

"Again, waiting for the newsflash," Harper drawled, inwardly bristling at the way Kaia casually spoke of Adam's flaws and failings, as if she knew him so well.

"Well, for one thing, what you may not know is that Adam has some secrets of his own that Beth might not be too happy to hear." A secretive smile crept across Kaia's face. Harper knew exactly what she was referring to, but any pleasure she might have drawn from taking Kaia down a peg was hollow. She'd caught a glimpse of Kaia-and-Adam, act one, and had yet to wash the painful images out of her mind. She didn't like to be reminded of act two, when they'd adjourned to a bedroom; Harper had, mercifully, missed the fireworks. But she could imagine. And did—often.

"Yeah, yeah, he slept with you," Harper said, the words slicing into her. "Big deal. Anyway, I can't use it."

Kaia's eyes widened, and Harper smiled, knowing that at least she'd taken the wind out of the other girl's sails, as hoped. But Kaia wasn't thrown off for long.

"So he told you? Interesting—and not too smart."

"Well, that's Adam, honest to a fault. Of course, he used to be loyal to a fault, too," Harper said, glaring, "before you got through with him."

"Do you want to fight about my popping your boy's cherry, or do you want to get him for yourself?"

"What's the difference?" Harper asked irritably. "I

told you, I can't use it. If Beth breaks up with him over this, he'll spend the rest of the year feeling guilty and chasing after her. That does me no good at all. And, not that I really care, but I imagine that Beth wouldn't be bouncing back too quickly either—I see her as the 'I can never trust a man again' type. After something like that, I don't think Kane would exactly be her type."

"Good thing I have a backup plan, then," Kaia said triumphantly. "One that turns Beth into the villain. Adam will be looking for a 'true' friend to turn to, and you'll be right there to pick up the pieces."

"Sounds perfect. Only one problem—Beth would never cheat on Adam. She doesn't have it in her."

"Oh, really?" Kaia smiled, and it seemed she was about to say something, but she stopped herself, paused for a moment, and then continued. "Well, I suppose you're right. And *we* know that, and *Beth* knows that, but there's no reason Adam has to. And all that really matters is what *he* believes."

"He accuses her—unjustly—she gets mad, we get mutual destruction." Harper nodded eagerly. "I like it. But how—"

She cut herself off at the sight of two drunken hulks looming over their table, one uglier than the other. (Although it was admittedly difficult to judge: Were buck teeth uglier than gold teeth? Was the jagged scar above the eyebrow uglier than an irregularly shaped red blotch covering the chin? Was mountain-man hair uglier than no hair?)

Baldy leered down at the two girls, his stained T-shirt exuding the stench of cheap beer. "You ladies are at our table," he slurred.

"'S *our* table," Mountain Man agreed. "Everyone knows that."

Baldy tried to squeeze into the booth with Harper, but with a yelp of anger and a sharp jab, she successfully pushed him away. He stumbled backward, but Mountain Man broke his fall.

"Wasn't nice," Mountain Man warned them. "You're sitting at *our* table, you must belong to us too. Move over."

Kaia wrinkled her nose and shot Harper a look of disbelief. "Why are these losers talking to us?" she asked.

Harper cringed at her choice of words—she'd spent enough time around Grace's roughnecks to know that the best tactic was to shut up and get out of the way. But she wasn't about to be bested by Kaia's bravado. So she mustered some of her own.

"I don't know—they must be as stupid as they are ugly," she said, forcing a laugh. It felt good.

"Who you calling stupid?" Baldy asked menacingly.

"You sure ain't too ugly yourself, babe," Mountain

Man leered, passing his greasy hand through Harper's hair. *That* was enough. She jumped up from the table—and suddenly realized she was taller than both of them.

"Listen, buddy, get the hell out of my face," she snapped.

"Who's gonna make me? You? Or your hot little friend?"

As Harper searched for the words that would end this fiasco before it went any further, a scruffy guy about her age came wandering over.

"We got a problem here?" he asked, getting in Mountain Man's face. "She asked you to leave her alone."

"Who asked you, shithead?" Baldy growled, stepping up behind their knight in scruffy armor.

It was over in an instant.

Scruff Boy punched Mountain Man in the gut and, before Baldy had a chance to react, gave *him* a shove hard enough to knock both men to the ground. As the two losers lumbered up to their feet and began advancing on him, they got a nasty surprise—a tap on the shoulder from the Cactus bouncer, a WWE reject who looked like he bench-pressed losers like them for a warm-up. And, apparently, a friend of Scruff Boy's.

Five minutes later the bouncer was back at the entrance, having barely broken a sweat, Mountain Man and Baldy were stumbling through the parking lot with a few fresh scars to show off to the ladies, and Scruff Boy? He was still standing there.

Harper looked him up and down—medium height, medium build, wildly curly black hair, and dark, catlike eyes. Kind of hot, really, beneath that stubble and the torn Clash T-shirt. She knew who he was, of course— she knew every guy in town. Especially the hot ones. He went to their school, barely (this was his second senior year in a row), played in a band, ran with a crowd that drank too much and smoked even more. Pretty much a total waste of space. But he had, after all, cleaned up their mess. They should probably be polite—

"Why are *you* still here?" Kaia asked him, curling her lip in disdain.

Or not.

"You two okay?" he asked, in a slow, zoned-out voice. "I'm Reed." He stuck out his hand for Kaia to shake—she left him hanging.

"We're fine," Harper jumped in, again not to be out-done. "So you can just run off back to . . . whatever it is people like you do."

He stood frozen in place, looking at them both with a mixture of disgust and disbelief.

"What are you waiting for?" Kaia finally asked. "A medal?"

"Actually, a thank-you," he informed her. "My mistake."

"You're right. It was," Kaia said, and turned back to Harper. "What was I saying?"

Harper watched the boy out of the corner of her eye. He stood there for another moment, as if waiting for them to let him in on the joke. Then reality sank in. He shook his head and trekked back across the bar to a booth crowded with deadbeat delinquents. They pounded him on the back and slammed him with high fives—impressed by the fight, she supposed. Good thing they hadn't paid attention to the aftermath. Reed Sawyer could take on two drunken thugs with ease, but apparently in Harper and Kaia, he'd met his match.

"You were about to blow my mind with your oh-so-perfect plan," Harper prodded Kaia, putting the whole sordid incident out of her mind.

Kaia laid it out for her, step by step, and when she was done, Harper leaned back and let loose a low whistle of admiration. It was breathtakingly perfect—beautiful, and a little complex, but if everything went smoothly, it would deliver the goods. She could already imagine herself in Adam's arms.

And if Kaia really came through, and she owed all her happiness to her worst enemy? Well, if it got her Adam, it was a debt she'd be willing to spend the rest of her life repaying. And knowing Kaia, that might be exactly how long it would take.

ℒ ℒ ℒ

The Wizard of Oz was playing at the Starview. It played there every year in October, and every year, Miranda and Harper went to the last showing and split a large popcorn and an overpriced box of Mike and Ikes. It was tradition, and had been ever since eighth grade, when they'd both desperately wanted to go but had been too embarrassed to admit it to each other. Finally, on the day the movie was set to close, they'd each secretly snuck off to the theater— only to run into each other in the lobby, both buying boxes of Mike and Ikes.

By now it was a ritual set in stone, down to the whispered comments they tossed back and forth during the show and the postmovie pizza and beer at Guido's. (The beer had been a tenth-grade addition, but in some cases, it was worth making a change.) It was tradition—fixed, beloved, and unbreakable. At least, until now.

Now Miranda stood at Harper's locker, waiting in vain for her friend to show, watching the minutes slip past and the other students fade from the hall, until only she stood there, patient and alone.

The movie started at five. By four, Miranda was done waiting. She'd already waited an embarrassing half hour too long.

And she wasn't about to go to the movie herself, not alone, not as if the past five years had never happened and she was still a gawky eighth grader too worried about her status to admit a geeky love for Munchkins.

No, apparently Harper had better things to do—probably some guy had sworn his everlasting love and she'd taken him out for a quick spin—"quick" being the operative word, since use 'em or lose 'em got tedious if you hesitated too long before moving from the former to the latter. Or so Harper always said.

Not that Miranda hadn't elimidated her share of lovestruck losers—it was just that the tan, dark, and handsome set didn't usually flock in her direction. At five feet one, maybe she was just too close to the ground for them to see her.

She was tired of being invisible and—apparently—forgettable. Why should Harper have all the fun? Miranda found her car, one of the last in the largely empty lot, and took off toward the strip mall on the edge of town.

Her new and improved look had waited long enough, and outfit number one was there, ready and waiting for her.

Was it too risqué? Did it make her boobs look big? Did the skirt make her ass look huge? Maybe. *So what?* she fumed silently, trying to drown out Harper's scoffing voice in her mind. At least it makes a statement. At least people will remember I'm there.

✒   ✒   ✒

Never return to the scene of the crime. If it worked for *Law & Order*, it worked for Beth, so she'd spent the last weeks studiously avoiding the newspaper office as best she could. Every time she set foot inside, even with other people around (and she made sure there were *always* other people around), she could feel the weight of memory pressing down on her. The small space, a refurbished supply closet that she'd petitioned the school to allocate to the newspaper, had felt so cozy, so warm and familiar—a place she'd fought for and won. It had been a home. Now it was just a dank and claustrophobic cave—every time the door closed, her heart sped up, her throat constricted. She felt trapped by those walls, just like she felt in French class every time Mr. Powell's eyes alighted on her. Sometimes their gaze locked before she could look away, and she felt his eyes boring into her, the way his tongue had when his arms were wrapped around her, pushing himself against her and—

No matter what she may have been fantasizing about in her most secret, most ridiculous daydreams, she never would have acted on it. Never.

She just wished she could go back in time and make sure it never happened.

But going back not being an option, she resolved to go forward. Forward meant acing AP French, and forward meant sticking it out on the newspaper, for the sake of her college applications, if nothing else. Forward meant looking him in the eye every day and never saying anything to anyone about what had happened, until she forgot it herself. Eventually she would forget. It had just been a kiss. One kiss. She *would* forget all about it. Soon.

And today moving forward meant returning to the newspaper office, alone. Doing what she'd signed on to do—run the paper, make it great. She forced herself to return, hating the sound of her key in the door, hating the sight of the couch she used to nap on, the table at which she'd spent so many hours lost in her work. She was so different now—but everything there, it was exactly the same. And maybe in the end, she just couldn't stay away.

Neither, it seemed, could he.

She'd spent half an hour staring blankly at the computer screen, trying to finalize the page-one layout for the next edition, but mainly just concentrating on keeping her body calm and still—she felt that if she relinquished control for even a moment, she'd start to tremble uncontrollably. Or just flee.

Maybe she'd known that he was on his way.

Because at the sound of the knob turning, the door opening, she didn't need to turn around—she knew it was him. Not by the jaunty footsteps or the faint whiff of his

Calvin Klein cologne. She'd just known. As if the room had suddenly gotten chilly, or the walls had begun to press in.

"Beth," he said quietly.

Still she didn't turn around.

"You've been avoiding me," he said, finally.

"You noticed," she said drily, her back to him. She focused on keeping the pain and panic out of her voice—she knew, somehow, that if she could pull this off, if she could face him without crumbling, prove to both of them that she could do it, that this could be the end of it.

"Beth, if I did anything that made you feel uncomfortable . . . If you thought that I—well, sometimes it's easy for people to get the wrong idea about situations, imagine that certain things happened, when they didn't, really. Blow things out of proportion . . ."

She grabbed the edges of the desk, pressing down until the tips of her fingers faded to white, and forced herself to take a deep breath and turn around slowly.

"What is it, exactly, that you think I imagined?" she asked in a measured tone.

"Well, you obviously thought that things somehow crossed a line, and if I sent you any confusing signals, I just want to apologize—I'd just hate to see you overreact."

"Overreact?" Her voice almost broke on the last syllable, and again she forced herself to breathe. She would not yell, and she would not cry, even if it killed her. She hoped that from across the room he couldn't see that she was shaking.

"You're obviously upset," he pointed out, taking a step toward her. "If we could just—"

"Stay away," she blurted out, jumping out of her seat and away from him.

He backed off, holding his hands out in front of him as if to demonstrate they weren't hiding a secret weapon. Of course, he didn't need one.

"Okay, okay, I'm back here, okay?" he retreated to the doorway. "Just tell me, what can we do to fix things here? How can I convince you I'm not the big bad wolf?" He cocked an eyebrow and gave her a patented Jack Powell grin, and Beth suddenly realized that this was a man who'd discovered that, with his accent and his dimples, he could get away with pretty much anything.

She also suddenly realized that he needed her help to get away this time—that he was running scared. She had the power, and she could use it.

"There's nothing you can do," she said simply. "Just stay away from me. I'm not dropping out of French and I'm not dropping the newspaper—but I don't ever want to be in a room alone with you again. So make sure that doesn't happen, or I'll make sure of it for you."

He took a step toward her again.

"Are you *threatening* me?"

She was almost as surprised as he was.

"I'm just explaining things for you," she replied. "Stay away from me, or I'm going to the administration."

"And say what?" he asked, in a low, dangerous voice.

"You know what."

He came closer, and closer, until he was looming over her, only a few inches away.

"That I came on to you? That I *wanted* you? That I fell madly in love with you and you rebuffed my nefarious advances?" he hissed, curling his lip in derision. "Is that what you'll say?"

She stayed silent, lip trembling, back now pressed against the wall, eyes searching for an escape. He was blocking her path to the door.

"Because I'll tell you what I'll say," he continued. "I'll say it's a silly schoolgirl crush gone out of control. That I made the mistake of getting close to you, helping you out, not realizing what a sad, pathetic, unstable little girl you really were. Prone to tears and hallucination." He smiled coolly. "What do you think they'll say to that? Who would you believe?"

"Stop," Beth begged, hating the soft, whispery sound of her own voice. "Just stop."

"Because *I* think they'll believe me," he pressed on. "I think they'll ask themselves, why would *he* ever risk everything for someone like *her*?"

Beth had no response—it was all she could do just to stand there, stare up at him, not lose control and break down. But her control was slipping. He reached a hand toward her, and she skirted away—but there was nowhere to go.

If he touches me, I'll lose it, she realized. *I can't stop myself.*

But she couldn't stop him, either, and he smiled cruelly and put a hand on her shoulder as she felt her knees buckle and—

"Am I interrupting something in here?"

Mr. Powell jumped back from Beth and spun toward the door. Kane stood in the doorway, one arm slung against the frame, a quizzical expression painted across his face.

"That's up to Ms. Manning." Powell turned back to Beth. "Are we done here?"

"We're done," she murmured, forcing herself to meet his gaze.

"Okay, then. I'll be happy to honor your request, Ms. Manning—but I'd advise you to remember what I said here."

Beth nodded, and Mr. Powell strode out of the room. As soon as he was gone, the last of Beth's energy disappeared, and she sagged against the wall.

"What was all that about?" Kane asked, hurrying over to her. He put an arm around her and guided her to a chair. "Are you all right?"

"I'm fine," she whispered, as a tear escaped from the corner of her eye and spattered on the table.

"Okay, that's obviously a lie, but we all know I don't feel all that strongly about the truth," he said gently. "So I can deal with that."

In spite of herself, Beth smiled. "What are you doing here?" she asked, hoping he wouldn't notice her surreptitiously wiping her nose with the edge of her sleeve. She brushed another tear away.

"Looking for you, actually. Swim practice let out early, so I thought I'd come see if I could bully you into another study session. I know we weren't due to meet until tomorrow, but . . ." He grinned and pulled a brown paper bag out of his backpack. "I even brought a bribe."

She looked inside and gasped in delight.

"For me?"

"Chocolate chip cookies and chocolate milk—that's right, isn't it?"

"That's perfect."

"Somehow, I think the vending machine cookies will be slightly less satisfying than Auntie Bourquin's fresh-baked best, but I figured—"

"No, Kane, it's perfect, really. It's incredibly sweet of you to remember."

She breathed in sharply and shook herself, trying to shrug off the dark fog that had come over her. She gave him her best attempt at a smile, and pulled out a notebook, opening it up to a blank page.

"The bribe worked—let's get to it. How about we start with geometry?"

Another tear spattered onto the page, and Kane put a tentative hand on her shoulder, dropping it quickly as she instinctively jerked away.

"Beth, stop for a second."

Reluctantly, she looked up from the page, where she'd already started drawing a series of triangles.

"Are you really okay?" he asked gently. "We don't need to do this now, if you're not up for it. I can go, if you want. Or I can stay, and we can just talk."

She didn't say anything, just looked at him, wondering how she'd missed it all these years, the sweet, sensitive look in his eyes, the soft, unquestioning openness. She'd always thought Kane was just—well, to be honest, a heartless bastard who cared only about himself. But this wasn't the face of someone who didn't care.

"Or we could just sit here and stare at each other in silence," Kane finally added. "I'm okay with that, too." He grinned. "Girls are often struck dumb by my wit and impeccable physique. It's okay, no need to be embarrassed."

She burst into laughter, and this time, she was the one to put a hand on *his* arm.

"It's okay," she told him. "We can do some work. I want to."

"Are you sure?" he asked, covering her hand with his. "Whatever it is, I just want to help."

Beth sighed, remembering the relief that had swept through her when she'd looked up to see him in the doorway, rescuing her.

"Trust me," she assured him. "You already have."

Adam froze in the doorway and just watched. Their heads bent together, his hand on hers, the grateful smile on her face.

He watched—and then he crept out as quietly as he had crept in.

Practice had let out early, and he'd thought Beth could use a pick-me-up. She'd been working so hard lately, and he knew she'd been planning to barricade herself in the newspaper office until nightfall. *Poor Beth*, he'd thought. *My poor, overworked, overstressed girlfriend.* Wouldn't it be nice to surprise her with an unexpected treat. So stupid.

He'd bought some cookies and chocolate milk from the vending machine by the gym—her favorite.

He'd rushed down the hall toward the office, already imagining the smile on her face when she saw him walk through the door, the squeal of delight at the guaranteed sugar rush. He loved to see her happy.

He'd tiptoed to the door of the office, oh-so-gently and oh-so-quietly turned the handle, eased the door open— and there they were. Kane and Beth, bent over their work together—though they obviously weren't working.

Kane was munching on a cookie, Beth was giggling— they looked comfortable together, like friends. Like more than friends.

Like they didn't want to be interrupted.

Adam hated himself for the tendrils of jealousy creeping through him and for the fact that he couldn't drive Kaia's mocking warnings out of his mind. He had nothing to worry about. He knew that. Knew that he could just say her name, or clear his throat, and they would look up and welcome him to the table, and together, they would eat cookies and slurp chocolate milk and complain about the SATs or their asshole swim coach or whatever. He could and he should, he knew that. And yet—

He didn't. He stepped backward, silently, away from them, and eased the door shut behind him. He walked a few paces down the hall, then slammed a fist into a locker in frustration. It didn't help. So he kept going, down the hall, out of the building, back home. Alone.

And inside the newspaper office, Beth looked at Kane, Kane looked at Beth, and, engrossed in the conversation, engrossed in each other, they never noticed a thing.

chapter six

IT HAD TAKEN HARPER ABOUT TWENTY-FOUR HOURS to notice that Miranda wasn't speaking to her—unanswered calls, unreturned messages, a cold shoulder in the hallway and an empty seat in the cafeteria. By Tuesday night it had become pretty clear to Harper that she'd somehow screwed up. She knew it would take less than ten minutes to get Miranda—the ultimate pushover, at least when it came to Harper—to forgive her for it. Too bad she didn't have the slightest clue what "it" was.

But maybe she could bluff it out.

After countless unreturned messages ("Rand, come on,

call me back—I'm sorry, I totally screwed up. Call me!"),
the phone finally rang.

"Do you even know what you're apologizing for?"
Miranda asked as soon as Harper picked up the phone.

Harper squirmed. Sometimes she was sorry Miranda
knew her so well.

"Of course I do," she said indignantly. "And I'm
sorry—I swear, I'll never do it again."

"What?"

"I said, I'll never do it again, I promise."

Miranda sucked in a sharp, exasperated breath. "No, I
heard you. I mean, *what* will you never do again?"

Harper paused. "Well, I'll never do anything like *this*
again, I'll tell you that much."

Miranda snorted. "You're unbelievable—you really
have no idea, do you?"

Harper crumbled under the pressure. "Okay, you got
me. No, I don't. But I'm sorry, I swear—just tell me what
I'm supposed to be sorry about."

"Well, *if you only had a brain*, maybe you could figure
it out," Miranda said cryptically.

"If I only had a—oh God, *The Wizard of Oz*. Shit,
Miranda, I totally forgot!"

"Uh, yeah."

"I really am sorry." And she was. Harper wasn't a slave
to tradition the way Miranda was, but she looked forward

to their *Wizard of Oz* trip each year. It was a chance to blow off steam, to pretend they were kids again, to gorge themselves on candy. Plus, she had to admit . . . she really liked the movie. "I totally suck," she admitted. "Let's go tomorrow, okay?"

"Harper, it closed," Miranda said harshly. "That's kind of the point, remember? We always go on the last day. We've only been doing it for like, five years?"

"Okay, I suck. I completely and totally suck. Is this it? Are you done with me? You are, aren't you?" Harper affected a voice of exaggerated desperation. When in doubt, make 'em laugh. "You're getting rid of me and finding a new best friend. Who is it, Katie? Eloise? You know she's a shrew, so I'd advise against her. Tara? You always liked her better anyway, didn't you? And why not? I'm a horrible, terrible person. . . ."

"Quit the melodrama, Harper. You're not funny."

"Not even a little?"

She was rewarded by a muffled laugh on the other end of the phone—and Harper knew she'd got her.

"Not even a little," Miranda confirmed, unconvincingly." In fact, you're right. You do totally suck. I should just find a new best friend." But Miranda's familiar playful sarcasm had replaced her tone of bitter anger.

"Yeah, it would probably be good for you—but when is something good for you ever any fun?" Harper asked.

"Point taken."

"So we're okay?" Harper abandoned the comedy for a second. Miranda had to know she was sincere. "I really am sorry."

"You should be—but yes, we're okay."

"I knew it. You can't live without me!"

"Don't press your luck," Miranda cautioned her. "So where were you, anyway?"

There was a pause—since she hadn't realized that she'd ditched Miranda, Harper hadn't bothered to come up with a good excuse. But what was she supposed to say, *I was out with our worst enemy, plotting a way to set up the guy you're crushing on with another girl?* In this case, it didn't seem likely that honesty would be the best policy.

"I was . . . at the dentist. It was an emergency."

"A tooth emergency?" Miranda asked dubiously.

"Yeah, I chipped a molar, and I managed to get the guy to see me right away. Thank God."

"It hurt a lot, huh?"

"It still does." Why had she said that? Now she was going to have to fake a toothache for the rest of the week. First rule of successful lying: Keep it simple, and never offer more information than necessary. She'd had a lot of practice.

"Must have been really horrible," Miranda said

sympathetically. "We're talking acute, throbbing, knives-digging-into-you pain?"

"Uh-huh." It was sort of true, if you counted the pain of having to lie to Miranda 24/7—and having to rely on Kaia, of all people.

"Brutal, agonizing pain?"

"Yeah."

Miranda laughed. "Good."

Payback came on Friday night. As the wounded party, Miranda got to pick the activity, and after a few days of careful thought, she'd settled on the perfect punishment. Karaoke. Both girls were equally averse to the torture and public humiliation that Karaoke Night at the Lasso Lounge represented, but Miranda figured it was worth sitting through an hour of off-key crooning to see Harper make a fool of herself in public. She'd been right.

"You aren't really going to make me do this," Harper complained, as a hefty man crooned Bruno Mars's latest hit up on the makeshift stage.

"Oh, I so am," Miranda replied with an evil laugh.

"This is cruel and unusual punishment, you know," Harper pointed out.

Miranda smiled sweetly. "What are friends for?" She pointed to the short line of would-be American Idols who had assembled by the stage. "Now get over there and show 'em what you're made of."

Harper glared at her, gulped down the last of her drink, and stalked off toward the line. "I hate you," she tossed over her shoulder.

Miranda just raised her drink in a one-sided toast. "Don't forget to smile!"

Then she leaned back in her chair and waited for the fun to start. This was going to be good.

Too many hours and too many drinks later, Harper and Miranda stumbled out of the bar on a karaoke high. Midway through her Cyndi Lauper spectacular, Harper had abandoned her embarrassment and belted out "Girls Just Wanna Have Fun" at the top of her lungs. She'd scored a round of thunderous applause and returned to the table flushed and ready for more. And after another margarita, Miranda had conceded to go with her, kicking off a marathon sing-along that took them back to the endless afternoons they'd spent as kids, choreographing dance moves to the latest on MTV. The humiliation factor was through the roof—but there was no one there to see them, and by that point in the night, they didn't even care. After a rousing, girl-power version of "I Will Survive," the karaoke machine had finally shut down, the lights went out, and Harper and Miranda were forced to seek a new adventure.

So phase two of the night was planned during the tail end of phase one, which meant that clear, sober thinking had been left far behind by the time Harper suggested they stop off for supplies.

The result of their giggly stumble through the twenty-four-hour convenience store?

A two-pound bag of Mike and Ikes (on sale for Halloween), a two-gallon bottle of Diet Coke and another of Hawaiian Punch (mixers), a six-pack of Jell-O pudding (because, well, just because—thanks to the two pitchers of margaritas back at the Lasso Lounge, they no longer needed a reason). And the pièce de résistance: a box of hair dye that promised to "change your color—and your life—in three easy steps." It was time for Miranda to become a bottle blonde.

"You said you wanted a change, right?" Harper asked, tossing the box into their shopping basket, despite Miranda's halfhearted protests.

They stumbled back to Harper's house with the goods—her parents were off in Ludlow for the weekend, visiting her great-uncle in his nursing home, a trip that Harper had easily resisted being guilted into. Great-Uncle Horace had no idea who she was and last time had insisted on referring to her as Millie, apparently the name of a British nurse who'd been "kind" to him during the war.

Harper's parents didn't mind her staying home alone,

as long as she had "that responsible Miranda" around to keep an eye on things. If they only knew.

One very messy and wet shampoo later, Miranda's hair was thoroughly coated with dye, and the two of them had nothing left to do but wait for it to dry. They fidgeted impatiently, leafing through magazines and flipping through the TV channels—Friday night was pretty much a home entertainment dead zone.

Miranda refused to look in a mirror until it was perfectly dry—she said she wanted to wait to get the full effect. And, as Harper watched with horror as Miranda's hair dried and the final color emerged, she concluded that postponing the inevitable could only be a good thing. But finally they could wait no longer.

"Okay, I can't stand it anymore," Miranda said. "How does it look?"

"Uh . . . it's different," Harper hedged. "It's definitely different."

"Well I *know* that—but how does it look? Oh, forget it. I need to see for myself."

She bounded up, but Harper leaped ahead of her and jumped in front of the mirror.

"Before you look, I just want to remind you of what you said before, how I'm such a good friend to you."

"Of course you are, Harper—this was your idea, wasn't it? I'm not going to forget that."

"That's what I'm afraid of," Harper murmured. But she stepped aside.

Miranda's scream would have woken up Harper's parents, had they been home—as it was, Harper suspected it might still have woken them up a hundred miles away in Ludlow. It might even have woken up Great-Uncle Horace—and he was deaf.

"Harper—what have you done to me?" Miranda cried, lunging toward her. Harper jumped away, searching for some large piece of furniture she could put between herself and the newly psychotic Miranda.

"Don't blame me," she protested. "I followed the directions. I think." She ducked unsuccessfully as Miranda threw a pillow at her head.

"Look what you've done to me!" Miranda yelled. She slumped down on the bed and burst into—well, Harper couldn't tell whether it was sobs or hysterical laughter.

"Are you . . . okay?" Harper asked tentatively, sitting down beside her.

"Okay?" Miranda asked, tears of laughter streaming down her face. "How could I be okay? I look like Kermit the Frog!"

Sad, but true.

Miranda's rust-colored hair had been changed in three easy steps, all right—her head was now topped with a frizzy mass of bright green tendrils, the color of celery. Or of everyone's favorite Muppet.

It was horrifying. Humiliating. And hilarious.

Unable to control herself any longer, Harper burst into giggles.

Miranda fell backward onto the bed, gasping for breath. "It's not funny," she complained.

"I know," Harper said, trying to force a solemn and sober look.

"Except that it is," Miranda admitted, breaking into laughter once more.

"I know," Harper agreed, laughing again herself. She felt a rush of relief that Miranda didn't want to kill her—but she worried about what would happen in the morning, when the alcoholic glee had washed out of her system and, sober and hungover, she still looked like a Muppet. Things might not seem so jolly in the light of day.

After all, it's not easy being green.

(Just ask Kermit.)

It was Friday night, date night, and things were going to be different. Beth was determined. Adam had been acting weird all week—though she wasn't even sure what would classify as "weird" these days. Stand-offish? Short-tempered? Irritable? How was that any different, really, from the way things were the rest of the time? When was the last time they'd been together—and *talked*—without it turning into a fight? It used to be so easy to talk to Adam, and now it was just easier not to.

But tonight really would be different. Tonight would be an actual date. Not a half-rushed hookup in her bedroom before her parents got home, not a stolen few minutes between classes or a stale slice of pizza after work. Tonight it was just the two of them, all night long. And it would be fun, and easy, no matter how hard she had to work at it.

She'd suckered Adam into taking her to the Frontier Festival, an annual carnival that passed through town every October, ostensibly to celebrate the harvest (though Beth was unsure what kind of harvest a mining town, much less a defunct mining town, had to offer). Really it was just an excuse for cotton candy, funnel cake, 4-H livestock contests, and a rickety Ferris wheel. Beth had loved it as a child, and had always dreamed of walking through the booths and crowds of squealing children on the arm of a handsome boy. Now she finally had one.

It started out just as she'd hoped. Hand in hand, they traipsed through the colorful booths, mocking the lame Wild West theme, squealing in fear and delight as the carnival rides swung them through the air, gorging themselves on cotton candy and corn dogs. Adam even spent ten dollars trying to win her a prize—but the water gun target shoot, the whack-a-mole, even the basketball free-throw game failed to cough up any booty. Finally Beth tried her hand at skee-ball, and in about five minutes had succeeded in winning Adam a stuffed pink elephant, which he accepted with a rueful but gracious grin. It was relaxing, carefree, fun, sweet—and it couldn't last.

Adam spotted him first, but Beth was the one to call him over. That was before she noticed the buxom brunette on his arm. Kane waved eagerly and hurried over to say hello, his Kewpie doll following close on his heels. In a moment everyone was introduced.

Beth, meet Hilary, a brainless idiot with a twenty-three-inch waist and a six-inch hollow space in her head.

You can't judge her before she even opens her mouth, Beth chided herself, appalled by her nasty knee-jerk reaction. She smiled at Hilary and, as sweetly as she could to make up for the evil thoughts swarming around her head, asked, "So, Hilary, do you go to Haven High too? I don't think I've ever seen you around."

Hilary giggled, and responded in a thin, airy voice. "Oh, no, I'm homeschooled—my parents think public school teaches you to be immoral."

Beth and Adam both shifted uncomfortably in silence. What, exactly, was one supposed to say to that?

No matter—Hilary wasn't waiting for an answer. She draped an arm around Kane's waist.

"Of course," she giggled again, "now I've got Kane for that. Right, sweetie?" She slapped him gently on the ass and he jumped in surprise, flashing Beth and Adam a bemused and slightly abashed look. At least, Beth read it as abashed—but maybe she was wrong, since the next thing he did was pull Hilary toward him and give her a long, hard kiss. How embarrassed by her could he be?

After a long moment he released Hilary, who looked up at him, flushed and adoring.

"I'm teaching her everything I know about bad behavior," Kane explained.

Hilary put on a fake pout and a grating baby voice. "And now I'm a bad, bad girl, aren't I?"

"You sure are," Kane agreed, pinching her ass.

"Ooh!" she squealed. "I'll get you for that." And she lunged toward him.

It was the obvious start of some kind of tickle slap fight that Beth was sure would soon end in another grope match—not something she needed to see.

"Come on, Adam," she whispered, tugging at his shirt. "Let's go."

They waved hasty good-byes and began to back away from the squealing couple.

"Off to win your lady love a bigger prize?" Kane called out from amid the tickle storm. He gestured to the small stuffed elephant Beth was holding in her arms;

Hilary was toting a stuffed pink panda about four times as large.

"Actually, I won this for *him*," Beth pointed out.

"A true champion, eh?" Kane called jovially. Then his voice grew serious and he locked eyes with Beth, ignoring the giggling and pawing going on around him. "I never had any doubt."

Beth tore her gaze away with difficulty.

"Let's go," she urged Adam again. "Now."

Once they were a safe distance away, Adam began to shake with laughter.

"He's a real piece of work," he said, shaking his head.

"Him? What about *her*?" Beth asked as they wandered toward the Ferris wheel.

"Ah, she's no different from any of the other girls he picks up. Smarter, maybe."

"Smarter? You've got to be kidding me." Beth rolled her eyes and climbed into a Ferris-wheel cart after Adam. They began to swing upward toward the stars.

"No, it's true—think about it, any girl with half a brain at our school is too smart to go near him."

"That's a nice way to talk about your best friend," she scolded him.

"What? He'd admit it himself—the guy's a player. Besides, you're the one always calling him a sleaze."

"That was before I got to know him."

"Trust me, Beth, if you knew him the way I do, you'd believe me. I love the guy and all, but I gotta call it like I see it." He put an arm around her shoulders and pulled her close to him, running a warm hand up and down her bare shoulders. Beth shivered, suddenly noticing the cool night air blowing past.

"How about we stop talking about Kane and his latest bimbo and just enjoy the view," Adam suggested.

"It is beautiful," Beth agreed, looking out over the glittering sprawl beneath them. A range of low-slung mountains loomed in the distance, silhouetted by the full moon.

They sat quietly for a moment until Beth couldn't take it anymore—the words boiled up inside of her and finally leaked out.

"I just don't see why he does it!" she exclaimed, flinging her arms up for emphasis.

"Who?"

"Kane—he's so much better than these girls."

"Why are you getting so angry?" Adam asked in frustrated confusion. "What do you care?"

"I just—I just want him to be happy. Don't you? He's *your* friend."

"That's right, he's *my* friend," he repeated. "And I can tell you that he is happy. I'm the one sitting up here while my girlfriend goes crazy over another guy. Too jealous of Kane to care whether I'm happy?"

"I am *not* jealous," Beth protested indignantly.

"Whatever."

"I just think he's a great guy," she insisted. "He deserves better."

"Like who? You?"

"Stop it, Adam," she said irritably. "If you don't want to talk about him anymore, we won't talk about him anymore. You don't have to make such a big deal about it."

He crossed his arms and peered out over the side, away from her. "Fine."

"Fine."

And so they didn't talk at all.

Kaia knew things. It was second nature now, after her long years of training—part skill, part talent, whatever. Everyone needs a hobby. In New York, after all those years with the same people, the same streets, the same hangouts, it had been easy. You just had to listen, ask the right questions, be in the right place at the right time, learn how to be invisible. This last, for Kaia, had been the hardest lesson to learn, as she'd made a life out of being seen, being *noticed*—but it turned out that didn't always serve her purposes. Knowledge was power, and when you were a teenager, held hostage by the arbitrary whims of adults who mistakenly thought they knew best, you needed all the power you could get.

After sifting through the skeletons in the closets of half of the Upper West Side, the denizens of Grace, California didn't really pose much trouble for Kaia's investigative skills, especially since, at the moment, she had very little else to do. So even though she'd been in town for only a month, she knew things, big and small.

She knew that the servants played poker together in the room above the garage every Sunday night—and that their drink supplies always came courtesy of the Sellers family liquor cabinet. She knew that Alicia, the married maid, was screwing Howard, Kaia's father's driver. She knew that the Haven High principal was having an affair with her English teacher, that Adam's mother was well deserving of her reputation as the town slut, that her gym teacher was an alcoholic kleptomaniac, that her middle-aged mailman was still emotionally debilitated by the tragic loss of his mother in 1987, and that the woman who ran the local post office was a thirty-seven-year-old virgin.

Of course she knew about Harper's and Kane's little crushes—that was child's play.

And she knew that every Friday night from eight p.m. to closing, the bar stool on the far left in the Prairie Dog Bar and Grill was occupied by one Mr. Jack Powell.

Yes, knowing things could come in handy.

It was a hole in the wall, with room for no more

than ten customers at once (though crowding was never a problem). The grill, if it had ever truly existed, must have broken long ago, for the only food available was the stale peanut and pretzel mix filling the spotted beer mugs spread across the bar, and the moldy cheese left as bait in the mousetraps in the corners. Other than the bartender, a smiling old man with no hair and plenty of rounded edges, Jack Powell was the only one there.

She sidled up to the bar and hopped onto the stool next to him. He was hunched over a mug of beer, reading a book. *No Exit*, by Sartre. How appropriate.

"Kind of a bleak choice for Friday night," she observed, peering over his shoulder at the tiny print.

He looked up in horror and practically fell off his stool at the sight of her.

"Are you stalking me now?" he asked drily, regaining his composure as she laughed in his face.

"Please—you should be so lucky. I'm here for a drink and some peace and quiet, just like you."

"And until a moment ago I thought I'd found it," he grumbled.

"Can I get a Corona?" she called to the bartender, ignoring Powell.

"Don't serve her," Powell instructed him. "She's under age."

The bartender winked. "Hey, buddy, I won't tell if you

won't." He slid a bottle down the bar toward Kaia. "On the house, beautiful."

"You must be pretty used to getting exactly what you want," Powell said in disgust.

"Pretty much," she agreed.

"You're fighting a losing battle this time."

"You think this is me fighting?" She shook her head. He could be so cute when he was being clueless. "Please—this is me on low gear, getting a drink. It's just good luck we two lonely hearts happened to run into each other."

"And you just happened to be wearing . . . practically nothing?" he asked sardonically, gesturing toward her barely-there silk top.

"So you noticed," she said with pleasure, running her fingers lightly along her bare breastbone. "And here I thought it was just my imagination, your staring at my chest all the time."

"It's a bit difficult not to, with your shoving it in my face like that."

"Jack, Jack, Jack." She shook her head ruefully. "You can insult me all you want. I'm not leaving."

"No, but I am." He closed his book and stood up, slapping a ten-dollar bill down on the bar. "Thanks, Joey," he called to the bartender.

"And where will you go?" Kaia asked. "Home? To sit alone in your pathetic little bachelor pad until you can

force yourself to go to sleep? Or maybe to the library—
would that be more your speed?"

"I'll be quite happy to go anywhere you're not," he
informed her. "Thanks for ruining my night."

"I'm the best part of your night, and you know it. Or
were you having more fun a few minutes ago, sitting here
alone in this cellar, mooning over your beer like a drunken
poet?"

"Fun doesn't seem to be in my vocabulary these days," he
admitted with a dispirited sigh. "This isn't the town for it."

"You're just not looking hard enough, Mr. Powell."
She put her finger softly to his lips and raised her other
hand to his temple—and for once, she noticed, he didn't
twist away. "Stop talking, for once, and open your eyes."

He raised his hands and gently removed hers from
his face. But he let them linger in his grasp for a moment
too long, and it was she who broke contact first—but not
before raising one of his hands to her lips and grazing his
knuckles with a gentle kiss.

He pulled away quickly.

"I'm seeing things pretty clearly right now," he said
sharply. "And I can see that it's time for me to go." He
slipped out of the bar and Kaia sat down again, sipping her
Corona thoughtfully.

He could run—but he couldn't hide.

Kaia would always know where to find him.

❧ ❧ ❧

It seemed the farther they got from the festival—and from Kane—the better things were. By the time they got back to Adam's house, Beth was smiling, a look of glazed contentedness on her face. Maybe it was just the slow descent from a cotton candy sugar high—but whatever the reason, Adam thought as she snuggled close to him, he'd take it.

"It's such a nice night," she said, taking his hand as she climbed out of the car. "I almost hate to go inside."

He checked his watch. There was only an hour left before her curfew, not enough time to go anywhere, but . . .

"How about we go around back," he suggested. He led her into the backyard and over to the large, flat rock that lay on the dividing line between his house and Harper's. He and Harper had played there when they were little and always—even these days—considered it "their" place. He snuck a guilty glance up at Harper's bedroom window, which overlooked the yard. She wouldn't mind—she would, in fact, never know.

Beth clambered up atop the rock and lay back on it, spreading her arms and looking up at the clear, starry sky.

"You could lose yourself in the stars," she sighed. "Out here, in the dark, you could forget the whole world, and just—be."

"I know exactly what you mean," Adam said, lying down next to her. "I could lose myself in you." He took her face in his hands and turned it toward him gently, kissing her forehead, her nose, her cheeks, her soft, smooth lips. She brushed her blond hair away from her face and pulled him closer to her, tangling her legs in his. The smooth rock surface was cool beneath his skin, but she was so warm, throbbing with heat as she grazed the lines of his body and began to rub the bare skin beneath his shirt.

"I'm sorry I was so . . . I'm sorry about tonight," she murmured.

"It was nothing. Forget it," he assured her, cradling her in his arms.

"I'm just stressed—there's so much to do, and no time, and—"

"Shh." She was trembling in his arms, and he put his hand to her cheek, then ran his fingers across her lips. "It's okay. I know. It'll be okay."

"I miss you," she whispered.

"We just need to make it through the SATs," he suggested. "And then maybe you can take a break for a while. We can take a break, focus on us. No stress, no SATs, no homework. Just us."

"It sounds perfect," Beth sighed. "I can't wait." She lay her head on his chest. "I could just lie here forever, listening to you breathe."

He ran his fingers through her hair and began softly massaging her back, rubbing and kneading her taut muscles, her tender skin.

"I wish you could," he whispered. "Next week. Just keep telling yourself that. You'll make it until then. *We'll* make it until then."

"I hope so," she whispered.

So did he.

chapter seven

"NO WAY IN HELL AM I GOING OUT IN PUBLIC LOOK-ing like this," Miranda wailed.

As Harper had expected, Miranda had awoken with a raging hangover and a far stormier outlook on being a green-headed monster.

"Well, on the bright side . . . ," Harper began.

"I don't want to hear it," Miranda interrupted her. "It's too early in the morning for bright sides."

"It's twelve thirty," Harper pointed out. They'd rolled out of bed a few minutes ago and were now slouched in front of the kitchen table, trying to cure their hangover with juice and a handful of aspirin.

"Am I in my pajamas? Am I eating Rice Krispies? Am I still waiting for my first cup of coffee? Then it's morning."

Harper, whose own head was throbbing with the pain of one margarita too many, was in no position to argue.

"Look, we'll fix this," she promised.

"You'd better," Miranda growled. "It's your fault I look like the Jolly Green Midget to begin with."

"We'll take care of it, I promise. The box said it washes out in twenty to twenty-five shampoos, right? So all we need to do is wash your hair twenty-five times in a row, and that should be that."

"That's a lot of showers. . . ."

"Do you *want* to go to school on Monday looking like a stalk of broccoli?" Harper asked wryly.

Miranda looked appalled at the thought. "Hey, it's not like we're in the middle of a drought or anything," she said, reconsidering. "Bring on the shampoo."

"Uh, actually, we're going to need to go get some more of that," Harper reminded her. They'd used the last of it the night before in their drunken beauty school efforts. But perhaps the less said about that, the better.

"We?" Miranda squawked. "Did I mention that I am *not* going out in public like this? Which part of that did you not understand?"

"Chill out—I'll go to the drugstore and get more shampoo. Just let me throw on some clothes."

"Fine," Miranda sulked. "I'll jump in the shower. Might as well get started."

The two of them scampered upstairs, Harper to hastily throw on some clothes and Miranda to single-handedly bring on a drought. As she pulled on a T-shirt, Harper idly picked up her cell phone and noticed she had a text message waiting for her from Kane. 1:37, ELEMENTARY SCHOOL PLAYGROUND. BE THERE. BRING ADAM.

Cryptic much? Harper thought grouchily. It was definitely too early in the morning for riddles. She called Kane immediately.

"What are you talking about?" she asked, without saying hello.

"Can't talk now—*Beth* and I are studying," he said meaningfully. "Just trust me—you won't want to miss this."

"But what—?"

"Can't *talk* now," he repeated. "Just be on time."

He hung up, and Harper sighed, casting a glance toward the bathroom door, where the water in the shower had just turned off.

"When you're out getting the shampoo, can you grab us some lunch, too?" Miranda called from behind the door.

Harper cradled her head in her hands. Really, what was she supposed to do? Jeopardize the whole plan just because Miranda was having a hair crisis? It wasn't even a tough call—she'd just need to come up with a good excuse.

"Rand, change of plans—I'm going to need to run you home," she said casually.

Miranda swung open the door and popped out, towel hastily wrapped around her dripping body.

"What? I must have heard you wrong, because I thought you said you were abandoning me."

"Rand—"

"But that can't be right. Not you, my best friend, who just ditched me five days ago and promised never to do it again and who—"

"Rand—," Harper helplessly tried again.

"*Who*, by the way, turned my hair *green*!" She grabbed some clothes and went back into the bathroom, slamming the door behind her. "So, lunch," she said. "I'm thinking pizza? Or Chinese food?"

"Stop acting like a baby, Miranda. I have to take a rain check. It's an emergency."

Harper waited in silence for several minutes, until finally a fully dressed—though still dripping—Miranda emerged from the bathroom.

"What kind of emergency?" she asked suspiciously.

"Well, not an emergency exactly—I mean, it's not life threatening," Harper hedged, thinking fast. "It's just, you remember that tooth problem I was having? That was the dentist on the phone—he says he can fit me in for a follow-up, but only if I come right away. Some kind of last-minute cancellation."

"Follow-up?"

"Yeah, my tooth is still killing me." Harper brought one hand to her jaw, hoping that Miranda wouldn't remember which side of her mouth the fake toothache was supposed to be on, since Harper no longer had any idea. "Of course, if you really need me, I guess I could just suffer through the pain. . . ."

Miranda heaved an exaggerated sigh.

"No, I can take a shower—or thirty of them—all by myself. I'm a big girl, after all."

"I'll come over tonight and we'll do final damage control, I promise."

"I can't wait to see the look on my mother's face when she sees this one," Miranda said with a sudden smile. "You know, it'll almost be worth it."

"You see? There's a silver lining after all."

Miranda shot Harper her patented Look of Death. "I said, *almost*."

"It's such a beautiful day," Kane had mused. "Why don't we do this study thing outside?"

Beth had reluctantly agreed. It's not that she didn't want to go outside—in fact, on a day like this, with a light breeze blowing and only a few wispy clouds in the sky, the last thing she wanted to do was sit inside and stare at fractions. But they had a lot to get through, and not much time. Being outside would be a distraction.

It was just so hard to say no to him.

They ended up in the playground of their old elementary school, stretched out on a picnic blanket between the swings and the jungle gym. The playground served as a park on the weekends, and laughing children swarmed all around them.

Still, Kane stayed focused. More focused even than Beth, who kept looking around at the playground equipment with something akin to longing. She came here by herself sometimes, at dusk, to sit on the swings and watch the sunset. It was a good place to think—surrounded by memories of a simpler time, all those games of tag and four square, the races she'd run, the games she'd lost and won, the swings she'd been on constantly, whooshing through the air as if she could fly.

She'd be going to college in a year, and there were very few parts of the town that she'd be sorry to see go. She'd been born here, grown up here, knew it inside and out. There were a few people she never wanted to leave behind—Adam, of course, her family, and—she looked at Kane—new friends too, the ones she'd missed getting to know all these years. But the town itself? She was ready to leave Grace in the past, never to be seen again. All except the playground. It was a special place. Her place. And really, it was all that remained of her childhood.

Kane yawned and stretched himself out on the picnic blanket, preening in the sun like a lazy and self-satisfied cat.

"Late night last night?" Beth asked sarcastically, trying her best not to admire his impeccable physique.

"I know, I know, Heather's a little—"

"*Hilary*," Beth corrected him.

"What?"

"Her name was *Hilary*," she reminded him with a reproachful glare.

Kane at least had the grace to blush.

"Ah, yeah. Hilary's a little—well, she's not like you. She's just . . . fun."

"So I'm not fun?" *Why do I even care what he thinks of me?* she asked herself.

"You're fun and so much more, Manning," he said languidly.

"And that means what, exactly?"

"It means you're cute when you're mad—anyone ever tell you that?"

"You're changing the subject," she pointed out, ignoring the compliment. That was just the kind of thing Kane said, after all, she reminded herself. Just the kind of guy he was. It didn't mean anything.

Kane sighed. "It means that you're fun, but that's not all there is. Girls like Heather—"

"Hilary."

"Whatever—they're a dime a dozen," he explained. "Girls like you? There aren't so many."

Now it was Beth who blushed. "I just hate to see you wasting your time, Kane. You deserve so much more."

"I can't believe this is coming from you, of all people."

"Why me, 'of all people'?"

"Come on, Beth," he said, looking away. "I know how girls like you see me. You think I'm a sleazy flirt. Not worth your time. Girls like you think I'm worthless."

"Not all of us," she murmured.

"What?"

She was suddenly struck by the unusual sincerity, the urgency in his voice. And she didn't like it.

"Let's just—uh—let's get back to work," she suggested, bending back over her notebook. "So, when the exponent is in the denominator, you want to . . ."

The problem was, she didn't know *how* she saw him anymore—but she suspected it was time to stop looking.

Adam had been surprised when Harper called suggesting they take a walk down to the old playground. Reminiscing about the past wasn't usually her thing—Harper was all about living in the moment.

But neither of them had anything better to do, and it couldn't hurt to go visit the site of some of their best exploits. Just because Beth was off somewhere studying with Kane, *again*, didn't mean he needed to sit around the house all day sulking. He needed to take his mind off of things—and no one did that better than Harper.

"Why do you keep checking your phone every five minutes?" he asked her, just after pointing out the spot where Danny Burger, fifth-grade stud, had wet his pants. In fear of ruining his too-cool-for-school rep, he'd promised the witnesses three packs of baseball cards each in return for their eternal silence—and then run the whole two miles back to his house. "Are you expecting a call?"

"No, I left my watch at home and I just want to see what time it is—I have a dentist appointment later. Let's walk a little faster," she suggested.

As they reached the gate of the small playground, Harper pointed toward a couple by the swings.

"Isn't that Beth? And Kane?" she asked.

Adam squinted at the couple—it was them, all right. Kane was pushing Beth higher and higher, and he could imagine the exuberant look on her face as she stretched her toes closer and closer to the sky. He'd seen it enough times himself.

Harper raised a hand to wave, but he grabbed it and stopped her.

"No, let's just—just wait, okay?"

She gave him a cryptic look, but shrugged in agreement. So they just stood at the fence and watched.

"What are they doing here, anyway?" Harper asked. "I thought they were studying."

Adam's stomach clenched. "Yeah, so did I."

"We should really get back to work now," Beth complained, breathless with exertion.

Kane checked his watch. One thirty-five.

Harper had better be out there somewhere, he thought.

It was the perfect setup—the picnic, the romantic frolicking on the swings. And that whole heart-to-heart on his dating life? Talk about an unexpected pleasure. So Beth was paying attention, was she? He'd been unsure of how to play it last night—too much macho pig with all the leering and groping? Would it erode all the hard work he'd put into changing her image of him?

But as soon as he'd seen the look on her face, he'd known he had her. She was disgusted, sure—but she also, for a split second, wanted to *be* Hilary, wanted to forget all her uptight, repressed, do-gooder rules and restrictions and just fall into his arms. It was a look he'd recognize anywhere.

One thirty-seven. Time for the coup de grâce.

"Just a couple more minutes, sarge?" he grinned down at her—and, surprise, surprise, she couldn't resist. "Just once down the slide," he suggested.

"Okay," she conceded. "But you first."

Perfect.

He slid down, waving as he went and then tapped her lightly on the shoulder. "Your turn, teach."

She climbed up the narrow ladder and stood paused at the top, looking down at him dubiously.

"This is a little higher than I remember," she said nervously.

"What are you, chicken?" he called up to her. "Five-year-olds slide down this thing. Don't worry, I'll be down here at the bottom to catch you."

He waited for her, and watched as she slid down the rusty and pitted metal, her blond hair cascading behind her, a grin of delight illuminating her flushed and open face. Kane had been with a lot of girls, but he'd never known any who could be made so happy by so little. In fact, he usually ran a little more toward the high maintenance end of the spectrum, girls who could accept a gold bracelet with an upturned nose and a faint "Thanks, I guess." But Beth—he shook his head in bemusement. Give her a freshly baked chocolate chip cookie, swing her through the air, it would be enough. She'd be happy. And it was real happiness, the kind that spills over its borders, pours into everyone around you. *That* he'd never seen before.

She slid with a squeal into his arms, and the momentum knocked them both backward onto the scraggly bed of grass, where they lay tangled in each other's arms, heaving with laughter. For a moment Kane even forgot why he was there, what he was doing, who was watching.

Then he remembered—and felt a sudden stab of an emotion so unfamiliar he barely recognized it: guilt.

Adam stood motionless, his face impassive, carved in stone.

Harper reached a tentative hand out toward him.

"Adam, I'm sure it's just—"

"Don't, Harper. Just—don't."

He was clenching the chain-link fence so hard that his knuckles turned white, and Harper could see a small muscle twitching just above his jawline—but those were the only exterior signs of whatever was churning within him at the sight of Beth and Kane rolling around on the ground in each other's arms.

"I'm sure it's nothing," he said quietly. "They're just taking a break. Nothing wrong with that."

Harper stayed silent, waiting for him to give her some sign of what to do next. Finally he pulled himself away from the fence, turned his back on the playground.

"Let's go," he said shortly "Let's just go."

Harper hated to see Adam in pain, much less to know that she was the one responsible for it—but in this case . . . well, wasn't it better for him to suffer a little pain now, if it would help him avoid a much greater pain later on, when he finally realized on his own that Beth was the wrong girl? Or when *she* left *him*, for college or for another guy or for no reason at all? *Just look at her*, Harper thought in disgust. Running around with Kane, throwing herself into his arms. The timing might have been a trick, but what they were looking at? That was real. That was betrayal.

And when you looked at it that way, she was doing Adam a favor. Just helping a good friend see the light.

Miranda had snuck into her house as quietly as she could.

It wasn't quietly enough.

At the sound of the door her mother came clattering down the stairs and, after a horrified tirade on the state of Miranda's head, let loose with the bad news: She needed some peace and quiet. Which meant she was sending Miranda's little sister, Stacy, to the Frontier Festival—in care of Miranda.

And she wouldn't take "No way in hell am I leaving the house like this" for an answer.

The festival turned out to be just as bad as she'd

expected. Hokey and crowded, it would have been punishment enough on its own—but with green hair? It was
torture. Everywhere they went, Miranda felt like people
were staring at her (perhaps because Stacy kept pointing at
her head and shouting, "My sister has green hair!"). *They
might as well put me in the freak show*, she thought drily.
Come one, come all, see the Amazing Human Chia Pet.

"Hey, it's the mean, green, fighting machine!" One of
the barkers suddenly called out. "Where are you going?"

She looked around. The screechy voice booming from
the megaphone could only be coming from the tall, gawky
boy manning a dunk booth—and it could only be directed
toward Miranda.

She shook it off. *Just keep walking*, she told herself.

"Come on, show us your stuff, Incredible Hulk style!"
he called. "Three throws for a dollar—I dare you."

"Randa, he's talking to you," Stacy pointed out, eyes
wide. As if she hadn't noticed.

"Forget it, Stacy. We're leaving."

"But—"

"What are you, scared? Where are you hiding your
wings, chicken?" When he started clucking, that was it.
Enough was enough. Miranda heaved a huge sigh and
turned her sister back around.

"Come on, Stacy, it's time to dunk a dunce."

The annoying barker—a tall, skinny teen with glasses

and a striped T-shirt that made him look like a live action Where's Waldo—grinned and collected their money, then scrambled up onto a wooden bench that hovered precariously over the tank of water. He waved cheerfully.

"Worried?" Miranda asked as her sister readied herself to take a throw at the bull's-eye target.

"Nah—how about you?" He snickered. "You're looking a little green in the gills there."

As the loser cackled to himself, Miranda leaned down to Stacy and encouraged her.

"Throw hard, sweetie—as hard as you can."

Ball one.

Miss!

"Nice try, ladies. I'm shaking in my moccasins."

Moccasins. She should have figured. This guy had loser written all over him.

Ball two.

Miss!

"One more shot—but you're winners either way."

"You'll give her a prize even if she doesn't hit the target?" Miranda asked, pleasantly surprised.

"No, of course not—but don't you feel like you've won just by meeting me?"

"Won what?"

"The game of life, of course."

"Only if you're the booby prize," Miranda muttered.

She grabbed the last ball from Stacy's hands. "Let me take this one, Stace."

Ball three.

Crack!

Splash!

Miranda and Stacy burst into uncontrollable laughter as the annoying loser flailed wildly in the shallow water, finally popping up for air.

"You think that's funny, do you?"

"Hilarious," Miranda agreed.

"Well, just remember you said that."

Before Miranda could figure out what he was talking about, he climbed out, soaking wet, and slammed his palm into a bright red panel by the tank.

"Better hold your nose," he suggested cheerfully.

Too late.

A bucket overturned over Miranda's head, unleashing a flood of icy water.

"What the hell!" she screamed, looking down at herself, post-tidal wave. Her clothes were soaked and sticking to her body, marred by a few light green streaks—apparently her hair was still water soluble.

"Language, language," water boy cautioned her with a smirk, pointing toward Stacy. "There are children here, you know." He grabbed a giant stuffed bear off the rack and handed it to the girl.

"Here you go, sweetie. Good job." He turned to Miranda. "And you."

"I get a prize too?" she asked, holding her arms out from her sides in a pathetic attempt to air dry. "I think you've already given me enough."

"You get the best prize of all." He scrawled something on a piece of paper and handed it to her.

She uncrumpled it and looked uncomprehendingly at what he'd written: *Greg—555-0133.*

"My phone number," he explained, a bright red blush spreading across his face and out to the tips of his oversize ears.

"Wha—?"

"I think your hair's cute," he spit out, eyes darting away in embarrassment. "And so are you."

Kaia shut off the TV in frustration. There were only so many hours of nothing on that she could take. But what else was she supposed to do? She'd read a book, read the latest issue of *InStyle*—twice—even done her homework (truly a move of last resort). And it was still only Saturday night. She'd pretty much burned her bridges for what passed as A-list social life around here, and she didn't have much interest in palling around with social climbers who thought that hanging with someone who used to be at the top of a social ladder was the next best thing to ever being there themselves. And what did that leave? Kaia, alone and bored in her father's palatial monstrosity of a midlife crisis (complete with pool table, hot tub, giant flat-screen TV). After a few weeks trapped in small-town hell, even the luxury oasis wasn't cutting it.

She wondered what was going on back at the home front. Kaia got a message or two a week from members of her old crowd (even, once in a while, an e-mail from her mother, complaining about the decorator's incompetence or her dermatologist's too frequent vacations). But that was about it.

Principle dictated that she wait for them to call her and describe how empty life was without Kaia. Boredom dictated that she call them and torture herself with the knowledge of the life she should be living.

Boredom—and masochism—won out.

"Kaia, we miss you so much!" Alexa fawned. (They had all fawned over her, back in New York, jockeying for favor as if hoping her light would shine down on them and redeem their pitiful lives. It was a horrible way to think about your friends—but then, Alexa and the rest weren't *really* friends, were they? So what did it matter?) "K, you missed the sale of the season yesterday. Bergdorf's—you would not *believe* the scene."

"Oh, I can imagine."

"I should have snagged you something, but it was just too crazy."

"Well, not much call for Marc Jacobs out here in the sticks, anyway," Kaia admitted.

"Oh, that's right," Alexa said, her voice dripping with pity. "Burlap sack is maybe more your speed these days, right?" A beat. "Just kidding, of course."

"Of course," Kaia said drily.

"How are the hotties out there? You climbed into bed with any cowboys yet?"

"A few. It's slim pickings, though. Like Presley Prep on a Monday morning." Showing up in homeroom at eight a.m. on a Monday, sans hangover, was basically admitting to the world that you'd spent the weekend poring over your stamp collection. Or, Kaia thought, looking around in self-pity, forming a permanent body-size lump in your couch, flipping aimlessly through the TV channels 24/7.

"Tell me about it," Alexa drawled. "But by Tuesday— totally yummy. Tyler was getting so jealous the other day when—"

"Tyler?" *Her* Tyler? Six-foot-two Kenneth Cole addict with a nasty sense of humor and a silver Ferrari?

"Uh, yeah," Alexa mumbled. "You know we've been seeing each other. You know, nothing serious."

"I *don't* know," Kaia corrected her coolly. "Maybe you should enlighten me."

"Oh, I already told you all about it. I'm sure of it. You remember—you said you didn't care?"

It was an utter lie. But pointing that out would violate the code, the code that forbade you to ever admit to caring. Not when you were with a guy, not when the guy moved on to someone else, not when your supposed friends stabbed you in the back.

Kaia didn't really care about the code—but then again, she didn't much care about Tyler or Alexa, either. So she let it pass.

"Actually, he's here right now," Alexa finally remembered to mention. "Want to say hello? Ooh, Tyler, quit it. I'm on the phone." There was a series of giggles, then a disconcerting pause during which Alexa and her Harvard-bound hottie were doing who knows what, then, "Sorry, I'm back, what were you saying?"

Before Kaia could answer, the doorbell rang—it was like a gift; from the gods.

Or possibly the delivery guy, waiting outside with the pizza she'd ordered. Either way, it was a sign.

"I was saying I have to go—hot party to get to," Kaia lied easily.

"Sure, sure—awesome to talk to you, K, we miss you so much here. Oh, Tyler, for fuck's sake, quit it. We think about you all the time. No, Tyler, I'm not talking to you, I'm talking to Kaia. *Kaia*. Tyler, stop it! I mean it!"

"Yeah, miss you, too," Kaia said dully, her voice

drowned out by giggles. She shook her head in disgust and hung up the phone.

Think about her all the time? Yeah, right.

She hated them all for a moment—her parents for forcing her into exile, the friends who'd left her behind even though she was the one who'd left, Harper and her cronies here, who had all the social capital that Kaia had worked so hard to accumulate in her old life. You can't take it with you, they say.

Ain't it the truth.

She shuffled down to the front door to collect her pizza and got another unpleasant surprise.

"It's you," the scruffy delivery guy grunted when she opened the door.

"Do I know you?" It seemed a highly unlikely—and highly disturbing— prospect.

"We've met. I rescued you?" He spoke slowly, his words spaced out as if he were in danger of forgetting which one came next. It was the kind of voice that you imagined saying "yo" or "dude" every other word—so much so that the words almost didn't need to be said. They were just implied.

Still, it was true, they'd met before. Under the dweebish Guido's hat and apron was the same grody guy she and Harper had blown off in the Cactus Cantina. *And now my night is officially complete*, she thought in disgust.

"Oh yeah," she grudgingly admitted. "What was your name? Weed? Seed?"

"Reed," he corrected her, glowering. "Hopefully next time you'll get it right."

Weed would have been more appropriate, she decided, judging from the smell hovering around him and the glassy look in his eyes. He reeked of pot.

"Hopefully there won't be a next time," she retorted.

"Fine with me, princess."

"I hope you don't treat all the people you *serve* in this manner," Kaia said haughtily.

"Not too many people home to serve on a Saturday night," he said with a sly smile.

Was *he* actually criticizing *her* social life? Or would that be giving him too much credit? Veiled insults take brain power, and Kaia was sure this guy was running on empty. She knew she should just shut the door and go back to her night, lame as it was—but there was something about this guy that held her in place. Maybe it was his deep, dark, intense gaze, or the way his soft lips curled up into a knowing smile—

She shuddered. Surely she hadn't sunk low enough to be attracted to a guy like *this*. Raw sex appeal notwithstanding, he was still a delinquent pothead. A delivery boy, she reminded herself. That was it.

"Better sitting at home eating shitty pizza than running around town *delivering* it like a servant on wheels," she pointed out, trying not to watch the way his body moved beneath his tight black T-shirt.

"Dude, at least I get paid," he countered. "If you think about it, you're kind of paying me to hang out with you." He snorted and shook his head, as if pitying her. "I can think of better ways to spend my money."

"You know what? Me too." She snatched back the couple dollar bills she'd given him for a tip and slammed the door in his face.

"And then he asked you out?" In her excitement, Harper almost dropped the phone. She flopped back onto her bed and kicked her legs in the air in triumph. This could be just the loophole she was looking for.

"He gave me his phone number," Miranda clarified. "It's not the same thing."

Details, details. "Okay, but he basically asked you out. Excellent."

"Um, were you not paying attention when I described what an annoying loser he was?" Miranda asked. "And did you miss the part where he dumped a bucket of water on my head?"

"Methinks the lady doth protest too much," Harper teased her. "Besides, that was just his way of flirting. Maybe he's a little shy and awkward. I think it's adorable."

"Since when do *you* find shy and awkward adorable?"

Harper's mind was racing. Sure, *now* she was betraying Miranda by helping Kane get another girl—if you wanted to look at it that way. But as Harper saw things, Kane had made it painfully clear that he wasn't interested. Just because she'd sworn a solemn oath to Miranda that she'd do everything she could to make it happen . . . well, what was she? A magician? It's not like she had any power over what Kane wanted.

The problem was just that Miranda might not see it that way. So if Miranda found some other guy to lust over in the meantime, someone who actually wanted her in return, and she got swept up in some torrid new romance? Well, she'd stop feeling so shitty about the Kane thing and Harper could stop feeling so guilty.

Problem solved.

"I say you go for it," Harper urged. "How long has it been since you've gone out on a date?"

"Can I plead the fifth?"

"Miranda," she said warningly.

Miranda sighed. "Okay, okay, too long."

"And why is that?"

"I don't know—because I'm fat? Because I have frizzy hair that now looks vaguely like seaweed? Because I'm so short that a guy has to fall over me before he notices I exist?"

"Shut up, loser," Harper snorted. "You know none of those things are true. Plenty of guys ask you out."

"Sucky guys."

"That's exactly what I'm talking about—you're too picky. They can't *all* suck."

"Oh, trust me—"

"No, I don't trust you. You've got these impossibly high standards that no guy could ever measure up to and then you complain about being alone. I'm tired of it."

"So I'm supposed to have *no* standards?" Miranda asked.

"No, you're just supposed to be realistic. To take a chance once in a while on someone who's not one hundred percent perfect."

"I don't think Kane's perfect—"

Harper rolled her eyes, glad Miranda couldn't see her through the phone. This was getting pathetic.

"Great. So there's *one* guy in all these years who measures up. You think maybe it's time to branch out a little?"

"Why are you yelling at me?" Miranda asked in a small voice.

"I'm sorry." Harper took a deep breath. "I'm not yelling. I just want you to be happy, Rand. So what if this guy's not the one? So what if he's not as hot or as charming as the Great and Powerful Kane? You don't have to marry him—just go out with him a couple times. Think of it as practice. And who knows," she continued, hating herself for it, "maybe you'll even make Kane jealous. You know guys always want what they can't have." She knew that was one idea Miranda would find impossible to resist.

"Okay . . . you got me. I'll do it. I'll call Greg and ask him to dinner."

"Fabulous." Harper grinned and looked out her window toward Adam's bedroom. She wondered what he was thinking about right now. Probably Beth. But even that wasn't enough to deflate her mood. "Good luck, not that you need it."

Miranda sighed.

"Thanks for the reality check, Harper. You're the best."

Harper hung up the phone and gave herself a mental pat on the back for a job extremely well done. Miranda would be distracted (and, as an added bonus, maybe even happy), leaving Harper free and clear to pursue her own agenda. Guilt free.

Was Harper the best?

Damn right.

Beth slammed her hand on the dining room table as another paper airplane whizzed past her head.

"Adam, give it a rest, I'm trying to concentrate."

"Okay, okay." He bent down over his book again and there was a moment of blessed silence. But then, just when

Beth had almost wrapped her head around the variables in a monstrously complicated word problem, a tiny ball of paper flew onto her book. When she looked up in irritation, another one hit her squarely in the forehead.

"Jesus, Adam, what are you, twelve years old?"

"What? I'm just trying to have some fun. You can't tell me you're not bored out of your mind."

"That's not the point," she snapped. "The SATs are in less than two weeks, and I *need* to get through this. I thought you did too—isn't that what you said?"

Actually, Adam had called to report his latest swimming victory, suggesting they go out on the town to celebrate. It was a huge moment for him—the swim team was going to the regional championships for the first time in a decade, and it was all thanks to Adam. Beth would have liked nothing more than to spend the night celebrating, to enjoy the fact that she was in love with such an amazing guy. But . . . she just didn't have the time. She'd set aside the night for SAT studying, and she couldn't break her schedule. Not this close to the test. Not even for Adam. But when she'd told him that, he hadn't gotten angry, or sulky, or any of the other reactions she'd expected. Instead, he'd invited himself over. A study date, just the two of them.

"I need to study," she'd warned him, wary that she'd be too distracted by his charming smile and silky blond hair.

"Hey, I'm taking the test too," he'd pointed out. "Don't I need to study?"

She'd been skeptical—but, after all, she'd been begging him all along to take the SATs more seriously. Who was she to object when he finally took her advice?

They had set up shop at the dining room table and, after a couple minutes of small talk, lowered their heads over their books.

For about five minutes. And then his attention span ran out.

The last hour had been insanely frustrating as she tried to keep her concentration and her temper. But she wasn't having much luck with either.

"I just thought we could take a little break," he whined, squirming under her disapproving gaze. "Have a little fun."

"There's no time for fun—not now," Beth said, gesturing at the intimidating piles of books, notebooks, and flash cards that lay scattered across the table. She hated the way she sounded, like such a humorless stick in the mud. But it was partly his fault—if he wasn't always such a baby, she wouldn't always have to be such a nag. It's not like she enjoyed playing the role. "Why can't you understand that?"

"Maybe because you seem to have plenty of time when it comes to Kane," he said sulkily.

"Is that what this is all about? Is that why you're here?" Beth sighed in exasperation. How had Adam gotten so disconnected from the things that really mattered to her, enough so that he couldn't understand the most important things in her life? Instead, they just had to have this same pointless conversation over and over again. Maybe that was what happened when you stopped talking, she thought sadly. You ran out of new things to say. "Are you really that jealous?"

"I'm not jealous at all" he said hotly. "I just don't understand what the deal is with the two of you."

"I told you—he cares about doing well," Beth insisted. "He *wants* my help."

"That's not all he wants," Adam muttered.

"What was that?" she asked sharply.

"I just think you need to ask yourself why he wants to spend so much time with you. Why are you so sure that he cares so much about the *test*?"

She stiffened—it infuriated her when he implied that the only thing she had to offer the world was her body. Why was he so convinced that all anyone could ever want from her was sex? Maybe because it was all *he* wanted? As always, she tried to suppress the fear—but these days, it never disappeared for long.

"Oh, I don't know—maybe because when I study with *Kane*, he actually works hard," she pointed out, and it was absolutely true. "He doesn't sit there fidgeting, throwing paper airplanes, and ignoring everything I say unless it's about football or TV. Now . . . who does that sound like to you?"

"Fine!" he said in a loud, sulky voice, looking away. "You caught me. I don't give a shit about this stupid test. I just wanted to spend some time with my girlfriend. Lock me up and throw away the key."

She shushed him and glanced down the hall—her mother was trying to sleep a bit before working a night shift, and the last thing Beth needed was to wake her up. They both held still for a moment, waiting—but no sound came from the bedroom. They were safe. And in the quiet pause, Beth's anger had seeped away. She closed her book, then reached over and closed Adam's, too.

"Adam, listen to me. You have nothing to worry about."

"You don't know Kane . . ."

"Maybe I do, maybe I don't. But I know myself," she said urgently. "*You* know me. Whatever it is you think he's after, he's not going to get it."

Adam looked down and didn't respond.

"You trust me, right?"

"I do, of course I do, it's just that—"

"Look. Remember last month, when you were spending all that time with Kaia?" she asked.

A wary, panicked look flashed across Adam's face. "Yes . . ."

"And I was insanely jealous?"

"That's right, you were," he said triumphantly, vindicated.

"And you got mad, because I didn't trust you—and you were right."

He looked down again, deflated.

"I should have trusted you," Beth told him, "because I know you'd never do anything to hurt me."

"I never would," he said urgently. "Beth, you know that. I love you."

"And I love you." She leaned across the table and gave him a soft kiss on the lips. "And you just have to trust that. Okay?"

"So what now?" he asked.

She laughed. "Now you get out of here and let me get my work done so that I can see you another time. *Without* the stupid books."

He rolled his eyes. "Are you sure?" he asked, coming around to her side of the table and massaging her shoulders. As always, she melted beneath his warm and sure touch. "Because you might want to keep me around—I tend to come in handy."

She swatted him with her notebook. "Don't tempt me," she begged. "Now come on, get out."

He shrugged and turned to go. But he didn't get very far.

"Okay, come back," she cried. "You got me—one more kiss."

It was a long one.

Adam drove home. With the sweet taste of Beth still fresh on his lips—and the image of her in Kane's arms still fresh on his mind. He knew Kane—the guy got anything he wanted. Anything. Anyone. Adam had to work for everything he got; but for Kane, victory came easy. And it came often.

Beth could deny it all she wanted—she could beg him to trust her a hundred times. But he couldn't help what he knew, and what he knew was that sometimes being in love, being trustworthy just isn't enough. Yes, he remembered back when he was spending all that time with Kaia. He'd sworn to Beth a million times that nothing would ever happen. And he'd meant it.

And it's not like he was some horrible person, he reminded himself. Kaia had just been there—the wrong girl, in the right place at the right time. He hadn't been able to stop himself. Sometimes he wasn't even sure he could blame himself—it had all seemed so inevitable. Sometimes, despite the best of intentions, things just happened.

And *that's* what he was afraid of.

chapter eight

THAT NIGHT, IT SEEMED LIKE SLEEP WOULD NEVER come.

Beth lay in bed, her body drained of energy, her mind spinning in circles, refusing to slow, refusing to relax. When had her life gotten so complicated? And what did it mean that the things that should have made her happy were the ones keeping her awake?

And, as long as she was asking meaningless questions that she'd never be able to answer, if she was so in love with her boyfriend, why did she sometimes wish he was someone else?

I wish I were someone else, she thought wistfully.

Someone who didn't care so much about always doing the right thing and getting the job done, someone who wasn't overwhelmed by commitments and responsibilities to everyone in her life. *Someone who wasn't tied down to the same guy, day in and day out*, her mind whispered. To trade lives with someone, just for a day—was that so much to ask?

What would it be like, she wondered, to have Kaia's life? Not her striking beauty, or her wealth—though at the thought of a life free of skimping, saving, and scrounging, free of bussing tables at the diner and watching her parents drag themselves home from work at three a.m., Beth often felt a sharp pang of jealousy. There were people who lived life without struggling for every dollar. She'd accepted that she wasn't one of them—and while she didn't care as much as she used to, she cared. A lot. But looks, money, clothes, those were just things, possessions—Beth didn't want to *have* what Kaia *had*, she wanted, at least sometimes, secretly, late at night, to *be* who Kaia *was*. Beth often watched her out of the corner of her eye, marveling at the girl who seemed to float above the fray, skimming across the surface of life, never getting her feet dirty. It was such an alien frame of mind that Beth couldn't imagine how the world must seem to her. But on nights like this, she longed for it.

The apathetic manner, the almost inhuman poise—

Kaia, she was sure, never fought with her boyfriends. Never questioned what she "really" wanted, and whether it was right or wrong. And, Beth was sure, never worried that her life was boring, that *she* was boring. Kaia was just like Kane in that way—and maybe, Beth suddenly realized, that was why she was so drawn to him, in spite of herself. And she was. Drawn to him. Even though she could only admit it to herself at times like this, alone, stranded between night and day, waiting for sleep—or sunrise.

It didn't matter, of course, because she was with Adam. Good, solid Adam. They were two peas in a pod. A perfect match. She knew that. She loved that. And yet . . .

He was the only boy she'd ever dated. The only boy she'd ever held. Not that she was bored. She was just . . . curious. And if she could, for just one day, abandon herself, if she could leave good, dutiful Beth behind, if she could borrow Kaia's mind, Kaia's life—then she could know what it felt like to live without consequences, without guilt, to take whatever she wanted, to have it all. Just a one-day vacation from her cookie-cutter life, from always doing the right thing. That was all she asked.

Just one wild day.

And one wild night.

What had happened to her wild nights?

Sprawled across her Ralph Lauren sheets, her comforter

kicked to the foot of the bed, Kaia opened her eyes with a sigh. She'd kept them closed as long as she could, hoping she could force sleep to come, but it wasn't working. She just wasn't tired—how could she be, when it was only one a.m. and she'd spent the night, like every night before it, lounging around her house?

Kaia's body was designed for a different life—she'd trained it well over the years, and by now it expected a steady influx of loud music, flashing lights, hot bodies, and cold drinks. Every night—all night. That had been her old life in her old world. She'd done her best to pretend that it had all disappeared when she left: the city, the social scene, her old friends. She preferred to think of it all as frozen in limbo, awaiting her return.

But when reality hit, it hit hard. The city was still bursting with life, her "friends" were still partying till dawn—and the only thing frozen in limbo was Kaia. She hated them for it, and she hated her parents for causing it. Most of all she hated the hours she spent every night, alone in the dark room, staring at the ceiling and wishing she could do something about the endless, deep quiet seeping into her bedroom from the desert outside. She could play music, turn up the volume on the TV, it didn't matter—somehow the desert silence managed to drown it all out. Made it impossible to forget how still everything was, and how empty—just like her life.

Most of the time Kaia clung to her memories of the past, to her hard-edged city persona, clung to it with a death grip, for fear of forgetting who she was and where she'd come from, fear of turning into a small-town zombie content with the simple life. But there were moments, fleeting but sharp, when she just wished she could let it all go. Everyone else in this stupid town was so happy, so satisfied—what must it be like, Kaia wondered, to be able to inhabit such a narrow world without feeling like the walls were closing in?

What must it be like to be Beth, too timid to complain about what you had, too dim to wonder if there might be something more? Kaia had been spending a lot of time recently watching Beth, wondering how her mind might work—and sometimes, to her horror, she'd actually wished she could, just for a moment, switch places with the girl. She had such a picture-perfect life—loving parents, loving boyfriend—all the things Kaia had never wanted, never thought she needed. And it was true, she didn't *need* someone lying beside her, holding her, whispering that he loved her and that everything would be okay. She didn't *need* to know if her mother missed her, or if her father would ever stop home for more than a night. That kind of thing was no more than a security blanket for the Beths of the world. It was just that late at night, alone and empty, Kaia sometimes wished she were one of them.

Beth, she was sure, didn't stay up nights desperate for excitement, searching for trouble. Beth wasn't constantly bored, restless, always on the hunt for the next hot spot, the next hot guy. Beth didn't spend every minute wishing she were somewhere else, doing something else. Being someone else. No, when your life was placid, when you had what you wanted, no more and no less, you slept like a baby. It was only when you were dissatisfied, when your life seemed empty and you had nothing to fill it with, that you tossed and turned. Until finally, as always, you gave up on sleep and turned on the light.

Adam awoke with a start and flicked on the light, gasping with the relief of escaping a nightmare. He didn't remember much of it, only that it had featured Beth and Kaia— and it had left him drenched in a cold sweat. He sat up in bed and took a few deep breaths, trying to wash all traces of the nightmare out of his mind so that he could safely fall back asleep.

His sleep had been filled with nightmares for weeks. They'd started the night after he slept with Kaia, and ever since Kane and Beth had started spending all that time together, his dreams had only gotten worse. Too much stress, he told himself, lying back down on the mattress. Adam had always liked to keep things simple. But now? Nothing was simple, not anymore. Certainly not his relationship with Beth. That was a minefield. When he was with her, he struggled over his every word, agonized over every action, searching fruitlessly for the magic combination that would put right whatever had gone wrong.

Nothing worked. And lately it seemed like everything that came out of his mouth just made things worse.

Kane, on the other hand, always knew the right thing to say. Adam could see it in Beth's eyes—"Why can't you be more like him?" She would never say it out loud, but he knew her well enough to read her thoughts, to know her desires. Kane was flashy, charismatic, Kane saw what he wanted and took it—and girls loved that. Adam had always thought Beth was different. But now . . . he wasn't so sure.

Just once, he thought in frustration, *just once, I'd like to know what it's like.* To win, every time, without trying. To effortlessly be the best, and have the world at your fingertips. Everything Adam had, he had only because Kane hadn't thought it worth the trouble. Kane got good grades without studying, beat Adam on the courts without breaking a sweat, could get any girl he wanted just by curling up a corner of his lip in that famous Kane smirk. Adam worked so hard, at everything—and yet time and time again, it seemed he was always coming in second.

But Beth hadn't been seduced by the flash or the glitter of Kane's charm—Beth had chosen Adam. She'd been repulsed by Kane, she always told him, and seduced by

Adam's straightforward manner, his honest appeal. It had been the first time he and Kane had ever gone head-to-head over a girl—and the first competition Adam had ever truly won. But it seemed the battle had never really ended. And maybe he hadn't won after all.

Adam had never wanted to be Kane, had never even much admired Kane. But if only he could just borrow a little of whatever it was that allowed him to lead a charmed life. Adam was sure that Kane would never have gotten sucked in by Kaia's act, would never have been fooled into believing anything she said. Kane would know exactly the right thing to say to get his girlfriend past the whole virgin issue—and he'd do it so smoothly that she would think it had been her idea. And Kane would never, *never* let another guy sweep his girlfriend off her feet. Kane didn't get brushed aside, ignored, overlooked. Ever.

Kane had "it," whatever it was. And Adam just didn't. Instead, he had a work ethic, a conscience, and a face that couldn't lie. And, for now, he had Beth.

But with Kane on the prowl, how long would that last?

How long could it last, this merry sidekick game, before she got fed up? Miranda lay flat on her back in bed, her eyes tracing the tiny cracks in the white ceiling paint. She'd stayed up late, shampooing and shampooing until finally she'd managed to wash most of the green out of her hair. She hoped.

And now she'd been lying in bed for the past hour, trying to work up some kind of excitement about this dunk-tank guy, trying to picture his body curled up against her in the bed, his hands crawling across her body . . . but it wasn't working. She kept losing her concentration, and his face kept morphing into Kane's. She didn't have to *work* at desiring Kane—it was the easiest thing she'd ever done. Imagining herself in Kane's arms seemed as natural as breathing. Maybe because she had so much practice.

She knew what Harper had said—and she knew Harper was right—but still, did she have to like it? She didn't see Harper forcing herself to date a loser, just because her first choice was "temporarily" unavailable.

But of course, that was Harper. Miranda sighed. You'd think she would be used to this by now. She'd been playing second fiddle to Harper since elementary school. "Partners in crime," that's what they always called themselves—but when she was alone, Miranda sometimes wondered. It didn't feel like a partnership. It felt like Harper was out for herself, leaving Miranda to follow behind, cleaning up her messes.

Miranda shook away such disloyal thoughts. Just because Harper could be a little thoughtless, a little self-centered at times, was no reason to question her commitment. Maybe there was only one problem in this friendship: Just maybe, Miranda was jealous. She would never have admitted it out loud, but there were times—*lots* of times—when she looked at Harper and asked herself, *Why not me?* They'd started in the same place as wild, spunky outcasts, gone through all the same experiences— and yet Harper had blossomed into this alpha queen, while Miranda, it sometimes seemed, had never blossomed at all.

What did Harper have that she didn't?

Beauty, she reminded herself.

Charisma.

Sex appeal.

And confidence.

Maybe that's all it was—Harper knew what she wanted, and she believed she deserved it. So she went out and did whatever it took. Miranda, on the other hand? She knew what she wanted, beat herself up about it, then sat on her hands and did nothing.

And, when it came to Kane, it seemed Harper agreed with her—she wasn't worthy. Didn't deserve the guy of her dreams, apparently. She deserved to settle for some- thing attainable, something subpar.

Miranda was no hanger-on, clinging to a friendship with Harper in the hopes that some small crumbs of desirability and popularity would fall to the ground at her feet. But a part of her was always waiting, wondering—when would

Harper turn to her and say, "It's your turn now"? When would she reveal her secret of success and teach Miranda how to be bold, beautiful, and . . . more like Harper?

After all, everyone knew Harper Grace had it all—so wasn't there enough to share?

Harper had never been very good at the sharing thing. Maybe it came from being an only child. Or maybe it just came from her utter disdain for almost everyone who crossed her path. Why should she share? Who was more deserving than her of having . . . well, anything?

Which isn't to say that there weren't a few exceptions—obviously there were some people worth her time and goodwill. Well, at least two: Miranda and Adam.

But then, she wasn't very good at sharing them, either. Which is why she'd hated Beth even before discovering her own feelings for Adam. Harper was supposed to be his top priority, and always had been. But when Beth showed up, everything changed. She'd stomped all over Harper and Adam's friendship, pulled him away; even if she hadn't been in love, Harper doubted she would have been able to stand it for very long.

She wouldn't have to wait much longer, Harper comforted herself. The next day, she was planning to put Kaia's plan into action. There was just one thing: What if it didn't work?

Harper rolled over in bed, kicking at her blankets in frustration. She hated thinking of Beth, wanting what Beth had—*Beth*, of all people. So boring, so dull—she was nothing, compared to Harper. And yet she had the one thing that Harper wanted the most.

And it wasn't just Beth. Kaia'd had him too.

It was infuriating, the way Harper couldn't stop watching her enemies—even her friends—and wishing she had what they had. She would never want Beth's life, Beth's bland and muddled personality. So why did she spend so much time wishing she could take Beth's place?

It was the same with Kaia, spoiled, self-centered, bitchy, *rich* Kaia. She had no friends, no life—but she had so much else. Harper looked around at her room with complete disgust. The shoddy pieces of furniture, shadowy silhouettes in the moonlight, were supposedly antiques, but to her they just seemed old and out of style. Her closet was bursting with imitation designer gear, discount shoes—and even those, her parents always claimed, were practically more than they could afford. Whereas Kaia was probably spread out on designer sheets beneath a mahogany four-poster bed, tucked away in a cozy corner of her giant estate. Kaia didn't have to buy Frada (imitation Prada), and she didn't have to worry that someone from school would spot her helping out at the family dry cleaning store on weekends.

Sometimes it seemed like everyone she knew had something she wanted. Money, men—it didn't end there. She was even jealous of Adam's good-natured honesty, Kane's car—and his complete lack of scruples. Even Miranda had something Harper occasionally longed for: obscurity. She didn't have to worry about people watching, judging her every move. She didn't have to constantly perform. She could just *be*.

It was as if everyone had *something*, something that made their lives better, special—and what did Harper have?

For one thing, she had the admiration of every kid in school. But, late at night, deep in the back of her mind, a small voice questioned what they saw when they looked at her. Was it real? Or did it all rest on an elaborate bluff?

Because if Harper really was who they said she was, if she really did have anything a girl could ever want, why did she lie awake so many nights wishing she were someone—almost *anyone*—else?

Anyone else might have lain awake all night, every night, struggling with his conscience, worrying about his betrayal of a friend, wondering if he was doing the right thing.

Not Kane.

No, as he stretched himself out along the couch and tucked a thin blanket over himself, his mind was untroubled, his conscience clear.

And he did have a conscience—despite his constant boasts to the contrary. True, it didn't get much of a workout. But it was, like everything else about Kane, fully functioning—and, he insisted to himself, in this case it just had nothing to say.

He flicked on the TV—he needed it to fall asleep, to fill the silence of his empty house—and closed his eyes.

So he was in hot pursuit of Adam's girlfriend. So what? First, as he'd pointed out to Harper, he and Adam weren't best friends. Spending time with people didn't automatically make you close, it didn't mean you could depend on them. He'd learned that the hard way, a long time ago. And he wasn't about to make the same mistake again. He liked Adam, liked hanging out with him—he certainly outclassed the rest of the Haven High gang of losers—but they didn't owe each other anything.

Second, Beth was just a girl. Sure, Adam would be broken up, for a while—but he'd recover.

And then, there was the third issue. The status of his so-called crime: Was it even possible to steal something that had already been stolen? Because Kane had spotted Beth first. Kane had pursued Beth first. And by the rules of the game—rules that, in the old days, Adam had readily agreed to—Beth had been his for the taking. Until Adam swooped in and took her away. Beth had forgotten. Adam had forgotten.

But Kane remembered.

She had chosen Adam over Kane. She'd fallen for Adam's good-boy looks, his good-boy charm. She'd brushed Kane away from her like a gnat and given herself to Adam. And ever since then, everything had been different. Adam was different, ignoring every other girl, most of the time ignoring Kane—all he wanted was Beth. To be with her, to talk about her, to hold her. Kane couldn't stand it. Partly because he hated to see a friend morph into one of those relationship pod people, jettisoning all the interesting parts of his personality. Trying his best to behave—to obey.

But more than that, Kane couldn't stand the possibility that Beth wasn't "just a girl," that she really was something special, something new—and that she belonged to someone else. Kane was not, by nature, a covetous person. Envy was too passive for him. To envy something, after all, you had to be sitting on the sidelines, watching what someone else had. Wanting it, longing for it, and powerless to get it.

Kane didn't do powerless. He didn't waste his time wishing he had someone else's life, someone else's possessions. He was who he was, he had what he had—and when he discovered something out there in the world that he needed? He took it.

chapter nine

HARPER DIDN'T USUALLY ASSOCIATE WITH BETH and her little clique during gym class. Of course she had to be nice to Adam's girlfriend, and *pretend* they were friends, but that didn't mean they needed to be bosom buddies. So usually, after suffering through the forty-five minutes of torture better known as phys ed, she stayed on the other side of the locker room, sliding out of her hideous orange and black uniform and back into her real clothes as quickly as possible so that she could get the hell out. (The girls' locker room, although lacking the overpowering stench of sweat ever-present in the guys' locker room, was still not the type of place in which you wanted to kick back and relax.) But today was different. Today she had a mission. Kane and Harper had conferred, and agreed: It was time to set Kaia's plan into motion.

She moved into position—a few feet away from Beth and the group of mousy blondes who surrounded her. When Beth, with her watered-down personality, managed to be the center of attention, you had to wonder about the quality of the company. Imagine a group that found the Queen of Bland riveting, Harper marveled to herself.

Far enough away to be unobtrusive, but close enough to . . . to do what she had to do.

She felt a small twinge of guilt about the whole thing, but quickly squelched it. She was doing all of them a favor, she reminded herself. Beth and Adam's rickety relationship was being held together by a Band-Aid—and it would be less painful for all involved if someone just ripped it off, nice and quick.

Lucky for them all, Harper was up to the task.

"God, if I never have to run laps again, it'll be way too soon," Marcy sighed, stripping out of her sweaty gym uniform.

"Who invented gym, anyway?" Marcy's best friend, Darcy, chimed in.

Beth laughed, letting the familiar chatter wash over her. It was the same every week with these girls: Gym sucked. School sucked. Guys rocked. Gym sucked. Rinse and repeat.

They weren't her friends, exactly—beyond Marcy and Darcy (one never went anywhere without the other), they weren't even friends with one another. But they were all dating guys on the team—the swim team, the basketball team, the lacrosse team, depending on the season. It didn't really matter. At a school this small, there was pretty much only one Team. And whatever the season, Adam was its captain. Which somehow made Beth—what, exactly? She was never sure. Not the most popular, certainly. That would always be Harper, who kept herself aloof from "the girlfriends" but still managed to gain their unadulterated admiration. Not the best liked—for Beth was unsure whether these girls actually *liked* anyone. She was certain, however, that if she and Adam ever broke up, the flock of giggling girls would disappear along with him. But at the moment she seemed to have a certain cachet. It was as if they were all drawn to one another by some elusive girlfriend pheromone, and hers was—by virtue of dating Adam, Big Man on Campus—the strongest. Maybe it was some kind of evolutionary reflex.

Or maybe you've just been spending too much time staring at your AP bio book, she thought, laughing at herself and her insatiable need to overanalyze everything. Why couldn't she just accept these girls for whatever they were? Comfortable acquaintances, just another perk of dating Adam, like free tickets to football games and a ride to school whenever she needed one.

So what if they were vain and vapid? It's not like she could afford to be choosy—she didn't have too many friends these days, beyond Adam. So she should probably stop being so judgmental and just take what she could get.

"So *are* you, Beth?" Marcy asked insistently.

"Am I what?" Beth asked in confusion, suddenly realizing all eyes were on her. She pulled off her gym uniform and began brushing out her long blond hair. Back in ninth grade, when she'd walked into the locker room for the first time, she'd been insanely bashful about letting the other girls see her change. Over the course of a few months, she even developed a system of contortions that would allow her to change from her clothes into her gym uniform and back again without revealing a square of naked flesh to anyone. Four years later the whole thing seemed ridiculous. She was totally comfortable now wandering around the locker room in her underwear—it was just another part of the high school experience, like cafeteria food. And trigonometry. She couldn't even remember what her problem had been. Of course, she mused, back then *no one* ever saw her naked, and the very thought of revealing herself to another person had made her skin crawl. Then came Adam.

"Are you going to the championships?" Darcy repeated

on behalf of her best friend. "You heard the student council got together enough funds to pay for a bus to take us all up to Valley Glen, right?"

"Yeah, I heard." Beth smiled, remembering how delighted Adam had been when she told him she would finally be there to see him swim. And hopefully, win. This year's regionals were being held at Valley Glen High, a huge school up north, and a school bus had been chartered to take half of Haven High along to cheer on the swimmers. (Given the football team's 0-9 record—three years in a row—Haven fans had plenty of time and energy on their hands.) It would be a long day, but Beth wouldn't miss it for anything. She knew how important it was to Adam. And seeing how much he wanted her there had just reminded her how much he loved her. And how much she loved him. Not that spending five hours on a bus with Marcy, Darcy, and the rest of the Haven High cheering section sounded particularly appealing to her—but it would be worth it to get to see Adam in action again, to show him that she cared. Besides, she'd promised him. She was, after all, his good luck charm. "I'm definitely going," she answered, grinning. "I can hardly wait."

"Looks like you won't have to," Marcy said.

"What do you mean?"

"Weren't you listening?" Darcy asked. "We were just talking about how great it is that they rescheduled the championships for this week."

"This week?" Beth asked in alarm. "But the SATs are on Saturday!"

"Exactly, that's what's so great—you know they're giving the seniors Thursday and Friday off."

"So we can *study*," Beth pointed out.

Darcy laughed. "Yeah, but who's actually going to do that? No, it's perfect—we'll ride up on Thursday morning, watch the meet, do some victory partying, and then ride back late that night. And we have all of Friday to sleep it off!"

"Are you sure about this?" Beth asked, her throat tightening.

"Yeah, Kyle just told me."

Kyle was Darcy's boyfriend, and the swim team's cocaptain. If he'd said it, it must be true.

Shit.

"I can't do that, I can't go away two days before the test," she cried. "That's insane."

"Breathe, Beth. It's no big deal. It's just . . ."

But Beth tuned out the rest of the prattle, her mind frantically racing to find a way around the problem. There wasn't one. She was just going in circles, always coming back to the same basic certainty.

She was going to have to back out—and Adam was going to freak.

❧   ❧   ❧

As the rest of the girls filtered out of the locker room, Harper lingered. Once she was on her own, she pulled out her phone and quickly flipped through the images she'd captured. Perfect. She'd gotten everything she needed— and more. This swim meet development was quite the windfall.

That had been the only flaw in Kaia's ruthlessly brilliant plan—the when. And now Beth had supplied them with the perfect solution. If Adam went out to Valley Glen and Beth stayed here . . .Well, if she'd had any doubts before about whether this was the right thing to do, they were gone now. Why else would all this good luck be raining down on her if this weren't exactly what she was meant to do? Why else was everything working out even better than expected?

It would be the ideal setup, but it would mean they had to move fast. And Kane, who was on the swim team too (at least when he felt like going to practice) would have to give up a shot at athletic glory—somehow, Harper was pretty sure he wouldn't care. Why would he want to go all the way to Valley Glen for a pathetic plastic trophy, when the real trophy would be right here, conveniently close to home?

She slipped out of the locker room and started texting Kane and Kaia. They needed to know that step one was taken care of and step two needed to happen ASAP. Beth had just dumped a giant gift in their laps. It would be a shame to let it go to waste.

Beth steeled herself all day for the inevitable. But when the moment came, she still wasn't ready. She sat in the car next to him, looking out the window as the familiar scenery whizzed by, nodding absently as he filled her in on the details of his day at school. She was too nervous to pay much attention, instead plotting out the conversation in her mind, striving for some angle that wouldn't cause an eruption. She'd yet to find one—but a couple miles from her house, she realized she just couldn't wait any longer.

"I've got bad news," she blurted out, interrupting some story about his history teacher's toupee.

He flicked his eyes off the road for a quick second, flashing her a look of concern. "What is it?"

"It's your swimming championships."

"Oh, right, I've been meaning to tell you, there was some kind of scheduling screw-up, so they changed the date and—"

"I can't go," she said flatly.

"What?"

Something suddenly occurred to her—and she didn't like it. "Adam, if you knew they'd changed the date, why didn't you tell me?" she asked suspiciously.

"I was about to," he said uncomfortably.

"It's two days before the SATs—you *knew* I wouldn't be able to do that."

"Yeah—wouldn't *want* to do that."

"Wouldn't want to blow the test, no," she agreed. He could be such a baby sometimes. "Look, I'll come see you some other time, I promise."

"Some other time? This is *it*, Beth, this is the time. It's the end of the season—it's the championships, for God's sake. I thought you understood that this was important to me."

"And the SATs are important to *me*," she retorted. "Look, it's not like I'm asking you not to go."

"No, you're just saying you can't be bothered to come along," he countered.

"Don't do that." She was getting so sick of having the same conversation again and again. Was she supposed to plan her entire life around him? "Don't try to make this about you and me. You know this test means everything to me."

"And I don't?"

She was running out of patience—if she wanted to spend the afternoon dealing with a whiny child, she'd be home babysitting her little brothers.

"Adam, it's not that I don't want to be there for you—but this is my life we're talking about here. I can't throw everything away for some stupid swim meet."

"Right," he muttered. "When it's something you care about, it's important. When it's something I care about, it's just stupid."

Beth sighed. "That's not what I meant, and you know it. I wish I could go, Adam, I do," she said desperately. "I just *can't*—I mean, if it were some other weekend. *Any* other weekend. This just isn't the time."

He gripped the wheel tightly. "It's *never* the time. You just don't get it, do you? You and me, we need—I need—can't you just *make* the time?"

"*You* just don't get it," Beth cried, as all the anger and frustration she'd been suppressing for the past few weeks bubbled to the surface and burst through. "Why do you have to be like this? Why can't you understand that this is my future we're talking about? It's your future too," she pointed out, even though she'd promised herself she would never bring this up, wouldn't try to force him to see what he was missing out on. "It wouldn't hurt you to do a little studying of your own. I mean, even Kane—"

She cut herself off, realizing as soon as his name came out of her mouth that she'd made a serious mistake. But it was too late.

"So that's what this is about?" Adam snarled. "I knew it."

"No, that has nothing to do with what this is about. Why can't you just let this go?"

"Are you seeing him tonight?" he asked in a low, calm voice.

"Yes, but—"

"And tomorrow?"

"Adam—"

"And I guess *he'll* be ditching the swim team, staying here with you for some hot and heavy studying while your boyfriend conveniently goes out of town?"

"You got me!" she cried. "You figured out my secret plan. As soon as you get out of town, Kane and I are just going to hop into bed together. That's all you care about, isn't it? Not spending time with me—keeping me away from him!"

Adam stared straight ahead at the road, fingers tightly clenching the wheel. The car suddenly felt very, very small. "I didn't realize that staying away from him would be such a sacrifice."

"I'm not your property, Adam. You don't get to tell me who to spend time with. And acting like this isn't the best way to keep me from cheating on you—or breaking up with you."

"What is the best way, then? You tell me. Because I'm beginning to think there isn't one. You're just going to do whatever you want to, no matter what I say."

"You're right," Beth spluttered, barely able to believe the words that were coming out of her mouth. She would *never* cheat on Adam—and she'd never throw away her relationship just to preserve some barely-there friendship with Kane. But that was *her* decision to make. Not his. "If you want someone who's just going to take orders from you, follow you around like you're her almighty ruler, you're dating the wrong girl."

"Maybe I am," he agreed angrily.

"You know what? Stop the car."

"What?"

"Stop the car. I'm getting out. I can't be around you when you're like this."

He glanced over at her incredulously. "You want me to stop the car and let you out on an empty road in the middle of nowhere?"

"Anything would be better than being stuck in this car with you," she said, her voice filled with spite.

"Fine." He swerved to the side of the road, slammed on the brakes, and the car skidded to a stop. "Get out. See if I care what happens to you."

"Oh, don't worry, I know you don't. You've made that painfully clear."

"Don't try to—"

But she slammed the door in his face, and his voice trailed off as he saw she was serious. She turned away from the car and began walking slowly down the narrow shoulder of the road. At that rate, it would take her an hour to get home from there—and it was getting dark.

✷ ✷ ✷

Adam knew he should pull up alongside her and try to persuade her to get back into the car. If that failed, he should drive beside her the whole way home, just to make sure nothing happened.

It was the right thing to do. He knew that.

And he really meant to do it, right up until the moment he put the car in gear and pressed a leaden foot down on the gas pedal. The tires screeched as the car peeled onto the road and sped past her solitary figure.

By the time he'd calmed down enough to realize what he'd done, she had long since disappeared into the dark distance. He could have turned around. Gone back for her.

But he didn't.

Kaia's favorite French film was part of a trilogy: *Bleu*, *Blanc*, and *Rouge*. She'd seen all three in a row during a foreign film festival at Lincoln Center. One rainy day, she'd barricaded herself in the theater and, shivering in her Anna Sui raincoat, she'd fallen in love. The best of the three, she'd decided, was *Bleu*. The plot was elegant and obscure: A young, beautiful woman loses everything, everything that matters. She is alone, disconnected, disenchanted, and free. Ultimate freedom, at the ultimate price. Death of the spirit—and, ultimately, a reawakening.

It was intense, it was sexy, and it was the way Kaia

wanted her world to be. Elegant, beautiful people, awash in a cool, bluish gray light, speaking in clipped sentences packed with suppressed passion and cryptic meaning.

So it was this DVD that she tucked into a picnic basket, along with some gourmet cheese imported directly from a small farm in the French Alps, and a bottle of Bordeaux snagged from her father's ample wine cellar, before setting off for Jack Powell's house. It was time for Little Red Riding Hood to pay a call on the Big Bad Wolf.

She wasn't completely sure that now was the time to make her final move—though it was quite obvious the move would need to be hers. He wasn't about to take the step. But was he ready yet? Oh, she saw the glint in his eyes when he looked at her, the hint of desire in his voice every time he told her to go away. And the spark between them when they'd touched the other night, that couldn't be denied.

Yes, she told herself once again. *He's ready.*

And so was she.

She wore a filmy black slip dress and strappy black kitten heels. And beneath it all, a custom-made camisole of red lace, and black panties with a red lace trim. She looked good, *all over*. And she knew it.

She rang the doorbell, savoring the nervous energy fizzing inside of her—it was rare, these days, that a guy could set her blood boiling with anticipation, that the thrill of the chase came paired with the arousing fear of rejection. It was one of the reasons she wanted this so badly. That, and the way his designer shirts hung on his sculpted body, the sound of his elegant British accent, his easy charm, his icy anger.

He was the complete package. And it was such a turn-on.

He opened the door, unlike her, dressed down for the night—adorably rumpled hair, tight jeans, Oxford T-shirt. His eyes widened when he saw what was waiting on his front doorstep.

"You," he said simply, blocking the entranceway to the house.

"Me." She smiled.

"You're out kind of late," he finally observed. "Won't Mommy and Daddy be wondering where their precious little one has run off to?"

"Daddy's off screwing his secretary in a Vegas hotel room, and Mommy's back in Manhattan, probably having a nice, long sleep courtesy of Dr. Valium," she informed him bitterly. "So . . . no."

"What's in the basket?"

She pulled out the wine. "Reinforcements."

He looked down the dark and deserted street.

"Did anyone see you? Does anyone know you're here?"

"What do you think?"

"I think you're trouble," he reminded her. "But as I recall, we've already had that conversation."

"Ad nauseam . . . are we ready for a new one?"

He looked her up and down, then sighed appreciatively. "You are *not* what I expected when I came out to this hick town."

"Ditto. So—what do you want to do about it?"

There was a pause, and a palpable tension in the air. This was the moment, she knew. He was on the brink, and it was now that he would either step back to safety—or grab her wrist and plunge them both into the depths.

He took a deep breath. "There are going to be some rules."

"Of course." She nodded, disguising her relief. Now they were getting somewhere.

"No one can know."

She rolled her eyes.

"No one," he repeated.

"Yes, sir." She saluted.

"No other guys."

"I don't see how that's any of your—"

"High school boys get jealous," he explained. "When they get jealous, they get curious. And *that* I don't need."

"Right. No extracurricular activities," she agreed. She

had the sneaking suspicion this wasn't the first time he'd had this conversation. He was too quick, too smooth.

"And no more of this stalking nonsense. I don't want you showing up in my classroom, in my bar, at my house— we meet *when* I say, *where* I say. I don't like surprises."

Kaia gave him a slow, simmering smile.

"Then you're going to hate me."

His face remained frozen. "Are we agreed?"

"Completely."

"You break the rules, and we end this," he warned her. "Immediately. I'm not some horny teenager who's so desperate to get some that I'm willing to throw my life away."

Could have fooled me, Kaia thought, wondering—not for the first time—what had brought a man like that to a town like this.

But if he wanted to believe he was in control, that was just fine with her.

"Your wish is my command, *Jack*."

"In that case, what are you waiting for?"

She took a step toward him, tilting her head up as if to seal the deal with a kiss, but he backed away and shook his head.

"Not out here," he chided her. "Never where people can see." He swung the door open a bit wider and stepped aside, ushering her in with an exaggerated sweep of his arm.

No matter, she could wait. For another minute or two, at least. And then, she thought, pausing in the doorway and marveling at his cocky good looks and the sizzling current of sexual tension flowing between them—then all bets were off.

She stepped inside the house, and Powell slammed the door shut behind her.

Waiting time was over.

chapter ten

THE NEXT DAY THEY MET AT DUSK.

When Kane pulled up in his silver Camaro, Adam was already on the court. He'd arrived a half hour before and had spent the time running up and down the length of the court, slamming the ball into the cool concrete, sinking shot after shot. Warming up. Practicing. Kane, he knew, had called him out here for a friendly game of ball. Nice and easy. That was the thing, wasn't it?

Adam slammed the ball against the backboard. Nice and easy. Story of Kane's life. You want something? You take it. Just like that. Kane, who got good grades without studying. Who had every girl chasing after him despite being an unapologetically sexist pig. Who was the best basketball player in town despite the fact that he was too lazy to practice, too above it all to join the team.

He won everything, always—every game, every argument, every girl. And all without even trying.

Adam slammed the ball again, harder.

Not this time. Everyone had to lose sometime. Everyone.

The game started off slow. Friendly. Nice and easy. But then Kane scored. And scored again.

And Adam began to simmer. And the angrier he got, the harder he tried, the harder he gripped the ball, the harder he threw it. What should have been a smoothly arced two-pointer became a spasmodic air ball; what should have been an easy layup bounced off the rim. And every time, Kane grabbed the rebound.

He shot.

He scored.

"Dude, what's up with you today? You're playing like a girl," Kane taunted him.

Adam ran past his opponent, giving him a hard shove with his left shoulder and grabbing the ball as Kane fell backward.

He shot and, finally, scored.

And it felt good.

"And your problem is . . . ?" Kane asked, picking himself up off the ground.

"No problem," Adam replied, suddenly whipping the ball toward Kane, whose lightening fast reflexes caught it just before it smashed into his nose.

"Hey, watch the face—I'm nothing if I'm not pretty."

"Tell me about it," Adam growled.

"Oh, I get it," Kane said, dribbling down the court with swift, sure movements.

"Get what?" Adam asked irritably.

He lunged for the ball, but Kane veered away, faking left, then cutting right as Adam's hands swiped uselessly at the empty air.

"You're tired of always coming in second," Kane said, tossing in another basket. "You're always the runner-up, I'm always the champ. You're tired of being a loser."

It was nothing more than their standard trash talk. They always did it. You got a rise out of your opponent, put him off his game. Kane, to be sure, had made a science of it—and used the same technique off the court to keep his opponents equally off balance. Today shouldn't have been different from any other day, but it was. Today Adam just wasn't in the mood.

"Shut up," he snapped, grabbing the ball away and dribbling it down the court. Kane hounded him, but Adam knocked him off balance again, this time with a sharp jab in the stomach.

Kane dropped to the ground with a soft sigh, as if all

the air had been let out of him, and Adam raced for the basket with a spurt of renewed, righteous energy. His path was clear, his mind was clear, and the basket lay straight ahead.

He got into position, readied the ball on his fingertips, imagining its perfect three-point arc ending in a nearly silent *swoosh*.

"By the way," Kane said nonchalantly, still on the ground where Adam had left him. "If I see your girlfriend tonight, should I tell her you say hello?"

Air ball.

After the basketball game ended—rather abruptly—Kane rushed home to shower and change, then drove right back to school. He met Kaia and Harper in front of the dark building, their figures illuminated by the low-watt yellowish lights. Kane pulled out his key—he had keys for almost every door in town—and they slipped inside.

There was always something about being in the school after hours, after dark. An illicit thrill, the undercurrent of tension and excitement—the possibility of getting caught. The halls that were so familiar and oppressive during the day transformed into a dark, shadowy no-man's-land for them to explore.

It made no sense—sneaking *into* school would likely get them into no more trouble than sneaking out of it, which all three of them did on a regular basis. But there was still something there—an unspoken feeling that just by being there at this hour, alone in the dark, they had somehow taken ownership of a side of the school its true owners had never known.

Of course, in a sense, they owned the school during the daylight hours too—so it wasn't a big leap of the imagination.

They crept down the hallway, single file, keeping an eye out for the janitor. Kane went first, leading the way, unable to stop dwelling on the game. It had been so easy to get a rise out of Adam—it was the kind of thing he did best. A skill that had always made him proud. At least in the past.

Next came Kaia, silently marveling at the excitement and nervous energy churning in her stomach, despite the fact that this little caper was far tamer than many she'd successfully pulled off on the East Coast. Maybe it had something to do with the night before—the touch of Jack Powell's body had lit up something inside of her, something that had lain dormant for a long time.

And finally, Harper. Decked out in trespassing haute couture (black faux-cashmere sweater, dark jeans, Sketchers sneakers in place of her usual heels, the better for softly padding through the empty halls). She gripped the bag holding Kane's digital camera tightly. Things were going so smoothly, so perfectly—was something about to happen to screw everything up? Or should she just accept that the universe was on her side, guiding her toward an inescapable destiny?

Kane led them to the girls' locker room, unlocked the door, and flicked on the lights. They squinted in the sudden brightness, then got down to business. Harper pointed out Beth's locker—it probably wouldn't matter much on the small screen, but they'd agreed that the backgrounds should match as exactly as possible.

Then Kaia took the camera and Harper stripped off her shirt—her height and body type were closest to Beth's, and again, they'd agreed this was best. She unbuttoned her jeans, but then paused.

"Bashful, Grace?" Kane asked, chuckling. His laugh echoed through the room, bouncing off the grubby linoleum and washing over them. He'd already stripped down to his silk boxers. "Come on, it's nothing I haven't seen before."

She sneered at him. Stripping down in front of Kane was no big deal—it was the camera she couldn't stop thinking about. And not just because, when it came to kinky fun, she'd never been into the whole Kodak moment scene. It was more that seeing the camera made it real. What they were about to do—and who it was going to hurt. Harper knew she could put a stop to the whole thing in a second—just call it off, send everyone home.

Instead, she peeled off her jeans.

"You do know how to sweet talk a girl," she said sarcastically. "I know we all look the same to you."

"Well . . . that may be true," Kane admitted. "But in this case, I mean *you're* nothing I haven't seen before. Or are we forgetting that fateful day after Shayna's eighth-grade birthday blowout?"

"Kane," Harper said warningly, shooting a glance at Kaia, whose affected veneer of boredom couldn't disguise her sudden interest. Harper and Kane had vowed never to speak of The Incident again. And never had—until now.

"I, for one, remember it *very* well," Kane mused. "You, me, a jug of grain alcohol. Good times, good times."

"Kane! Shut up." She balled up her jeans and threw them at him. He caught the denim missile easily and tossed it back to her.

"Chill out, I'm just trying to lighten things up. Just reminding you that my arms are not such an alien place for you to be."

Harper rolled her eyes. "I'll never understand how you manage to get anyone to fall for that dirtbag 'charm' of yours," she complained.

"Ask Beth—she's falling for it, hook, line, and sinker."

At that, Kaia cleared her throat and waved the camera in the air.

"Guys? Speaking of Beth, maybe we should get a move on with the task at hand? Much as I'm enjoying the Harper and Kane show, I don't really need to spend the rest of the night watching you two practice flirtatious banter."

Kane nodded. "You're right, enough flirting—"

"*That* was flirting?" Harper interjected. "We really are in trouble."

"Like I was saying," Kane continued, staring down Harper, "enough flirting, down to business." He mugged for Kaia and the camera. "Come on, I'm ready for my close up, Ms. DeMille."

"Okay then, hotshot, let's get started. Nice and slow."

The next hour passed in a blur, a steamy montage of sexy poses and ever-changing camera angles.

Here was Harper draped in Kane's arms, her head resting on his bare chest.

Flash, click.

And Kane tracing his fingers down Harper's bare back.

Click.

Harper and Kane pressed together, their lips locked in a kiss.

Click.

And more, and more, and more.

Not that Harper was enjoying the rubbing and the pressing and the groping and the kissing of the fake hookup. And not that Kane was turned on by the warm, supple body writhing in his arms, her mind committed to someone else, her body all his. Kaia, certainly, could not have been taking a secret thrill from the voyeurism of it all, playing the puppet master, barking out commands, suggesting poses, capturing it all on film.

All three of them, they assured themselves, would never sink low enough to actually enjoy the depravity.

Still, when the pictures were all taken, the arms and legs untangled, the clothes back on, all three were sorry to see the evening end.

"Well, it's been fun, ladies," Kane said, grabbing the camera and flipping appreciatively through the stills they'd captured. "You look *good*, Grace."

"You're not going to start chasing after *me* now, are you?" Harper asked, feigning disgust.

"Oh, don't be so full of yourself. You may look good," he pointed out, "but I look better."

"On that note, should we get out of here?" Kaia suggested. "I think we got what we needed."

"Here's my cell, Kane." Harper handed over her phone, with its own stock of photos still intact. "So you're sure you can actually make this work?"

"Have no fear—my Photoshop skills are second only to my carnal skills—and you've got personal confirmation of those."

"Gross, don't remind me," Harper complained, smacking his chest good-naturedly. "Come on, let's go—I think after that, we could all use a drink."

They crept out as silently as they'd crept in, and drove off together into the dark night, the cell phone and digital camera safe and sound in Kane's bag. It was the dynamite that would blow Beth and Adam's relationship apart—and the fuse had just been lit.

The dunk tank guy, Greg, had been only too eager to take Miranda for dinner, and they'd met at seven that night at the one nice restaurant in town. It turned out he was a junior (a bit embarrassing, but not nearly as bad as if he'd been a sophomore), and when he wasn't dressed like a cowboy, he was at least passably cute. Or at least acceptable. The ears were still too big and the thick-framed glasses still a no go, but she could at least handle the freckles. After all, they matched her own.

The dinner itself had gone, well . . . okay. Miranda was wearing the sexy new outfit she'd impulse bought the other day, and while she was still slightly afraid it made her look like a thick-trunked tree, she told herself she probably looked okay. And Greg, once you stripped away the nervousness that apparently made him act like a dick, was a pretty nice guy with an easy laugh. He seemed fun, witty, smart, and—what should have been the best part—totally into Miranda.

And that was the problem. Yes, it was great to be adored, but it wasn't enough. Because when she looked at him, all Miranda could think was: *Yeah, he's okay.*

As they walked toward the coffee shop together, he took her hand—and she let him. It wasn't unpleasant, it was just—neutral. *Maybe this is how it's supposed to be*, she told herself. Girl likes boy, boy likes girl—maybe the sparks come later. Maybe love at first sight is for suckers and romantic comedies. Maybe, out in the real world, being smart and nice and funny and kind of cute was enough. No wild heartbeats, no movie-star good looks, no rapt gazing into each other's eyes—just good food, good conversation . . . and an okay time.

That's what she told herself, at least, as they strolled through the night hand in hand. And she was almost convinced. Then they stepped inside the coffee shop.

And there he was.

Movie star good looks.

Her heart beating wildly.

Her gaze drawn inexorably to his.

Kane. And in an instant, she remembered what it was to feel, to want, to crave the touch of someone's hands, his lips, to glow under the warmth of his smile, to light up when he was around, to suddenly forget the existence of everyone else in the room. In the world. To look at other girls, foolish girls, and think, *How can they not see what I see?*

There was one guy in that room who made Miranda catch her breath with desire—and it wasn't the one she'd come in with.

He sat at a table with Harper and Kaia. (It was only later that it would occur to her to wonder what Harper—supposedly home studying—was doing out with Kane, or what either of them was doing with Kaia, of all people. But that was later.)

"Miranda!" Kane called out, catching sight of her and Greg and waving them over.

Miranda pulled Greg over to the table to say hello. She tried not to drool.

"Small world," she commented.

"Small town" Kaia snorted, and excused herself to get more sugar for her, as she put it, "sorry excuse for a macchiato."

"What are you guys doing here?" Miranda asked.

Harper shot Kane a cryptic look. "Study break," she said quickly. Then she noticed what Miranda was wearing, and her eyes widened in surprise. "That shirt—I thought—when did you get it?"

Miranda did a little twirl. "You like?"

"It's . . ."

"It's ravishing," Kane said with an approving grin. "No offense to your date here, but you keep dressing like that and he's going to have himself some serious competition."

Miranda flushed with pleasure. It was the first time Kane had ever given her a compliment on how she looked—maybe the outfit had done its job. Maybe Kane would finally start seeing her in a new light, as more than just a snarky brainiac. Or maybe Harper was right, and seeing her with another guy had made him jealous and—

Oh, right. Another guy.

She suddenly remembered Greg, who was standing quietly, obediently beside her. Shit.

They'd decided on coffee instead of alcohol, since Kane had a long night of Photoshopping ahead of him. And it had seemed a fine choice—until Miranda and her date walked in. Harper almost spat out her mochaccino at the site of her. In *that* outfit. Fortunately, it seemed Miranda was too dazzled by Kane's presence to wonder what the trio was doing there together. That was the silver lining—the black cloud, of course, was that Harper could tell from the queasy look on Miranda's face that this Greg thing wasn't going to work.

Not a big surprise—Greg was scrawny, gawky, and worst of all, bland. Under normal circumstances, Harper would have given him the big thumbs down—Miranda could do way better.

But these weren't normal circumstances, and she was going to have to take what Miranda could get. Which, at the moment, was a geeky, gawky loser. That, however, was a problem for another time—for tomorrow. Tonight she was still riding high on her triumph, and once Miranda was gone, she could continue celebrating in peace.

As Kane and Kaia bantered flirtatiously back and forth about who had the hottest drink, Harper zoned out, letting the conversation wash over her. The plan was set in motion now, and it was only a matter of time before the big payoff. She didn't know how she was going to make it through the next couple days, hoping that nothing went wrong, that no one—including herself—lost their nerve, and knowing that by the end of the week, if all went according to plan, she and Adam would finally be together. And when that happened, she knew, she would stop all this ridiculous worrying about what she'd done and who she'd betrayed—because being with Adam would feel so right, it would justify anything that had happened along the way. She couldn't wait.

Kane lifted his mug and proposed a toast.

"To getting what we want," he proclaimed, "by any means possible."

They clinked glasses and drank up. Harper smiled weakly, suddenly glad he hadn't suggested an alternate toast: "To getting what we deserve."

"Can you guys just shut up for one second?" Beth screamed in frustration. But it was no use. Her bratty brothers

487

continued their hyperactive race through the house, hollering and squealing as they clomped up and down the stairs. Disaster was inevitable. Whether it would be one of the twins colliding with a heavy piece of furniture or Beth's head exploding (or some combination of the two, featuring an irate babysitter and a blunt object), she didn't know. But she did know she couldn't take this much longer. The stress of the SATs always looming over her, the fight she'd had with Adam eating away at her, and now, these brats. The world was conspiring to drive her insane.

Not that she didn't love her little brothers.

And maybe, if their house had been fully stocked with all that stuff supposed to keep five-year-olds in check— X-Box, cable TV, DVD collection—she wouldn't have minded spending day after day after day with them. But her family couldn't afford any of that stuff. So the twins just had Beth—and each other. Normally, Adam would be here, occupying the twins with one of those lame magic tricks they loved, or teaching them how to tie different kinds of knots. Adam was an only child, and always claimed he was jealous of her "adorable" little brothers. "If you think they're so cute," Beth usually responded, "take them home with you. Please." But she had to admit that, when Adam was around, even *she* found her brothers kind of cute—he brought something out in them. And in himself.

But she and Adam weren't speaking to each other—hadn't since the day before, when he'd left her in the middle of the highway and sped away, covering her in a cloud of dust. She was on her own with the babysitting thing tonight, and that meant she had two options: continue to yell and scream, which would neither get the twins to shut up nor get her any closer to that perfect score—or bribe them with ice-cream sundaes.

As always, it worked like a charm. Jeff and Sam, who, when they were silent, looked almost cherubic with their big blue eyes and curly blond hair, sat side by side at the table in front of their heaping bowls of ice cream, chocolate sauce, and a cherry for each. Their legs dangled several inches from the floor, swinging back and forth as they dug into their frozen treasure.

"Bethie, can I ask you a question?" Jeff asked, slurping down a spoonful of rocky road.

"Sure," she said, expecting to have to explain why the sky was blue or why Daddy smelled strange and acted so funny when he came home late at night.

"Is Kane your boyfriend now?"

"What? No, of course not," she said quickly. Kane had been over at the house a lot lately, studying—but she hadn't realized that her brothers had noticed.

"He's just a friend."

"I like him," Jeff said.

"Me too," Beth replied.

"But I like Adam better."

"Adam stinks, I like Kane," Sam countered. Beth knew he was just trying to get a rise out of his brother—but still, it hurt to hear.

"Sam, take that back!" she scolded him.

"No way," Sam said, grinning, seeing he'd made her mad. "Adam stinks. Kane's way better."

"Adam is!" Jeff yelled.

"No, Kane!"

They went back and forth, louder and louder, until finally Beth pulled away both their ice-cream dishes and held them high in the air.

"No more, unless you guys behave!" she threatened.

They shut up immediately, and she handed back the bowls.

"But Beth," Sam asked quietly, "which one do *you* like better?"

They both stared at her, their eyes filled with curiosity, and Beth shifted uncomfortably in her seat. It was just too weird to hear the question coming out of her little brother's mouth, the same question that Adam had been pestering her with one way or another for weeks. The same question that kept bouncing up in her mind no matter how hard and how many times she tried to push it away.

"I like them *both*, Sam, in different ways."

"But who do you like *better*?" Jeff repeated insistently.

She ignored the question and skipped over to the refrigerator. When in doubt, distract.

"We almost forgot—who wants whipped cream!"

Greg pulled the car to a stop in front of Miranda's house.

"So," he said awkwardly, turning off the ignition and staring straight ahead as if afraid to look at her.

"So," she repeated, giving him a half smile. Part of her wanted to throw open the door, jump out of the car and never look back. But it would be so rude, even cruel . . . and a part of her was just a little curious to see what would happen if she stayed.

So she did.

"I had a great time tonight," he said hopefully, twining his fingers with hers.

"Me too," she replied—it was only polite. She looked down at her hand, linked with his, as if it belonged to someone else.

He touched her cheek with his other hand. "I'm really glad you agreed to go out with me."

He was so earnest, it was painful. "You've got really pretty eyes," he whispered. "You know that?"

Oh God, just kiss me already, she thought, stifling a laugh. But she just smiled sweetly. "Thanks."

And then, even though she'd been waiting for it, he took her by surprise. One moment his face was a foot away, the next it was on hers, bumping awkwardly against her nose, and then their lips were suctioned together. There was no wave of passion, not even a ripple. Instead, she just observed, as if from very far away.

His lips were oddly soft and very wet.

She'd never before noticed how strange kissing was, really. All that squishing and sucking and smacking together. Where your tongue goes and what your hands should be doing. She'd never really thought about it before.

But then, she supposed, you probably weren't supposed to be thinking very much, during. You certainly weren't supposed to be thinking about your unfinished chem lab or yesterday's episode of *General Hospital* while his fingers were crawling up beneath your shirt, hungrily grasping at your bare skin. And you probably shouldn't be thinking about another guy.

But Miranda was—and wished that those were his arms wrapped around her, his breath hot against her neck.

But then again—

It was dark inside the car, and they were just shadowy silhouettes pressed against each other. He could be anyone. She could be anyone. When she closed her eyes, there was only the feel of a body next to hers, of a solid chest and broad shoulders, of warm flesh and hard muscle.

When she closed her eyes, they were two strangers coming together in the dark.

When she closed her eyes—he could be anyone.

chapter eleven

"SO I THINK I'M GOING TO DITCH OUT ON THIS whole swim meet thing," Miranda said, stretching herself out on Harper's living room couch.

"What do you mean, 'ditch out'?" Harper asked lazily. She was curled up in a worn orange armchair, feeling far too relaxed and contented to get upset about Miranda's last-minute change of heart. "Why wouldn't you go?"

"I don't know." Miranda, who'd been playing a game of 'should I or shouldn't I eat this' with a bag of Chips Ahoy! for the last twenty minutes, finally pushed the unopened bag away in disgust. "With the SATs and all, it just seems like maybe I should stay home and study—"

"The SATs aren't until Saturday," Harper pointed out. "We'll get back from Valley Glen Thursday night—you'll have all day Friday to study." They'd had this conversation already, a few days before, and Harper had thought the matter was closed.

"Yeah, but I'll be totally wiped, and it's probably better if I—"

"Miranda, what's *really* going on?" Harper interrupted, shaking her head. It's not like Miranda's presence on Thursday was at all crucial to the plan—but she didn't like last-minute changes, not this late in the game. Not when everything was moving along so perfectly.

Miranda flushed and looked away. "I just think it'll be weird," she admitted. "Greg's going, and I don't want to . . . I think it's better if I just stick around here. I'm sure I can find someone who wants to do some last-minute cramming." She laughed ruefully. "There's always Beth—I'm sure she's not going anywhere two days before the SATs, and—" Miranda suddenly caught a glimpse of Harper's face, which had almost completely drained of color. "What?"

But Harper was struck speechless for a moment, as she felt her whole plan begin to unravel.

"Just to avoid this guy Greg, you'd stay home and"— she could barely bring herself to say it—"study with *Beth*?"

"Well, I was kind of joking about the Beth thing,"

Miranda allowed, "but actually, it doesn't seem like the worst idea in the world."

"Except that it is," Harper countered heatedly—and then caught herself. She couldn't have Miranda staying home and screwing everything up. She couldn't leave Beth with a potential alibi. But what was she supposed to tell Miranda?

Obviously not the truth.

"So exactly what was so wrong with this guy?" Harper asked, stalling for time as she desperately tried to figure out how to get Miranda on that bus and safely out of town.

"There was nothing *wrong* with him," Miranda clarified, sounding exasperated. "I just don't think I need to be with a guy I'm not really that into."

"Okay, *first* of all, hooking up in a car does not qualify as being 'with' him, so just take it easy. Second of all, you've only been on one date—that's, what, four hours? You have no way of knowing whether you're into him or not." Harper cringed at her own words, since she'd only needed thirty seconds with Greg to determine he was a loser. But in principle, she reasoned, it was sound advice. So what if she and Miranda, experts in snap judgment, had never followed it before? There was a first time for everything.

"I know that when I stood him next to Kane, it wasn't pretty. Doesn't it seem like the guy you're with—excuse me, on a date with—should at least seem like the most appealing guy in the room?"

Uh, not when you have no chance in hell of getting the one you really want, Harper thought. But she couldn't say that.

"Miranda, you know that old song, 'If you can't be with the one you love, love the one you're with'?" she said instead.

"No, and if you start singing, I'm walking out right now."

"No singing, I promise. Just a suggestion—give the guy another chance. Forget you ever saw Kane last night."

"What were you all doing there, anyway?" Miranda asked suspiciously. "I thought you were staying in."

"Oh?" Well, at least this time she'd known it was coming, and she'd had some time to prepare. "Yeah—uh, Kane told me he was going out with Kaia to talk about . . . their history project, and I invited myself along. You know, to keep an eye on him—for you!" *You are an evil person—and, all of a sudden, a shitty liar,* she told herself. She hoped Miranda would buy it.

"Well, thanks, I guess," Miranda said grudgingly. "I can't believe you were willing to subject yourself to a night with Kaia just to keep him away from her. For me."

"Well, believe it." Please, please believe it.

"So you *do* still think I've got a chance?" Miranda asked, her voice filled with a new hope.

It was a hope that Harper knew she should shoot down immediately, for Miranda's sake, if not for her own. But if she was going to get Miranda to this swim meet, Harper was going to need to use some bait. And she had just the thing.

"I think . . . it can't hurt to find out. And this whole swim team championship could be your perfect opportunity."

"Why—is Kane coming?"

"He's on the swim team, isn't he?" Harper replied carefully. It was a true statement . . . it just didn't actually answer the question. "You can spend some time with him, be there to support him. And as for Greg—how do you think Kane will feel, seeing some guy chasing after *you* for a change?"

"I don't know if it's such a good idea, Harper," Miranda said dubiously. "Having the two of them side by side? It might not be—"

"I saw the way Kane was staring at you in that coffee shop, Rand," Harper broke in, throwing caution to the wind. "Seeing you with another guy? It made him look at you in a whole new way."

"I thought so too!" Miranda crowed.

Harper smiled weakly, feeling like a sticky gob of something you peel off the bottom of your shoe. It wouldn't be so bad, she told herself. Maybe once she spent some more time with this loser, Miranda would decide she actually liked him—maybe she'd finally forget all about Kane. When you thought about it, Harper was doing Miranda a service—Kane was a sleazebag, not good enough for her best friend. Things were bad enough now, with Miranda chasing after him so pathetically—but she'd be much, much worse off if she ever got what she wanted. Kane was bad news.

Miranda needed someone good, someone solid. Really, if she knew what Harper was up to, if she knew the *whole* story, she'd have to be grateful. She'd have to say thank you.

But maybe it was better not to risk it.

They arrived at the school at seven the next day, just after sunrise. The swim team, riding in a separate van, had already left, and Miranda and Harper found themselves lost amid a sea of rabid Haven High fans. It had been a long time since either of them had attended a school sporting event—now, trapped in a rowdy crowd of students waiting to get on the bus, they remembered why they'd stayed away.

"Miranda! Hey, over here!" The two girls looked over toward the sound of the voice to see a life-size foam cactus pushing through the crowd—and heading straight toward them. "Hey, I was hoping you'd be here," the cactus-guy called, bobbing his head awkwardly—thanks to the costume, his arms were both stuck rigidly out from his body, as if in a permanent double-handed wave.

"Do we know this loser?" Harper muttered to Miranda, as the cactus approached.

Miranda just sighed.

"Hi, Greg. When you said you were coming, you didn't mention you'd be—" She gestured to his elaborate green foam costume. It was too horrible for words.

"I'm the mascot," he explained, a wide smile breaking out on his face. "I'm supposed to bring some cheer for the cheering section."

"Well you certainly brought *us* some morning cheer," Harper said snidely, smirking at Miranda.

Miranda just sneered back—then yelped in dismay as Greg's thorny arm wrapped around her and pulled her toward the bus.

"Our chariot awaits, madame," he told her gallantly. "You can help me lead the fight song."

Harper stifled a laugh and tried her best to ignore the pleading look in Miranda's eyes as Greg dragged her away. She knew she should probably feel guilty, but she couldn't help it: All she felt was a rush of anticipation and excitement, and the warm certainty that everything was finally falling into place, exactly as she'd planned.

She found a seat for herself on the bus and watched

out the window as they pulled out of the lot and onto the open road. The road stretched ahead of them, and Grace soon fell behind—and as the miles wore on, her heart grew lighter and lighter. It was all going to work. By the time the bus returned to Grace, late that night, everything would be different. And Harper would have everything she'd ever wanted. It felt like she'd been waiting a lifetime; but only a few hours more, and her wait would finally be over.

The pit stop was, almost literally, a pit.

It was a gas station in the middle of nowhere, a lonely gray outpost in the gray desert landscape. It looked abandoned, a wreck of a building that faded into the washed-out sepia tones of the scrub-brush-covered land. But after three hours on the road, cramped together in a tiny van with nothing but drab scenery, dirty jokes, and a scratched-up music CD to keep them entertained, the swim team was ready for a break. And they weren't picky.

Besides, at least there was a bathroom—unisex, and looking as if it had only recently been introduced to indoor plumbing, but semifunctional nonetheless. There was a small convenience store area by the cash register, where the coffee looked like it should have been dispensed by the ancient, rust-encrusted gas pumps, but it was coffee.

And there was even cell reception. Just in one spot,

behind the semi-outhouse and a few feet from where the owner had tethered a sallow, swaybacked horse, but one spot was all Adam needed.

He couldn't do it, couldn't leave town without at least *trying* to talk things out with Beth. Or rather, he had left town, without saying a word, and it was killing him. He would go no farther.

"Hello? Beth?" he shouted when she picked up the phone, trying to make himself heard through the static.

"Adam? Is that you?"

"Beth?" He could barely hear her.

"Where *are* you?" she asked, her voice punctuated by static and silence. "You're cutting in and out."

"Beth, I wanted to apologize." It took a great deal of effort to get the words out—since really, it was the last thing he wanted to do.

"What? You want to what?"

"I'm sorry!" he shouted.

"Did you say you can't hear me? I can't hear you, either."

"Beth, I just want to . . ."

She interrupted, but her response was incomprehensible. There was too much static, too many moments of dead air.

"Adam, I—you, but you—if—and then Kane—"

"What? What about Kane?"

"—have to go, Adam—later?"

"Beth, wait!" he called uselessly.

Disconnected.

"Nervous?" Harper asked, hoping that her voice sounded normal and that Adam wouldn't notice the desire throbbing beneath her carefully casual smile. They stood at the edge of the Olympic-size pool, waiting for Adam's heat to start, and as Adam shifted his weight from one foot to the other and anxiously watched his teammates finish up the butterfly relay, Harper watched . . . Adam.

He was wearing nothing but tight orange briefs and an orange and black swim cap with goggles strapped around his head. His tan skin glistened, still wet from his warm-up laps. Harper's eyes traced a path down his taut biceps, his chiseled abs, the angular curves of his muscles. . . . His body was like a work of art.

"Not really," he murmured, looking out at the huge crowd of screaming spectators. "It's just a meet, just like any other."

The lie was obvious in his face, but Harper didn't call him on it.

"Good," she said warmly. "Nothing to be nervous about."

He looked past her into the distance for a moment, a wistful look crossing his face.

"I just wish . . ." His voice trailed off, but Harper knew what he was thinking. He wished that Beth were there. Sweet, loving Beth, his little good-luck charm, always there to support him in his time of need. But she wasn't there now, was she?

Better get used to it, she warned him silently.

"Never mind," he said, shaking it off. "It's going to be fine. I'm going to be fine."

"You're going to be great," she corrected him—and suddenly, without fearing what he would do or think, threw her arms around him. *Just a friendly hug*, she told herself, pretending not to notice the warm touch of his bare skin against her body. *For now.* "Good luck," she murmured.

"Thanks, Harper," he whispered, clutching her tightly. "I'm glad you're here."

So was she.

Adam loved swimming. He loved the way his body sliced through the water, he loved the harsh, unforgiving rhythm of the strokes, and he loved the feel of his muscles working in concert, disconnected from his mind, from worries of speed or victory, just pushing and pushing, toward their limit. And, on good days, beyond.

But most of all, he loved the silence. When he dove off the edge and slipped beneath the water, the noise of the world dropped away. The screams and cheers of the crowd disappeared, and the universe narrowed to a single bluish tunnel of water. Nothing mattered except his body and his breathing, and forcing his limbs to cut through the water, surging ever ahead. He could shut out all the background noise of his life, shut off his mind, and just focus. Just be.

But today, with so much riding on this race—and with so many problems waiting for him back on dry land—he worried that the water wouldn't work its familiar magic. As he stood poised at the edge of the pool, waiting for his moment, he couldn't get the noise to stop, couldn't find his focus. It wasn't just the screaming crowd, or the yells of his teammates. It was the sound of Beth's voice in his head, telling him she wouldn't be there. Telling him she'd rather stay home, with Kane. Faces flashed through his head: an apologetic Beth, a smirking Kane, and then Harper, with such a look of calm and comfort that he almost believed her, for a moment, that everything would be okay. At the thought of Harper, the voices almost quieted, and the rapid pounding of Adam's heart subsided—but only for a moment. Because thinking of Harper cheering for him on the sidelines reminded him of Beth's absence. And that led him back to Kane. He couldn't escape it, the sound of his own thoughts and fears. He couldn't clear his mind, couldn't concentrate, and then—

The sharp report of the starting gun.

A dive off the edge, the sharp pain of cold water slamming into him.

A new world, silent and awash in blue.

His mind shut down, his body took over—and Adam finally let go.

They'd had a marathon study day, cramming last-minute vocab and equations into their heads for hours on end until even Beth felt like her brain was about to melt.

"I'm totally burnt," she finally said, throwing down her pen. "How about a break? We can pick up with this again in the morning."

"You?" Kane asked with mock incredulity. "My faithful taskmaster is actually suggesting we stop early? How *inconceivable*!"

"Hey, I can be *stupefying* sometimes."

They both burst into laughter at the ridiculously unnecessary use of SAT words.

"God, we have turned into complete SAT nerds, haven't we?" Beth moaned through her laughter.

"Harvard, here I come." He looked serious suddenly. "And it's all thanks to you."

"Oh, no, Kane," she said, blushing. "I don't even know why you wanted my help in the first place—you're such a quick study. I barely had to do anything."

"You did plenty," he insisted. "And I still can't believe

you were willing to waste so much time on a screwup like me, not when you had so much else you needed to take care of."

"It was my pleasure," Beth assured him. "What would I have done without the company?"

They sat across the table from each other, silent for a moment. The air was charged with tension. Beth stared into his eyes, wanted to look away, but couldn't. She didn't know what she was doing or feeling—but she knew it was dangerous.

"Well, I don't know about you," she said finally, with a forced joviality intended to break the intensity of the moment. Her too-loud voice seemed to echo in the still room. "But I'm *voraciously ravenous*. You want to meet back here early tomorrow?"

Kane smiled. "Actually, I think I've got a better idea— meet me at the northeast corner of Dwyer Park in an hour? I've got a little surprise for you."

"Tonight? Don't you have a hot date or something?" She winced inwardly at the thought of him groping yet another bimbo—or worse, someone actually substantive, someone he could really fall for.

She stopped herself, suddenly—that wouldn't be worse, that would be *better*. She wanted the best for Kane, she reminded herself. He should be with someone good, someone substantive—someone else.

"There's nowhere I'd rather be tonight than with you," he assured her. "Now, I know I'm only a poor stand-in for Adam—"

"Forget about Adam," she said, a little more harshly than she'd intended. "You're right. We've been working hard, and we deserve to celebrate—you and me."

"Okay, then don't forget," he said, heading toward the door. "Dwyer Park, northeast corner, one hour. Can't wait."

Neither could she.

Adam raised his trophy over his head one more time, and the Haven High fans sent up a deafening cheer. He'd been grinning so hard, and for so long, that his face felt stretched out of shape, but he couldn't stop. Third place in the four-hundred-yard IM at regional championships—it was better than he'd ever expected to do. And if he was disappointed to have lost out on first place by only a few seconds—well, his beaming teammates and the adoring crowd had wiped such thoughts from his mind.

He turned to Harper, who'd been standing loyally by his side all day long. She'd been there to wish him luck before his races, and had greeted him with a howl of triumph every time he'd pulled himself out of the pool. After his big event, the four-hundred IM, he'd swept her, soaking wet, into a tight hug—relieved the race was over, relieved he had someone with whom to share his victory.

Together, they'd watched the rest of the heats, cheered on his teammates, waited through the interminable award ceremony. And when Adam had stood to receive his two-foot-high trophy, Harper's shouts of encouragement had risen above the noise of the crowd.

The meet had cleared his mind, worn him out. He had no energy, no will, to think about his problems, to worry—instead he just relaxed and enjoyed himself. And enjoyed Harper. It was so easy between the two of them. They'd been friends for so long that they didn't have to *try* when they were together, they didn't have to wonder or worry about what the other was thinking. They could just laugh and talk—just be together.

"Come on," he urged her, throwing an arm around her shoulders and pulling her along. Now that the meet was over, the hosting high school was throwing a big, all-school pizza party—and he wanted to get there before all the pepperoni was gone.

Harper leaned against his shoulder and smiled up at him, and Adam marveled for a moment at the warmth and sincerity that filled her eyes. He knew there were a lot of people at Haven High who had their doubts about Harper—but if they only knew her like he knew her . . .

"Actually," she hedged, giving him a mischievous grin, "I have a better idea."

As she explained, Adam laughed and shook his head—

leave it to Harper to find her Valley Glen equivalent and snag an invitation to the Pit, a secluded clearing in the nearby woods that was apparently *the* place to hang, if you were into that whole good music, warm beer, no adult supervision thing. (And who wasn't?)

"She promises it's better than it sounds," Harper wheedled. "A bunch of them are headed over there now—"

"We don't even know these people," Adam said hesitantly "And you don't want to miss the bus."

"It's close by—we'll be back with plenty of time to spare," she promised, pressing closer to him. "No one will even notice we're gone."

Adam shrugged his shoulders and nodded. He supposed that he should stick around for the pizza thing, bond with his teammates—but suddenly, laughing it up with the guys, watching them stuff their faces with pizza and smash soda cans against their foreheads, didn't have much appeal. Not compared to sneaking off somewhere mellow and secluded, somewhere with Harper.

Besides, at this point Adam would have agreed to pretty much anything. He felt strange—weirdly relaxed, loose. It took him a moment to place the unfamiliar sensation, but then he got it: He was happy.

Beth didn't know what to expect when she walked up to the park—really a dusty brown square in the middle of town with a sprinkling of sallow, brittle grass that the town replanted, to no avail, every winter, only to see it all die off by the end of summer. There was a rickety band shell at the other end, which tonight was festooned with banners advertising: GRACE NOTES IN CONCERT! ONE NIGHT ONLY!

She smiled and shook her head. This town got more ridiculous with every passing day.

When she found Kane, he waved and, with a flourish, pulled a daisy from behind his back.

"What's this?" she asked, giggling.

"A flower for the lady," he said. "Just the beginning—follow me, please." He led her through the park toward a picnic blanket that was laid out with a cornucopia of delicious-looking food—heaping sandwiches, cheese, fresh-baked bread, chocolate-covered strawberries, and a bottle of red wine in the center. Kane sat down and gestured for her to do the same.

"You did all this?" she asked, eyes wide.

"I'm a man of many talents," he said, pouring her a glass of wine. "I figured it was the least I could do to thank you."

"It's amazing," she breathed. And it was: the food, the warm breeze, the starry sky. "This is just what I needed—how did you know?"

"Like you said, I'm a quick study. But that's not all."

He looked at his watch. "The entertainment portion of our evening should be starting just . . . about . . . now—"

Suddenly a low base line began booming out of the speaker propped up a few feet behind them, and a moment later a four-part harmony broke into the familiar strains of "Blue Moon," one of Beth's favorite oldies.

She looked up at the band shell and, sure enough, four old men in silver vests and bowler hats—the Grace Notes, she assumed—were crooning away. In the darkness Beth could barely see any of the other picnickers, and it felt like they were singing just to her.

"Did you know about this?" she asked Kane.

"I saw the fliers earlier this week," he admitted. "Thought it could be fun."

"I wouldn't think this was quite your speed," she told him, laughing—she'd been laughing so much these past few weeks.

"Hey, we can leave if you want," he offered, starting to get up.

"Leave? Are you crazy?" She grabbed his arm and pulled him back down again, taking a sip from the glass of wine. She almost never drank—but this was, after all, a special occasion. The wine trickled down her throat, warm, sweet, and delicious. "This is wonderful, Kane— thank you." She leaned over and hugged him. For just a moment too long.

They sat side by side in the moonlight, enjoying the food and the wine, letting the music wash over them, laughing, talking—and then, as the night wore on, quiet. And close.

And when Beth's cell phone rang, she didn't answer it—didn't even check to see if it might be Adam.

And when she shivered, and Kane slowly, tentatively put an arm around her and pulled her close to his warm body, she didn't move away.

chapter twelve

ADAM CAME BACK TO THE SMALL CAMPFIRE AND plopped down next to Harper, who passed him a joint. "Everything okay?" she asked quietly.

Adam, who didn't usually go for pot, inhaled deeply and hoped that if it was going to mellow him out, it would work fast.

"Fine," he said shortly.

He didn't know why he'd had to ruin a perfectly good day. He'd been in a great mood, tired but happy—so he'd let his guard down, called Beth to share the good news of his victory.

There was no answer.

Was she screening? Was she out?

He didn't know, and he supposed it didn't matter. What mattered was that he was here now, free, and if he didn't stop stressing, the moment was going to pass him by.

He looked good-naturedly around at the small group of Valley Glen high schoolers who'd gathered at the Pit. Their names and faces may have been different from the familiar Haven High crowd, but they seemed familiar—Adam had never felt so instantly at home. An old Jay-Z album was booming through the tinny speakers of an old boombox, and Adam leaned his head back, enjoying the way the driving beat enlivened the still, dark woods. He and Harper were perched on a thick log in front of the improvised campfire, next to Miranda and her new guy, who had tagged along when Harper and Adam sneaked away from the pizza bash. It was just like being back in Grace—only better, because here Adam wasn't the center of attention, wasn't the big man on campus, carrying the burden of everyone's hopes and expectations. Here he could just sit back and watch the action from the sidelines.

"I'm glad you dragged me out here," he confided to Harper in a low voice, leaning close to her ear.

She favored him with a warm grin. "Me too, Ad."

Suddenly filled with a burst of affection and gratitude for his oldest friend, he swept her into a bear hug.

"What would I do without you, Gracie?" It was what he'd called her sometimes when they were kids, because it was funny to watch her get red in the face and throw things at him. He knew she secretly loved it.

"Good thing you'll never have to find out," she promised him in a muffled voice.

"Dude, get a room!" one of the random Valley Glen guys called out.

Adam looked up, suddenly realizing everyone was looking at him. Maybe he wasn't the center of attention out here—but he wasn't invisible, either. He flushed hotly and jumped up. "You guys think we need more beer?" he asked Harper and Miranda. "I think we need more beer. I'll go grab some." He jogged off in the direction of the massive coolers.

No one here knew him, of course—and it seemed unlikely that Miranda or her random guy would run home and start spreading gossip. And, Adam reminded himself, there was nothing to gossip about—he and Harper were just friends. Everyone knew that. But still, if someone got the wrong idea, and somehow Beth got wind of it . . . that was really all he needed, for word to get back to Beth that he'd been up here macking on Harper.

On the other hand . . . he pictured her and Kane back in town together, curled up on a couch, studying, ignoring her ringing phone. Maybe she wouldn't even care.

And maybe he didn't either.

✎ ✎ ✎

"Can I talk to you for a second?" Miranda hissed as soon as Adam was gone. It wasn't a request.

"What is it?" Harper asked, visibly annoyed.

She was annoyed? Let her try spending the day fending off the advances of a *human cactus* who had all the sexual chemistry of a rock. *Then* she could talk to Miranda about feeling annoyed.

"Not here," she whispered, and dragged Harper off deeper into the woods, away from the rest of the group—away from Greg. "I cannot believe you," she told Harper, once they were a safe distance away from the group.

"What?" Harper asked wearily.

"What do you mean, 'what'? What's the deal with telling Greg we were coming out here and inviting him along? Like I didn't have enough trouble staying away from him all day long?"

"I don't know," Harper mused, "he's kind of cute without the cactus outfit. Aren't you having fun?"

"No, that would be *you*," Miranda said slowly. "We're talking about *me* now—something I know you have some trouble wrapping your brain around."

"What's that supposed to mean?"

"It means you dragged me along on this stupid trip, when I could have been home studying—and now I'm stuck out here in the middle of nowhere while you and

Adam gaze into each other's eyes and Greg tries to stuff his hand down my shirt."

"Well, that's why I invited Greg along," Harper pointed out defensively. "To keep you company. Besides, you didn't have to come. I told you that you could stay for the pizza thing. We could have met up later."

"Right, like I was going to spend the night with those mindless drones. I *thought* we were going to be hanging out together."

"So here we are," Harper pointed out, "together. What are you complaining about?"

She just wasn't getting it. But she would.

"I don't know, maybe about the fact that you totally lured me out here under false pretenses," Miranda snapped. "Or have you forgotten your little plan," she lowered her voice to a whisper, "to make Kane jealous? Somehow, I don't think it's going to work—because, gosh," Miranda widened her eyes and craned her neck around in exaggerated confusion. "I don't see him *any-where*, do you?"

"Very funny. Like I knew he was going to pull a no-show? Besides, is your life all about Kane now? Wherever he goes, you follow?"

"That's not the point, Harper, and you know it. The point is that you suckered me into coming up here, then ignored me all day, and stuck me with . . . *the mascot*. Do you know what people must be thinking when they see us together?"

"So that's all you care about now?" Harper asked. "He's not good enough for you? And I thought I was supposed to be the shallow one."

Miranda recoiled—maybe because, deep down, she recognized a sliver of truth in Harper's words. Greg was sweet, funny—but he'd spent the day acting like the court jester, not caring that everyone was laughing at him. Maybe he didn't mind being the center of ridicule, but Miranda wasn't looking to become Mrs. Class Clown anytime soon. Still, Harper, of all people, had no right to accuse her—not now, not after today.

"Did you ever think that maybe I just don't like spending time with some guy who's chasing after me when I know I'm not interested?" she asked.

"Did it ever occur to you that I'm doing you a favor?" Harper retorted.

"Oh?"

"Maybe if you give this guy a chance, instead of chasing after something you can't have, you could actually be *happy* for once. Though I know that would just screw with your whole view of the universe."

Miranda snapped. Harper had deceived her, ditched her—and now, instead of apologizing, was acting like Miranda was making the whole thing up? Just looking for an excuse to complain? Miranda had been the model friend—always there when Harper needed her, always ready to support her wild ideas, sympathize with her ridiculous problems. And what did she ask for in return? Not much: a little companionship, a little understanding. What did she get? Nothing. No, worse—she got an endless day with dull-as-dirt Greg, while Harper did what she wanted, as usual, with no apologies and apparently no regrets. Because things were different for Harper, right? Because she played by a different set of rules.

That had always been the understanding, at least—and Miranda was fed up.

"Look who's talking!" Miranda yelled. "I'm not the one chasing after a guy who's already got a girlfriend. And is totally in love with her. You want to talk to me about pathetic and hopeless?"

"That's different," Harper said hotly.

"Why? Because you're Harper Grace and you always get what you want? And meanwhile I'm supposed to settle for second-best?"

"That's not what I said."

"But it's what you meant. It's what you always mean. But why? Why should I have to settle for someone I think is just okay? Why can't I hold out for something that's really amazing? Don't you think I *deserve* something amazing?"

"Of course you do, Rand," Harper said sincerely.

"Then why the hell does everyone always want me to *settle*?"

"I don't," said a low male voice behind them.

They spun around to see Greg standing a couple feet away. He'd obviously heard everything—or, at least, enough.

"I just came to see if everything was all right," he explained awkwardly.

Miranda took a step toward him. "Greg—," she began in a faltering voice, but broke off, not sure what to say.

"No, I get it," he told her, his face impassive—but it was obviously taking him a great deal of effort to keep it that way. "You don't want to settle—that's fair. You think you deserve better." He shrugged and bit down on his lower lip. "So do I."

And he walked away, back toward the school.

Miranda and Harper stood frozen in place for a moment, and then tears began leaking down Miranda's face.

"I can't believe he—Harper, I feel so terrible, and he—" She stopped, her voice choked off by sobs, and Harper wrapped her in a tight hug.

"I'm a terrible person," Miranda whimpered.

"No, you're not," Harper assured her.

"I'm going to be alone forever—I deserve to be alone forever."

"No you don't, Rand! Look, here's what I think. You just need to—"

She was stopped by the sound of her cell phone ringing. They both looked down at it—Kaia.

"Why's she calling you?" Miranda asked.

But Harper had already answered the phone.

"Kaia? Can we do this later? Or—no, okay, I understand. Just give me a sec."

She took the phone away from her ear. "Miranda, I have to take this," she said lamely. "I'm sorry."

Tears still streaming down her face, Miranda looked at her best friend in shock.

"You're kidding, right? You're going to leave me here so you can talk to *Kaia*?"

Harper looked confused for a moment, then looked away.

"I'm sorry, I just have to." She gave Miranda another hug, but Miranda pulled away.

"This won't take long," Harper promised. "I'll meet you back by the fire, and we'll talk the whole thing out. I swear."

"Whatever." Miranda turned away, her shoulders shaking. "Have fun talking to Kaia. Tell her I say hello," she added bitterly.

Harper didn't respond, and when Miranda finally turned around, she was gone.

Harper hurried back to the clearing and knelt by Adam's side, handing him her cell. "Adam, there's a call on my phone that I think you need to take," she whispered urgently.

"What? What do you mean?" He looked at the phone in confusion.

Harper pulled him away from the campfire and led him off into the woods, away from everyone, stopping when they'd reached a cluster of low-hanging trees.

"Just trust me, it's important—something you're going to want to hear."

She left him alone and, bewildered, Adam put the phone to his ear. The reception was shockingly clear.

"Hello?"

"Adam, it's Kaia."

"Kaia? Jesus, what the hell are you calling me for? And on Harper's phone?"

"Adam, don't hang up—please. This is serious."

She sounded desperate and, against his better judgment, he took his finger off the end button. For the moment.

"You've got one minute—talk," he said gruffly.

"I don't know how to tell you this," she began hesitantly. "I went into school today—it was open, you know, and I wanted to do some laps in the pool, and, well, I didn't think there'd be anyone else there, but—"

She stopped.

"Spit it out," he ordered.

"They were there when I came in," she said haltingly. "In the locker room. All over each other."

"Who?" But he thought he knew. A hollow space opened inside of him as he waited for the words to be spoken aloud, to make it real.

"Beth and Kane."

There it was. Three syllables. Funny that it took so little to ruin everything.

"And I'm supposed to believe that? From *you*, of all people?"

He wanted to believe she was lying—but couldn't. He was the one who'd been lying, to himself. All along, telling himself there was nothing to worry about.

Stupid.

"Why would I lie about this, Adam? Look, I know I've treated you . . . poorly in the past."

He let out a barking laugh. *That* was the understatement of the year.

"But I have a lot of respect for you," she said, emotion filling her voice. "You don't deserve this."

"Kaia, I'm not throwing away a two-year relationship on your say-so," he said hollowly.

"I thought you'd say that," she responded. "I've got proof."

He looked at the phone's screen, and a moment later there they were, right in front of him—Beth and Kane, in each other's arms. Naked. Entangled.

The screen was small, the resolution poor, but he could make out Beth's hair, her face, the mole on her left shoulder blade. He could see her kissing Kane, rubbing his bare chest, letting him lick her neck and—he turned the phone off. Hanging up on Kaia, shutting out the nightmarish pictures. He'd known it was true, yes, but to *see* it?

The images were seared into his brain. He smashed his fist into the ground, a volcano of rage erupting within him. He slammed the phone into the ground as hard as he could and stomped on it, imagining it was Kane's neck he was crushing beneath his heavy boot.

"Adam, are you okay?" Harper asked tentatively, emerging from behind the trees.

"Go away, Harper," he said in a strangled voice. No one should see him like this.

"Adam?"

"I just need some time alone, okay? I just—please, Harper, go."

She nodded and backed away.

"You know where to find me when you need me," she promised.

Promises—what were they worth to him anymore? Adam sank onto the ground and laid his head in his hands.

Was this his fault? Had he started it, sleeping with Kaia in the first place?

No.

A cold certainty filled him, a righteous rage—this was no one-time thing, no harmless fling. This was Beth, his Beth, so innocent, so trustworthy—*supposedly*—and Kane, his best friend, his bro, his loyal and true ally. This was an affair, a dirty, scummy, poisonous affair between two heartless traitors who'd betrayed him and everything he thought was real.

He wanted to scream.

He wanted to hit something, someone.

He wanted to cry.

But instead, he just sat there on the cold ground, immobile, silent.

It was all over now, all of it. There was nothing left.

When it became clear Adam had hung up on her, Kaia tuned off the phone with a satisfied grin. He could deny it all he wanted, but she knew he'd believed her the moment the words were out of her mouth. He'd believed it before she even picked up the phone. The pictures were just gravy—but they'd definitely sealed the deal.

"Kaia, I'm getting bored in here. Why don't you come back to bed?" the languid, British voice called to her from the bedroom—where the handsome British man who owned it lay sprawled across his silk sheets, waiting for her.

"Be right there!" she called. "And I've got a surprise for you."

She stopped in the small kitchen and pulled a can of whipped cream and a jar of chocolate syrup out of the fridge. Powell always said he didn't like surprises, but this one would be too sweet to resist. She gave herself a quick once-over in the hallway mirror and then, laying her phone on the counter, headed down the hall to begin her night for real.

I've done my part now, she thought, sending a telepathic message out toward Kane and Harper, who were about to reap the benefits of a carefully laid plan. *Your turn—just don't screw it up.*

Eventually, the anger had seeped out of him.

Or rather, the anger was still there, like acid, burning a hole deep inside of him, but all his energy had washed away, and he felt slow, heavy, weighed down by a deep sadness. And he knew then that he didn't want to be alone.

He walked back toward the Pit to find Harper—but she found him first. She was sitting on the ground by the side of the trail. Waiting for him.

"You're always there when I need you," he marveled, his voice breaking midway through the sentence.

"Oh, Adam," Harper moaned. "Kaia told me—I'm so sorry, I—"

"Please, stop," he said quietly. "Let's not—just stop."

A tear trickled down his face and she caught it with her fingertip as it rolled down his cheek, then pulled him into a hug. He leaned against her, crying silently in her arms, deeply ashamed, and knowing that there was no one, *no one* in the world he would allow to see him like this. No one but Harper. He leaned against her, and she held him up. Like always.

"I broke your cell phone," he murmured into her hair.

"I don't care about that," she said, pulling back and looking him in the eye. "I care about you." She gently pressed her hand against his cheek. "Let's take a walk," she suggested. "I think you need some air."

She put an arm around him and led him down the forest trail and away from the pit. They walked in silence, past the silhouetted trees and shadows cast by looming rock formations. The night was bright, the moonlight filtering in through a canopy of leaves. At the edge of the woods they turned to make sure the Grace bus and van were still there, silently waiting in the parking lot. Then they walked along the perimeter of the woods, listening to the whispering wind and the distant howling of a coyote.

Adam, lost in a world of his own thoughts and regrets, noticed none of it.

Finally, Harper led them over to a square, flat rock that lay tucked between a cluster of saplings.

"Just like our rock," she said, scrambling up onto it and pulling him after her. They lay back on the cool granite and stared up at the sky—and she was right, it did feel for a moment like they were back home, in the backyard, a million years ago, when it had been just the two of them and everything had been so simple.

His mind dipped through the past, skidding across memories of long-ago days. So many moments that had brought him to this one. And Harper—he turned his head to look at her and realized she was staring at him, eyes awash in love and sympathy—Harper had been there for almost all of them. She was the one constant in his life. His father gone, his mother useless, his girlfriend and his best friend—

No, there was only Harper. Loyal. True. Just thinking about her, just lying there so close to her made the anger subside, made the world seem almost bearable, made the red tide of pain and betrayal recede.

She reached over and took his hand, squeezing it gently, and he squeezed back, then shifted onto his side and looked at her. For the first time, *really* looked at her. And realized what he'd been missing. Slowly, wordlessly, he sat up, pulled her up beside him, then tipped her chin up, closed his eyes, and melted into her.

The moment their lips met, it was as if he'd been waiting forever to hold her in his arms, and he drank her in hungrily, urgently, needing the contact, the pressure of her arms around him, her lips on his, their bodies entwined. He didn't need Beth, he thought angrily. And he would prove it.

Time stretched—and it felt like they'd been on the rock, folded into each others' arms, forever, would be forever—

And then Harper pushed him away

"I can't, Adam," she whispered.

"Harper—" He reached out for her.

"No, not like this," she protested, sitting up and drawing away from him.

"Is it too fast? Is it—"

"It's too soon, Adam," she said tenderly. "You're hurt. You're angry." She brushed his hair out of his face and kissed him on the cheek. "When we do this . . . *if* we do this . . . I don't want it to be because you want to get revenge on Beth."

"I'd never *use* you, Harper," he protested.

"I know that—don't you think I know that? But I think . . . I think we should wait. Until you know what you really want."

I want you. That's what he wanted to say. But the words choked in his throat because he knew she was right. And she didn't deserve that. He didn't deserve that.

He lay back on the rock again, sighing.

"I'm so fucked up, Harper," he admitted. "How did things get so fucked up? I don't know what I'm supposed to do now. I just don't know."

She kissed him softly on the lips and then lay back beside him, taking his hand.

"We'll figure it out, Adam. Together."

The night had seemed interminable. Harper had disappeared into the woods, and Greg had refused to listen to her apology, so Miranda had picked her way through the forest, following the narrow path back toward Valley Glen High School. Alone. She'd made her way to the parking lot and stood by the empty Haven bus. Alone.

Finally, the pizza party had ended, the Haven High fans had surged into the parking lot and boarded their bus and the van, and now Miranda was speeding toward home. And, slouched down in a seat right behind the driver, peering out the window into the darkness, she was still alone. Completely and utterly alone.

She hadn't noticed whether Harper, Adam, and Greg had made it back in time, and she didn't really care. It's not like any of them were worried about her, wondering where she was or if she was all right. Harper's amazing disappearing act had made that pretty clear.

No, she was on her own—and maybe, she thought

bitterly, she'd better get used to it. After all, who understood her? Who was there for her when *she* needed someone to lean on? Good old Miranda, always there to lend a sympathetic ear, always ready to give advice—but when was it ever *her* turn? When she was the one who needed help, who needed some support, then there she was—alone.

What was the point of putting everything you had into a friendship when all you got back was . . . well, nothing?

She leaned back against the worn leather of the bus seat, trying to get comfortable, trying to ignore the shouts and laughter coming from the seats behind her. She closed her eyes, willing herself to be tired, to lose herself in sleep. But her mind refused to relax.

It was a five-hour ride back home, and she had nothing to do but curl up in the dark, wide awake, and contemplate the misery of her own existence.

Good thing she had enough material to last her the rest of the night.

They rode home on the van together, side by side, hand in hand. Adam had decided he was in no shape to ride on the rowdier fan bus with most of the team. As the van pulled onto the road, he wrapped an arm around Harper, pulling her close, then closed his eyes and leaned his head back against the seat. She snuggled up against him, her head on his chest, and listened to his heart, beating in time with the gentle rocking of the van.

She felt so warm, so safe with him by her side. And the taste of him was still on her lips—she'd waited so long for him to look at her like that, to hold her like that. Which had made it all the harder to push him away. Even harder than it had been to watch him in all that pain, to watch him raging against himself and the world and know that she could end it for him with just a few quick words—but that doing so would cost her everything. So she'd stayed silent, played the loyal and dutiful friend— and it had worked. Better, and faster, than she'd ever imagined.

It didn't matter how she'd gotten here, she reasoned. All that mattered was that she was here now, and she was close, so painfully close, to getting everything she wanted. She just had to be careful—she couldn't rush it, couldn't let him rush it. Patience, time—and then, the big payoff.

As the night wore on, a deep quiet settled over them. Harper closed her eyes and breathed in Adam's close-ness; in the quiet dark, it felt like they were all alone in the world. Together. She leaned against him, her cheek resting on his chest, rising and falling with his steady breaths, slowly drifting off to sleep. After so much time and energy spent planning the next step, looking toward tomorrow, and the day after that, Harper had finally found herself in a moment she could enjoy for what it was, a moment she wished would last forever.

If only it could.

chapter thirteen

ADAM AWOKE THE NEXT MORNING WITH A SICK feeling in the pit of his stomach. It was as if, even before he was fully awake, even before his mind had wrapped itself around the horror of the night before, his body had known that something was deeply, deeply wrong. When he'd staggered home last night at three a.m., a part of him had wanted to call Beth, to drive over to her house, bang on the windows until she let him in, shake her until she admitted what she'd done.

He'd wanted to call her last night, the moment he'd found out. But he'd stopped himself. It wasn't because he was afraid he'd say something he shouldn't—it was because he wanted to see her face, wanted her to be there right in front of him when he told her exactly what he thought of her. He didn't want anything—not static, not some misplaced twinge of pity or forgiveness—to get in the way.

He knew that this moment, coming face-to-face with her, would be the hardest one to get through, that if he were going to crack, were going to buy the inevitable denial and tearful "have pity on me" routine, it would be then. But he also knew that if he could get through the encounter without breaking, he could be rid of her forever.

It was Harper who'd convinced him, who'd persuaded him to wait until he'd calmed down and his head was clear—or at least until morning. And now morning was here. A storm of anger was still simmering just beneath the surface—he was almost afraid to pick up the phone. Once he released himself, once he let out all the emotion he'd been bottling up since the night before—he didn't know how he'd stand it.

But he couldn't do nothing. That would be worse.

So Adam rolled out of bed and called her, suppressing his nausea and affecting a cheerful, innocent voice.

"I'm so happy you called!" she said.

"I missed you!" she said.

"I can't believe you won!" she said.

Adam choked out a few terse sentences. He was fine. He was tired. He wanted to see her.

"I want to see you, too!" she gushed. "I'm stuck at work all day, but tonight we're going to Bourquin's, for some last-minute studying. Meet me there?"

We?

Perfect.

Beth shifted her weight back and forth outside the coffee shop, then began to pace along the front of the restaurant. Kane waved at her through the glass window, and she gave him a weak smile.

She couldn't wait for Adam to arrive. These last few days had been so confusing—her and Adam not speaking, Kane always underfoot, and then last night, in the park . . .

She just needed to see Adam again, soon, to talk to him, touch him, remind herself that he was real, that *he* was her life, that everything else was just—just misplaced emotion. She'd been stressed, things had been weird between them for so long, but now it could all be over. The SATs were tomorrow morning, and after that, she promised herself, she'd stop. Take a break from overachieving, just for a little while, take a break from the dutiful-daughter routine, change her shifts around at the restaurant. She'd even promise not to see Kane again, if that's what it took. She and Adam would have the chance, finally, to be together, to heal. One more night, and she'd be all his—she couldn't wait to tell him.

Adam had spent the day cleaning out the garage, hoping to keep his mind off things. It was all he could do to keep from running down to the diner and confronting Beth— but he'd decided it would be better to wait. That night, she and Kane would be together. Which meant he could kill two birds with one very large stone.

For hours upon hours he had sorted through the junk in the garage, boxing up most of it to be taken down to the town dump. Just before taping up the last box, he'd slipped his new trophy inside, then closed the lid again. He didn't need a reminder of the day before sitting on his shelf, mocking him. He didn't need to remember how happy he'd been, how good he'd felt about himself and his life, before everything came crashing down. The trophy was nothing but garbage now—just like his relationship.

As the sun set Adam walked over to the coffee shop—it was a long way, but then, he had a lot of energy to burn. He saw her before she saw him. She stood just under the neon sign, her features lit softly by the bluish glow. Angelic, he might have thought in a different life. She looked at her watch and began pacing. She was waiting for him—or maybe she was wondering how much time she'd have to waste on him before getting back to her secret lover.

Bile rose within him, and for a moment he thought he might be sick. But then he forced away the image of her and Kane (when he closed his eyes, he imagined them screwing everywhere—on her bed, in his car, in the locker room, on the basketball court—her poison had tainted everything and everywhere in his life). He needed to be calm. Strong.

Things were going to get worse before they got better.

"Adam!" she called, as soon as she spotted him approaching. "I'm so glad to see you—I missed you!" She ran over to give him a hug, but when she tried to kiss him, he turned his face away.

"Are you still mad?" It seemed an unnecessary question. She'd been hoping that a couple days away had made him realize he had nothing to worry about, that she and Kane were just friends. And that was it, she thought, pushing away the memory of last night. That was it.

"Now, why would I be mad?" his voice sounded strange. Hard. "Did you and Kane have a good time without me?"

"It was horrible," she lied. "All we did was study. I'm so burnt out—I just need to get some sleep."

"Yeah, I bet you do. I bet you're *real* tired."

"What?" What was he getting at?

"Just drop it, Beth," he said harshly.

"What?"

"The innocent act. The little miss perfect shit. It's tired, and I'm not buying it anymore."

"What act? Why are you being like this?" She reached out a hand to him, but he shrugged it off, jerking away as if her touch burned.

"Don't touch me," he said sharply.

Beth took a step back. Her heart was thumping in her ears, and a sense of dread had settled over her.

"Adam, what's going on?"

"I guess you thought I'd never figure it out."

"Figure what out?" she asked.

"You must think I'm an idiot or something."

"Of course I don't—what are you—?"

"Just shut up already!" he roared. "I can't stand it anymore. Stop looking at me like you give a shit, stop acting like you're all confused, all pure and sweet and innocent—I know all about it, all about you and . . . him."

He jerked his thumb toward the window of the coffee shop—Kane was inside, looking out with obvious concern.

"This again?" Beth asked, tears welling up at the corners of her eyes. "I told you, there's nothing going on."

"And I told *you*—I know everything. Kaia *saw* you,

Beth. I guess you thought you'd be safe, but she saw you. And she told me everything."

Beth's mind skidded across the last forty-eight hours—what could Kaia have seen? What could she have said to make him this angry? The night in the park, it had just been innocent. It might have looked . . . but it had been innocent. Completely. And besides—*Kaia?*

"Kaia? You're yelling at me because of something Kaia told you?" Beth asked incredulously. "Kaia's a liar and a bitch, Adam, you're the one who told me that. Why would you believe anything she has to say? Why would you believe her over me?"

"Oh, *Kaia's* a liar? *Kaia's* a bitch?" He forced a laugh. "That's a good one, Beth. You know, I didn't believe her either, not at first. I defended you—I defended your *honor*." He laughed again, bitterly. "Good thing for her, she had *pictures*."

Pictures? Beth's heart leaped into her throat. What could there even be pictures of? They hadn't even kissed. There had been one moment when—but no. Whatever she may have imagined doing, *nothing* had happened. Nothing.

"Adam, nothing happened," she protested. "You've got to believe me. This is just a huge misunderstanding. If you'll just listen to me—"

"I'm done listening to you," he snapped. "I'm done

with your lies. Do you have any idea what it felt like? To see you with him? I should have turned last night with Harper into a Kodak moment for you, then maybe you could see how it feels."

Beth, who already felt as if she'd been punched in the stomach, staggered back and had to lean against the wall for support.

"Harper? You and Harper?"

He looked surprised for a moment, as if not realizing he'd said it aloud. Then his face twisted into an ugly smile.

"That's right, Harper. But why should you even care? I hope to hell you do." He glared at her, and she couldn't bring herself to look away. "I hope it hurts."

It was as if Adam had disappeared into the desert, and some heartless, unfeeling monster had returned in his place. Beth was reeling.

"So, what—you get a phone call or something from *Kaia*, of all people, and then without even bothering to talk to me, you just jump into bed with someone else? What's wrong with you?" she cried.

"You are *not* the victim here," he spat. "So you can just knock off the tears. It's not going to work."

She lunged forward and grabbed both of his hands tightly in hers. If she could just make him stop for a minute. Think. Before throwing everything away.

"Adam, just wait—can we just—"

"Enough!" He shoved her backward, and she stumbled back against the wall. "Don't touch me again, Beth. I mean it."

That was when she knew. It was over. This person, this thing in front of her who spit out all this hate and anger and venom, who took Kaia's word over hers, who let Harper—

She couldn't even think about it. Couldn't even look at him.

"Just go, then, Adam," she said wearily through her tears. "If that's how you feel, why don't you just go?"

"One more piece of unfinished business," Adam replied, looking over her shoulder. She turned—Kane stood in the doorway. "Everything okay out here?" he asked with concern.

"Hey, bro, everything's just fine. Why don't you come on out for a little talk?" Adam said heartily.

Kane looked back and forth between the two of them.

"It doesn't *look* fine," he said hesitantly, walking toward Beth, who was now slumped against the wall, her head in her hands. He put a hand on her shoulder. "Beth, are you—"

"Don't touch her," Adam snapped, knocking Kane's arm away roughly.

"What's your problem?" Kane asked, turning to face him.

"You were," Adam said. Suddenly, he punched Kane in the face, hard, knocking him to the ground. "But not anymore."

As Kane moaned in pain and Beth looked on in horror, Adam slowly turned his back on them and walked away

"She's all yours now," he called over his shoulder. "You two deserve each other."

Kane lay on the ground for a moment, moaning—with a few small whimpers thrown in, just for effect. (Not too many, though—it wouldn't do to have her thinking he was some kind of wimp.) Then he slowly pulled himself up and walked over to Beth, who was frozen in place, staring after Adam's disappearing figure.

Kane said a silent congratulations to Kaia and Harper— apparently, everything had gone like clockwork. His turn now.

He put a comforting arm around Beth, trying to still her heaving sobs.

She leaned against him for a moment, burying her face in his chest and crying. *It's going to be a bitch to get all of that snot out of the fabric,* he thought. *But after all this hard work, what's a little more?* So he held her, wishing his hands could stray downward, but he held back, just rubbing her shoulder blades and making comforting noises. Patience, he counseled himself.

"Beth, maybe you want to go inside and talk?" he finally suggested.

At the sound of his voice, she looked up in alarm, almost as if she'd forgotten he was there. She twisted away from him.

"I—I have to go," she said, wild eyed, backing away from the restaurant.

"Okay," he said quietly, trying to calm her down. It unsettled him, somehow, to see her like this. It wasn't that he felt guilty, he insisted to himself. Or that he couldn't stand to see her hurt. It was just—unsettling. Guys and crying don't mix, he decided. That was all. "Let me get my keys. I'll drive you home," he offered.

"No—no!" she yelped. "I just need to be by myself. I just need to go."

"Beth, I'm not letting you wander out there by yourself," he said in alarm. "Not when you're . . . like this."

But it was too late—she'd run off into the darkness.

Once she was safely gone, he shook his head and shrugged.

So he'd have to wait. Another day, maybe two. Not a problem. He could be patient. Now that everything was in place, there was nothing standing in his way, he just had to wait.

She'd come back.

They always did.

Harper was antsy. She knew she should study—she might not care about the SATs, but it couldn't hurt to spend a couple hours at least *looking* at her books, just so she could say she'd done something.

But she was too excited to concentrate. She couldn't just sit there and study, not while she was stuck in this weird limbo between triumph and actually reaping the benefits of her victory. She couldn't sit still, couldn't stay inside—she wanted to dance, to leap, to drink, to show the world that she was the girl who had everything.

She wanted, in essence, to go out.

Adam was off somewhere with Beth, breaking her heart, she hoped.

Kane, if he was smart, was lurking about, ready to pick up the pieces.

Miranda, she was pretty sure, wasn't speaking to her. A problem for another day.

She supposed she could call up some of the girls, just choose some names at random from her phone and sucker them into going out—but she didn't want that. She didn't want to have to make up an excuse, to have to pretend that today was just another day when in fact today was *the* day, the start of everything, the day the world was about to open up for her. She wanted someone who would celebrate with her—and know what she was celebrating.

With surprise, she realized what it was—she wanted Kaia.

As she whirled under the lights of Grace's only "dance club"—a large and half empty bar that played cheesy eighties hits on Friday nights, Kaia was surprised to discover that she was actually having something akin to a good time.

Jack Powell was in for the night. Friday nights were his, and his alone, he'd informed her, and she'd figured that meant she'd be spending a quiet night at home watching TV and painting her nails. (Let these small-town losers study for the SATs—she'd aced the test last spring with the help of Ivy Bound, an intense one-on-one prep program for mediocre rich kids. So Kaia couldn't care less what happened in the morning.) And then Harper had called, and here they were, downing poorly mixed Cosmos and flailing their arms around to old-school Madonna—two material girls out on the town. For what it was.

And why not? Hadn't they triumphed over the forces of good and managed to win the fair-haired couple over to the dark side? Harper looked happier than Kaia had ever seen her, and Kaia knew it was more than the vodka.

So let her be happy, Kaia thought. She doesn't deserve it, but then, who the hell does? Why not Harper? Why not all of them?

Harper swung her arms around Kaia and they belted out the lyrics of the chorus together, at the top of their lungs.

"Don't get any ideas," Harper shouted, trying to make herself heard over the music. "I still can't stand you!"

"Don't worry, the feeling is mutual," Kaia yelled, grinning. She spun around and raised her arms above her head, twisting and turning to the steady beat.

It was a scene Kaia would have been hideously embarrassed to witness back in New York, much less participate in—the only people who danced to eighties music were bridge-and-tunnel chicks trolling for men in the big city, and men with gold teeth and bad breath looking for their next lay.

No, the number one rule of her life in the Big Apple: Only losers look like they're having fun. Boredom is the new chic.

But here? There was no one to see her—no one who counted, at least. There was only her, Harper, the flashing lights, the drinks, the steady beat and the vibrating floor. She closed her eyes and let the music fill her up, sweeping over her and carrying her body away.

Adam had left a sweatshirt in her room the last time he was there. The last time—maybe it was just that, the last time he would ever be there. Beth moaned and curled up into a tight ball, burying her face in the soft cotton of the shirt. It still smelled like him.

She closed her bloodshot eyes and breathed in deeply, letting herself pretend, for a moment, that he was in the room, lying down beside her, his arms around her, that she was safe.

But it was no use. Her bed was empty—and a sweatshirt, a scent, a thinning memory, was all she had left.

It came in waves: the sadness, the terrifying feeling of being completely alone, completely out of control. It came in waves—she'd heard the phrase before, but never really understood what it meant. That when they came, the powerful feelings swept over her, knocking her down and tossing her about as if she'd been caught by the blast of a wall of water. It lifted her off her feet, spun her, slammed her into the ground, and dragged her, tired and teary and confused, to shore, to safety, to the relative peace that would rule until another wave swept in and knocked her down all over again.

There were moments, brief moments, where she thought she would be okay, that all the pain and sorrow sweeping over her would end, that it would drag her down, but not forever. And then there were other moments, long, interminable moments, when she feared she would drown.

He was drowning—in anger, in despair, in indecision, in regret.

Had he done the right thing?

Was he a complete hypocrite? Sleeping with someone else and then dumping on Beth for doing the same? Had he made a horrible mistake?

Adam sat on the floor of his bedroom, door shut tight, loud music drowning out the rest of the world—if only it could drown out his thoughts. But they were too loud.

In front of him sat a pile of pictures, pictures that Beth had given him over the past couple years, pictures of the two of them together, happy.

There they were in the mountains, and there, in another, curled up together on the couch. Beth, cheering in the stands at one of his basketball games. Beth, cheeks flushed, eyes radiant, balanced on her toes to give him a kiss on the cheek. Beth, elegant and lovely, in her silver evening gown at last year's spring formal.

He held the last picture in his hands—it had always been his favorite and, until this evening, had sat on his desk in a silver frame. It had been taken just after they'd started going out. They were in the park. It had been a rare, beautiful day—cool air, brilliant blue sky. Even the grass had seemed lush and green. Adam had swept Beth up in his arms, dangling her above the ground, and she was laughing, trying unsuccessfully to get away, her hair billowing in the wind, her face filled with joy—his face filled with love. It was how he always thought of her—open, happy, laughing, so in love with him, so hopeful about the future. She'd believed in them—believed in him.

He held the picture, wondering: Had he made a mistake? Thrown away something too precious, too perfect to lose?

But then he remembered that these weren't the only pictures, that these images no longer told the whole story. He looked out the window, to Harper s dark bedroom only a few feet away, and remembered who he could count on—and who he couldn't, who had taken everything good in his life, everything he'd thought was real, and stomped on it. Destroyed it.

This picture in front of him that he'd loved so much— it was a lie. Everything he'd loved had been a lie.

He tore the picture in half, right down the middle, and threw it aside.

He was done with lies, forever.

chapter fourteen

THE NEXT MORNING HARPER RAN OUT THE DOOR AT
eight a.m. sharp to meet Adam, who was driving her to
school for the dreaded test. She was still hungover from
the night before, and she expected he'd look even worse,
but instead, Adam was clean shaven and bright-eyed, and
had a wide smile on his face. Too wide, Harper decided,
but if he wanted to pretend nothing had happened, she'd
respect that and go along with it. For a while.

"Excuse me while I have a heart attack," he joked when
she climbed into the car. "Harper Grace? *On time?* Will
wonders never cease?"

"Hold the applause and let's get going," she sighed,

squinting in the bright morning sun. "The sooner we get started, the sooner we can get this thing over with."

"Amen to that," he agreed, and shifted the car into gear.

The whole ride was like that—pleasant small talk, strange and unnerving only because it was so utterly and completely normal. As they pulled into the lot, they passed right by Beth's car, but Adam said nothing—maybe he hadn't noticed.

The car pulled to a stop, and they got out. Harper took a deep breath. "Well, should we go face our future?"

She began to walk toward the school, but Adam grabbed her hand and pulled her back to the car.

"Wait," he said, smiling. "I have a present for you."

He pulled a small, hastily wrapped package from his pocket and handed it to her. She ripped off the wrapping.

"A new cell phone?" she asked, surprised.

"To replace the one I broke," he explained, blushing. "Sorry, again."

"Oh, Adam, you know, I don't care about the phone," she assured him. "I mean, thank you—this is so sweet, but—how are *you* doing?"

He shrugged and looked away. "Okay, I guess."

She took a step closer to him and put her hands on his shoulders, forcing him to look her in the eye. "How are you *really* doing?"

Slowly, carefully, as if afraid it might hurt, he smiled. A real smile, this time.

"I think I'm really okay," he told her. "Now."

And he leaned toward her, and they kissed, and it was sweet and soft and perfect—and again, she forced herself to push him away.

"Adam, I told you—," she protested.

He wrapped his arms around her waist and pulled her close to him, bending his lips to her ear, and whispered the words she'd been waiting so long to hear.

"I don't want revenge," he promised. "I want *you*."

She didn't think it would hit her so hard.

One minute, Beth was on her feet, barely awake, barely functional, but still upright, moving forward.

And the next, there they were, Adam and Harper, locked in each other's arms.

It was as if all the breath was sucked from her lungs, all the energy leeched from her body. The world narrowed to a pinhole vision—all she could see was him, with her, those familiar hands all over another body. She knew every inch of him, could almost feel what he was feeling as Harper wrapped herself around him. She wanted to throw up—instead she staggered, would have collapsed, but a pair of strong arms caught her halfway to the ground.

Kane.

"Beth, you look terrible," he said, helping her up and putting his arm around her. She leaned against him gratefully.

"Thanks," she said weakly as they shuffled toward the school. "A girl always likes to hear that." She did look terrible, she knew that. She'd cried all night, and it showed. When she'd looked in the mirror this morning, she had barely recognized the pale, gaunt face looking back at her with dead, hopeless eyes. "You don't look so great yourself," she added, gesturing toward the angry, enflamed skin around his left eye.

"You should see the other guy," Kane joked—then looked appalled, as he realized what he had said. "Beth, I'm sorry, I didn't mean—"

"It's okay." But it wasn't. It might never be.

"Beth, I want you to know, if you need—"

She put up a hand to silence him.

"Can we not do this now? I just need to—I just need to make it through the test."

It was as far ahead as she could bear to look. The future, which started in three hours, would take care of itself.

Three hours.

One hundred eighty minutes.

Too many questions to count—and a whole future riding on every answer.

Miranda bit nervously on the eraser of her number two pencil. Maybe she should have spent a little more time studying and a little less time partying. Too late now.

Kane tapped his toes, checked his watch, and waited for the time to run out. After all that time pretending to be an idiot, it was almost a pleasure to run through the test, fill in all the answers with ease, and kick back and relax. But he wished the clock hand would move just a little faster. He had things to do.

Kaia filled in the bubbles at random, making pictures with the dots and trying to spell out as many words as she could with the letters *A, B, C, D,* and *E.* Who knew, maybe she'd score even better this time. If so, she could patent the method and drive the Ivy Bound assholes out of business.

Harper fidgeted. This sucked. Stuck inside, alone, trapped behind a desk, when Adam sat somewhere behind her. Was he watching her? she wondered. Did he finally want her as much as she wanted him? As soon as this thing was done, they were heading home—her parents were out for the day, and she and Adam had a *lot* of catching up to do. Now it was just a matter of running down the clock.

Adam didn't want to be there. The test didn't mean anything to him—he wasn't going anywhere, test or no test. He knew that. So why waste his time? He watched Beth, a few rows in front of him, her blond head bent intently over the page. *I hope it was worth it to you*, he thought bitterly. It had all started with this stupid test. *I sure as hell hope it was worth it.*

The numbers and words swam in front of her, blurred by tears. Beth's mind was fuzzy with fatigue, and it was all she could do to keep her heavy lids from slipping shut. To sleep would be such bliss—to forget all of this, to forget about him, a few rows back. Was he looking at her? Or was he looking at Harper? She didn't even know how many sections she'd already finished, only knew that the test had dragged on forever—and that her answer sheet was still almost completely blank.

She'd heard that you got six hundred points just for filling in your name. . . . She was going to need it.

Free at last, Miranda thought, stepping out of the stuffy school and breathing a relieved breath of warm, fresh air. But her celebration was short-lived, for what good was celebrating when you were all alone?

Harper, who she still wasn't speaking to, was a few steps ahead. When they hit the parking lot, Adam ran up to her and swept her off her feet with a hug and a passionate kiss.

Big surprise, Miranda thought. *Harper gets everything she wants. Again.*

And there, only a few feet away, were Beth and—of all

people—Kane. On another day Miranda might have been heartbroken—but today? Today she just accepted the new development and moved on. She was in the kind of mood where the worst-case scenario seemed pretty much the only option—which meant she wasn't much surprised when it happened.

Beth looked like she'd been hit by a train (small wonder, considering the way her boyfriend, or maybe ex-boyfriend, Miranda supposed, was all over Harper). But it looked like Kane was disgustingly determined to cheer her up.

No, Miranda wouldn't waste her time worrying about Beth. Or any of them. Why should she? They all had someone—and then there was her. As always.

Alone.

Beth had pushed Kane away, and, thinking she wanted to be alone, needed to be alone, she'd driven over to the old elementary school playground, her place, the place that always felt like home.

But as soon as she stepped through the opening in the chain link fence, she knew she'd made a mistake.

Beth had thought she would want to be there. She thought it would remind her of life beyond Adam, of childhood, of happiness. But the past suddenly seemed bleak—because all that hope had led her here, to the empty present. The playground didn't wrap her in the soft arms of memory. It didn't fix anything. It was just a cold, strange place, made all the stranger by the fact that it was so familiar, that it was completely unchanged.

She was the one who'd changed.

She walked over to the swings, always her favorite spot, and sat down on one, pushing herself back and forth. Even the swings felt wrong, off. The seat was too tight, her legs were too long, scraping the ground. She was too old, and her body no longer remembered what to do, how to be that child who swung so high, pumping her legs, scraping the sky. *That's what happens when you get older*, she realized. You feel a little sick as the swing sways back and forth, but not enough to stop, and only at one point, when you've gone as far back and as high up as you can, and you're almost parallel with the ground, you stop in midair, then lurch back into motion a moment before your stomach does, swooping toward the ground. You wonder whether your swing could flip over the metal bar at the top, swing you all the way around, and throw you to the ground, bruised and broken. When you were a kid, you thought it could happen—but you weren't afraid. All grown up, you know it can't happen—but you're filled with fear. You swing slower, instead of pumping for the sky. You don't jump off—you slow yourself to a stop. You'd never fling yourself into the air in midswing, because you're no longer dreaming of flying. You're just worrying about how you're going to land.

This is what it means to get old, Beth thought. *To grow up. To be alone.*

It sucked.

"I thought I'd find you here."

It was Kane, appearing in front of her as if from nowhere. He always appeared just when she most needed someone, as if he somehow knew.

He sat down on the swing next to her.

"Should I ask how the test went?" he asked hesitantly.

She didn't know if it was the reminder of the bombed SATs or just the warmth and concern in his voice, but she burst into tears.

"I'll take that as a no," he said, and scooped her into his arms. And this time she let him hold her, let him comfort her, melted into his warm, strong body, let herself be supported by someone else—because she could no longer do it herself.

He rubbed her back, gently kissed the top of her head, and then—and she knew it was coming, hadn't she always known it was coming?—he tilted her face toward him and kissed her.

She was about to pull away. But then she thought of Adam and Harper, of facing another moment on her own all by herself, of drowning.

She was so tired, too tired to think, too tired to resist.

She pulled back for a moment and looked into his eyes. They were warm and caring. She took a deep breath, and kissed him—and let herself go.

What did she have left to lose?

Kaia stood by the fence at the end of the playground, watching and smiling.

Happily ever after, she thought—or, at least, happy for another couple weeks until the whole mess blows up in their faces.

She looked again at Kane and Beth, one of the more mismatched twosomes she'd ever seen. All four of them were flirting with disaster, and Kaia was more than happy to help things along. It passed the time, after all.

Besides, she was good at it—making trouble, causing chaos. She may not know how to make herself happy—but she was damn good at making other people miserable.

And she was just getting started.

Turn the page for a sneak peak at

seven deadly sins
VOL 2.

"Pride"

THEY WANTED HIM. ALL OF THEM. HE KNEW IT.

And he loved it.

Kane Geary had developed many gifts in his eighteen years of life, not least of which was a finely tuned radar for the appreciative stares of beautiful women. And tonight, he could feel their eyes on him, their gazes drawn to him from all over the restaurant. The luscious redhead in the back booth, stealing glances over her date's sloping shoulders; the trim blonde waiting for the bathroom, zeroing in on his chiseled pecs; their perky waitress, shamelessly grazing his shoulder as she leaned across him to lay out their food—even the age-weathered brunette up in front was joining in the fun, catching his eye with a wink every time her balding husband's back was turned.

Seated on the edge of Chez Jacques's spacious dining room, which bustled with the well-bridled enthusiasm of a small-town Saturday night, Kane was, quite simply, the center of attention. Which was exactly how he liked it. Not that Kane was an attention-grabber, one of those tedious people who talked too much, too fast, too loudly. That would be too obvious. And far too much work. Instead, he waited, knowing that his smoldering good looks and effortless grace would eventually and inevitably draw the world to him. Or, more specifically, draw the girls.

They came in all shapes, colors, and sizes, and they wanted only one thing: him. Which meant that Kane could take his pick. And he usually did.

This time, he thought, smiling at the blond beauty sitting across the table from him, *I may be onto something*. Beth Manning seemed to have it all: brains, personality, body by Barbie . . . and, as of two months ago, she had him.

She was, to put it mildly, an unlikely choice. Haven High's resident most-likely-to-succeed, a power player when it came to AP classes and extracurriculars, a nobody when it came to anything else. Beth was the world's original "nice girl," and Kane knew that until recently, dating him had never crossed her mind. Nice girls didn't date Kane Geary. They stuck with people like Adam Morgan, Mr. All-American, earnest, good-hearted, and sweet as apple pie. But now Adam was history, and Beth was all his.

All it had taken was a little hard work, just a few surreptitious pushes in the right direction . . . and here she was. Tossed aside by her beloved boyfriend, who'd caught her cheating. With Kane. Or, at least, Adam *thought* he'd caught her. Kane smirked. You'd think that after their years of friendship, Adam would have realized that when it came to Kane, what you see is rarely what you get. But Adam hadn't bothered to look deeper; and Kane hadn't hesitated before swooping in to claim his prize.

And what a prize. Perched primly on the edge of her seat, her hand on his, his foot grazing her leg beneath the table. Gazing at him with those open, grateful eyes—as if a dinner at Chez Jacques, the overpriced "French bistro" whose chef and menu were about as French as McDonald's french fries, was proof of his boundless love. Yes, it was "the best restaurant in town"—but when your town was a dusty assortment of liquor stores and burned-out buildings like Grace, California, and when most local cuisine tasted as if a handful of desert dirt and cacti had been tossed in for "local flavor," best restaurant in town wasn't saying much. Not that Beth seemed to realize it. Kane supposed that a lifetime in Grace—or perhaps a year with Adam—had dulled her expectations. Or at least her tastebuds.

She'd temporarily dispensed with her daily uniform, a bland T-shirt and jeans, and was instead wearing a low-cut satin dress, a pale sky blue that matched her eyes. With her long blond hair swept into a loose knot at the nape of her neck and the long silver earrings he'd given her swaying gently with her every graceful move, she looked like a model. Gorgeous, elegant—perfect. And should he expect any less?

Kane could see the question in the envious gazes of his female admirers: What does *she* have that I don't?

One thing, ladies, he responded silently, suppressing a smile. *For the moment—me.*

"What are you thinking?" she asked him, tucking a stray hair behind her ear. It had become a familiar question. Good ol' Adam was pretty much an open book—it must be somewhat unnerving for her, Kane supposed, to be dating someone with any kind of inner life, someone with secrets. And Kane didn't mind her asking—as long as he didn't have to give a real answer.

"I'm just thinking how beautiful you look tonight," Kane told her—a half-truth being the best kind of lie. "I'm thinking how incredibly lucky I am to have ended up with someone like you."

Beth giggled, her face turning a faint shade of pink. "I'm the lucky one, Kane," she protested.

He couldn't argue with that.

For Harper Grace, Saturday night traditionally meant three things: booze, boys, and boredom. She would hit a lame bar with a lame guy, flash her crappy fake ID at an apathetic bartender, and down a couple of rum and Cokes before finding a secluded spot for the inevitable not-so-hot 'n' heavy make-out session with Mr. Wrong. It had seemed a risky and adventurous formula a few years ago, but the love 'em and lose 'em act had gotten old, fast. Grace was a small town, too small—and after a few years of the same bars, the same guys, the same post-date conversation with her best friend, Miranda (usually concluding with, "Why would you ever let me go out with such a loser?"), the thrill was gone.

But, now . . . Harper glanced to her left. Adam's wholesome good looks were just barely visible in the dim light cast by the flickering movie screen. His bright eyes, his wide smile, the shock of blond hair that set off his perfect tan—it was too dark to see the details, but no matter. She knew them all by heart.

Now, things were different, Harper reminded herself, leaning against Adam's broad shoulder and twirling her fingers through his. There was no more need for cheap thrills, because she had the real thing. Adam Morgan, her next-door neighbor, her oldest friend—her soul mate, if you believed in such things. Which, of course, she didn't. But she believed in Adam—and she believed that after all the effort she'd put into winning him, she fully deserved her prize. They'd been together only a couple months, but already, he never spoke of his year with The Bland One anymore. The dreamy gaze that used to bloom across his face at the mere mention of Beth's name was gone. Knowing—or believing—that his perfect little angel had hopped into bed with someone else had had its effect. Adam had finally wised up and realized that the right person for him had been there all along, a loyal friend and next-door neighbor, just waiting for her time to come. Unlike Beth, *Harper* would never let him down, never mistreat him, never lie to him—unless, she conceded, it was for his own good.

So what if she was spending her night in a dark theater watching an endless Jackie Chan marathon rather than preening in front of the adoring masses, Haven High girls hoping that her polite acknowledgment might secure them a berth on the A-list, brawny bouncers and bartenders attracted by her billowing auburn hair like moths to a flame and hoping against hope she would ditch her date and fall into their open arms? (It had been known to happen.) So what if she had to watch what she said 24/7, to make sure none of the nasty thoughts constantly popping into her brain slipped out in Adam's presence, lest he begin to think she really was as much of a power-hungry bitch as the rest of their school believed her to be? And so what if, in order to get what she wanted, she'd had to screw over the people she loved the most, and sacrifice whatever shreds of integrity she may have had left after four years in the Haven High trenches?

None of that mattered now. Not now that she had Adam. Strong, handsome, kind, wonderful, *perfect* Adam.

She'd waited so long—but it had been worth it. All of it.

"What are you thinking?" he whispered, slinging an arm around her and drawing her close. She nestled against him, laying her head against his shoulder. He was always asking her that, and she was still delighted by the novelty of being with a guy who actually cared what she was thinking, who was focused on getting into her mind rather than into her bed.

"I'm thinking this—you, us—it's all too good to be true," she admitted. And though it was intended as a lie, the words had the ring of truth.

"It's true," he assured her, and kissed her gently on the forehead.

I'll reform, Harper decided, leaning against his warm

body. No more party girl. No more shallow, superficial bitch. She would be the girl Adam wanted her to be—the girl he seemed to think, deep down, she really was. And who knew? He could even be right.

After all, anything's possible.

Miranda was bored.

She'd tried to tell herself that having all this free time on her hands was a good thing. She could use some space—a nice long stretch of empty hours every now and then would give her a chance to do all the things that she wanted to do. She wouldn't have to accommodate anyone else—not her mother, not her little sister, not Harper, none of the people who usually saw fit to dictate the what, when, and how of Miranda's life. She'd just do her own thing. She was a strong, smart, independent woman, right? (This month's *Cosmo* quiz had confirmed it.) Enjoying your alone time was right there in the job description, and she'd been certain she was up to the task.

But it was time to face facts. These last few weeks she'd read plenty of good books, watched all her favorite movies, taken so many "relaxing" bubble baths that she was starting to grow gills—and enough was enough. She was bored. Bored out of her mind.

It's not like she needed to spend every minute of every day with Harper. Miranda was a best friend, not some parasite who needed a constant infusion of Harper's energy to thrive. They needed *each other*, equally—or so Miranda had thought. Apparently, she'd thought wrong. Because here she was, alone. *Again.* On yet another Saturday night, playing Internet solitaire while Harper lived it up with the love of her life. So much for late-night rendezvous at the bar of choice, or Sunday brunches where they dissected every moment of the lame night before. No more of the late-night distress calls Miranda had complained about so much—never admitting, even to herself, how good it felt to be needed.

Not that Miranda begrudged her best friend her happiness—not much, at least.

"You wouldn't believe it, Rand," Harper told her. Constantly. "It's better than I ever could have imagined. Having him there for me? Always? It's amazing. It's so perfect. You'll see."

Sure, Miranda would see for herself. Someday. Maybe. Until then, she was growing intimately familiar with the whole outside-looking-in thing, turning herself into an impeccable third wheel in under a week. She'd always been a quick study.

Harper refused to elaborate on how it had happened, how one day Beth and Adam were going strong, and the next, Harper was the one in his arms, Beth kicked to the curb.

Not that vapid blondes like Beth ever stayed single for long—thirty seconds later, there she was, Kane Geary's latest conquest, floating along by his side as if she'd been there all along.

No, it was girls like Miranda who stayed single—for what seemed like forever. In all the years she'd longed for Kane, had he given her a second look? Had he ever once considered that her wit and charm might be worth ten of his bimbos, despite her stringy hair and lumpy physique?

No—guys like Kane, they never did. Probably never would.

Her computer *dinged* with the sound of a new e-mail, and she opened it warily, expecting spam. More offers to increase her girth or introduce her to some "Hot XXX Girls NUDE NUDE NUDE." Who else would be sitting in front of their computer on a Saturday night but the people trying to sell that shit—and the people who actually bought it?

LOOKING FOR LOVE IN ALL THE WRONG PLACES? read the banner headline.

Great. Even cyberspace knew how pathetic she was.

Join MatchMadeInHaven.com, Grace's first teen Internet dating site! Find your true love with the click of a mouse! After all—you've been lonely too long. . . .

You can say that again, Miranda thought bitterly. And, for just a moment, she considered it. No one would ever have to know, she reasoned, and maybe, just maybe, this was her ticket to coupledom. Maybe there was someone out there, just like her, waiting for the right girl to come along. Could she really complain about being alone if she hadn't done everything in her power, *everything*, to fix the problem?

And then she caught herself, realizing the depths to which she was about to sink.

What are you thinking? she asked herself sternly, shaking her head in disgust. *You're not that desperate.*

At least, not yet.

They ate in silence.

The dining room table was large and long, too big for just the two of them. Kaia sat at one end, her father at the other, and for most of the meal, the quiet was punctuated only by the distant chattering of the maids in the kitchen and the occasional clatter of a silver Tiffany fork against the edge of Kaia's Rafaelesco plate. She saw her father wince at each *clang* and *scrape*—it didn't inspire her to be more careful.

Kaia would rather have been in the cavernous living room, eating take-out in front of the giant flat-screen TV, as usual. When you got down to it, she would have preferred to be back home in New York, eating in a chic TriBeCa bistro. Even holing up in her New York bedroom with a three-day-old bag of Doritos would have been preferable to having even one more meal in Grace, CA. Good food didn't change the fact that she was in exile, a prisoner, beholden to her parents' stupid whims. She didn't want to be stuck in the desert, stuck in his pretentious, *Architectural Digest* wannabe house, and she certainly didn't want to be stuck at the hand-crafted mahogany dining room table facing the man who was keeping her there, And despite her perpetual inability to read him, she was pretty sure he didn't want to be there either. Yet there they sat, one night a month.

And the night stretched on, interminable.

"So, how's school?" her father finally asked.

"I wouldn't know," she answered lightly.

"Kaia . . ."

The warning note in his voice was subtle, but clear. *He talks to me like I'm one of his employees*, she thought, not for the first time.

"School's fine. Delightful," she offered. "I go every day. It's a truly wonderful experience. I'm simply learning ever so much. Is that what you want to hear?"

He sighed and shook his head. "I just want to hear the truth, Kaia. And I want to hear that you're happy."

"Sorry to disappoint, *Father*, but those are two different things—and, at the moment, they're mutually exclusive. You and Mother have seen to that."

His lips tightened, and Kaia braced for an angry response, some of that famous Keith Sellers temper, quick as lightning and just as deadly, but he kept it together. Barely. "This year isn't supposed to be a punishment, Kaia."

"Then why does it feel like one?"

"It's supposed to be a break," he continued, as if she hadn't spoken. "To give you and your mother some space. To give you some time to think about what you want your life to be."

"I want my life to be back to normal," Kaia spit out, immediately regretting it. She'd vowed not to let her guard down. Bad enough that she'd almost cried on the day he'd cut up all her credit cards—and *had* cried on the day her mother had shipped her off to the airport. She'd refused to give them the satisfaction of knowing she cared.

"Oh, Kaia. I wish I could help," he said, almost sounding like he meant it. "Maybe if I spent some more time at home. . . ."

"You really want to help?" Kaia asked, allowing a note of near sincerity to creep into her voice. She'd been waiting for the right moment for this, and there was no time like the present—right? "How about a temporary reprieve," she suggested. "Winter break's coming up, and I thought, maybe, just for a couple weeks—"

"You are *not* going back to the East Coast," he cut her off. "Not for two weeks, not for two days—you know the terms of our agreement."

"Agreement, right," she muttered. "Like I had a choice."

"What was that?" he snapped.

"I said, if this isn't a punishment, why do I feel like I'm in prison?" she asked, loud and clear.

"Katherine, that's quite enough whining for tonight." His measured tone masked an undercurrent of tightly bottled rage. The famous Keith Sellers temper was famous for a reason.

"It's *Kaia*," she reminded him.

"I named you *Katherine*," he countered, rising from the table. "I *let* you call yourself by that ridiculous name, but you'll always be Katherine, just like I'll always be your father, whether you like it or not."

"Trust me, I know," Kaia snarled. "If I could change that, along with the name, I would have done it a long time ago."

By the time he roared at her to go to her room, she was already out of her seat and halfway up the stairs.

Just another warm and fuzzy family dinner at the Sellers house.

Bon appétit.

It was almost midnight before Kaia's father had gone to sleep and she was able to sneak out of the house. She was still fuming about the way her parents felt they could run her life. They were mistaken. They could ship her across the country and strand her in the desert, but they couldn't stop her from slipping out of the mansion, driving twenty minutes down the deserted highway, pulling to a stop in front of a squat, nondescript gray house, and scurrying up the walkway, head down to shield her face from prying eyes. They couldn't stop her from throwing open the door and falling into her lover's arms.

Her *lover*—she liked the sound of that. She'd had her share of guys, but never one she'd call a *lover*. The term was too adult, too mature for the puny prep school boys she'd toyed with back east—it was reserved for a man. And now she'd found one.

"*Je m'oublie quand je suis avec toi,*" she murmured into his neck.

I forget myself when I'm with you.

He hated when she spoke French to him; it was too much of a reminder of his day job, and of their roles in the real world, beyond the walls of his cramped apartment, where he was a French teacher, she a student. He didn't want to remember—and she never wanted to forget.

The delicious scandal, the secrecy—why else was she

there? It didn't hurt that he was sophisticated, worldly, movie-star handsome, that at least when they were alone in bed together, he treated her like a goddess—but really, the thrill of the forbidden had always been, and remained, the biggest draw. He was too shallow, too vain to be anything other than an object of illicit desire. She had no fairy-tale illusions of love—and knew he felt the same.

It's why they worked so well together.

"What are you thinking?" he asked idly, though she knew he didn't really care.

"I'm thinking you're a superficial, conceited, despicable human being, taking advantage of a sweet young girl like me." To Jack Powell, she could always speak some form of the truth—because the things they said to each other would never matter. Neither of them was in this for good conversation.

"And you're a callous, duplicitous, licentious girl who's out only for herself," he retorted in his clipped British accent, and kissed her roughly. "I can't get enough of you."

It was a match made in heaven—or somewhere a bit farther south.

ROBIN WASSERMAN is the author o
the Seven Deadly Sins series, the Cold
(*Frozen, Shattered, Torn*), *The Book of Blo*
The Waking Dark. She lives in Brooklyn

f *Hacking Harvard*,
Awakening trilogy
od and Shadow, and
, New York.